The MAP of BONES

FRANCESCA HAIG

HARPER
Voyager

HarperCollins*Publishers*
1 London Bridge Street
London SE1 9GF

www.harpercollins.co.uk

Published by Harper*Voyager*
An imprint of HarperCollins*Publishers* 2016
1

A catalogue record for this book
is available from the British Library

ISBN: 978-0-00-756312-8

This novel is entirely a work of fiction.
The names, characters and incidents portrayed in it are
the work of the author's imagination. Any resemblance to
actual persons, living or dead, events or localities is
entirely coincidental.

Set in Jansen Text
Typeset by Palimpsest Book Production Ltd, Falkirk, Stirlingshire

Printed and bound in Great Britain by
Clays Ltd, St Ives plc

MIX
Paper from
responsible sources
FSC FSC C007454
www.fsc.org

FSC™ is a non-profit international organisation established
to promote the responsible management of the world's forests.
Products carrying the FSC label are independently certified
to assure consumers that they come from forests that are managed
to meet the social, economic and ecological needs
of present and future generations,
and other controlled sources.

Find out more about HarperCollins and the environment at
www.harpercollins.co.uk/green

This book is dedicated, with love and gratitude, to my parents, Alan and Sally, who shared with me their enduring passion for words.

PROLOGUE

Each time he came to me in dreams, I saw him as I'd seen him the first time: floating. He was a silhouette, blurred by the tank's thick glass, and by the viscous fluid in which he was submerged. I could see only glimpses: his head slumped against his shoulder; the curve of his cheek. I couldn't see his face clearly, but I knew it was him, the same way that I would know the weight of his arm across my body, or the sound of his breath in the darkness.

Kip's torso curled forwards, his legs hanging. His suspended body was a question mark that I couldn't answer.

I would have preferred anything to those dreams – even the memory of his jump. That came to me often enough in the daytime: his half-shrug, before he leapt. The long fall. How the silo floor was the mortar that made his bones a pestle, grinding his own flesh.

When I dreamed of him in the tank it was a different kind of horror. Not the spreading blood on the silo floor, but something worse: the immaculate torture of the tubes and wires. I had freed him from the tank myself, months ago. But ever since I'd watched him die in the silo, my dreams encased him once again within the glass.

The dream shifted. Kip was gone, and I was watching Zach sleeping. One of his hands was thrust out towards me. I could see the gnawed skin around his fingernails; I could see his jaw, roughened by stubble.

When we were very small we'd shared a cot, and slept each night curled together. Even when we were older, and he'd begun to fear and despise me, our bodies never unlearnt that habit of closeness. When we'd outgrown our shared cot, I would roll over in my own bed and watch how he, sleeping on the far side of the room, would roll too.

Now I stared again at Zach's sleeping face. There was nothing on it to show what he had done. I was the branded one, but his face should have worn some kind of mark. How could he have built the tanks, and ordered the massacre on the island, and still sleep like that, open-mouthed and oblivious? Awake, he had never been still. I remembered his hands, always moving, tying invisible knots in the air. Now he was motionless. Only his eyes were twitching as they followed the movements of his own dreams. At his neck, a vein pulsed, keeping count of his heart's beats. My own, too – they were the same thing. When his stopped, so would mine. He had betrayed me at every opportunity, but our shared death was the one promise that he couldn't break.

He opened his eyes.

'What do you want from me?' he said.

I had fled from him all the way to the island, and back to the deadlands of the east, but here he was, my twin, staring at me across the silence of my dream. It was as if a rope bound me to him, and the further we ran from each other, the more we felt it tighten.

'What do you want from me?' he said again.

'I want to stop you,' I said. Once I would have said I wanted to save him. Perhaps there was no difference.

'You can't,' he said. There was no triumph in his voice – just a certainty, hard as teeth.

'What did I do to you?' I said to him. 'What have you done to us?'

Zach didn't answer – the flames did instead. The blast came, its white flash ripping through the dream. It stole the world and replaced it with fire.

CHAPTER 1

I woke from flames, a scream bursting from me into the darkening air. When I reached out for Kip, I found only the blanket, chalky with ash. Each day that I tried to adjust to his absence, I'd wake to find my forgetful body rolling towards his warmth.

I lay back in the echo of my own scream. I dreamed of the blast more often now. It came to me in sleep, and sometimes when I was awake. I understood more than ever why so many seers went mad. Being a seer was like walking on a frozen lake: each vision was a crack in the ice underfoot. There were many days when I felt sure I would plunge through the brittle surface of my own sanity.

'You're sweating,' said Piper.

My breath was fast and loud, and refused to be slowed. 'It's not hot. Do you feel feverish?'

'She can't talk yet,' said Zoe from the other side of the fire. 'She'll stop carrying on in a minute.'

'She's running a fever,' Piper said, his hand on my forehead. He reacted like this whenever I had a vision. At my side quickly, crowding me with his questions before the visions had even had a chance to dissipate.

'I'm not sick.' I sat up, brushing his hand away, and wiped my face. 'It's just the blast again.'

No matter how many times I'd endured the vision, there was no preparing for it, and no lessening its impact. It made my senses bleed into one another. The sound of it was absolute blackness; the colour a white that shrieked in my ears. The heat went beyond pain: it was total. The size of the flames was beyond any measure: the horizon was consumed, the world snatched away in an instant of flame that lasted forever.

Zoe stood and stepped over the crumbs of the fire to pass me the water flask.

'It's happening more often, isn't it,' Piper said.

I took the flask from Zoe. 'Have you been counting?' I said to Piper. He didn't reply, but kept watching me as I drank.

Until that night, I knew I hadn't screamed for weeks. I'd worked so hard at it. Avoiding sleep; taming my convulsive breath when a vision came; clenching my jaw until my teeth felt as though they would grind each other down to dust. But Piper had noticed anyway.

'You've been watching me?' I said.

'Yes,' he said, not flinching from my stare. 'I do what I have to do, for the resistance. It's your job to endure the visions. And it's mine to decide how we can use them.'

It was me who broke the gaze, rolling away from him.

For weeks our world had been made of ash. Even after we'd left the deadlands, the wind still blew from the east, loading the sky with a burden of black dust. When I rode behind Piper or Zoe, I saw how it settled even in the elaborate contours of their ears.

If I'd cried, my tears would have run black. But I had no time for tears. And who would I cry for? Kip? The dead of the island? All who were trapped in New Hobart? Those still suspended, out of time, in the tanks? There were too many, and my tears were no good to them.

I learned that the past is barbed. Memories snagged at my skin, relentless as the thorn bushes that grew by the deadlands' black river. Even when I tried to recall a happy time – sitting with Kip on the windowsill, on the island, or laughing with Elsa and Nina in the kitchen at New Hobart – my mind would end up at the same point: the silo floor. Those final minutes: The Confessor, and what she had revealed about Kip's past; Kip's jump, and his body on the concrete below me.

I found myself envying Kip's amnesia. So I taught myself not to remember. I clung to the present, the horse beneath me, its solidity and warmth. Leaning with Piper over a map sketched in the dust, to calculate our next destination. The indecipherable messages left in the ash by the lizards that dragged their bellies across the ruined earth.

When I was thirteen and freshly branded, I'd stared at the healing wound in the mirror and said to myself: *This is what I am.* Now I did the same with this new life. I tried to learn to occupy it, as I'd learned to inhabit my branded body. *This is my life*, I said to myself, each morning, when Zoe shook my shoulder to wake me for my shift as lookout, or when Piper kicked dirt over the fire and said it was time to move again. *This is my life now.*

After our raid on the silo, the whole Wyndham region was so thick with Council patrols that before we could travel back to the west we had to head south, picking our way through the deadlands, that vast canker on the earth.

Eventually we had to let the horses go – unlike us, they

couldn't survive on lizard flesh and grubs, and there was no grass where we travelled. Zoe had suggested eating them, but I was relieved when Piper pointed out that they were as thin as us. He was right: their backbones were sharpened like the peaked spines of lizards. When Zoe untied them they galloped off to the west on legs that were nothing more than splints of bone. Whether they were fleeing us, or just trying to get away from the deadlands, I didn't know.

I'd thought I knew the damage that the blast had wrought. But those weeks showed me the wreckage anew. I saw the skin of the earth peeled back like an eyelid, leaving scorched stone and dust. After the blast, they say most of the world was like that: broken. I'd heard bards singing about the Long Winter, when ash had shrouded the sky for years, and nothing would grow. Now, hundreds of years later, the deadlands had retreated to the east, but from our time out there, I understood more of the fear and rage that had driven the purges, when the survivors had destroyed any of the machines that were left after the blast. The taboo surrounding the remnants of the machines wasn't simply a law – it was an instinct. Any rumours or stories of what machines had once been able to do, in the Before, was overshadowed by the evidence of the machines' ultimate achievement: fire and ash. The Council's strict penalties for breaking the taboo never had to be enforced – it was a law upheld by our own revulsion; we shuddered away from the fragments of machines that still surfaced, occasionally, in the dust.

People shuddered away from us, too, we Omegas in our blast-marked bodies. It was the same fear of the blast and its contagion that had led the Alphas to cast us out. To them, our bodies were deadlands of flesh: infertile and broken. The imperfect twins, we carried the stain of the blast in us, as surely as the scorched earth of the east. They chased us far away from where they lived and farmed, to scratch an existence from the blighted land.

Piper, Zoe and I had emerged from the east like blackened ghosts. The first time we washed, the water downstream ran black. Even afterwards, the skin between my fingers was stained grey. Piper and Zoe's dark skin took on a greyish tone that wouldn't wash away – it was the pallor of hunger and exhaustion. The deadlands weren't something that could easily be left behind. When we headed west, we were still shaking ash from our blankets each night when we unpacked them, and still coughing up ash in the morning.

*

Piper and I sat near the entrance to the cave, watching the sun shrug off the night. More than a month earlier, on the way to the silo, we'd slept in the same hidden cave, and perched on the same flat rock. Next to my knee, the stone still bore the scuff-marks from where Piper had sharpened his knife all those weeks ago.

I looked at Piper. The slash on his single arm had healed to a pink streak, the scar tissue raised and waxy, puckered where stitches had held the wound closed. At my neck, the wound from The Confessor's knife had finally healed, too. In the deadlands, it had been an open wound, edged with ash. Was the ash still there, inside me, specks of black sealed beneath the scar's carapace?

Piper held out a piece of rabbit meat skewered on the blade of his knife. It was left over from the night before, coated with cold fat, congealed into grey strings. I shook my head and turned away.

'You need to eat,' he said. 'It'll take us three more weeks

to get to the Sunken Shore. Even longer to get to the west coast, if we're going to search for the ships.'

All of our conversations began and ended at the ships. Their names had become like charms: *The Rosalind. The Evelyn.* And if the hazards of the unknown seas didn't sink the ships, then sometimes I felt that the weight of our expectations would. They were everything, now. We'd managed to rid the Council of The Confessor, and of the machine that she was using to keep track of all Omegas – but it wasn't enough, especially after the massacre on the island. We might have slowed down the Council, and cost them two of their most powerful weapons, but the tanks were patient. I'd seen them myself, in visions and in the awful solidity of reality. Row after row of glass tanks, each one a pristine hell.

That was the Council's plan for all of us. And if we didn't have a plan of our own, a goal to work for, then we were just scrapping in the dust, and there'd be no end to it. We might forestall the tanks for a while, but no better than that. Once, the island had been our destination. That had ended in blood and smoke. So now we were seeking the ships that Piper had sent out from the island, months before, in search of Elsewhere.

There were times when it felt more like a wish than a plan.

It would be four months at the next full moon since the ships sailed. 'It's a hell of a long time to be at sea,' Piper said as we sat on the rock.

I had no reassurance to offer him, so I stayed silent. It wasn't just a question of whether or not Elsewhere was out there. The real question was what it could offer us, if it existed. What its inhabitants might know, or do, that we couldn't. Elsewhere couldn't just be another island, just a place to hide from the Council. That might offer us a respite, but it would be no solution, any more than the island was. There had to be more than that: a real alternative.

If the ships found Elsewhere, they'd have to make their way back through the treacherous sea. If they survived, and if they weren't caught attempting to return to the captured island, then they should be returning to a rendezvous point at Cape Bleak, on the north-west coast.

It felt like such a tenuous chance: *if* piled on *if*, each hope feeling flimsier than the last, while Zach's tanks were solid, multiplying with each day that passed.

Piper knew better, by now, than to push against my silences. He kept staring at the sunrise, and went on. 'When we've sent out ships in the past, some of them made it back to the island, months later, with nothing to show for the journey but damaged hulls and crews sick with scurvy. And two ships never came back.' He was quiet for a moment, but his face betrayed no emotion. 'It's not just a question of distance, or even storms. Some of our sailors have come back with stories of things we can barely imagine. A few years back, one of our best captains, Hobb, led three ships north. They were gone for more than two months. It was nearing winter, when Hobb got back – and there were only two ships by then. The winter storms we're used to on the west coast are bad enough – we didn't even make crossings to the island in winter, if we could help it. But further north, Hobb told us the entire sea up there had started to freeze solid. The ice crushed one of the ships, just like that.' He opened his hand wide, then closed his fist. 'The whole crew was lost.' He paused again. Both of us were looking at the frost stiffening the grass. Winter was on its way.

'After all this time,' he said, 'do you still believe that *The Rosalind* and *The Evelyn* could be out there?'

11

'I'm not sure about belief,' I said. 'But I hope they are.'

'And that's enough for you?' he said.

I shrugged. What would 'enough' mean, anyway? Enough for what? Enough to keep going, I supposed. I'd learned not to ask for more than that. Enough to get me to fold my blanket at the end of each day's rest, stuff it back into my rucksack, and follow Piper and Zoe once more onto the plain for another night of walking.

Piper held out the meat again. I turned away.

'You need to stop this,' he said.

He still spoke as he always had: as if the world was his to command. If I'd closed my eyes, I could imagine he was still giving orders in the island's Assembly Hall, rather than squatting on a rock, his clothes torn and stained. There were times that I admired his self-assurance: its audacity, in the face of a world that did its best to show us that we were worthless. At other times, it baffled me. I'd caught myself watching how he moved. The last few weeks had left him thinner, his skin stretched a little too tightly over his cheekbones, but it hadn't changed the defiant jut of his jaw, or the spread of his shoulders, unafraid to occupy space. It was as though his body spoke a language that mine could never learn.

'Stop what?' I said, avoiding his gaze.

'You know what I mean. You're not eating. You barely sleep, or talk.'

'I'm keeping up with you and Zoe, aren't I?'

'I didn't say you weren't. It's just that you're not yourself anymore.'

'And since when are you an expert in what I'm like? You hardly know me.' My voice was loud in the morning stillness.

I knew it wasn't fair to snap at him. What he'd said was

true enough. I'd been eating less, even now we were out of the deadlands and the hunting was good. I ate just enough to stay well, to travel fast. On frosty days, when it was my turn to sleep, I cast the blanket off my shoulders and offered myself up to the cold.

I couldn't explain any of this to Piper or Zoe. It would mean talking about Kip. His name, that single syllable, caught in my throat like a fish bone.

His past, too, stopped me at the brink of words. I couldn't speak about it. Since the silo, when The Confessor had told me what Kip had been like before the tank, I carried her news with me everywhere. I was good at secrets. I'd hidden my seer visions from my family for thirteen years before Zach exposed me. I'd concealed my visions of the island from The Confessor for the four years of my captivity in the Keeping Rooms. On the island, I'd hidden my twin's identity from Piper and the Assembly for weeks. Now I concealed what I knew about Kip. The knowledge that he had tormented The Confessor as a child, and delighted when she was branded and sent away. That he'd tried, as an adult, to track her down and pay to have her locked in the Keeping Rooms for his own protection.

How could he be such a stranger to me, when I could identify each of his vertebrae under my fingertips, and I knew the precise curve of his hip bones against my own?

But at the end, in the silo, he'd made the choice to die, to save me. These days, it seemed that was the only gift we had to offer one another: the gift of our own deaths.

CHAPTER 2

Halfway to the Sunken Shore, Zoe led us to a safehouse at the edge of the plains. Nothing moved in the cottage but the wind, banging the front door, which had been left open.

'Did they run, or were they taken?' I asked, as we walked through the empty rooms.

'Either way, they left in a hurry,' said Zoe. In the kitchen, a jug lay in pieces on the floor. Two bowls sat unwashed on the table, velveted with green mould.

Piper was bending to look at the door latch. 'The door was kicked in, from outside.' He stood. 'We have to leave now.'

And even though I'd looked forward to a night of sleeping indoors, I was glad to leave those rooms where all noise was muted by dust. We retreated into the long grass that grew right up to the house itself, and didn't make camp until we'd walked all day, and half the night.

Zoe was kneeling over a rabbit that she'd caught the day before, skinning it while Piper and I lit a fire.

'It's worse than we thought,' said Piper, leaning forward to blow on the timid flame. 'Half the network must've been infiltrated.'

It wasn't the first ruined safehouse that we'd seen. On the way to the silo we'd come across another safehouse, where nothing remained but blackened beams, still smoking. The Council had taken prisoners on the island, and the resistance's secrets were being wrung from them.

As Zoe and Piper took stock of what we knew, I sat in silence. It wasn't that they excluded me from conversations – rather that their talks were full of shorthand references to people, places and information that they shared, and that I had never encountered.

'No point in going past Evan's place,' Piper said. 'If they took Hannah alive, then they'll have got him too.'

Zoe didn't look up from the rabbit. She stretched it out on its back, grasped its back legs with one hand, and ran her knife down the line of exposed white fur. The stomach fell open like two hands parting.

'Wouldn't they pick up Jess, first?' she said.

'No. She never dealt with Hannah directly – she should be safe. But Evan was Hannah's contact. If she's taken, Evan's done for.'

The resistance network on the mainland had been larger and more intricate than I'd ever realised. At how many other safehouses did broken doors now swing onto empty rooms, the latches smashed? The network was like a woollen jumper with several loose threads, each one threatening to unravel the entire thing.

'Depends how long Hannah held out for,' Zoe said. 'She might've bought him some time to get clear. Julia lasted three days when they took her.'

'Hannah's not as strong as Julia – we can't assume she managed to last that long.'

'Sally had no contact with Hannah, either. And some of the western cells should still be intact,' Zoe went on. 'They reported straight to you – there were no links with the eastern network.'

I spoke up. 'I never realised how much of the resistance was going on here, on the mainland.'

'You thought the island was the only thing that mattered?' Zoe said.

I shrugged. 'That was the main thing, wasn't it?'

Piper pursed his lips. 'The thing about the island – it mattered that it existed. It was a symbol – not just for the resistance, but for the Council too. It was a signal that there could be a different way. But it was never going to be big enough for all of us. Even in those final months, we were having to turn down some requests from refugees – until we'd built up our capacity. Added to the fleet, sorted out the supply situation.' He shook his head grimly. 'It was never going to be the final answer.'

Zoe interrupted him. 'Most people on the island did nothing. They felt like great rebels just for living out there, but that was it. They might have joined the guards or done a few shifts in the lookout posts, but not many of them were actually actively contributing – coming to the mainland to help with rescues; running the safehouse network; monitoring the Council's movements. Even some of those in the Assembly with Piper – they were happy enough to sit about in the Assembly Hall, looking at maps and talking about strategy, but you wouldn't catch half of them making the crossing. The mainland was where the hard work still happened – but once they'd made it to the island, most people never came back.'

'I wouldn't have put it like that, but Zoe's right,' Piper said. 'A lot of people on the island were complacent. They thought being there was enough. It was those on the mainland, or working the courier ships between the two, who did most of it. Zoe did more than most, and she's never even been to the island.'

I looked up quickly. 'Really? I was sure that you had,' I said.

'They never wanted any Alphas setting foot on the place – even I understood why.' Zoe was hunched over the rabbit. She pulled the fur from the flesh as if peeling off a glove. 'Why did you think I'd been there?'

'I guess because you dream about the sea all the time.'

I didn't realise I knew it, until I heard myself say it. In all those nights that we'd slept close to one another, I'd shared her dreams, the same way I'd shared her water flask or her blanket. And her dreams were all of the ocean. Perhaps that's why it hadn't struck me before: I was used to it, after my years of dreaming of the island. Used to the sea's restlessness, and its shifting register of greys, blacks and blues. In Zoe's dreams, though, there hadn't been any island, nor any land at all: just the churning sea.

One minute Zoe was squatting by the fire, the rabbit's flaccid body in her hands; the next her knife was at my stomach.

'You've been snooping in my dreams?'

'Stand down,' said Piper. He didn't shout, but it was a command nonetheless.

The blade didn't budge. Her other hand had grasped a handful of my hair, her knuckles jabbing against my skull, holding me in place. The blade had gone straight through my jumper and shirt, and was pressed flat against my stomach; I felt its cold indentation on my skin. My head was twisted back and to the side. I could see the rabbit on the ground where she'd dropped it, its wrung neck and open eyes.

'What the hell have you been doing?' she said. As she

leaned closer the blade became more insistent. 'What did you see?'

'Zoe,' warned Piper. He wrapped his arm around her neck, but he didn't fight her – just held her, and waited.

'What did you see?' she repeated.

'I told you. Just the sea. Lots of waves. I'm sorry – I can't control it. I didn't even realise until just now.' I couldn't explain to her how it worked. How my awareness of her dreams wasn't an eavesdropping, any more than I'd eavesdropped on the sea while on the island. It was just there, a background noise.

'You said it didn't work like that,' she said, her breath hot on my face. 'You said you couldn't read minds.'

'I can't. It's not like that. I just get impressions, sometimes. I don't mean to.'

She shoved me backwards. When I'd steadied myself, I put my hand to my stomach. It came away red.

'It's rabbit blood,' Piper said.

'This time,' said Zoe.

'If it makes any difference,' I said, 'you know what I dream about.'

'Everyone within ten miles knows what you dream about, the way you scream and carry on.' She tossed the knife down next to the half-skinned rabbit. 'That doesn't give you the right to poke around in my head.'

I knew how it felt – I would never forget the sense of violation that The Confessor's interrogations had left me with. How my whole mind had felt sullied by her probings.

'I'm sorry,' I called after her, as she walked away towards the river.

'Let her go,' said Piper. 'Are you OK? Show me your stomach,' he said, reaching out to lift my jumper.

I swiped his hand away.

'What was that about?' I said, staring after Zoe.

He picked up the rabbit and shook the dirt from its flesh. 'She shouldn't have done that – I'll talk to her.'

'I don't need you to talk to her for me. I just want to know what's going on. Why did she react like that? Why is she like this?'

'It's not easy for her,' he said.

'Who has it been easy for? Not for me, that's for sure. Not for you, or any of us.'

'Just give her some space,' he said.

I waved at the plain surrounding us, the pale grass stretching for miles, and the sky so big that it seemed to have encroached on the earth itself. 'Space? There's nothing here but space. She doesn't have to be in my face every moment.'

I got no answer but the rasping of the grass in the wind, scratching at the underside of the sky, and the moistened scrape of Piper's knife on the rabbit's flesh as he finished the skinning.

Zoe didn't come back until after dawn. She ate in silence, and slept on the far side of Piper, instead of her usual spot between us.

I thought of what she'd said earlier: *once they'd made it to the island, most people never came back.* Is it Piper she's thinking of, I wondered, when the sea floods her sleeping mind? The sea that he crossed for the island, leaving her on her own, after all that she'd given up to be with him.

CHAPTER 3

I'd first heard Piper and Zoe mention Sally, and the Sunken Shore, when we were still in the deadlands. They were meant to be resting, but I could hear their raised voices from the lookout spot. It was dawn; I'd volunteered to take the first watch, but when I heard them arguing I left the lookout post and headed back to the fire.

'I never wanted to drag Sally into this,' Zoe said.

'Who?' I said.

They both turned to face me. It was the same movement, doubled. And the same expression: the same angle to their eyebrows, the same appraising eyes. Even when they were arguing, I felt like an intruder.

Piper answered me. 'We need a base, with someone we can trust. The safehouse network's crumbling. Sally will give us shelter, so we can start to muster the resistance and send people to Cape Bleak to seek the ships. Outfit new ships, if we need.'

'I've told you before,' said Zoe, still ignoring me and addressing only Piper. 'We can't get Sally involved. We can't ask her. It's too dangerous.'

'Who is she?' I asked.

'Zoe told you about how we got by, as kids, after we were split?'

I nodded. They'd been raised in the east, where people used to let twins stay together a little longer. Piper had been ten when he'd been branded and exiled. She'd run away to follow him. The two of them had survived by stealing, working, and hiding, with some help from sympathetic Omegas along the way, before they'd finally joined the resistance.

'Sally was one of the people who helped us,' he said. 'The first one. When we were really young, and needed it most.'

It was hard to imagine Zoe and Piper needing help. But I reminded myself of how young they'd been – even younger than I'd been when my family sent me away.

'She took us in,' said Zoe. 'Taught us everything. And she had a lot to teach. She was old when we found our way to her, but years before that she'd been one of the resistance's best agents, working in Wyndham.'

'In Wyndham?' I thought I must have misheard. No Omegas were allowed to live in an Alpha town – let alone in Wyndham, the Council's hub.

'She was an infiltrator,' said Piper.

I looked from Zoe to Piper, and back again. 'I've never heard of them,' I said.

'That was the idea,' Zoe said impatiently.

'It was the resistance's most covert project,' Piper said. 'It wouldn't be possible these days. This was back when the Council was less strict about branding, especially out east. We're talking about fifty years ago, at least. The resistance had managed to recruit a few unbranded Omegas, with deformations minor enough that they could be disguised, or hidden. For Sally, it was a malformed foot. She could jam it into a normal shoe, and she trained herself to walk straight on it. It hurt her like crazy, but she got away with it for more than two years. There were three infiltrators, right inside the Council chambers. Not as Councillors, but as advisors or assistants. They were right in the thick of it.

'The Council hated infiltrators more than anything.' Piper smiled. 'It wasn't even the information that they managed to find out. It was the fact that they managed to do it – pass themselves off as Alphas, sometimes for years. Proof that we're not that different, after all.'

'Sally was the best of any of them,' Zoe said. 'Half of the current resistance was built on the information she got out of the Council.' When she spoke of Sally, Zoe had none of her usual sarcasm, or the raised eyebrow that could sharpen a single word into a weapon. 'But she's ancient now,' she went on. 'She can hardly walk. Hadn't worked for the resistance for years, even by the time we came to her. Too risky, apart from anything else. She was top of the Council's wanted list for a long time, and they knew what she looked like. I don't want to get her involved.'

'We're all involved, whether we want to be or not,' said Piper. 'The Council will come for her, soon enough. They won't care that she's old, or frail.'

'She's managed to stay hidden from them for all these years,' Zoe said. 'We can't drag her into this.'

He paused, and then spoke more quietly to her. 'You know she'd never turn us away,' he said.

'That's why it's not fair to go to her.'

He shook his head. 'We don't have any other options. Not after what I did on the island.'

I could see it again: the blood thickening between the stones of the courtyard.

'The Council would never have spared the island if you'd

handed Cass and Kip over to The Confessor,' Zoe said.

'I know that,' Piper said. 'But we can't assume that the rest of the resistance will understand that. You saw how they reacted at the time. When that many people are killed, people cast around for someone to blame. We can't know how they're going to take it when we reappear, especially not with Cass. We don't know if it will be safe for her. If we're going to reconnect with the resistance, we need to start with somebody we know we can trust.'

She turned away from me again, and looked only to Piper. 'Sally's been through enough,' she said.

'She'd want us to go to her,' he said.

'You brave enough to try telling her what she'd want?' said Zoe, with a slow smile. Piper smiled back at her. He was like her reflection.

*

At each settlement we passed on the journey to the Sunken Shore, we did our best to spread the word about the Council's plans for tanking Omegas. Above all, we tried to warn them away from turning themselves in to refuges. These huge, secure camps were supposed to be the Council's protection for struggling Omegas – a place where any Omega would be given food and shelter, in exchange for their labour. They were a last resort for Omegas, and a reassurance for the Alphas themselves. A guarantee that however much they might restrict Omegas to blighted land, and however high they raised their tithes, we would not take them with us into starvation. But for years now, those who entered the refuge gates had not been allowed to leave. The refuges were expanding rapidly, and had become nothing more than tank complexes.

But time and again, when we tried to pass on this news at settlements, we were met with silence. Wary stares and crossed arms. I remembered how Kip and I had started the fire outside New Hobart: how it had taken on its own momentum as it built and spread. Spreading the word of the Council's tanks was more like trying to light a fire in rain, with sodden green twigs. It wasn't the kind of tale you could just share with a stranger in a tavern, as if it were no more than gossip about a neighbour. We could only risk raising the topic with those who were sympathetic to the resistance – and who would admit to that, after the massacre on the island? The Council, after years of denying that the island existed, was now spreading the word of the island's defeat. The blood on its streets had rendered it safe: a cautionary tale, rather than a threat.

And the cautionary tale was working. People were warier than ever. When we approached settlements, people straightened in the fields and watched us coming, their hands firmly on their pitchforks and spades. We ventured into Drury, a large Omega town, but both times we entered taverns the noisy conversations stopped, as if the sound were a lamp suddenly extinguished. At every table, people turned to the door to assess us. Their loud conversations never resumed – whispers and mutterings replaced them. Some people would push back their chairs and leave as soon as they saw Zoe's unbranded face. Who in the taverns within would dare to discuss the resistance with three ragged strangers, let alone a group that included an Alpha and a seer?

The most frustrating encounters weren't with those who refused to talk to us, but those who seemed to believe us, but still did nothing. In two of the settlements, people listened to our story, and seemed to understand how it made sense of the Alpha's treatment of us. That the tanks were the endpoint to which the Council's policies of the last few years had been heading. But the question we heard, again and again, was *What are we supposed to do about it?* Nobody wanted to shoulder the new burden of this news. They had enough burdens already. We saw it, everywhere we went: the lean faces, the bones of eye sockets thrust forward as though trying to escape the skin. The settlements where shanties and lean-tos propped one another up. The people with teeth and gums stained a livid red, from chewing areca nut to distract from their hunger. What did we expect these people to do with the news we told them?

Two days after we'd found the abandoned safehouse, and my fight with Zoe, Piper left at dawn to scout a small Omega town further west on the plain. He returned before noon, sweat darkening the front of his shirt despite the cold.

'The Judge is dead,' he said. 'It's all over the town.'

'That's good news, isn't it?' I said. The Judge had been ruling the Council for almost as long as I could remember, but he'd been under the control of Zach and his allies for years. 'If he's just a puppet, what difference does it make if he's finally died?'

'It's not good news if his death only clears the way for someone more extreme,' said Zoe.

'It's worse than that,' Piper said. He pulled a sheet of paper from his pocket. Zoe took it and opened it. I squatted on the grass next to her to read it, trying not to think about her knife at my guts, two nights before.

'*Council leader killed by Omega terrorists,*' the headline read. In smaller print, underneath, it continued: '*Terrorists from the self-styled Omega "resistance" movement yesterday assassinated the twin of long-serving Council leader, The Judge.*'

I looked up at Piper. 'Is it possible?'

He shook his head. 'Hardly,' he said. 'Zach and his cronies

have had The Judge's twin locked up for half a decade – that's how they've been controlling him ever since. It's all a set-up. They've just decided they don't need him anymore.'

'So what's changed? You always said they needed him because people wanted the Council led by someone who seemed to be moderate.'

'Not now. Listen.' He grabbed the poster and read from it out loud:

'In his fourteen years as Council leader, The Judge was a staunch protector of Omegas. This latest outrage by Omega agitators raises pressing security concerns for those serving on the Council –'

'As if they haven't all had their twins locked up for years, if not tanked,' scoffed Zoe.

Piper kept reading. *'– and indeed for all Alphas. This attack on the very head of our government is further proof that the growing threat of Omega dissidents endangers both Alphas and Omegas. The General, reluctantly stepping forward to fill The Judge's role, expressed her sadness at his untimely demise. "Through this cowardly act, these terrorists have robbed the Omegas of a steadfast ally, and have demonstrated the ruthlessness and brutality of those who claim to be agitating for Omega 'self-determination', and who are willing to kill their own kind in order to undermine the work of the Council."'*

'They've killed two birds with one stone,' he said, tossing the paper on to the grass. 'They've got rid of him, finally, and by pinning it on us, they've stoked the anti-Omega sentiments, strengthened their own argument against the moderates.'

'So it's The General in charge now,' I said.

'*Reluctantly stepping forward*, my arse,' said Zoe. 'She's been pushing for this for years. And The Reformer and The Ringmaster will be neck deep in the whole scheme.'

None of the Councillors went by their real names. In the past, they'd chosen their Council names to disguise their identities and protect themselves from attacks on their twins. These days, when nearly all the Councillors kept their twins imprisoned in the Keeping Rooms, if not in the tanks, the elaborate names were just pageantry. Each of the names was a statement, a way of announcing to the world their agenda.

The General; The Ringmaster; The Reformer. I remembered the trifecta of faces from Piper's chart on the island: the three young Councillors who were the real power in Wyndham. The Ringmaster, his smile half-hidden by his mass of dark curls. The General's angular face, her cheekbones unforgiving. And Zach, The Reformer, my twin. His face frozen in the artist's pen-strokes. The person who I knew best, and not at all.

'The three of them have already been running things for years, really,' Piper said. 'But it's a bad sign, that they felt able to get rid of The Judge once and for all. They're confident enough of their support that they don't even need to hide behind him anymore.'

'More than that,' Zoe said. 'You've heard it, everywhere we go – the unease after the numbers who died at the island. I'd bet that even some Alphas were a bit restive about the killings. A stunt like this with The Judge shores up their own support – makes it seem as if it's a righteous battle, against an Omega resistance that's ruthlessly aggressive. Justifies their own brutal tactics.'

It was a network of fear, expertly manipulated by the Council. Not only the Omegas' fears, but the fears of the Alphas too. I had seen how they cringed away from us, how they viewed us as walking reminders of the blast, our deformed bodies a poisonous residue. The fact that my mutation wasn't visible didn't make any difference: the Omega brand on my face had been enough to provoke spits and insults from Alphas who'd passed through my settlement when I was a teenager. Alphas had always shunned us, even in good times. Then came the drought years, when I was a child, and even Alphas had gone hungry. And the year the harvests failed, when I was at the settlement. People turn on one another when they're hungry and afraid, and the Council had made sure that it was the Omegas that they blamed. This lie about The Judge's death was just the latest part of the narrative that the Council had been constructing for years: that it was us against them.

I picked up the paper, still warm from being crushed in Piper's pocket. 'It's all accelerating, isn't it. The Council's got everyone running scared. Alphas and Omegas both.'

'They don't have The Confessor anymore,' he said. 'Or her machine. Don't forget what we've achieved.'

I closed my eyes. The one thing I ought to have been grateful for – the fact that Zach no longer had The Confessor's cruel brilliance at his disposal – I couldn't even think of without losing my breath, the raw pain of it like a boot to the guts. Her death was Kip's death.

'How much do you know about The General?' I asked them.

'Not enough,' said Zoe. 'We've been monitoring her since she came on the scene. But it's been decades since infiltrators were able to penetrate the Council fort. It's harder than ever to get into Wyndham, let alone close to the Council.'

'What we do know is all bad news,' Piper said. 'She's militantly anti-Omega, just like The Ringmaster and The Reformer.'

It still jarred, to hear Zach spoken of by his Council

name. In the silo, The Confessor had said, *I had another name once.* I wondered if my twin ever thought of himself as Zach anymore. I suspected not – he would have wanted to leave it behind, along with the unsplit childhood that he'd been forced to share with me.

'The General's better established than either of them,' Piper went on. 'They all started young, not that it's unusual in the Council. That place is a snake pit – plenty of Councillors don't live long. But The General's the sharpest of the lot, politically. She got her start working for The Commander. The rumour was that she got her place by poisoning him.'

I remembered The Commander's death being announced when I was still living in the settlement. *Untimely*, the Council's bulletin had said. Timely enough for The General, it seemed.

'The General's never disputed those stories,' Piper said. 'True or not, it suits her to be feared. Every time she's come up against opposition, it's ended badly – and never for her. Scandals, disgrace, backstabbings – sometimes literally. One by one, everyone who's opposed her has been silenced, or driven out. The only reason The Judge lasted as long as he did was because he was useful to her and the other two – a popular figurehead for them to use.'

'Why her, as the new leader,' I said, 'and not The Ringmaster, or Zach?'

Piper was squatting, his elbow on his knee. 'The Ringmaster came to the Council via the army,' he said. 'He's got a huge following amongst the soldiers, but he's less of a political operator than the other two. They need him – he's been there longer, and he's got the common touch, and the loyalty of the soldiers, who see him as one of their own. But the word is that he's less radical. Don't get me wrong – he's still notorious. He runs the army, for one thing, so when it comes to enforcing Council rule, he's been the driving force for years. But although he's brutal, he's not the one driving the big reforms. Most of the worst changes – pushing the settlements further and further from decent land; the tithe increases – they seem to have originated with The General. And the tightening up of registrations came from The Reformer. Probably The Confessor too, working behind the scenes with him.'

'And what do you know about how Zach fits in to it all?'

'Less than you, probably,' Piper said.

Once, I would have agreed with him. I would have argued that I knew Zach better than anyone. Now, there was a distance between us that I couldn't breach. Between us lay The Confessor's body, and Kip's. All the silent people floating in those round glass tanks.

Piper continued. 'The Reformer's always seemed like an outsider – it comes from being split late, and not raised in Wyndham like the other two. But he had The Confessor, and that made him hugely powerful. I think the tanks are his pet project – and the database, too. He's never been smooth, like The General is – she can charm as well as intimidate. The Reformer's just as ruthless, though, in his own way.'

'You don't need to tell me that,' I said.

Piper nodded. 'But now that he's lost The Confessor, allegiances might have shifted.'

I remembered how Zach had let me escape, after Kip and The Confessor's deaths. I could still hear the waver in his voice, as he'd shouted at me to go before the soldiers arrived. *If they find out you were involved, that'll be it for me.* Was it The General or The Ringmaster he feared? Or both? Before the silo, I might have convinced myself that, on some level, Zach had wanted me set free. But whatever part of me could have believed that had been left on the silo floor, along with Kip.

'We need to get to Sally's quickly,' Piper said. 'We don't have a choice. From there, we start mustering the resistance, seeking the ships. They've wiped out the island; they've got rid of The Judge; they're dismantling the resistance network, bit by bit.'

The sky above us, sulky with clouds, took on a new and pressing weight, and I felt that the three of us were very small. Just three people on the wind-scoured plain, against all the Council's machinations. Each night, as we trudged through the long grass, there were more and more tanks being readied in the refuges. Who knew how many they'd tanked already. And more people were arriving at the refuges every day.

I couldn't claim that I understood Zach anymore, but I knew enough to know this: it would never be enough. He wouldn't be satisfied until we were all tanked.

CHAPTER 4

The next night, well after midnight, I began to sense something. I was jittery, and found myself scanning the darkness around us as we walked. Once, when Zach and I were little, wasps had made a nest in the eaves of our house, right outside our bedroom. For days, until Dad found the nest, a buzzing and scraping had kept us awake, lying in our small beds and whispering of ghosts. What I felt now was like that: a high-pitched buzz at the edge of my hearing, a message that I couldn't interpret, but that soured the night air.

Then we passed the first sign for the refuge. We were about halfway between Wyndham and the southern coast, skirting the wagon road. But we passed close enough to the road to see the sign, and crept nearer to read it. The wooden board was painted in large white letters:

Your Council welcomes you to Refuge 9 – 6 miles south.
Securing our mutual wellbeing.
Safety and plenty, earned by fair labour.
Refuges: sheltering you in difficult times.

It was illegal for Omegas to attend schools, but many managed to scrape together the basics of reading, learning at home, as I had, or in illicit schools. I wondered how many of the Omegas who passed the refuge's sign could read it at all, and how many of those would believe its message.

'*In difficult times,*' Piper scoffed. 'No mention of the fact that it's their tithes, or pushing Omegas out to blighted land, that make the times so hard.'

'Or that if the difficult times pass, it makes no difference,' added Zoe. 'Once people are in there, they're in for good.'

We all knew what that meant: the Omegas floating in the nearly-death of the tanks. Trapped in the horrifying safety of those glass bellies, while their Alpha counterparts lived on unencumbered.

We kept clear of the road, following it from a distance amongst the cover of gullies and trees. As we approached the refuge I found myself slowing, my movements sluggish as we drew closer to the source of my disquiet. By dawn, when the refuge itself came into view, walking towards it felt as though I was wading upstream through a river. In the growing light, we crept as close as we dared, until we were peering down at the refuge from a copse at the top of a rise only a hundred feet away.

The refuge was bigger than I could have imagined – it was the size of a small town. The wall surrounding it was higher even than the wall the Council erected around New Hobart. More than fifteen feet high, it was built of brick rather than wood, with tangled strands of wire along the top like nests thrown together by monstrous birds. Within the wall, we could glimpse the tops of buildings, a jumble of different structures.

Piper pointed to where a huge building loomed on the

western edge. It took up at least half of the refuge, and its walls still had the yellow tinge of fresh-cut pine, bright against the weathered grey wood of the other buildings.

'No windows,' Zoe said.

It was only a few syllables, but we all knew what it meant. Within that building, row upon row of tanks waited. Some would be empty, and some still under construction. But the sickness loitering deep in my gut left me in no doubt: many had already been filled. Hundreds of lives submerged in that thick, viscous liquid. The cloying sweetness of that fluid, creeping into their eyes and ears, their noses, their mouths. The silencing of lives, with nothing to hear but the hum of machines.

Almost all of the refuge's sprawling complex was entombed within the walls. But at the eastern edge was a section of farmed land, surrounded by a wooden fence. It was too high to climb easily, and the posts were too closely spaced for a person to slip through, but there was room enough to show the crops in their orderly lines, and the workers there, busy with hoes amongst the beets and marrows. Perhaps twenty of them, all Omegas, bent over their work. The marrows had grown fat – each one larger than the last few meals that Piper, Zoe and I had eaten.

'They're not all tanked, at least,' Zoe said. 'Not yet, anyway.'

'That's what, six acres of crops?' Piper said. 'Look at the size of the place – especially with that new building. Our records on the island showed that thousands of people have turned themselves in at the refuges each year. More than ever, lately, since the bad harvest and the tithe increases. This refuge alone would have upwards of five thousand people. No way they're being fed from those fields – it'd barely be enough to feed the guards.'

'It's a display,' I said. 'Like a minstrel show, a pretty picture of what people think a refuge is. But it's all for show, to keep people coming.'

There was something else about the refuge that unsettled me. I searched and searched for it, until I realised that it was an absence, not a presence. It was the almost total lack of sound. Piper had said that there were thousands of people within those walls. I thought of the sound of the New Hobart market, or of the island's streets. The constant noise of the children at Elsa's holding house. But the only sounds reaching us from the refuge were the strikes of the workers' hoes on the frost-hardened earth. There was no background hum of voices, and I could sense no movement within the buildings. I recalled the tank chamber I'd seen at Wyndham, where the only sound had been the buzz of the Electric. All those throats stoppered with tubes like corks in bottles.

There was movement on the road that led east past the refuge. It wasn't mounted soldiers – just three walkers, moving slowly, and laden with packs.

As they drew closer, we could see they were Omegas. The shorter of the men had an arm that ended at the elbow; the other man limped heavily, one twisted leg gnarled like driftwood. Between them walked a child. I'd have guessed he was no older than seven or eight, although he was so thin that his age was hard to tell. He looked down as he walked, guided only by his hand held tightly by the tall man.

Their heads looked too large on their thin bodies. But it was their packs that pained me most. Those bundles, tightly wrapped, would have been carefully chosen. A few treasured possessions, and all the things they thought they'd need, in the new life they'd embarked upon. The taller of the men had a shovel across his shoulders. From the other man's pack hung two cooking pans, clattering with each step.

'We need to stop them,' I said. 'Tell them what's waiting for them in there.'

'It's too late,' Piper said. 'The guards would see us. It would all be over.'

'And even if we could get to them without being seen, what could we say?' Zoe said. 'They'd think we're mad. Look at us.' I looked from Zoe to Piper, and down at myself. We were dirty and half-starved. Our clothes were ragged, and had never shed the grey stain of the deadlands.

'Why would they trust us?' Piper said. 'And what can we offer them? Once, we could have offered them safety on the island, or at least the resistance network. Now, the island's gone, and the network's collapsing by the day.'

'It's still better than the tanks,' I said.

'I know that,' Piper said. 'But they won't. How could we even begin to explain the tanks to them?'

A gate in the stone wall opened. Three Council soldiers in red tunics stepped forward, to await the new arrivals. They stood casually, arms crossed, waiting. And I was struck once again by the ruthless efficiency of Zach's plan. The tithes did the work for him, driving the desperate Omegas to the very refuges that their tithes had helped to build. Inside, the tanks would swallow them, and they would never emerge.

To the east, in the field behind the wooden palings, I saw a sudden movement. One of the workers was waving. He had run close to the fence and was waving frantically to the travellers on the road. He swung both arms back the way the walkers had come. There was no mistaking his meaning: *Away. Away.* There was such a gulf between the violence of the action, and the silence in which it was conducted. I didn't know whether he was a mute, or whether he was just trying to avoid the notice of the guards. The other workers in the field were watching him – a woman took a few steps towards him, perhaps to help him, perhaps to stop him signalling. Either way, she froze, looking over her shoulder.

A soldier was running from the wooden building behind the fields. He tackled the waving man quickly, felling him with a blow to the back of the head. By the time a second guard had reached them, the Omega was on the ground. They dragged his motionless body back to the building and out of sight. Three other soldiers emerged into the field, one walking along the inside of the fence, staring at the remaining workers, who bent quickly back to their tasks. From a distance the whole thing had been like a shadowplay, unfolding quickly and in silence.

It was over in moments, the soldiers' response so efficient that I didn't think that the new arrivals even saw the disturbance. Their heads were still down, and they were walking steadily towards the soldiers waiting at the gate, just fifty feet away. Even if they had seen the man's warning, would it have saved them if they'd turned and run? The guards could have overtaken them in no time, even on foot. Perhaps the warning had been futile – but I admired it nonetheless, and winced to think of what would be happening to the waving man now.

The two men and the boy reached the gate. They paused there, in a brief conversation with the guards. One of the guards held out his hand for the shovel that the tall Omega carried; he handed it over. The three of them stepped forward and the soldiers began to drag the gates closed. The taller of the Omega men turned back to stare along the plain. He couldn't even see me, but I found myself raising my hand, and I echoed the frantic wave of the farming man. *Away. Away.* It was pointless – my body's instinct, as futile and as unstoppable as a drowner's underwater gasp for air. The gates were already closing, and the man turned away and stepped into the refuge. The gates clashed shut behind him.

We could not save them. Already more would be on their way. In settlements nearby, they would be weighing the decision, and thinking of what they might pack. Closing the doors of houses to which they would never return. And this was only a single refuge – all over the land there were more, each one being equipped with its tanks. Piper's map, on the island, had shown nearly fifty refuges. Each one, now, a complex of living death. I couldn't look away from the new building. It would have been intimidating even if I didn't know what it contained. Now that I did, the building was a monument to horror. Only when Piper nudged me, and began to pull me deeper into the copse, did my lungs stutter back into breath, a juddering intake of air.

*

A few miles from the refuge, Piper thought he saw a movement through the scrub to the east. But by the time he got there he could find only some trampled grass, and no trail to follow in the dry terrain. The next day, when Zoe was taking the watch while Piper and I slept in the cover of a hollow, she heard a chaffinch's call, and woke us both, whispering that early winter was the wrong season for a chaffinch to sing, and that it could have been a whistle, a signal. I drew my knife while I waited for her and Piper to circle the perimeter of our camp, but they found nothing. We struck camp early that day, leaving before sundown and avoiding open ground, even when night had come.

At midnight, we crossed a valley pierced by the remains of metal poles from the Before. Bent but not felled by the blast, they curved above us, forty-foot ribs of rust, as though we were traversing the carcass of some vast monster, long dead. A jostling wind had blown all night, making it hard to speak; here in the valley the wind was noisier than ever as it shredded against the poles.

We were just beginning the climb from the valley's base when the man sprang from behind one of the rusted posts. He grabbed me by the hair, and before I could scream he had spun me around, his other hand pressing a knife to my throat.

'I've been looking for you,' he said.

I dragged my eyes from the hilt of his blade. Piper and Zoe had been just a few steps behind me. Both had their knives out now, poised to throw.

'Let her go, or you die here,' said Piper.

'Have your people stand down,' the man said to me. He spoke calmly, as if Zoe and Piper, bristling with knives, were barely a concern to him.

Zoe rolled her eyes. 'We're not *her people*.'

'I know exactly who you are,' he told her.

The knife at my throat sat precisely where The Confessor's knife had left its scar. Would that thickened strip of skin slow the blade, if he cut me? I craned my head to the side to try to see his face. I could make out only his dark hair, not tightly curled like Piper's or Zoe's, but massed in loose whorls. It reached his jaw, tickling the side of my cheek. He ignored me, except for his attentive knife. Slowly I turned my head further. Each movement pressed my neck more firmly into the knife blade, but at last I could see his eyes, fixed on Piper and Zoe. He was older than us, though still probably under thirty. I'd seen his face somewhere before, though the memory felt insubstantial.

Piper worked it out before I did.

'You think we don't know who you are?' he said. 'You're The Ringmaster.'

I knew, now, where I'd seen him: in a sketch on the island. Those few marks on a page had become flesh. The full lips, and the smile lines outside each eye. From up close, as he clasped me tightly, each one was a ridge of moonlight on his darkened face.

'Stand down,' The Ringmaster said again, 'or I'll kill her.'

Three figures stepped from the darkness behind Zoe and Piper. Two of them held swords; the third a bow. I could hear the creak of the bowstring, pulled taut, the arrow pointed at Piper's back. He didn't turn, though Zoe pivoted to face the soldiers.

'And if we do stand down, what's to stop you killing her then?' Piper asked evenly. 'Or all of us?'

'I won't kill her unless I have to. I came to talk. Why do you think I came without a big squadron? I've taken a risk to find you, talk to you.'

'What are you doing here?' Again, Piper's bored, impatient tone, as he might sound when chatting in a tavern with a tiresome companion. But I could see the tendons in his hand drawn wire-tight, and the careful angle of his wrist, as he held the knife poised above his shoulder. The blade itself was a tiny dart of silver in the moonlight. If I hadn't seen those knives in action, I might have thought it looked beautiful.

'I need to talk to the seer about her twin,' The Ringmaster said.

'And do you always start a conversation with a knife to the throat?' asked Piper.

'We both know this is no ordinary conversation.' The Ringmaster, behind me, was perfectly still, but I saw the tiny movements of his soldiers. The light moving on the blade of one man's sword, as he inched closer to Piper; the tremor of the archer's bow as the arrow was pulled back further.

'I won't talk to you while you're threatening us,' I said. With each word I felt his knife, rigid against my neck.

'And you need to understand that I'm not a man who makes idle threats.' He raised the blade, so that my chin was forced upwards. I could feel the pulse of my neck against the steel. The blade had been cold at first, but was warming now. Zoe was moving, very gradually, so that she stood back-to-back with Piper, facing the soldiers behind him. The soldier with the bow was only a few feet from her, one eye narrowed as he squinted down the line of the arrow at her chest.

When Piper moved, everything seemed to unfold very slowly. I saw how he released the blade, his arm extending, one finger pointing at The Ringmaster like a denunciation. Zoe launched at the same time, her two knives hurled at the archer as she dived to the side. For an instant the three blades were in flight, and the arrow too, slicing through the air where Zoe had stood a moment before.

The Ringmaster swiped Piper's knife from the sky with his own blade. The noises came in quick succession: the clash of his blade against Piper's; a shout from the archer as Zoe's knife hit him, and the clang as her second blade struck one of the poles. The arrow had passed my left shoulder and been lost to the darkness.

'Hold,' The Ringmaster shouted at his men. I clutched at my neck, where his knife had sat, and waited for the pain and the gush of loosened blood, its hot spurt through my fingers. It never came. There was just the old scar, and my pulse thrashing underneath my own grip.

CHAPTER 5

For several seconds we were all motionless. The Ringmaster crouched in front of me, his knife pointed at Piper, who held his own dagger only an inch or two from The Ringmaster's. Zoe, with two more throwing knives drawn, stood with her back to Piper. Beyond her, the archer was grimacing, clutching the knife lodged by his collarbone. The other two soldiers had moved in, swords outstretched, just beyond the reach of Zoe's vigilant blades.

I groped for the knife at my belt, but steel scraped on steel as The Ringmaster sheathed his blade. 'Stand down,' he said, with a toss of his head at his soldiers. They dropped back, the injured man swearing. I couldn't see his blood but I could smell it: the unmistakable raw-liver stench that reminded me of skinned rabbits, and of the bodies on the island.

'I think we understand one another,' The Ringmaster said. 'I came to talk, but you know now that if it comes to blades, I'll stand my own.'

'Touch her again and I'll cut out your tongue,' said Piper. 'You won't be talking then.'

He moved past The Ringmaster and grabbed me, drawing

me back to where Zoe stood. Her knives were lowered but not sheathed.

'Leave us,' The Ringmaster shouted to his soldiers, with an impatient wave. They withdrew until the darkness and distance hooded their faces, and I could no longer hear the wounded archer's laboured breathing.

'You're OK?' Piper said to me.

My hand was still at my neck.

'He could've slit my throat,' I whispered, 'when you threw the knife.'

'He was never going to kill you,' Piper replied. 'Not if it was so important to him to talk to you. It was a ploy.' He spoke up now, so that The Ringmaster could hear him. 'Just posturing, to impress upon us what a big man he is.'

I looked up at Piper and wondered what it must be like to be so certain of everything.

Zoe was surveying the valley. 'Where are the rest of your soldiers?' she said to The Ringmaster.

'I told you – I brought only my scouts. Do you have any idea what would happen if word got out that I'd met with you?'

I turned. His men were watching us warily from twenty yards away. The swordsmen still had their blades drawn. The injured man had dropped his bow and leaned against one of the bent metal poles, but then jerked upright again as though the touch of the taboo remnant was more painful than the dagger in his flesh.

'How did you find us?' I swung back around to face The Ringmaster. 'The Council's been searching for months. Why you, and why now?'

'Your brother, him and The General, think their machines allow them to keep track of everything. Maybe it worked well enough when they had The Confessor and her visions to help out. They never had time for old-fashioned methods. They could've learned a lot from the older Councillors, or some of the senior soldiers, if they'd taken the time to listen, like I did. I've been paying urchins in half the settlements from Wyndham to the coast, for years. When you need updates from the ground, a greedy local kid with the promise of a silver coin is worth more than any machine. Sometimes it's a waste of money – often enough they bring me nothing but rumours, false alarms. But every now and again you get lucky. There was an unconfirmed sighting of you at Drury. Then someone came to me, said three strangers had been seen in Windrush. The interesting bit was that there was an Alpha girl with two Omegas. I've had my scouts tracking you for four days.'

'Why?' Piper interrupted him.

'Because we have things in common.'

Piper laughed, the sound somehow louder in the darkness. 'Us? Look at yourself.'

The Ringmaster might have travelled away from Wyndham, but he still had the plush appearance of a Councillor. Somewhere, not far from here, would be a tent, carried and erected by his soldiers, and outfitted with clean bedding. While we'd travelled on foot, thigh-deep in drifts of ash, or footsore over rocky hills, he would have ridden. His men probably fetched him water to wash in – his face and hands showed none of the grime that marked the three of us. And by the look of his rounded cheeks, he'd never had to pick the grubs off a mushroom that was his only meal at the end of a long night of walking, or spend ten minutes scraping the last scraps of flesh from a lizard's thorny carcass. Our hunger was a garment that we could not remove, and as I looked at his well-fed face, I joined in with Piper's laughter. Zoe, behind me, spat on the ground.

'I know why you're laughing,' The Ringmaster said. 'But we have more in common than you know. We want the same thing.'

It was Zoe's turn to laugh. 'If you knew what I'd like to see done to you and the other bastards on the Council, you wouldn't be saying that.'

'I've told you already – you're making a mistake if you assume we're all the same.'

Piper spoke. 'You're all happy to sleep in feather beds while Omegas suffer. What difference does it make to us if you bicker amongst yourselves about the best ways to screw us over? You kill one another, periodically, but things don't get any better for us.'

'Things have changed.'

'Let me guess,' Piper said. 'You care about Omegas, all of a sudden?'

'No. Not at all.' His honesty stopped even Zoe, who'd been on the point of interrupting him.

The Ringmaster continued, making no pretence of shame. 'I care about Alphas. I want to do what's best for them. That's my job, just as yours is to act in the best interests of your own people.'

'I'm not in charge of the Assembly anymore,' Piper said. He gestured at himself – his ragged clothes, his dirty face. 'Do I look like the leader of the resistance to you?'

The Ringmaster ignored him. 'What The Reformer and The General are doing now, or trying to do, is a risk to all of us – Alphas and Omegas alike.'

'What are you talking about?' I said.

'Don't play coy with me,' he said. 'You escaped from Wyndham fort through the tank rooms. You know they're resurrecting the machines, the Electric. And I suspect you know more than you'd admit about The Confessor's database, too – I've never swallowed The Reformer's story that it was The Confessor's twin, alone, who killed her.'

I said nothing.

'For years I worked closely with The General, and The Reformer too,' he said. 'I was even willing to tolerate his closeness with The Confessor.' There was a curl of distaste in his upper lip. 'She was useful, at least. But there came a stage when our agendas diverged. It's become clear to me that your twin and The General no longer give any credence to the taboo. They pay lip service to it – they know that's what the public demands. But they're pushing at it. Always pushing.

'They've been working as secretively as they can, but they can't do it all alone. Over the past year or more, some of the soldiers from their personal squadrons have come to me. They've seen the things they're guarding: the tanks. The database. I rose up through the army, unlike The Reformer or The General, for all that she's taken a soldier's name for herself. I understand the soldiers, the ordinary people. I know how deep the taboo runs. Your twin and The General are so enthralled by their ideas, they've under-estimated how much most people hate and fear the machines.'

'More than they fear the Omegas?' I asked.

'It's all the same thing,' he said. 'People know that. The machines caused the blast, caused the twinning, and the Omegas.'

That was how he saw us: as an aberration – a horror to be listed along with the blast. A problem to be solved.

He went on. 'When The Confessor was killed, and her database trashed, I hoped that might be the end of it. But your brother's and The General's enthusiasm for the machines is unabated. It's already gone too far. The Judge was the last one on the Council with the power to openly oppose them. Even when they had his twin, towards the end, he still stood firm on the taboo, because he knew the public wouldn't stand for it if he didn't. So they killed his twin, and him, as soon as they figured they didn't need him anymore.'

'What about the others on the Council?' Piper said. 'Do they know what The Reformer and The General are doing? What they're planning?'

'Not many. Most have given their tacit approval: they're not looking too closely. They're happy to benefit if it works, and they don't want to be implicated if it all goes wrong.'

What a luxury it would be, I thought, to choose ignorance. To shrug off the burden of knowledge.

'Then there are those with no choice,' he said. 'Those who didn't get to their own twins before The Reformer and The General did.'

'What about your twin?' I asked.

'I have her,' he said. 'Not in the Keeping Rooms, but under guard, with soldiers I can trust.'

I tensed my neck muscles against the shudder that rose in me. There were still nights when I dreamed I was back in the cell at the Keeping Rooms, the formless days passing, and me trapped forever, a prisoner of time.

'You think that's better than the Keeping Rooms?'

'It's safer,' he said. 'For her and me. The way things are at the moment, I don't think I could protect her in Wyndham. Not even in the Keeping Rooms.'

'Why have you sought us out?' I said.

'For the last few years, since I realised the extent of their obsession with the machines, I've been trying to gather information, learn as much as I can about their plans. I've tried using other seers. There's only a handful of them.

Their powers vary so much – some are of no practical use, and most of them are broken.' He said it so offhandedly, as though when the madness claimed us, a seer was no more than a cartwheel with a broken spar, or a rusted bucket.

'You, though.' He turned back to me. 'From what I hear, you could be of some use. And if you're working with the resistance,' he nodded at Piper and Zoe, 'then there's even more to be gained from some kind of cooperation.'

'I've told you,' Piper said, enunciating each syllable slowly. 'I'm not in charge anymore.'

'You don't want to work to stop the tanks, then?'

'What is it that you think you want from us?' I interrupted.

The four of us were circling one another, a wary dance amongst the poles, while his soldiers watched from a distance.

'I need your help,' he said, 'to stop your twin and The General, and their pursuit of the machines.'

It seemed absurd. He was a Councillor, soldiers and money at his command, and powerful beyond what any of us, ragged, thin and exhausted, could imagine.

'You want help?' Piper said. 'Then ask your Council cronies.'

The Ringmaster laughed. 'You really think we're one big happy family, sitting around the Council chamber backslapping one another?' He turned from Piper to me. 'When you were in the Keeping Rooms, who did you think The Reformer was protecting you from? A Councillor's greatest enemies are those closest to him – those with the most to gain if he slips from power. Look at what happened to The Judge.'

'Why would we help you manoeuvre against them?' Piper said. 'You've only come to us because you're being edged out of power, and you're desperate.'

'Edged out of power?' The Ringmaster met Piper's gaze. 'You'd know how that feels.'

I interrupted him. 'You chose to work with them, before the machines drove you apart. Why would we work with somebody who hates Omegas?'

'Because I can offer your people a better life than the tanks. The refuge system has worked well for decades, as a humane way of dealing with the Omega problem. Maintained by tithes, it's a workable solution. Without your brother and The General, things could continue the way they used to.'

'That's why I could never work with you,' I said. 'There isn't an *Omega problem*. Only those problems that the Council's created for us: the tithes. Pushing us further and further out, to land where nothing will grow. The branding, and all the other restrictions that make it nearly impossible to live.'

'That's all immaterial now. We both know the only thing that matters is stopping the tanks.'

'Then why didn't you just come with more soldiers,' I said, 'and take me back to Wyndham? With me as your prisoner, you know you could force Zach to do whatever you like.'

'I would have, if I'd thought it would do me any good. Thought about killing you, too, to take him out altogether.' He was as unapologetic as his blade itself, whose indentation I could still feel on my throat. 'A few months ago, it might have worked. But it's bigger than your brother, now. He allied himself too closely to The Confessor. Now she's gone, it's weakened his standing. The General's been around for longer than him; she's better established on the Council. When the two of them killed The Judge, she grabbed power, and she's not going to let it go. If I threaten The Reformer, or even kill him, it's not going to put a stop to this. And if The General even suspected that we were using you as a hostage to control your twin, she'd kill him herself.'

Before I escaped from Wyndham, Zach had said to me: *I've started something, and I need to finish it.* But he was caught up now, as if trapped in the workings of one of his own machines.

'Anyway,' The Ringmaster went on, 'you're more use to me out here, as a contact with the resistance.'

'I won't be used.'

I was thinking of Piper, and what he'd said to me, just a few days ago: *It's your job to endure the visions. And it's mine to decide how we can use them.* I was tired of men who saw me as a tool to be wielded.

'We could benefit each other,' said The Ringmaster. 'We want the same thing.'

'No we don't.' This accusation cut me more than his blade had done. 'You want to be rid of us, just like Zach does – you just disapprove of his methods.'

'Perhaps our goals diverge eventually, but right now, we both want to stop what's happening with the tanks. So the question is, how important is that to you?'

'I won't help you.'

Piper talked over me. 'If we were to help you, what could you offer us in exchange?'

'Information. The kind of insider details that could help the resistance to stop the tankings. The General and The Reformer might be freezing me out, but I still have access that you could only dream of.'

'Information alone's no good to us, if we can't even act on it,' I said. 'There might have been a time when secret information-gathering and hiding away was enough. But our people have bled and died on the island. If you want to stop the tankings, you need to rally those soldiers loyal to you, and help us.'

'You ask too much,' he said. 'If I take arms against your brother and The General, it's open war. People will die – yours as well as mine.'

'People have already died,' I said. 'And more are going to be tanked – all Omegas, eventually. It's worse than death.'

'I'm willing to help you stop it. Why won't you do the same?' His voice was persuasive – I could imagine him holding forth in the Council Hall. 'These machines are powerful in ways we can't even understand. Who knows what the tanking could do to us?'

He was looking me in the eyes and I knew his concern was real. But I also knew that he only feared for the Alphas. His 'us' didn't include the Omegas in the tanks. We were nothing more than the background noise. And I reminded myself, too, that he controlled much of the army. I thought of the soldiers I'd seen in New Hobart, whipping an Omega prisoner until the flesh of his back split like overripe fruit. I thought of the soldiers who had attacked the island. Had they reported to him, followed his orders?

'You should be against the tanks because it's wrong to torture people by keeping them underwater and half-dead,' I said. 'Because it's an unspeakable crime. Not because of your fear of what the machines could do. Not because of the taboo.'

'I'm not without compassion,' he said. 'Stopping the machines benefits Omegas too. Your people, more than anyone else, are victims of what the machines wrought.' He looked pointedly at Piper's left shoulder. 'I'm not one of the idiots who swallows the Council line about Omegas as evil deviants. I understand that you're more to be pitied than hated.'

'We don't want your pity, or need it,' said Piper. 'We need your help. Your swords, and your soldiers.'

'We both know that can't happen.'

'Then we have nothing further to talk about,' I said.

He scanned my face. I didn't look away.

'You'll change your mind,' he said. 'When you do, come to me.'

He made to turn away, but I called after him.

'You want us to trust you,' I said, 'but you haven't even told us your real name.'

'You know my name,' he said.

'Not your Council name. Your real name.'

'I already told you.' His voice was granite – it yielded nothing. 'What would it change, if I told you the name my parents gave to me? Why would that be any truer than the name I chose for myself?'

I refused to be dismissed by him. 'Why choose The Ringmaster then?' I said.

He raised his chin slightly, appraising me.

'When I was a child,' he said, 'a minstrel show came through our town. They put on a hell of a show: not just bards, but jugglers and acrobats too. A horse that danced on its hind legs to the music, and a man who'd trained snakes to crawl all over his body. It felt like half the town turned out to watch. It was the most amazing thing I'd ever seen. But when everyone else was oohing and aahing at the dancing horse, and the man who walked on stilts, I was watching the man who introduced them. I saw how he got us hyped up for each act, and how he jumped in to cut an act short if it wasn't grabbing us. He orchestrated the whole thing. The performers were impressive enough, in their own way, but the Ringmaster was the one running the show. He had the audience performing like that dancing horse, by the end, and they filled his hat with coins without thinking twice.

He bent closer, as if he were telling me a secret. 'I never wanted to be the man on stilts, or the snake-charmer. I wanted to be the Ringmaster: the one who makes things happen. That's what I am now. You'd do well to remember it.'

He stepped back, and began to walk away to where his soldiers waited, barely visible in the darkness.

'Tell me why we shouldn't kill you now,' Zoe shouted at his back.

'That's what your twin would do,' he said, turning to me. 'The Reformer would have a knife in my back before I got three paces away.' He gave a grin – the quick twist of the mouth, a flash of teeth like the glint of a blade. 'I suppose it's a question of how alike you are.'

And it was a kind of courage, to turn his back on us and take those steps. His soldiers were too far away to help him. His death would be a matter of moments. I knew exactly how Piper would draw back his arm. The precise movement with which he would throw the knife: his arm straightening; the knife not tossed but released, unwavering, to bury itself in the back of The Ringmaster's neck.

'Don't do it.' I grabbed Piper's raised arm, his muscles taut beneath my fingertips. He didn't shift when I wrapped my hands around his forearm. His knife was poised, his eyes following The Ringmaster's path amongst the broken ghosts of poles. Next to him, Zoe had a knife raised too, assessing the soldiers waiting beyond The Ringmaster.

'Give me one good reason why he should live,' said Piper. 'No.'

He looked down at me, as if hearing me for the first time.

'I'm not going to play that game,' I went on. 'It's the same thing you asked me on the island, when the others wanted me dead. I won't do it – trading lives, weighing lives against others.'

'He's a risk to us, now,' Piper said. 'It's not safe to let him live. And he's a Councillor, for crying out loud. A terrible man.'

All of that was true, but I still didn't release Piper's arm.

'The world's full of terrible people. But he came to talk, not to harm us. What gives us the right to kill him, and his twin?'

In the silence that followed, The Ringmaster's words rang in my head: *I suppose it's a question of how alike you are.*

The Ringmaster had almost reached his soldiers when Piper shook free of my arm and strode after him.

'Wait,' Piper commanded.

The soldiers rushed to surround The Ringmaster, who had turned back to face Piper. The swordsmen had their weapons raised. Even the archer, his right hand still clutching the knife hilt buried in his shoulder, had drawn a dagger from his belt and raised it towards Piper with his shaking left hand.

'You have something of ours,' Piper said, leaning forward and calmly pulling Zoe's blade from the archer's flesh. The man inhaled sharply and gave a strangled curse, but under The Ringmaster's impassive gaze he didn't retaliate, just pressed his hand tighter against the wound. Fresh blood surged between his fingers and spilled down his knuckles.

The Ringmaster nodded once at Piper, then looked beyond him to me.

'When you change your mind, come to me,' he said. Then he turned and walked away, calling his soldiers to follow him.

CHAPTER 6

'You need to learn to fight,' Zoe said the next morning. Piper was on lookout, and Zoe and I were supposed to be resting, but our encounter with The Ringmaster had left us both edgy.

'I can't,' I said.

'Nobody's suggesting that you're going to become some kind of super-assassin,' she said. 'But Piper and I haven't got time to save you every five minutes.'

'I don't want to kill.' I remembered the blood smell from the battle of the island, and how each death had been doubled for me, my visions showing me not just those slain in the battle, but also their twins, ambushed by their own deaths.

'You don't have a choice,' she said. 'People like The Ringmaster – they're going to keep coming for you. You need to be able to defend yourself. And I can't always be here. Piper either.'

'I hate the idea of it,' I said. 'I don't want to kill. Not even Council soldiers. What about their twins?'

'You think I enjoy it?' said Zoe quietly.

I was silent for a few moments. Finally, I said, 'I won't fight unless I'm being attacked.'

'Only a few times a week, then, the way you're going lately.'

When she raised one eyebrow like that, she reminded me of Kip.

'Get out your knife,' she said.

From its sheath at my belt, I pulled the dagger that Piper had given to me on the island. It was about as long as my forearm, the blade sharp on both sides, and narrowing to a vicious point. The hilt was wrapped in leather, wound tightly and sweat-darkened to almost black.

'Could I learn to throw it, like you and Piper?'

She laughed, taking the dagger from me. 'You'd be more likely to take your own ear off. This isn't a throwing knife, anyway – not balanced right.' She spun it casually between her forefinger and thumb. 'And I'm not giving you any of my knives. But you can learn some basics, so you won't be completely useless if we're not around to save you.'

I looked up at her. Despite our arguments, it was hard to imagine her not being around. Her sarcastic asides were as familiar to me now as her wide shoulders, her restless hands. When we sat around the fire at night, the flick of her blade on her fingernails was as normal as the cicadas' rasping.

'Are you thinking of leaving?'

She shook her head but dodged my eyes.

'Tell me the truth,' I said.

'Just concentrate,' she said. 'You need to learn this stuff.' She tossed my dagger on the ground. 'You won't need that for now. And forget about high-kicks or backflips or any of that dramatic-looking stuff. Most of the time it's grappling, close and ugly. There's nothing pretty about fighting.'

'I know that,' I said. I'd seen it on the island: the clumsiness of desperation. Swords slipping in bloodied hands. Bodies that became slashed sacks, emptied of blood.

'Good,' she said. 'Then we can get started.'

For the first few hours, she wouldn't let me use my blade at all. Instead, she showed me how to use my elbows and knees to strike in close quarters. She showed me how to drive my elbow backwards into the guts of an attacker holding me from behind, and how to throw my head back and upwards to connect with his nose. She taught me how to bring my knee up to bury it sharply in an assailant's groin, and how to throw my whole body weight behind the sideways jab of an elbow to the jaw.

'Don't hit *at* somebody,' she said, 'or you'll make no impact. Hit *through* them. You have to follow through. Aim for a spot six inches under the skin.'

I was sweaty and tired by the time she let me try with the knife. Even then, at first she didn't teach me anything but defence: how to block a strike with my blade, shielding my hand with the hilt. How to stand side-on so that I presented a smaller target, and to keep my knees bent, legs wide, so that I couldn't easily be knocked over.

Then she got to the blade itself. How to strike without signalling it beforehand. How to go for the arteries between groin and thigh. How to make a low slash at the stomach, and how to twist the blade on the way out.

'I don't want to know this,' I said, grimacing.

'You're enjoying it,' she said. 'For once you're not slouching around. You haven't looked this animated in weeks.'

I wondered if it were true. There was a satisfaction in the mastery of each move, in feeling the actions become familiar. But at the same time I was repulsed by the idea of gutting anyone. Could actions and their consequences be so neatly separated? The movements permitted no uncertainty, and no ambiguity: you did them. That was it. All morning we'd repeated them, again and again. It was comforting, in the same way that biting my nails was comforting: a mindless action that gave some respite from thought. But when I bit my nails, all I ended up with was my own fingers raw-tipped and sore. The routines Zoe was teaching me would leave a body sundered, robbed of blood. Somewhere a twin, too, would bleed out, and it would be my hand dealing that double death.

Zoe resumed the fighting stance, waiting for me to mirror her.

'There's no point if you don't practise,' she said. 'It needs to be so that your knife's in your hand before you realise you need it. It needs to feel seamless – so it comes to you without thinking.'

I'd seen how she and Piper moved, and fought – their bodies fluid, not responding to their thoughts but becoming their thoughts. It was true what she'd said – *There's nothing pretty about fighting* – and I knew that however striking Zoe's and Piper's movements, the results were the same: blood, death. Flies swarming on sticky bodies. But I still found myself admiring the certainty of their bodies as they inscribed their answers on the world with a blade.

It was past noon when we stopped.

'Enough,' she said, when I clumsily blocked her final parry. 'You're tired. That's how stupid mistakes happen.'

'Thank you,' I said, as I slipped my knife back into my belt. I smiled at her.

She shrugged. 'It's in my interests to give you a better chance of getting yourself out of trouble, for a change.' She was already walking away. She was a door, forever slamming shut in my face.

'Why are you like this?' I called after her. 'Why do you always have to cut me down and stalk off?'

She looked back at me.

'What do you want from me?' she said. 'You want me to hold your hand, and braid your hair? Have we not given you enough, me and Piper?'

I couldn't answer. More than once, she'd proved that she was willing to risk her life to protect me. It seemed petty to complain that she didn't also give me her friendship.

'I didn't mean to see your dreams,' I said. 'I couldn't help it. You don't know what it's like, being a seer.'

'You're not the first seer,' she said, and she walked away. 'I doubt you'll be the last.'

*

It was dawn, two days later, when the bards came. We'd made camp just a few hours before, at a spot Zoe and Piper knew. It was a forested hill overlooking the road, with a spring nearby. Since The Ringmaster's ambush we'd been edgy, flinching at every sound. To make it worse, for two days it hadn't stopped raining. My blanket was a sodden load, dragging my rucksack until the straps chafed at my shoulders. The rain had thinned to a drizzle when we arrived, but everything was soaked and there was no chance of a fire. Piper took the first lookout shift. He spotted them in the tentative dawn light – two travellers making their way along the main road, in the opposite direction from where we'd come. He called us over. I'd been wrapped in a blanket in the shelter of the trees, and Zoe had just returned from a hunt, two freshly-dead rabbits swinging from her belt.

The newcomers were still only small figures on the road when we heard the music. As they drew closer, through the thinning fog we could see that one of them was thrumming her fingers on the drum hanging by her side, sounding out the rhythm of their steps. The other one, a bearded man with a staff, held a mouth organ to his lips with one hand, exploring fragments of a tune as they walked.

When they reached the point where the road curved away, they broke with it, instead heading up the hill through the longer grass, towards the woods where we sheltered.

'We need to leave,' said Zoe, already shoving her flask back into her bag.

'How do they know the spot?' I asked.

'The same way that I do,' Piper said. 'From travelling this road many times before. They're bards – they're always on the road. This is the only spring for miles – they're heading right for it.'

'Pack your things,' Zoe said to me.

'Wait,' I said. 'We could talk to them, at least. Tell them what we know.'

'When are you going to learn that we need to be more cautious?' Zoe said.

'In case word gets out?' I said. 'Isn't that what we've been trying to do? We've been trying to spread the word ever since we left the deadlands, and we're getting nowhere.'

'It's one thing for word to get out about the refuges,' Piper said. 'Another for word to get out about us, and where we are. If it had been Zach, and not The Ringmaster, who found us the other day, we'd all be in cells by now, or worse. I'm trying to protect you, and keep us all alive. We don't know who we can trust.'

'You saw what happened at the refuge,' I said. 'And there are more people turning themselves in every day, thinking it's a haven. We could stop them, if we could spread the word about what really happens there.'

'And you think two strangers can do it better than us?' Piper said.

'Yes,' I said. 'We need people who travel without raising suspicion. Who draw a crowd to hear them wherever they go. People who can make the news catch on, so it starts to spread by itself.' An Omega bard could count on a welcome at any Omega settlement, and an Alpha bard could expect to be hosted at any Alpha village. Bards were the roaming memory of the world. They sang the stories that would otherwise be buried along with their subjects. Their songs traced the love stories of individuals, and the bloodlines of families, and the history of whole villages, towns, or regions. And they sang imaginary tales as well: great battles and fantastical happenings. They played on feast days, and at burials, and their songs were a currency accepted all over the land.

'Nobody's listening to us,' I said. 'They listen to bards. And you know how it works. Songs spread like fire, or plague.'

'They're not exactly positive things,' Zoe pointed out.

'They're powerful things,' I said.

Piper was watching me carefully.

'Even if we can trust the bards, it would be a lot to ask of them,' he said.

'Give them the choice,' I said.

Neither Zoe nor Piper spoke, but they'd stopped their packing. The music was drawing nearer. I looked back down the hill to the pair approaching. The bearded man wasn't leaning on his staff; instead, he swung it loosely in front of him, back and forth, sweeping the air for obstacles. He was blind.

When they reached the edge of the woods, Piper called a greeting to them. The music stopped, the sounds of the forest suddenly loud in the new silence.

'Who's there?' called the woman.

'Fellow travellers,' said Piper.

They stepped into the clearing. She was younger than us, her red hair plaited and reaching all the way down her back. I couldn't see her mutation, though she was branded.

'You heading north, to Pullman market?' the man asked. He still held the mouth organ in one hand, the staff in the other. His eyes weren't closed – they were missing altogether. Below the brand on his forehead, the skin stretched uninterrupted across his eye sockets. His hands had extra fingers, unruly offshoots from every knuckle, like a sprouting potato. Seven fingers, at least, on each hand.

Piper avoided his question. 'We're leaving tonight, when it's dark. You'll have the clearing to yourselves.'

The man shrugged. 'If you're travelling at night, then I shouldn't be surprised you don't want to tell us where you're headed.'

'You're travelling at night, too,' I pointed out.

'Night and day, at the moment,' the woman said. 'The market starts in two days. We were delayed at Abberley when the flooding swept the bridge.'

'And I always travel in the dark, even if the sun's shining.' The man gestured to his sealed eye sockets. 'So who am I to judge you for it?'

'Our travel's not your business,' said Zoe. The woman stared at her, and kept staring, taking in Zoe's unbranded face, her Alpha body. I wondered whether my scrutiny of the bards had been so obvious.

'True enough,' the man said, unflustered by Zoe's tone.

He and the woman moved to the centre of the clearing. He didn't take her arm, but guided himself with his staff. Watching him negotiate the unseen world reminded me of how it felt to be a seer. When I'd navigated the reef, or the caves under Wyndham, my mind had been groping the air for directions, reaching out before me just as the bard's staff did.

He settled on a fallen log. 'One thing I don't understand,' he said. 'If you're travelling at night, you're avoiding the Council patrols. But you don't move like Omegas.'

'One of them's not an Omega,' said the woman, shooting another look at Zoe.

'She's with us,' said Piper quickly.

'It's not just her.' The blind man turned to face Piper. 'It's you, too.'

'I'm an Omega,' Piper said. 'Our companion here is, too – your friend will tell you that. The other lady may not be an Omega, but she's with us, and isn't looking for any trouble.'

'What did you mean, they don't move like Omegas?' I asked the man.

He swung his head to face me. 'Without eyes, you get good at listening. I'm not talking about hearing the sound of a limp, or crutches. That's the obvious stuff. But it's more than that. It's the way Omegas walk. Most of us sound a little slumped. We've all copped enough blows, missed enough meals, to keep our heads low. Most of us, you can hear it in our steps: we don't step high, or wide. We drag our feet: a little bit of shuffling. A little bit of flinching. The two of them,' he gestured towards Piper and Zoe, 'they don't sound like that.'

I was amazed that he could tell so much just from the sound of their movements, but I knew what he meant. I'd noted the same thing when I met Piper for the first time on the island: the unabashed way that he held himself. Most people on the island had begun to shed the diffidence that the mainland stamped on Omegas, but Piper wore none of it. Even now, thin and with the knees of his trousers blackened and fraying, he moved with the same loose-limbed confidence as he always had.

The man turned back to Piper. 'You don't move like an Omega, any more than the Alpha lady does. But if you're on the road with an Alpha, I'm guessing your story's not an ordinary one.'

'You heard what they said: their story's not our business,' said the woman, pulling his arm. 'We should go.'

'Surely we've covered enough miles for a rest?' he said, planting his staff in front of him.

'Why are you so keen to stick around?' Zoe asked him. 'Most Omegas keep well clear of us. Of me, anyway.'

'I told you,' he said. 'I'm a bard. I collect stories, the way some people collect coins, or trinkets. It's my trade. And even a blind man can see that there's a story here.'

'It's a story we can't share with just anybody,' said Piper. 'It'd mean trouble for us, as you well know.'

'I'm not one to talk to Council patrols, if that's what you mean,' said the man. 'Even a bard gets a hard time from the Council these days. They're no friends of mine.'

'There's talk that the Council wants to stop Omegas from being bards at all,' the woman added. 'It's all the travelling around that they don't like. They like to keep tabs on us.'

'I'd challenge the best of the Alpha bards to play as well as me,' said the man, flourishing his extra fingers.

'The soldiers would have your fingers off if they heard you say that,' said the woman.

'We're not about to tell them,' said Piper. 'And if you can keep quiet about having seen us here, I don't see why we can't camp together for the day.'

The woman and Zoe still looked wary, but the blind man smiled.

'Then let's make camp. I could use a rest. I'm Leonard, by the way. And this is Eva.'

'I won't tell you our names,' said Piper. 'But I won't lie to you, at least, and give false names.'

'Glad to hear it,' Leonard said. Eva sat next to him and began pulling their things from her rucksack. She had some nuggets of coal wrapped in waxed paper and still dry.

'Fine,' said Zoe. 'But we need to cook quickly – we're still too close to the road to risk a fire once this fog's cleared.'

While Piper stoked the fire and Zoe sat sharpening her knives, I joined Leonard on the log.

'You said the others didn't move like Omegas.' I tried to keep my voice low enough that the others wouldn't hear. 'What about me?'

'You neither,' he said.

'But I don't feel like them. They've always been so –' I paused. 'So sure. So certain about everything.'

'I didn't say you were like them. I just said you didn't walk like other Omegas.' He shrugged. 'Girl, you're hardly here.'

'What do you mean?'

He paused, and gave a laugh. 'You walk like you think the earth begrudges you a space to plant your feet.'

I thought of the moment after Kip's death, when Zach had found me slumped on the platform at the top of the silo. The air had been so heavy. If Zach hadn't begged me to run, to save his own skin, I doubted I'd have managed to drag myself upright and leave. All these weeks and all these miles later, I hadn't realised that I was still hauling the weight of the sky with each step.

CHAPTER 7

We ate the rabbits, as well as some foraged mushrooms and greens that Eva pulled from her bag.

'Are you a seer as well?' I asked her while we ate.

She snorted. 'Hardly.'

'Sorry,' I said. Nobody wanted to be mistaken for a seer. 'I just couldn't see your mutation.'

Leonard's face had turned serious.

'She has the most feared mutation of all,' he said. 'I'm surprised you haven't spotted it already.'

There was a long pause. I scanned Eva again but could see nothing unusual. What could be more feared than being a seer, with its promise of madness?

Leonard leaned forward, and gave a stage whisper. 'Red hair.'

Our laughter startled two blackbirds, that took off, screeching.

'Look more closely,' Eva said. She turned her head to the side and lifted her thick braid. There, nestled into the back of her neck, was a second mouth. She opened it briefly, baring two crooked teeth.

'Only shame is that I can't sing out of it,' she said, letting her braid drop. 'Then I wouldn't need Leonard for the harmonies, and I wouldn't have to put up with his grumbling.'

When the fire was extinguished and the sun risen, Leonard cleaned his hands carefully before he took up his guitar.

'Can't get rabbit grease on the strings,' he said, weaving his handkerchief between his clustered fingers.

'If you're going to be making a racket, I'd better keep watch,' said Zoe. 'If anything comes along the road, we'll need to see them before they hear us.' She looked up at the tree above her. Piper dropped to kneel on one knee and she climbed, without speaking, on to his bent leg, balanced for a moment with a hand on his shoulder, and then jumped up to grasp the branch. She swung herself upwards, feet pointed and body tucked. I could see what Leonard had meant, when he'd talked about the way she and Piper moved. The ease with which they inhabited their bodies.

When I envied Zoe, though, it wasn't her unbranded face I coveted, or her confidence. Not even her freedom from the visions that shredded my mind. It was the way that she and Piper moved together, without even speaking. The closeness that didn't require words. There'd been a time when Zach and I had been like that, long before we were split, and before he'd turned against me. But after all that had happened since, the intimacy of that shared childhood seemed as distant as the island. It was a place to which we could never return.

Eva took up her drum, and Leonard's right hand plucked at the strings, tickling the music out of the instrument, while the fingers of his left hand moved more slowly.

He'd been right, I knew, when he'd told me that he'd heard my hesitant footsteps. I'd been taunting my body with cold and hunger. Avoiding every consolation, because there would be no consolation for the dead I'd left in my wake. But this music was a pleasure that I couldn't dodge. Like the ash that had plagued us in the east, the music would not be denied. I leaned back against a tree and allowed myself to listen.

It was more noise than we'd permitted ourselves for weeks. Our lives had become so muted. We crept at night, wincing at the breaking of twigs beneath our boots. We hid from patrols, and talked often in whispers. We were at risk, every moment, until it began to feel as though sound itself had become something we had to ration. Now, even the most flippant of the bards' songs felt like a small act of defiance: to hear the music ringing out. To permit ourselves something more than bare survival.

Some of the songs were slow and sad; others were raucous, the notes sizzling and jumping like corn kernels in a hot pan. Several had lyrics bawdy enough to set us all laughing. And when I glanced away from the fire, I saw that even Zoe's feet, hanging from the branch high in the tree, were swinging in time with the music.

'Did your twin have the talent for music as well?' I asked Leonard, when he and Eva stopped for a drink.

He shrugged. 'All I have of her is a name on my registration papers. That and the town where we were born.' He fished the worn sheet of paper from his bag and waved it at me, laughing. 'They can't make up their minds, the Council. Can't do enough to keep us separate, but then they make us carry our twins around in our pockets, everywhere we go.' He traced the paper as if he would feel the word under his fingertip. '*Elise*, it says. That's what Eva tells me – she can read a little. But that's my twin's name, on there somewhere.'

'And you don't remember anything about her at all?'

He shrugged again. 'I was a baby when they sent me

away. That's all I know of her: those marks on paper, that I can't even see.'

I thought again of Zach. What did I have of him, now? I had been thirteen when I was branded and sent away. Not long enough for me, and too long for him. During my years in the Keeping Rooms, he'd come to see me, but only rarely. When I'd last seen him, in the silo after Kip and The Confessor's deaths, he'd seemed fevered, frantic. He had been hissing, cut loose, like the electric wires that Kip and I had slashed.

When the next song started, my mind was still lingering in the silo with Zach, hearing again the tremor of terror in his voice when he'd told me to run. Eva had swapped her drum for a flute, so it was only Leonard's voice tracing the words. It was mid-morning, the sun through the trees casting stripes on the clearing. It took me a moment to realise what Leonard was singing about.

> *They came in dark ships*
> *They came at night*
> *They laid The Confessor's kiss*
> *On each islander's throat with a knife.*

Piper stood up. To my left, Zoe dropped quietly from the lookout tree to the ground. She moved closer to where we sat in a circle around the ashes.

'I heard they didn't kill them all,' Piper said.

Leonard stopped singing, but his fingers on the guitar never hesitated, the tune continuing to unfurl from his hands.

'Is that what you heard?' he said. The music played on. 'Well, songs always exaggerate.'

He went back to the song.

72

They said there was no island
They said it wasn't true
But they came for the island in their dark ships
And they're coming next for you.

'You'd want to be careful who's listening, when you sing that song,' said Zoe. 'You could bring down trouble.'

Leonard smiled. 'And you haven't got trouble already, the three of you?'

'Who told you about the island?' said Piper.

'The Council themselves are putting the word out,' Leonard said. 'Spreading the news that they found the island, crushed the resistance.'

'That song you're singing is hardly the Council's version, though,' said Piper. 'What do you know of what happened there?'

'People talk to bards,' he said. 'They tell us things.' He strummed a few more chords. 'But I'm guessing you didn't need to be told about the island. I'm guessing you know more than I do about what happened there.'

Piper was silent. I knew that he was remembering. I'd seen it too. Not only seen it, but heard the shouts and whimpers. Smelled the butcher's block scent of the streets.

'No song can describe it,' said Piper. 'Let alone change it.'

'Maybe not,' said Leonard. 'But a song can at least tell people about it. Tell them what the Council did to those people. Warn them what the Council's capable of.'

'And scare them away from getting involved with the resistance?' Zoe said.

'Perhaps,' said Leonard. 'That's why the Council's telling their version. I like to think my version might do something different – perhaps help people to realise why the resistance is so necessary. All I can do is tell the story. What they do with it is up to them.'

'If we gave you another story to tell,' I said, 'you know it could be dangerous for you.'

'That's for us to decide,' Eva said.

Piper and Zoe didn't say anything, but Zoe stepped forward to stand beside Piper. Piper took a deep breath, and began to talk.

The bards put down their instruments while they listened. Leonard's guitar lay on its back across his knees, and as we talked I imagined that it was a box we were filling with our words. We didn't tell them about my link with Zach, but we told them everything else. We told them about the tanks, each one a glass case filled with terror. The missing children, and the tiny skulls in the grotto beneath the tank room at Wyndham. And the expanding refuges, and the machines that we'd destroyed with The Confessor.

When we'd finished, there was a long silence.

'There's good news in there too,' Leonard said quietly. 'About The Confessor. We passed near the Sunken Shore last week. She was from round there, they say, so there was a lot of talk about the rumour that she'd been killed. But I hadn't dared to believe it.'

'It's true,' I said, looking away from him. I didn't want to see Leonard's answering smile. He didn't know the price Kip had paid for this good news. The price I was still paying.

'And the rest of it – about the tanks. Is it really true?' said Eva.

Leonard answered her before we could.

'It's all true. Hell on earth, it's too far-fetched to make up.' He rubbed at his absent eyes. 'It explains everything. Why the Council's been driving up the tithes and the land restrictions, these last few years. They're pushing us toward the refuges.'

Francesca Haig

'And do you think you could put it in a song?' I said.

He reached down to place a hand on the neck of the guitar. 'There's a song in your story, that's for sure, though it won't be a pretty one,' he said. He hoisted up the guitar, stroking along the top with his thumb, as if waking it gently.

'Like Cass said: it'll be dangerous, spreading the word,' said Piper.

Leonard nodded. 'True enough. But it's dangerous for all of us, if word of the tanks and the refuges doesn't spread.'

'It's a lot to ask of you,' I said.

'You're not asking it of me,' Leonard said. There was no music left in his voice as he spoke – his words were grave and quiet. 'But you told me what you know. And now that I've heard it, I have an obligation.'

*

For hours, while I took my shift at the lookout post, I could hear Leonard and Eva working on the song. First they built the tune itself. The occasional word reached me: *No, try this. Hold off on the chord change until the chorus. How about this?* But mainly they didn't talk. It was a conversation that took place in music. He'd pluck out a tune, and Eva would echo it, then play with it: varying the melody, adding harmonies. For hours they sat together, passing the tune back and forth between them.

Even when Eva had settled down to rest, Leonard kept working, adding the words now. He sang slowly, trying out different versions of the words. He was stringing them onto the growing melody like beads on a string, sometimes unthreading and rearranging. When Piper relieved me at the lookout post, I fell asleep listening to Leonard's singing, the gravelled edge of his deep voice.

75

When I woke later, the moon was rising in the darkening sky, and Leonard was still playing. I walked down to the spring. The music followed me all the way to the water, which might be why Zoe didn't hear me coming. I saw her standing close to where the stream burst from the rock, about twenty feet ahead of me. She was leaning against a tree, one arm wrapped loosely around it, her head resting on the trunk as she tilted her face upwards. She swayed slightly to the music that filtered through the trees. Her eyes were closed.

I'd seen Zoe naked, when we washed at rivers. I'd seen her asleep. I'd even shared her dreams, her sleeping mind a window onto the sea. But I'd never seen her as unguarded as at that moment. I turned away, as if I'd seen something shameful, and began to retreat. She opened her eyes.

'Are you spying on me?'

'Just fetching water,' I said, lifting the empty water flask like a flag of surrender.

She turned back to the spring. When she spoke, she didn't look at me. 'There used to be a bard who came through our parents' village, a few times a year. She played the violin like nobody you've ever seen. Piper and I were only tiny, then – we used to sneak out after bedtime to listen.'

She said nothing more. I hesitated before speaking – I was remembering her blade at my stomach, after she'd learned that I'd seen her dreams.

'If you want to talk –' I said, eventually.

'You're meant to be the expert on the future,' she interrupted, striding towards me and grabbing the flask. 'Concentrate on that. That's what we need you for. Keep your nose out of my past.' She knelt at the spring and wrenched the stopper out before filling the flask.

We stood facing each other. I watched the water drip from her wet hand, and I tried to come up with words that she couldn't throw back at me.

Before I could speak, the music stopped suddenly. From up the hill, Piper was calling to us. Zoe strode past me and didn't look back.

'The song's not finished yet,' Leonard warned us, when we were gathered around him and Eva. A fog had descended with the darkness, and Piper had rekindled the fire. 'It'll change, too,' he added, 'as we travel, and as other bards take it up. If a song's alive enough, it changes.' I remembered the different versions of songs that I'd heard. The song about the blast, which changed from bard to bard, or from season to season.

Leonard began quietly, his fingers strumming a series of almost cheerful chords on the guitar. There was none of the intricate fingerpicking that had impressed me when he'd performed for us earlier. 'I've kept it simple,' he said, as if he could see me staring at his fingers. 'If you want it to catch on, it has to be something that any bard could play, without fifteen fingers.'

As the tune went on, melancholy notes were slipped in like contraband, so that by the time they reached the chorus, the tune had soured. Eva's melody parted from Leonard's, her voice climbing to new and mournful highs, as his stayed steady and low. Their voices counterbalanced and resonated, until the space in between the notes was thick with longing.

> *There's no refuge in the refuge,*
> *No peace behind those gates.*
> *No freedom once you turn to them*
> *Just living death, where the tanks await.*

They throw you in a cage of glass
Not living, and not dying.
Trapped inside a floating hell
Where none can hear you crying.

Oh, you'll never be hungry, you'll never be thirsty
And the Council's tanks will have no mercy.
Oh, you'll never be tired, you'll never be cold
And you'll never ever ever grow old,
And the only price you'll have to pay
Is to give your life away.

They drive us to the blighted land
Then bleed us with their tithes,
And if you go to the refuge
They'll take your very lives.

The taboo has been forsaken
Within the refuge walls.
The machines have been awakened
And the Council plans to tank us all.

Oh, you'll never be hungry, you'll never be thirsty
And the Council's tanks will have no mercy.
Oh, you'll never be tired, you'll never be cold
And you'll never ever ever grow old,
And the only price you'll have to pay
Is to give your life away.

When Leonard and Eva had played for us in the morning, we'd whooped along with some of the fast jigs, and clapped after some of the pieces where Leonard's fingers had been at their swiftest. But none of us clapped now. The last notes slipped away, between the trees that encircled us like a gathered crowd. Our silence was the song's best testament.

I wanted to send something into the world that wasn't fire, or blood, or blades. Too many of my actions in recent months were bloodstained. The song was different – it was something we had built, rather than destroyed. But I knew that it was still a risk. If Leonard was caught, the song would hang him as surely as any act of violent resistance would. If Council soldiers heard him sing, or traced the treason back to him, the song would wind itself around his neck sure as a noose, and it would be his dirge, and Eva's. Their twins', too.

'It's a brave thing that the two of you're doing,' I said to Leonard, as we were packing up the camp in the dark.

He scoffed. 'People fought and bled, on the island. I'm just an old blind man with a guitar.'

'There are different kinds of courage,' said Piper, emptying a flask of water on the fire, to ensure no telltale embers remained.

We said farewell to Leonard and Eva when we reached the road. A quick pressing of hands in the dark, and they were gone, heading east while we went west. Leonard was playing his mouth organ again, but distance rapidly dampened the music.

Over the next few days I found myself humming the chorus as I sharpened my dagger, matching the blade's rasp to the beats of the song. I whistled the tune as I gathered wood for the fire. It was only a song, but it took hold in my mind like the ragweed that used to take over my mother's garden.

CHAPTER 8

I'd never seen anything like the Sunken Shore. When we arrived, after five nights of walking, it was dawn. Below us, it looked as if the sea had crept gradually inwards, the land surrendering in messy increments. There was no clear point where the sea met the land, like in the steep cliffs that Kip and I had seen on the south-west coast, or even in the coves near the east coast's Miller River. Instead there was only a jumble of peninsulas and spits, divided by inlets that grasped inland like the sea's fingers. In some places, the land petered out into swampy shallows before giving in entirely to the sea. Elsewhere, low islands were humped with straggled grey-green growth that might have been grass or seaweed.

'It's low-tide now,' Piper said to me. 'Half of those islands will be under by noon. The shallows of the peninsulas too. If you get caught out on the wrong spit of land when the tide turns, you can find yourself in trouble.'

'How does Sally live here? They haven't allowed Omegas to live on the coast for years.'

'See out there?' Piper pointed to the farthest reaches of the broken coast, where the spits of land gave way to the water, a series of loosely linked islands barely keeping above the encroaching sea. 'Right out there, on some of the bleaker spits, it's too salty to farm and too swampy for good fishing, and paths are there one minute and gone in the next tide. You couldn't pay Alphas to live out there. Nobody goes there. Sally's been hiding out there for decades.'

'It's not just the landscape that keeps people away,' Zoe said. 'Look.'

She pointed out, further still. Beyond the scrappy spits of land, something in the water was glinting, reflecting the dawn back at itself. I narrowed my eyes and peered out. At first I thought it was some kind of fleet, masts massed in the sea. But they ignored the sea's shifting and stayed perfectly motionless. Another glint of light. Glass.

It was a sunken city. Spires impaled the sea, the highest of them reaching thirty yards above the water. Others were barely glimpsed - just shapes at the surface with angles too precise to be rocks. The city went on and on, some spires standing alone, others clustered near to one another. Some seemed still to have glass in windows; most were just metal structures, cages of water and sky.

'I took Sally's boat out there once, years ago,' Piper said. 'It goes on for miles – the biggest of the Before cities that I've seen. Hard to imagine how many people must have lived there.'

I didn't need to imagine. I could feel it, now that I was staring at the glass-sharpened sea. I could hear a submerged roar of presence, and absence. Did they die by fire, or water? Which came first?

We slept for the day on a promontory looking over the patchy welter of land and ocean. I dreamed of the blast, and when I woke I didn't know where I was, or when. When Zoe came to rouse me for the last lookout shift before nightfall, I was already awake, sitting up with my blanket wrapped around me and my hands clutched together to quell their shaking. I was aware of her watching me as I walked to the lookout post. My movements felt jerky, and my ears still rang with the roar of the ravenous flames.

It was high tide, the sea had engulfed most of the furthest spits, leaving a network of tiny hillocks and rocks jutting out, so that the water was curdled by specks of land. The sunken city had disappeared altogether. Then, as the darkness advanced, I watched the tide retreat again. Lamps were lit in the Alpha villages on the slopes below us.

It wasn't the underwater city that I was thinking of, as I watched the tide go out, the sea slinking away like a fox from a henhouse. I was thinking of Leonard's passing comment that The Confessor had come from the Sunken Shore. Somewhere, only a few miles down the sloping coastline, was the place where she and Kip had grown up. She would have been sent away when they were split, but Kip had probably stayed on. This strange landscape would have been his home. As a child, he would have roamed these same hills. Perhaps he'd climbed up to this very viewpoint, and seen the tide go out, as I saw it now, more and more of the land being exposed to the moon's gaze.

When it was full dark I woke Zoe and Piper.

'Get up,' I said.

Zoe gave a low groan as she stretched. Piper hadn't even moved. I bent and yanked the blanket off him, throwing it down at his feet as I headed back to the lookout point.

We couldn't risk a fire, within sight of the villages below, so we ate cold stew in the darkness. While Piper and Zoe packed up their things, I stood with my arms crossed, kicking at a tree root. Finally we moved off down the hill, towards the rich green slopes that edged the deepest inlets. We walked in silence. When, after a few hours, Piper offered me the water flask, I grabbed it without speaking.

'What's got you in such a foul mood?' said Zoe shooting me a sideways look.

'I'm not,' I said.

'At least you're making Zoe seem like a ray of sunshine in comparison,' Piper said. 'It's a nice change.'

I didn't say anything. I'd been gritting my teeth ever since we'd come within sight of the sea.

I remembered the day that Kip and I had first seen the ocean. We'd sat together, on the long grass overlooking the cliffs, and stared as the sea lapped at the edges of the world. And if he'd seen it before, he didn't remember – it had been new to both of us.

Now I knew that the sea would have been a daily sight for him. He would have been used to it – probably didn't even glance at it as he went about his daily business. The sea, which we'd sat and marvelled at together, would have been as familiar to him as the thatched roofs of his village.

It wasn't only Kip that I had lost. Even the memories of what we had shared were being snatched from me, rendered false by what I'd learned about him.

Safest not to remember, I told myself, walking faster. Safest not to disturb the drowned city of my memories.

*

We had to navigate carefully through the unforgiving landscape. We weren't only avoiding the Alpha villages, but also the inlets and fissures that penetrated even into the high slopes. Several times the route in front of us opened up into dark water, the gash of a crevasse. We walked all night, with only a brief rest at dawn. It was past noon when we left Alpha country and reached the edge of the straggling flatlands and the sea-mired spits. I stopped and looked back, one last time, at the Alpha villages behind us.

'I heard it too,' Zoe said, 'when Leonard mentioned that The Confessor came from here.'

Piper was walking ahead of us, out of earshot. Zoe, one foot up on a rock, was waiting for me.

'I figured you'd be curious, when we got here,' she said.

'It's not just that,' I said. I remembered her face at the campsite, when I'd caught her swaying with the music. I kept my eyes on the ground as we walked together. And for the first time, I ventured to say out loud what The Confessor had told me about Kip's past. I needed to speak it. And I offered my secret to her like an apology, because I had intruded on her secret dreams.

I told her everything The Confessor had told me: how Kip had been cruel, and had delighted in having her branded and driven away. How, later, when he could afford it, he'd tracked her down and tried to arrange to have her locked in the Keeping Rooms for his own protection.

I told Zoe how Kip's past had tangled everything that I felt. When I looked at the Sunken Shore and tried to imagine his childhood, I couldn't recognise him at all. Instead of recognising Kip, I was recognising Zach. Zach and Kip had shared the same resentment and anger at having a twin who was a seer and refused to be split. I'd been fleeing from Zach, but the more I thought of Kip's past, the more I saw Zach in him. And The Confessor – I had feared her most of all, but when I'd heard about her childhood, I recognised my own story. She'd been branded and exiled, just like me.

Everything was backwards. Everything was doubled, a mirror facing a mirror so that the picture regressed infinitely, and no end was possible.

When I'd emptied myself of words, Zoe stopped walking, turning again to face me, blocking my way.

'What did you hope I was going to say to you, when you told me this?' she said.

I had no answer.

'Did you think I was going to let you cry on my shoulder,' she went on, 'and tell you it was all OK?'

She grabbed me, shook me slightly.

'What difference does it make?' she said. 'What does it matter what he was like? Or The Confessor? There isn't time for you to indulge in all of this soul-searching. We're trying to keep you alive, and not get killed ourselves. We can't do it with you moping around. You're slipping further into the visions, too. We've both seen it – how they get to you. How you scream and shake, when you see the blast.' She shook her head. 'I've seen it happen before. You need to fight it. And you can't do that if you're obsessing over Kip. You're still alive. He's dead. And it sounds like he wasn't such a great loss after all.'

I hit her, full in the face. I'd struck out at her once before, months ago, when she'd made a similarly disparaging comment about Kip. But that had been a chaotic grappling in the half dark. This was more precise: a single punch to the face. I didn't know which of us was more surprised. Nonetheless, her instincts didn't let her down: she ducked to the left, deflecting most of the blow, my fist grazing along her cheek and ear. Even so, my knuckle cracked against something hard – her cheekbone, or jawbone – and I heard myself yelp.

She didn't strike back, just stood there, one hand raised to the side of her face.

'You need to practise more,' she said. She rubbed her cheek, opened her mouth wide to test the pain. A red mark was surfacing on her jaw. 'And you're still not following through enough.'

'Shut up,' I said.

'Open and shut your fingers,' she instructed, watching me as I winched my fist open and closed.

She took it and turned it over, methodically bending each finger. 'It's just bruised,' she said, dropping my hand.

'Don't talk to me,' I said. I shook my hand, half expecting to hear the rattle of bones knocked loose.

'I'm glad to see you angry,' she said, smiling. 'Anything's better than having you wandering around like a ghost.'

I thought of Leonard's words to me. *Girl, you're hardly here.*

'Anyway, it's not even me who you're angry at,' she said.

'You don't know what you're talking about.' I shouldered past her to follow Piper, who was nearly out of sight.

She called after me. 'You're angry at Kip. And it doesn't even have anything to do with his past. You're angry at him because he jumped, and left you behind.'

*

We walked in silence for hours. The peninsula that Piper led us to was really a string of islands, linked tenuously by a thin strip of land. The tide was already beginning to creep up the sides of the isthmuses, leaving just a narrow passage from one island to the next. In mid afternoon we set out across the final strip of stones, the last island ahead of us. It loomed tall, even now that the sea had claimed its lowest reaches. The tide was almost at its highest; the only way to reach the island was across a slim thread of rocks, already slippery with spray.

Piper was still ahead of us, already half way to the island. I turned back to face Zoe, who was just behind me.

'When are you going to tell him about Kip?'

'Keep moving,' she said. 'This path'll be underwater in a few more minutes.'

I didn't move.

'When are you going to tell him?' I said again. A wave splashed my leg, a shock of cold.

'I figure you'll do it yourself, soon enough,' she said, pushing past me and clambering onwards on the slippery rock.

I should have been relieved. But now the secret was once again mine, so was the responsibility. I'd have to tell him myself. And to say it out loud again felt like an incantation: as if each time I uttered the words, I made Kip's past more real.

CHAPTER 9

Piper and Zoe had paused on the brink of the final island. Piper blocked the way, crouching at the point where the isthmus met the wooded slope.

When I tried to edge past him, he stood and yanked at my jumper, pulling me back. 'Wait,' he said.

'What are you doing?' I said, shaking him off.

'Look,' he said, crouching again and peering at the path. I bent to see what he was so intent on.

He pointed out the strand of wire stretched across the width of the path, six inches above the ground. 'Stay down,' he said. Zoe, beside him, squatted on her heels. He leaned forward and tugged the wire.

The arrow passed a foot above our heads and disappeared into the sea. Piper stood, grinning. Somewhere on the island ahead of us, a bell was clanging. I looked back to the water. The arrow had not even left a ripple. If we'd been standing, it would have gone straight through us.

'She'll know we're coming, at least,' said Zoe. 'But she won't be happy that you wasted an arrow.'

Piper bent and pulled the wire again. Twice slowly, twice

quickly, and slowly twice more. Up the hill, the bell sounded out the rhythm.

Three more times, as we crossed the island, Piper or Zoe halted us so that we could step over trip wires. Another time, I felt the trap even before Zoe warned me to step off the path. When I bent to examine the ground, I could sense a kind of insubstantiality to it: a confusion between air and earth. Crouching, I saw the layer of long willow twigs woven together and covered with leaves.

'There's a six-foot drop under there,' Piper said. 'Sharpened stakes planted at the bottom, too. Sally made Zoe and me dig it, when we were teenagers. Was a bitch of a job.' He set off ahead of me. 'Come on.'

It took us nearly an hour to cross the island, making our way up the forested slope and avoiding the traps. Eventually we ran out of land. The island had climbed to a peak at its southern edge, where a cliff dropped away to the sea in front of us. There was nothing beyond but the waves and the unlikely angles of the submerged city.

'There,' said Piper, pointing through the final trees. 'Sally's place.'

I could see nothing but the trees, their pale trunks blotched with brown like an old man's hands. Then I saw the door. It was low, and half-concealed by the boulders that clustered at the cliff's edge. It stood impossibly close to the end of the bluff – it looked like a doorway into nothingness, and was so faded and battered by the coastal winds that the wood was bleached to the same shade as the salt-parched grasses around it. It had been built to take advantage of the cover of the boulders, so that at least half of the building must have hung out over the edge of the cliff itself.

Zoe whistled, the same rhythm that Piper had sounded

on the warning bell: two slow notes, two quick, and two slow.

The woman who opened the door was the oldest person I'd ever seen. Her hair was sparse enough that I could see the curve of scalp beneath it. Around her neck, the skin was draped like a cowl. Even her nose looked tired, drooping at the tip like melted candle wax. I was fairly sure that her forehead bore no brand, but it was hard to tell: age had branded her now, her forehead cragged with wrinkles. The loose flesh of her eyelids hung so low over her eyes that I imagined they must disappear altogether when she smiled.

But she wasn't smiling now. She was looking at us.

'I hoped you wouldn't come,' she said.

'Nice to see you too,' said Zoe.

'I knew you wouldn't come unless you were desperate,' the woman said. She came forward, a lurch in her step. Both legs were twisted, the joints gnarled and fused. She embraced Zoe first, and then Piper. Zoe closed her eyes when Sally held her. I tried to picture Zoe and Piper as they must have been when, ten years old and on the run, they first came to Sally. I wondered how much the old woman had seen them change. The world was a flint on which they had been sharpened.

'This is the seer?' Sally said.

'This is Cass,' said Piper.

'I haven't stayed safe all these years by bringing strangers into my home,' she said.

She had to balance her speech with her breathing, so the words came slowly. Sometimes she paused between each syllable, the noisy breaths taking their time. Each breath a sigh.

'You can trust me,' I said.

She stared at me again. 'We'll see.'

We followed her inside the house. When she shut the door behind us, the whole building shook. I thought again of the cliff underneath us, and the sea clawing at the rocks.

'Relax,' said Piper. I hadn't even realised that I was clutching the doorframe. 'This place has been here for decades. It's not going down the cliff tonight.'

'Even under the weight of an uninvited guest,' added Sally. She turned away and shuffled into the kitchen. Her footsteps on the floor were hollow – only wood between her and the cliff's plunge. 'Since you're all here, I suppose I'd better get some food ready.'

As she busied herself at the table, I looked at the closed door by the stove. No noise came from within, but I could feel, like a draught on the back of my neck, another presence in the house.

'Who else is here?' I said.

'Xander's resting,' Sally said. 'He was up all last night.'

'Xander?' I said.

Sally raised an eyebrow at Piper.

'You didn't tell her about Xander?'

'Not yet.' He turned to me.

'Remember I told you, on the island, that we'd had two other seers? And the younger one had been brought to the island before he was branded?'

I nodded.

'Xander was useful for undercover work,' Piper went on, 'but we didn't want to involve him in anything too important.'

'Was he too young?'

'You think we had the luxury of sparing the young ones that kind of responsibility?' He laughed. 'Some of our scouts on the mainland were barely in their teens. No – and it wasn't even that Xander couldn't be trusted, really. We never thought he'd deliberately betray us. But he was always volatile.'

'It got worse, in the last few years,' Zoe said. 'But even before that, he was always jumpy. Skittish, like a horse that's seen a snake.'

'It was a shame,' said Piper.

'A shame for him, to be so troubled?' I asked. 'Or for you, that you couldn't use him as you'd have liked?'

'Can't it be both?' Piper said. 'Anyway, he did what he could for us. We based him on the mainland. Even without his visions, it was useful to have someone unbranded who could pass for an Alpha. And sometimes his visions came in useful, too. But we had to bring him here, in the end. He couldn't work anymore, and Sally said she'd take him.'

'Why do you keep talking about him in the past tense? He's here now, isn't he?'

'You'll see soon enough,' Sally said, hobbling across the kitchen and opening the door to the room beyond.

*

A boy sat on the bed, his back to us. He had thick dark hair like Piper's, tightly curled, but it was longer, and stood in high tufts, like the peaks of beaten egg whites. The window above the bed looked out over the water, and the boy didn't turn away from it as we entered.

We moved closer. Piper sat next to him on the bed, ushering me to sit beside him.

Xander was perhaps sixteen. His face still had the softness of a child. Like Sally, he was unbranded. When Piper greeted him, he didn't look at us, or respond at all. His eyes darted from side to side, as if following the flight of some invisible insect above our heads.

I wasn't sure whether what I sensed about him was evident to everyone, or whether it was only seers that would feel it. The brokenness inside him. Sally had said that he was resting, but there was no rest here. Only terror. The frantic buzzing of Xander's mind was like a wasp trapped in a jar.

Zoe hung back in the doorway. I saw her mouth tighten as she watched the fidgeting of Xander's long fingers, ceaselessly kneading the air. And I remembered what she'd said to me, about how the visions affected me: *I've seen it happen before.*

Piper stilled one of Xander's hands with his own.

'It's good to see you again, Xander.'

The boy opened his mouth, but no words came. In the silence, I could almost hear the discordant jangling of his mind.

'Do you have any news for us?' Piper asked.

Xander leaned forward, until his face was close to Piper's. He spoke in a whisper. 'Forever fire. Hot noise. Burning light.' The words chased one another out.

'He's seeing the blast more than ever,' Sally said. 'Day and night, now.'

'He never used to be as bad as this,' Piper said. 'What's changed?'

'Move over,' I said to Piper.

'Maze of bones,' muttered Xander.

I looked up at Sally. 'What does that mean?'

'Search me,' she said. 'Sometimes he talks almost normally. Other times, he comes up with stuff like that. The fire, most of the time. Sometimes stuff about bones.'

'Noises in the maze of bones,' Xander said.

His eyes had stilled a little, staring abstractedly at the corner of the ceiling. I placed my hands on the sides of his head, and stared into his eyes.

I didn't want to force myself into his mind. I still remembered how it had felt when The Confessor had tried to probe my thoughts in the Keeping Rooms. After each session with her, my mind had felt like a dollhouse that had been picked up and shaken, everything scattered and rattling. I understood Zoe's fury, when she learned that I'd stumbled into her dreams. But I had to admit that I was also curious about what I might discover from Xander. I was desperate to see if what he saw was the same as what I saw. To confirm, I hoped, that I was not alone in the visions of fire that my mind hurled at me. If I was searching for anything in the jumble of his mind, I suppose it was a glimpse of myself.

His eyes remained blank as I groped towards his thoughts. Occasionally his mouth seemed to be trying to form words, but they didn't take shape. Stillborn, they stayed at his lips, empty shapes incapable of sound.

His mind was burnt out. Everything charred and gone, broken down to ashes and dust. This was what remained, after the flames had exploded too many times in his mind: ash, and smoke, and words sheared of their meanings, rattling loose in his head.

'It's the visions of the blast that've done this to him,' I said.

It wasn't the strangeness of his state that unsettled me, but its familiarity. I'd felt it myself, this madness, scratching around the edge of my mind like a rat in the rafters. It was always there. At times, particularly in the Keeping Rooms, or when the blast visions had become more and more frequent, it had been emboldened, almost crept into sight.

'Flash. Fire. Forever fire,' Xander blurted again. He didn't say the words – they uttered him. As each word burst from him, he convulsed. He looked startled at the sounds emerging from his own mouth.

'You know it happens to seers, eventually,' I said, trying to keep my voice even. I had lived with that knowledge for as long as I'd known what I was. But encountering the residue of Xander's mind still left me with a chill in my guts, my fists curled so tightly that my nails cut into my palms.

He was rocking backwards and forwards now, his arms wrapped around his knees. I recognised, in his scrunched body, that futile attempt to hide from the visions, as if making yourself smaller would somehow spare you. I remembered curling like that myself, as a child, with my head tucked down towards my chest and my eyes clamped closed. It didn't work, of course. Xander was right: *Forever fire.* It would never go away. The blast would haunt all of us seers, always. But why did it burst into our dreams more often now, enough to drive Xander to this?

'Let him rest,' Sally said, stepping forward and cupping Xander's chin in her hand. She lifted the blanket that had fallen from him, and tucked it again around his shoulders.

As we were leaving, he opened his eyes and, for a moment, fixed them on me.

'Lucia?'

I looked at Piper for an explanation. He'd glanced up at Zoe, but she didn't meet his eyes. She crossed her arms in front of her. Her face shut down.

'Lucia?' said Xander again.

Piper looked up at me. 'He must be able to tell you're a seer. Lucia was a seer too.'

The older seer from the island, branded. She'd drowned, Piper had said. A shipwreck in a storm, on the way to the island.

'Lucia's gone,' Piper said to Xander. 'The ship went down more than a year ago. You know that already.' His voice was too brisk, too loud: his attempt to sound casual was jarring.

We left Xander gazing out the window, watching the sea swap its colours with the sky. His hands twitched and twisted constantly. I thought of Leonard's hands on his guitar strings. Xander's hands were kept busy on the unseen instrument of his madness.

'What will you do with him?' I asked Sally, when she'd closed the door to the bedroom.

'Do?' She laughed. 'You say it like I have choices. As if there's anything I could do, other than just keep surviving. Keep him safe.'

Even from the next room, I found Xander's presence exhausting. The churning of his mind, from behind the closed door, made me feel seasick. When Sally sent us out to gather firewood and mushrooms, I felt guilty at my own relief.

Piper and I knelt together at the base of one of the trees, where mushrooms clustered thickly. Zoe was gathering wood nearby. Piper spoke quietly, so that she wouldn't hear.

'You've seen Xander – what being a seer has done to him.' He looked up at Zoe, twenty yards away, and dropped his voice even further. 'It happened to Lucia too.' At the mention of the dead seer's name, his voice caught, his eyelids closed. For a single moment I felt as though we were standing on different islands, and the tide had swallowed the neck of land between them. 'Towards the end,' he added. Then he looked quickly back at me and went on. 'Now you're having more and more visions of the blast, too. So why hasn't it happened to you yet?'

I had often wondered this myself. There were times

when I'd felt my sanity coming loose like a bad tooth. When the flames erupted within me again and again, I had wondered how it was that I still managed to function. Now I'd seen how the words bubbled out of Xander like water from an overheated pan, and wondered how long it would take before my own visions brought me to the boil. Did I have years, or months? When it happened, would I know?

When I asked myself why it hadn't happened already, I always came up with the same answer, though it wasn't an answer that I could share with Piper: it was Zach. If there was some streak of certainty in me, something that held me together when the visions tried their best to tear me apart – then it had its roots in Zach. If there was a strength in me, it was my stubborn belief in him that had formed it. Zach had been the steady point in my life. Not a force for good – I'd seen too much of what he'd done to believe that. But a force, nonetheless. I knew there was no part of me that had not been shaped by him, or against him. And if I allowed myself to slip into madness, then I could neither stop him nor save him. It would all be over.

*

Back inside, we helped prepare the meal. Occasionally, from the bedroom, we could hear Xander hurling syllables at the night air. *Bones* and *fire* slipped under the door. He might be mad, but he saw clearly enough what the blast had made of our world. Bones and fire.

'How long have you been living here?' I asked Sally, as I helped her pluck the brace of pigeons that she'd thrown on to the table. With each tug at the feathers the greying flesh stretched, leaving a clammy film on my fingers.

'Years. Decades. Time gets slippery, when you're as old as me.'

It's slippery for seers, too, I wanted to say. I was jerked between different times, without any say in it. After each vision I'd wake, gasping, as if the future were a lake I'd been dragged down into, before surfacing back in the present.

'I've thought about leaving here, sometimes. It's no place for an old woman. I used to be able to scramble down to the shore and do some fishing. These days I just set snares, and grow what I can. I never want to eat another potato, that's for sure. But it's safe here. The Council's looking for a lame old woman. I figure this place isn't going to be an obvious choice.'

'And your twin?'

'Look at me,' she said. 'And believe me, I'm even older than I look. If there'd been registrations when Alfie and I were split, no doubt the Council would have got to me that way. But things were different then. They didn't have us all pinned down in their records, the way they do now. And wherever he is, my brother's had the sense to lie low, take care of himself.'

She got up and crossed to the stove. When she passed Piper, her hand paused for a while on his broad shoulder. When he first came here, as a child, his hand would have been as small as hers. Smaller, probably. Now she had to stretch up to reach his shoulder, and her hand rested there like a moth on a bough.

When we ate, Xander sat at one end of the table, swinging his legs and staring at the ceiling. Piper carved the pigeons, severing the wings with a long, curved knife. Watching him, it was hard not to think of all the knives he'd wielded. The things he'd seen, and the things he'd done.

But the meal dragged me back to the room. Sally had stuffed the pigeons with sage and lemon, and the meat was soft and moist. It bore no resemblance to the meat we'd eaten on the road, cooked quickly over furtive fires, the outer flesh scorched and the middle still cold and springing with blood. We didn't talk much, until there was nothing left but a forlorn cluster of bones, and the moon had climbed past the window to hang above us.

'Piper told me about how you infiltrated the Council,' I said to Sally. 'But he didn't tell me why you stopped.'

She was silent.

'They were exposed,' Zoe said. 'Not Sally, but the two other infiltrators working with her.'

'What happened to them?' I said.

'They were killed,' said Piper abruptly, standing and beginning to gather the plates.

'The Council killed them?' I said.

Zoe's lips thinned. 'He didn't say that.'

'Zoe,' cautioned Piper.

'The Council would've killed them, eventually,' said Sally. 'Given how much they hated infiltrators, they would never have let them live, even when they'd finished torturing them for information. They didn't get a chance, though, with Lachlan – he managed to poison himself first. We had capsules to take if we were caught. But they searched Eloise before she had a chance, and took her capsule away.'

'So what happened to her?'

Piper stopped clearing away. He and Zoe were both staring at Sally. Sally looked straight at me.

'I killed her,' she said.

CHAPTER 10

'Sally,' said Piper quietly. 'You don't have to talk about this.'

'I'm not ashamed,' she said. 'I know what they'd have done to her. It would have been worse than death – far worse – and they'd have killed her at the end of it anyway. We all knew the deal. We were the heart of the whole intelligence network – if we cracked, half the resistance would fall. All our contacts, all the safehouses, all the information we'd gathered and passed on over the years. It would have been disastrous. That's why we had the capsules.'

She was still looking at me. I wanted to tell her that I understood. But it was clear that she didn't need my understanding. She wasn't looking for forgiveness, not from me or anyone else.

Sally's choice had been harder even than Kip's, perhaps, because it wasn't her own death that she had to bestow. I thought, again, of Piper's words to Leonard: *There are different kinds of courage*.

'They were denounced in the main Council Hall,' she said. 'I was up in the gallery when it happened, talking to some Councillors. Lachlan and Eloise never had a chance:

the soldiers were waiting to swoop. There were at least four soldiers to each of them. Lachy got to his capsule as soon as they had him cornered – he had it on a strap around his neck, like all of us. But after he started frothing and thrashing, they realised what had happened, and pinned Eloise down.'

Her voice was steady, but when she pushed her plate aside, the knife and fork clattered slightly with her hand's tremor.

'I was waiting for them to come for me,' she said. 'I'd slipped my own capsule into my mouth – had it in between my teeth, ready to bite down.' I could see her tongue move to the side of her mouth, tasting the memory. 'But it never happened. I was braced for it – if anyone had been watching me, they'd have seen that something was going on. But nobody was. Everyone was just staring at all the chaos down below. For a moment I just stood there, watching what was happening. Lachy was on the floor by then, thrashing around, blood coming out of his mouth. It's not an easy death, poison. And there were four soldiers holding Eloise, arms pinned to her sides. I was staring down like everyone else. And I realised the soldiers weren't coming for me. Whoever found out about Lachy and Eloise hadn't discovered there were three of us.'

Piper placed his hand on her arm. 'You don't need to go through this all again.'

She gestured at me. 'If she wants to throw her lot in with the resistance, she needs to know what happens. What it's really like.' She turned and looked squarely at me. 'I killed her,' she said again. 'I threw my knife, got her in the chest. It would have been a quicker death than Lachy's. But I couldn't stay to watch. It's only because of all the chaos, and because I was up on the gallery, that I managed to get out of there at all, and even then it meant going through a stained glass window and down a thirty foot drop.'

'That's when she smashed her foot,' said Zoe. 'Her good foot – and it's never recovered. But she managed to get on a horse, and made it out of Wyndham, to the nearest safe-house.' She laid her hand on Sally's other arm, so that she and Piper framed the old woman. 'And they said the first thing she did when she stumbled in, bleeding, was to spit out the poison capsule. She'd had it in her mouth the whole time, ready to bite down if they caught up with her.'

Piper picked up the flow of Zoe's story, without pause. 'They searched for her for years,' he said. 'There were posters everywhere. They used to call her *the Witch*.' He laughed bleakly. 'As if that's what it would take for one of us to pass as an Alpha. The idea that we had some kind of magic was less threatening to them than the idea that we weren't so different to them after all.'

Zoe joined his laughter, but I was watching Sally. She wasn't laughing. Could her shattered foot really be the only damage from that day? Could you sink a dagger into the chest of a friend and not find something changed inside you?

'It was you who taught Piper and Zoe to throw knives?' I said.

She nodded. 'You wouldn't think it, to look at me now, but I used to be able to split a cherry from fifty yards.'

I'd seen Zoe's and Piper's skill with knives. That was Sally's legacy, then: this knack for killing. I didn't know if it was a gift or a burden.

*

That night, after Sally had settled Xander back in the bedroom, we told her everything that had happened since the island, and everything that we knew about the Council's plans. She questioned us carefully. Sometimes she closed her eyes as we answered. Each time I began to wonder whether she'd fallen asleep, she would open her eyes suddenly - an owl's stare - and ask another question. Her questions were specific and deliberate. How many days since we saw the burned-out safehouse? How many guards had we counted at the refuge? How many patrols had we seen, since leaving the deadlands? What had The Ringmaster said, about the alliance between The General and The Reformer?

It was gone midnight when she went to the bedroom to sleep. We laid our blankets out close to the stove. I tried not to think about the thin layer of planks between us and the sea. There were no sounds coming from the room where Sally and Xander slept, but behind the closed door I could feel the scurrying of his mind. When I finally slept, I dreamed of Kip drifting in the tank. I woke into a grief as thick as the liquid that filled his ears and mouth. It left me silent, stranded far from words, or even from screams. When I'd managed to calm my breathing, I stood and tiptoed to the small window by the door. It looked away from the cliff to the trees.

'We don't need to keep a watch,' Piper whispered. 'The tide'll be high until dawn. And even if somebody came by boat, there are the traps. Make the most of it.'

'It's not that,' I said. 'I just can't sleep.'

I could barely make him out as he crossed the room, stepping carefully over Zoe, who rolled over with an impatient grunt. He joined me at the window.

'You need rest,' he said.

'Stop fussing over me. I'm not an old lady.'

He laughed, a deep chuckle. 'Sally is, and I wouldn't dare to fuss over her.'

'You know what I mean. You're always hovering, always worrying.'

'I'm looking out for you. Isn't that what Kip used to do?'

I didn't respond.

'It's not such a bad thing,' he said, 'to have somebody watching out for you.'

When I thought of someone watching over me, all I could think of was The Confessor, and her merciless scrutiny.

'I don't want to be watched,' I said. 'I only want to be left alone.'

'I see how you punish yourself,' he said quietly. 'You don't have to make up for what happened. That's not your responsibility.'

I drew a little closer. I didn't want Zoe to hear us, but my whisper was the hiss of fat in a pan.

'Which thing don't I have to make up for? The people who died on the island? The people trapped in New Hobart? Kip, dying to save me? Or everyone who's suffered because of Zach? Or are you somehow offering me some magical free pass for all of them?'

It was his turn to be angry. 'You give yourself too much credit,' he said. 'It's not all about you, or even about Zach. He's not even running the Council – it's The General who's in charge now. And this is a war. The people who died on the island knew the risks of being in the resistance. And, in the end, even Kip made his own decision. You think you're being selfless, taking it all on yourself, but you're being arrogant. How will it help them, or anyone, you being so hard on yourself, being miserable?' He was leaning towards me, but I avoided his gaze. 'This is your life,' he said, 'not the aftermath of your life.'

I wished he'd been wrong. It would have been easier if

I could snap at him again. But the word lodged in my head, as undeniable as toothache. *Aftermath*. That's what this was: not living, but reeling. I'd staggered out of the silo, and I was still staggering.

I stared out of the window and watched the stars drag their trails of light across the sky.

'It takes time to get over what's happened,' I whispered eventually.

I heard him exhale. 'How much time do you think we have?'

*

At dawn, over breakfast, Piper was pressing Sally about the latest news from the resistance.

'It's bad – but you know that already,' she said. 'Of the ships that landed safely, everyone on them is scattered. Then there were raids, in the weeks that followed. You know what it's like – it spreads. Each raid gives them a few more people to interrogate.' There was such a gulf between her personality and her body. Her words had sharp edges, but they emerged breathy and slightly slurred. She leaned on the table as she stood up, straightening her legs with a small sigh.

'We always took care,' said Piper. He rubbed the side of his face. 'Kept all the cells working separately. Limited the contacts. It shouldn't have unravelled this fast.'

Sally nodded. 'You kept things in good order. Better, even, than in my day. But no system's perfect. For now, everyone's been told to steer clear of the old safehouses, the old routines.'

'Who gave the order?' Zoe said. 'Who's leading the Assembly?'

'Assembly? Nothing so formal as that, since the island.

They're all scattered, those who lived, and there's plenty who've gone to ground, too scared to be part of any resistance after what happened out there. But those who're left are following Simon.'

Since the attack on the island, if Piper had smiled at all it was brief, and muted. But now he grinned widely.

I remembered Simon. Of the Assemblymen on the island, he was the one who'd seemed closest to Piper. Often, when Piper had sent for me, I'd arrive to find him closeted with Simon, talking together over maps and scrolls. Like Piper, he'd seemed a soldier rather than a courtier: his three arms were muscled and scarred. Where some Assemblymen and women had dressed in rich fabrics, Simon had worn a weathered tunic patched with leather. It was he, on the island, who had defended the north tunnel, long after there was no hope that we could defeat the Council invaders. Although Simon and the rest of the Assembly had opposed our escape, it was his defence of the tunnel that had bought me and Kip the time we needed to make it off the island.

'The last I saw of him he was punching me in the face,' Piper said. 'That was on the island, after I'd told the Assembly that I'd let you go.'

'And you're still happy he's in charge?' I asked.

Another grin. 'There were others who would have done worse. Some were arguing that they should leave me on the island, at the mercy of the Council soldiers. Simon spoke up against that, at least. If nothing else, he knew we needed all the strong seamen and fighters we had to get those last few of us off the island. He spoke up for me, when the others turned on me. But then there was the final scramble for the boats, and I didn't see him after that. He wasn't on my boat to the mainland. I wasn't even sure he'd made it off the island.'

'Where is he?' Zoe asked Sally.

'He's not stupid enough to stay in one spot for long,' Sally replied. 'Not since the safehouses started to fall.'

'But you know he's alive? You know where he is?'

'Elena came through here last week, headed further east. She'd seen him recently.'

'Where?'

Sally ignored his question. 'Are you so sure Simon will want you to go to him? You're not exactly popular, after what happened on the island.'

'I don't care whether I'm greeted with open arms. I can still help.'

'And what if you're greeted with blades?' Sally said. 'I heard what happened out there. You made a choice, on the island, to break with the Assembly. You walk back into the resistance now, and they could turn on you.'

'They might,' said Piper calmly. 'But I won't be walking in there alone. You're coming with me.'

Sally shook her head. 'I'm not involved anymore. You know that. Taking Xander in and keeping him safe is the most that I can do.'

'We're all involved,' Piper said. 'And you said it yourself: the network's crumbling. The safehouses are falling, one by one. You think they won't come for you, one day soon? This place, and your traps, won't keep you safe forever. Come with us, and I can protect you. Xander too.'

Sally looked at him appraisingly for several moments. Then she gave a slow laugh. 'I taught you well,' she said.

'What do you mean?'

'You always have an agenda. You can say all you like about wanting to help me, to keep me and Xander safe. But really you need me, to guarantee that the resistance won't turn you away.'

Piper didn't deny it. 'You know how people view you. You're the hero of the infiltrators. You can help to reunite the resistance.'

'Whatever I was then, I'm an old woman now,' she said. 'You're asking me to leave my home. And we both know you'd be a fool to promise you could keep me safe. There isn't any safe – not these days.'

She looked past him to where I sat.

'This stuff Piper and Zoe told me about,' she said to me. 'The tanks, and the refuges. You saw it yourself?'

I nodded.

'In a vision? Like Xander has?'

I was about to protest, to claim that my visions were different. But it would have been a lie. They were the same – the only difference was that I had somehow managed to keep my head above the water of my visions, while Xander had gone under.

'Yes,' I said. 'I saw the tanks in the flesh, too, under Wyndham. But it's the visions that have showed me the rest of them. Hundreds of tanks. Thousands.'

She nodded slowly. 'When Lucia had visions, she always said they weren't straightforward.'

'She came here? Lucia?'

'Piper and Zoe brought her here once, a few years back. But she was already losing it then.'

'She served the resistance faithfully, for years,' said Piper, his hand striking the table. 'You've taken care of Xander for long enough to see the toll that it takes.'

'Just move on,' said Zoe quickly. 'We don't need to talk about that.'

I turned back to Sally. 'Lucia was right. It's not straight-forward. I see things, but I can't always work out exactly what they are. Or when.'

'But you're sure about the tanks?' Sally said.

'Yes. I've seen them.'

Sally looked from me to Xander. He sat at the foot of the table, a piece of bread untouched on his plate. His hands were twisting in their secret choreography.

'She seems sane enough,' said Sally to Piper and Zoe.

'I'm right here,' I said. 'Don't talk about me like I'm a child.'

'This is too important to worry about manners,' snapped Sally. 'You're asking people to risk everything, just because of some visions.'

I kept my voice calm. 'Do you realise what we could all be risking if you don't believe me?'

Sally spoke to Piper, but she was still staring at me.

'I've been fighting this war for more than eighty years. Do you really think one girl can change anything?'

'No,' said Piper bluntly.

It was the same answer that I would have given, but hearing it from his lips, in his matter-of-fact tone of voice, still knocked the breath from my lungs.

'Not by herself,' he went on. 'She's going to need our help. Mine, and Zoe's. But that's not enough. Yours, too, so we can bring the resistance back together, find the ships. Perhaps send out new ships. I don't know if Cass can find Elsewhere, or bring down the Council. But I think she's our best chance. And I sure as hell know she won't be able to do it without us.'

Sally was still staring at me. I should have been used to scrutiny. I was raised in a house crammed tight with suspicion. Zach watching me, our parents watching both of us. Even now, Piper monitored my every movement. But Sally's stare went right through me. She looked at me, and I knew she saw Xander. His broken words, his restless hands.

'Then we should leave at dawn,' Sally said. 'Simon's near the coast, in the collapsed quarry inland from Hawthornden, where half the fleet's at deep anchor. We'll go by boat, at least at first. And I suppose I'd better show her the Ark paper.'

CHAPTER 11

'What are you talking about?' I said.

Sally stood. 'It's something I found, more than forty years ago, when I was undercover in Wyndham.'

She walked to the fireplace and knelt down. I moved to help her, but Piper stilled me with a touch of my shoulder. He let her do it herself: carefully lifting up the corner slate to remove a large envelope, browned and spotted with age. She stood, just as slowly, and returned to the table. It took her a few minutes to rifle through the various papers there, before selecting one and placing it on the table between me and Zoe.

'I found it in The Commander's inner office, when I was able to get an hour alone in there,' she said.

I'd heard Piper mention The Commander only a few days earlier, when we'd been talking about The General. The Commander had been The General's mentor, and it was he whom she was rumoured to have killed.

'I'd managed to steal the key to his document chest.' She smoothed the paper down. It crackled, stiff, beneath her hands. 'This is a copy,' she went on. 'The original was ancient

– I'd never seen anything so old. It was on strange paper, too: thinner than I'd ever seen, and so perished that bits were crumbling away with mould. There were whole sections missing, or impossible to read. Even the writing was different – tiny and precise, not like any other printing I've seen. I couldn't risk stealing the page itself – not just because The Commander might have missed it, but also because I was afraid it would just fall apart if I smuggled it out in my pocket. So I copied all the writing that I could make out, before The Commander's chambermaid was due to come back.'

I bent over the paper. The handwriting was messy, flecks of ink freckling the paper where Sally's hasty nib had snagged. But it wasn't the rushed writing that made the document hard to read, so much as the unfamiliar words.

Yr. 6, June 5th. MEMORANDUM (14c) FOR THE INTERIM ARK GOVERNMENT: STRATEGIES FOR SPECIES VIABILITY

As noted in Appendix 2 (REPORT ON SURFACE CONDITIONS OUTSIDE THE ARK, from Expedition 3a), the detonations' impact on climate exceeds even the most pessimistic pre-war models, in terms of both the scale and duration of the nuclear winter. Diffuse light penetrates the ash clouds for 2-4 hours per day, but visibility levels remain extremely poor, and agriculture largely untenable. Surface temperature shows a drop of . . .

I looked up. 'They're talking about the blast. The Long Winter.' I disbelieved my own words, even as I heard them echo in the kitchen. 'This is from back then?'

Nothing remained from the Long Winter but the stories

and songs passed down by bards. Each version was slightly different, but the essence was the same: the sky so thick with ash that darkness sat over the world for years. Neither crops nor babies would grow, and the survivors had barely clung on. It seemed impossible that the paper Sally had found could come from that time.

'What is it, this *Ark*?' I said. 'Where are they writing from?'

'Keep reading,' Piper said.

I traced the paper with my finger as I read.

. . . *earlier expeditions reported principally on the acute effects of the radiation (A.R.S). Amongst the few survivors located by Expedition 3, secondary effects of radiation are now in evidence. At the most minor, these include continued ulceration and sloughing of skin,*

more significantly, proliferation of cancers (some tumours already manifesting.

Given the adverse conditions on the surface, and the ongoing effects of radiation on surface survivors, the effectiveness of the Ark, and its importance in preserving hope of species viability, is clearer than ever

and the severity and scope of the radiation confirms the Interim Government's decision to keep the Ark sealed, and to minimise expeditions and all other ascents to the surface until significant improvements are made against the key environmental indicators already laid out in Appendix F. . .

'All this talk of *the surface*,' I said. 'They're not out there, are they? They're watching it from somewhere else.' I looked up at Piper, and he nodded.

'They saw it coming,' he said. 'They knew the blast was coming, and they built the Ark to lock themselves away and be shielded from it.'

That single piece of paper changed everything. All my life, I'd thought the Before was a time. Now I knew that it was also a place.

*

'Where could they possibly have hidden?' I said. 'The whole world burned.'

I knew better than anyone how absolute the destruction of the blast had been. I'd seen it myself, time and time again. The world turned to flame.

'Underground,' Piper said. 'They mention *ascents to the surface*. His finger hovered over the words. 'Think about it. They had technology that we can't even imagine, and time to prepare.'

Sally nodded. 'Best as we can figure, it was a kind of haven for them – for some of them, anyway. Probably those in charge.'

'But that's not the most important bit,' Piper said. He reached out to turn the page over. 'Look at this.'

Efforts continue to establish contact with allied nations. Both radio and satellite receivers sustained significant damage in the detonations. Reconstructing the radio transmitters and receivers may be feasible, but is not currently a priority, given the extent of the damage, and the challenges presented by surface conditions. Any communications would also depend on allied nations themselves having functioning equipment. Additionally, the high levels of atmospheric ash are likely to disrupt satellite and radio communications for the foreseeable future (see Appendix F).

A taskforce has therefore been convened to explore the feasibility of a naval or air expedition. The destruction of the Ark's aircraft hangar and the fires still burning at the fuel storage reservoirs make
another obstacle to air reconnaissance is the thick ash currently limiting visibility.

Re. naval reconnaissance: Surface Expedition 3 confirmed the total destruction of the harbour at

reported that one of the ships stored in Hangar 1 may be salvageable.

To provide the greatest chance of reaching survivors (let alone survivors in a state to provide us with aid), we will be prioritising those nations not thought to have suffered direct strikes. It has been judged futile to reach out to

Nonetheless, we remain optimistic that, if there are survivors in allied nations, we will be able to resume contact . . .

Half of the words were incomprehensible to me. But nestled amongst the unfamiliar language was a single idea that I grasped at like a rope thrown to a drowning man.

'Elsewhere,' I said.

Sally nodded. 'They knew it existed. And they knew where it was. More than one place, by the sound of it – those *allied nations*. The people in the Ark were trying to reach out, trying to make contact after the blast.'

And they'd had means of reaching out that we could only imagine. Things like *satellites* and *aircraft*. Could they really have had vehicles that had flown through the sky? It seemed fantastical. But I remembered what The Ringmaster had said: *these machines are powerful in ways we can't even understand.* And if the people of the Before could produce the blast, then I couldn't conceive of any limits to their powers.

'Just because there was once an Elsewhere, in the Before, that doesn't mean it's survived,' Zoe said. 'They say that right there.' She jabbed at the paper. '*If there are survivors.* They had no idea how badly Elsewhere was damaged.'

She was right. The words *direct strike* were loaded with death, even four-hundred years after they were written. And we had no way of knowing whether the Ark-dwellers had succeeded in making contact with Elsewhere, or what they might have found there. If our own ships could ever find another land, would it be any different to the charred landscape of our own deadlands?

'It's still the only confirmation we've ever had that Elsewhere exists at all,' said Piper. 'Maybe you understand, now, why I always argued so hard for the ships to be sent.'

When I thought of *The Rosalind* and *The Evelyn*, I felt the sails of my heart filling. The ships had not been sent out to wander blindly beyond the edges of our maps and into the formless sea. They had something to seek

*

'There was only this single piece of paper?' I asked, turning to Sally. 'Nothing else?'

'I barely finished copying it in time, before I had to get out of The Commander's chambers,' she replied. 'But that was the entire thing – at least all of it that was legible. I went through all the other papers locked in the chest, and there was nothing that looked similar, or that mentioned any Ark. And I never heard The Commander talk about it – but I didn't have access to his most private meetings. Eloise and Lachy were supposed to go back there the next afternoon, to search the papers in his desk, while I was taking notes for The Commander in a Council session. But I never had a chance to meet with them and hear whether they found anything – they were denounced the day after.'

'Do you think they were seen trying to search his rooms?' I said.

She looked down, and then back at me. 'Not a week goes by that I don't think about it, even now. But we were in danger every day – I'll never know for sure what it was that gave them away.'

'And you told the resistance about this paper?' I said.

'I'm not stupid,' she said. 'I sent an urgent report, the same day I found it. A woman called Rebecca was leading the Assembly then. After everything had died down, once I'd escaped, she came back from the island specially, to meet with me about it. We both knew, even then, how important it was.'

I couldn't take my eyes from the paper. The single sheet, unfolded on Sally's table, contained different worlds and different times. The Ark, a haven for the Before, hidden somewhere in the After. And new lands, beyond the dead-lands to the east, and the unforgiving sea to the west. But we still didn't know whether Elsewhere had survived the blast at all, or if it was just a land of bones and dust.

'What did Rebecca do?' I said.

'What could she do?' Sally shrugged. 'Like you said: it was just one piece of paper. We had nothing else to go on. I'd been run out of Wyndham, and Lachy and Eloise were dead. It's one thing to hear that this Ark existed – it's another to find it. Every Assembly leader since then has known about the Ark; some of them even sent out boats, like Piper, to search for Elsewhere. But none of them have been able to find anything.'

'We had a lead a few years back, from one of our sources in New Hobart,' Zoe said. 'An urgent report that some papers had come to light that might be linked to the Ark. But the Council got wind of the rumour at the same time – swooped in and crushed the whole cell. Since then, nothing.'

I thought of Elsa, who had taken in me and Kip at her holding house during our time in New Hobart. She'd never talked about her dead husband, except once when I'd asked her about the island: *My husband used to ask questions*, she'd said. I remembered how the air in the holding house kitchen had thickened with fear when I'd raised the topic of the resistance. The panic of Elsa's assistant, Nina, as she'd rushed from the room, and Elsa's refusal to discuss it.

I would probably never have the chance to ask her directly whether he'd been involved in the resistance. The Council had seized New Hobart. Kip and I had escaped, but it was a prison now, not a town.

'Make no mistake,' Piper said. 'The Council will have been searching for the Ark, and Elsewhere, if they haven't found them already. And they have far more resources than we have – and probably more information, too.'

I looked back at the paper. 'You don't think they could still be alive, the people in the Ark?'

Sally shook her head 'Four hundred years, and there's not been as much as a rumour, let alone a sighting. They died down there.'

'Maze of bones,' muttered Xander from his seat by the window. 'Fire, forever.'

Piper looked away from Xander to scrutinise my face. 'Can you feel anything?' He was leaning towards me, the tips of his fingertips resting on my knee. 'Any sense, from the paper, of where Elsewhere could be? Or of where the Ark itself was?'

'It didn't work when we tried this with Lucia, or Xander,' Zoe said.

'She's not the same as them,' Piper said.

Zoe shifted irritably. I wondered whether she was thinking the same thing as me: *not yet*.

Once, back on the island, Piper had asked me to look at a map and see whether I could help him find Elsewhere. I'd come up with nothing. This time, though, it might be different. Back then, Elsewhere had been nothing but a hope. Now, in the form of this creased sheet of paper, we had some kind of proof that it existed, or at least that it once had. I picked up the page and closed my eyes.

I tried to think of flying. I couldn't even begin to picture what the *aircraft* of the Before might have looked like, or how they could have worked, but I did my best to imagine myself soaring out beyond the edges of the land, and over the sea. I tried to see the island, as I remembered it, a blemish on the blankness of the sea. Then, further, to the north, where I imagined the winter ice sheets that Piper had told me about. To the west and the south, where nothing but sea unfolded under me. I willed myself to feel it: the glimpse of another coast, coming into view below.

But I wasn't flying; I was drowning. Water rose around me, closing over my face. When I opened my mouth to scream, I expected to taste the sharp salt of ocean, but instead, all I could taste was sweetness, a taste so saccharine and artificial that it tipped over into foulness. I would know that taste anywhere.

I couldn't move. When I strained my eyes to the right, I could see a face next to mine. It was hard to make out through the viscous fluid. Hair floated over half the face. Then the liquid shifted, and the hair drifted to the side. It was Elsa.

I shouted. Piper's hand on my arm brought me back to the room. When I looked down, my hands were shaking, the paper that they clutched fluttering like the wings of a moth.

'What did you see?' Zoe said.

I stood, moving slowly against the weight of the news that held me down.

'They're going to tank them all,' I said. 'Sealing the town was only the beginning. They're going to tank everyone in New Hobart.'

'This isn't about New Hobart,' said Piper. 'Concentrate on Elsewhere. And the Ark.'

'I can't,' I said. 'I could feel it. I could see Elsa, under-water.'

Piper spoke gently. 'You must have known it would come to that, ever since they captured the town. They were never going to just release them.'

He was right. The gradual tanking of those who turned

122

themselves in to the refuges was never going to be enough for Zach. The city was already a prison. Soon it would be a ghost town, like the submerged city in the sea beyond the Sunken Shore.

'I know you're worried about your friends there,' Piper said. 'But we can't free New Hobart. That would mean open war – a war that we can't win. The only way we can help Elsa and the others is by finding the Ark, or finding Elsewhere. So you need to concentrate. This is bigger than New Hobart.'

'New Hobart,' Xander echoed.

We all turned. I hadn't heard Xander cross the room to stand behind me.

'The soldiers are searching,' he said.

'In New Hobart?' I said.

'New Hobart,' he said again, but it was impossible to know whether it was a confirmation, or just an echo.

'Don't worry,' Piper said. 'They were looking for Cass. They didn't find her – she got out.'

I remembered the posters that had been nailed up all over the town, with my face and Kip's sketched on them.

'No,' said Xander. He spoke impatiently, as though we were children, or simpletons. He looked straight at me. 'You're not what they're looking for.'

I felt my cheeks flush. 'You're right. It wasn't me – or not only me. The Confessor was looking for Kip, most of all.' At the time, I'd failed to realise this – and it had blinded me to Kip's real identity. 'But it's finished now. They can't hurt him anymore.'

'It's not finished,' said Xander. He paused, still looking at me, his head cocked to one side. For a few seconds he said nothing. I wanted to grab him, to squeeze the words from him like the last drops of juice from a lemon. He turned back to gaze out of the window. 'Maze of bones,' he said quietly, and then would say no more.

*

That afternoon, while Piper sat with Xander, and Sally packed, Zoe took me outside to practise fighting. She was letting me do more drills with the dagger now, though it felt like she stopped me every few seconds to tell me what I was doing wrong. *Keep your eye on my blade, not yours. Faster. Watch your wrist – block a strike like that and you'll break it. Get on the higher ground – see how it slopes there. You don't want to find yourself fighting uphill.*

I could never match Zoe, her blade darting like a lizard's tongue, but the dagger that Piper had given me was beginning to feel like my own, rather than a borrowed weapon. I was used to its weight now, and the angle where its hilt met the blade. Knew how tight to grip the handle to block a strike, and how to loosen my wrist when I wanted to swipe at my opponent.

I saw a movement at the window of the house. It was Xander, his mouth slack on one side, his eyes unfocused. He was gazing right at where we stood, but whatever he was seeing it wasn't us.

Zoe took advantage of my distraction, coming at me faster so that I was driven a few steps back down the slope.

'Concentrate,' she said. 'You yielded the higher ground again.'

I nodded, testing my dagger's weight in my hand before circling her again.

The blast came, scorching my sight with flames.

It only lasted a moment, but Zoe slipped past my guard. The tip of her dagger came to rest, very gently, on my chest.

'If that happens in a fight, you're a dead woman.' She stepped back, blade lowered.

'It was the blast.' I didn't know how to explain to her that when the blast visions came, we were all dead, in a world turned to cinders. 'I think it's being around Xander,' I said, glancing back at the window. 'It sets the visions off even more than usual.'

'So concentrate harder,' she said.

I raised my blade, and we circled each other once more. She lunged, and I blocked. I swept my blade at her shoulder, and she darted backwards. Then the blast came again, an aftershock, a flash of whiteness that hit me like a seizure. My knife dropped to the ground.

Zoe threw down her own blade.

'There's no point practising if you're like this,' she said.

'I'm trying,' I said. 'You don't know what it's like, having the visions.'

She followed my gaze to the window. 'I'm trying to help you. Do you want to end up like him?'

I picked up my dagger again, and she did the same. We sparred until it was almost dark, but Zoe was quieter, not correcting me as often, or pushing me as hard. There was no point. We both knew that the greatest threat to me couldn't be fought with blades.

CHAPTER 12

It was too dangerous to sail through the sunken city by night, so we left just before dawn, bags loaded with all the food that we could carry. Sally didn't even look back as she closed the door behind her. She was concentrating on calming Xander, who had begun to whimper as we led him from the house, and would only walk if Sally held his hand and coaxed him forwards.

It took us a long time to reach the boat. There was a path, of sorts, zig-zagging down the face of the cliff, but over the years it had half crumbled with disuse. In the end, Piper had to carry Sally, though she grumbled and insisted she could manage by herself if we weren't hurrying her. Zoe and I, between us, helped Xander. He refused to look down at where the narrow path was shedding its edge beneath our feet, and clamped his eyes shut, his limbs stiff. Stones clattered from the path as we walked, and the sea was so far below us that I couldn't hear them land. The sun had risen by the time we reached the boat, tucked into a cave above the high-tide line. The boat hadn't been used for years, and when we carried it to the water a family of mice scuttled from a nest in the sail. Piper checked the hull before we set off, running his hand over the flaking planks and testing the ropes, stiffened into the loops where they'd been curled.

The boat was bigger than either of the dinghies that Kip and I had used, and had two small sails, rather than one. Sally and Xander sat in the stern. Xander had calmed now, gazing over the boat's side at the quiet sea. Once Piper and Zoe had rowed us through the rocks close to the peninsula, Piper handled the sails deftly, shouting his orders to me while Zoe took the tiller. We had to go carefully, to avoid the wreckage of the submerged city that punctured the dark water for miles. The tide was high, and only the tallest buildings emerged. The others lay in wait just below the surface. We passed so close to one of the towers that I could see pieces of our reflection in the broken glass that still clung to the rusted frame. I saw the fear on my own face, pale in the mirrored dawn.

Only when we were out of the clutches of the Sunken Shore, and we were making good speed, did I notice Zoe. She was standing in silence at the back of the boat, clutching the tiller so tightly that her knuckles stood out white on her dark hands.

'You OK?' I asked. I didn't dare to mention her sea dreams. The memory of her furious reaction was a splinter lodged in me, too sharp to touch.

'I don't like being at sea,' she said, and turned away from me to watch the wake of churned water behind us.

For the daylight hours, we stayed out of sight of the shore, only creeping closer once the sun had set. The wind was kind to us, and we moved fast. Zoe remained silent, but Xander made up for it with his periodic babbling. At one point, in the late afternoon, he began screaming about fire and muttering about the maze of bones. It kindled the flames in my own head, and I found myself on the floor of the boat with my head in my hands, the blast tearing at the walls of my sight, and the boat's unsteadiness only shaking my mind further. Until the vision passed, Piper put his hand on my back and I tried to concentrate on that single patch of warmth, the one steady thing in the rocking world.

Sally kept a lookout for patrol ships. I couldn't think of the Council's black fleet without a shudder, remembering the sight of them massed near the island. The moon was at its highest when Piper dropped the sails, and he and I rowed the boat close to shore to land on a rocky beach, the pebbles noisy underfoot as we dragged the boat up to the long grass where we could conceal it.

I took the first lookout shift, and even after Piper relieved me I could barely sleep. There was little cover from the drizzle, and I was lying between Zoe and Xander. All night, his dreams of fire jostled in my mind with Zoe's dreams of the sea. When we rose at dawn, and began the walk inland, I strode ahead, keen to get away from both of them.

We could only move at Sally's pace, and when she flagged, Piper and Zoe took turns to carry her. I watched her clinging to Piper's back, and noted how patiently his right arm hoisted her when she kept slipping down to the left, where there was no arm to support her. I saw his blade-scarred hand holding her leg, and thought I'd never seen his touch so gentle.

By nightfall we were in craggy, open country. Sally couldn't keep walking through the night, and we made camp in a stand of pine trees by a shallow creek. I went to the creek to wash, and when I came back to camp, my hair still wet, I saw Piper crouching near the fire, knife raised behind his head. For a moment I froze, scanning the trees for signs of an ambush. I couldn't see the others through the pines – only Piper, his eyes fixed on something out of my sight. Then he let the knife fly, and I heard Zoe give a whoop of triumph, and they both laughed. I stepped into the small clearing. A target was carved on a tree trunk, studded now with their knives. Zoe was grinning as she retrieved the knives. Sally and Xander were by the fire, watching the game.

'No need to ask who won, then,' I said.

'Piper's setting the snares tonight,' said Zoe, wiping her knife blade against her trousers. 'And taking first watch. He's already lost two rounds in a row. He's throwing so badly you're lucky he didn't hit you on your way back.'

She handed Piper back his daggers. I settled on the ground next to Sally and Xander, and watched Piper and Zoe as they played another round. Zoe went first, standing behind the line that they'd scraped in the earth, while Piper watched from the other side of the clearing. The first time Zoe edged one foot over the line, Piper laughed at her and she denied cheating. The second time she did it, he let fly one of his own knives, skewering her bootlace to the ground so that she couldn't snatch her guilty foot back.

'Try denying that,' he said to her with a smile. She bent to pull the knife free, swearing when her bootlace snapped.

'Pity you can't throw that accurately when you're aiming for the target,' she said, and handed it back to him.

He laughed, and she stepped back behind the line.

I laughed too. But even as I watched Piper and Zoe playing their target game, my neck was tense. She was laughing now, but I'd seen her slit a man's throat and leave his body in the dust. Piper was rolling his eyes at Zoe's latest throw, but I'd heard him speak of killing a man as casually as I might talk of plucking a pigeon.

Watching Piper and Zoe, I couldn't forget that even their games were made of blades.

*

After another day of walking, it was midnight when we crested a large hill, and saw the quarry below us. It was a scar on the hills, a gouge nearly half a mile long, the white clay bright under the moonlight. It started off shallow, a series of clay pits and chalky pools, but in the middle it became a gully, carved more than a hundred yards deep. On the northern side were sharp cliffs, seamed with red stone; on the southern side, whole sections of the wall had given way, slumping down and carrying with them boulders and trees that now lay, half-buried, in the rubble mounds that had engulfed half of the pit. A wide, well-kept road passed only a mile to the west, but the quarry itself must have been abandoned for decades – its base was thickly wooded, where the landslides had spared it.

We were able to edge within a few hundred yards of the quarry's mouth, under the cover of trees and ditches, but there was no way to get closer without being exposed. To the east, where one or two Omega shacks were dotted, there were fields stretching close to the quarry's eastern side, but they'd long ago been harvested, so offered us no cover. On the quarry's western edge there was a scattering of trees, but nothing thick enough to conceal our approach.

I stared at the quarry's steep sides. 'If the Council's already been here, then we'll be walking straight into a trap.'

'If the Council had already been here, I doubt they'd have left Omega sentries on the lookout,' said Zoe quietly. 'Look.'

She pointed west. Piper saw it before I did: the figure

perched high in an oak tree, where the woods petered out. The sentry was watching the road to the west, but when he turned periodically to scan the woods on each side, I could see his profile. He was a dwarf, bow slung across his shoulder.

'It's Crispin,' said Piper. 'And he won't be the only sentry. The others?'

'Haven't seen them yet,' Zoe said. 'But I'm thinking that hay shouldn't be sitting out, months since the harvest.' She gestured to a small stack of bales in a field to the east of the quarry. 'I'd bet there's a watch post under there. That'd give them a view of the whole eastern perimeter.'

'I didn't train my guards to be slack,' Piper said. 'They should've spotted us already.'

'Careful,' Sally said to him. 'Simon's guards. Not yours anymore.'

'I'm not likely to forget that,' said Piper. But he was already moving off towards the oak, stealthy but quick. We followed as he led from tree to tree. He got to within forty feet of the tall oak before he broke cover, stepping forward loudly.

'Crispin,' he shouted up at the platform. 'Give the signal – tell Simon he's got visitors.'

The watchman hid his surprise well, turning swiftly and notching an arrow to his bow.

'Stand where you are,' he shouted. From where we stood, looking up, his face was bisected by the bow, one eye squinting tight.

Piper gave him a wave, turning his back to the oak as he marched off towards the quarry's mouth.

'Stand where you are,' called the man again. He drew back the arrow further, the bowstring quivering. 'You're not in charge anymore.'

'If I was,' Piper said, 'you'd be whipped for not spotting us earlier.'

Zoe had caught up with Piper now, the two of them striding toward the quarry with the same long gait. She called back to the sentry: 'And tell your friend in the hay bale to pick a less flammable spot next time. If I were a Council soldier with an arrow and matches, he'd be nicely cooked by now.'

Crispin moved quickly, and my body tensed, braced for the whirr of the arrow, a sound that had impaled my dreams ever since the attack on the island. Instead, Crispin dropped the bow and brought both hands to his mouth, the better to amplify his whistle. Three long low notes, repeated – a rough approximation of a barred owl. An answering whistle came from the quarry below.

The path meandered between the clay pits and the mounds of earth, the collapsed walls on the southern side becoming more menacing as we walked deeper into the quarry. The moonlight barely penetrated here, and twice I slipped in the wet clay. The guards emerged one by one from amongst the pits and rubble heaps, and ran towards us. I recognised the three-armed silhouette of Simon in the lead, an axe in one of his hands. But as he drew close enough for me to see his face, he began to look less like the man I remembered. I could make out no obvious injury from the battle on the island, but something had happened to transform him. In the moonlight his face was grey and puffy. Where he used to move with a soldier's vigour, now he walked with a slow determination, as if against a tide.

Whispering broke out amongst his guards as they assembled around us. Then they saluted. At first I thought they were saluting Piper, as they used to do on the island. But it wasn't him they were looking at, as they all raised their hands to their foreheads. It was Sally, limping beside me, Xander leaning on her arm. If she noticed the guards' response to her, she didn't acknowledge it.

Simon stopped a few feet from where we stood. The others, six or seven of them, fanned around us. There were no more salutes now. They were all armed; the woman nearest to me had a short-sword in her hand. She was close enough that I could see the dent on the blade, where another sword had left a snarl in the steel's edge.

Simon stepped forward.

'It's just the five of you?' He addressed Piper.

Piper nodded. 'We have important information that you'll need.'

'You've come to tell me what to do next?' Simon said.

Sally sighed. 'I brought him here, Simon. Hear him out.'

'Does Sally know what you did?' Simon said to Piper. 'Does she know about the island?' He was staring at me now. I had become a shorthand for a massacre. A single glance at me was loaded with meaning. Heavy with blood.

'She knows,' said Piper. He didn't break his gaze, and his jaw didn't retreat from its usual jut.

Sally spoke impatiently. 'Don't make this into a pissing contest. This fight's going to need us all.'

Simon's gaze was fixed on Piper. There was only a foot or two between them. I'd seen them together many times on the island, and seen them debating heatedly, but never like this. The space between them was stacked with the island's dead. The air was thick with remembered screams, and the sound of arrows in flesh.

'He's a traitor,' muttered one of the men beside Simon.

'Thinks he can walk back in here, after what he did?' added the woman beside him.

We were completely encircled. Zoe stood with her hands

on her hips; it looked casual enough, but I knew how quickly she could dispatch death from the knives at her belt. We were outnumbered here, though. I looked at Simon again. For all his exhausted appearance, his arms were still knotted with muscles. The leather-wrapped handle of his axe was stained black, and I remembered the smell of blood that had filled the island's crater, and knew it wasn't only sweat that darkened the leather.

'I haven't come here to grovel.' Piper was looking at Simon, but he made sure to speak loudly enough for the assembled guards to hear. 'I stand by my decision. You've seen what the Council's capable of – they were never going to spare the island, whether or not I handed over Cass and Kip.'

'We paid too great a price for one seer,' said Simon.

'The minute you start thinking of people in terms of price, we've already lost,' I said. 'And it wasn't just me. It was Kip, too.'

'What difference does it make?' Simon said.

'He killed The Confessor,' I said. 'It cost him his life, but he did it. And we destroyed the machine that they were using to keep track of all of us, and to decide who lived and died, and who should be tanked.'

Simon turned to Sally. 'I'd heard the rumour that The Confessor had died. Is it true?'

Sally nodded. 'I believe them. She's dead. And the machine that relied on her – it's finished too.'

'But you still betrayed the Assembly,' Simon said to Piper. 'Killing The Confessor, or dragging Sally along now, doesn't change that.'

Sally shrugged Xander's hand from her arm and stepped closer to Simon. The ring of weapons around us lowered slightly as she spoke. 'I've fought for this resistance since I

135

was fifteen, Simon, and in that whole time, I've never been dragged anywhere. I've seen and done things that you can't imagine, and I'm no stranger to hard choices.' She paused for breath. 'Piper made a hard choice on the island. It was the right one. I've come here to vouch for him. But it makes no difference that I vouch for him and Zoe.' I noticed that she made no mention of me. 'That doesn't matter. What matters is that you need them.'

'She's right,' Piper said to Simon. 'I have information for you. There're things we need to talk about, and things you need to do.'

The woman close to me tightened her grip on the sword hilt.

'You don't get to tell me what I need to do,' said Simon. 'But I'll hear your news.' He turned away. 'You'd better come inside.'

There was a pause, and then the guards around us stepped back. The scraping sound, as they sheathed their weapons, was protracted, reluctant. Simon kept his axe in hand as we followed him further into the quarry.

In the deepest part of the excavations, amongst the low trees that clustered there, was a handful of tents, staked out wherever the trees and boulders provided shelter from anyone looking down from above. Simon and his guards had been here for some time; long enough that the paths between the tents were worn down to shallow trenches of boot-clutching clay.

When Simon led us to his tent, I noted that the guards took up positions at the door before it had even fallen closed behind us.

Inside, both Piper and Zoe had to duck under the sagging roof. Simon, axe in hand, stood by the lamp at the far side of the tent and waited.

As soon as the door was closed, he sprang at Piper. Zoe drew back her throwing arm quicker than my intake of breath, but Piper's laughter disarmed us both. Simon was embracing him, the two of them chest to chest, and patting each other resoundingly on the back.

'I'm sorry about that,' Simon said, with a jerk of his thumb outside. 'But you saw how most of them feel. If I'm to keep my authority, they need to see that I don't just lay down the red carpet for you.' He squeezed Piper's shoulder once more. 'I hoped you'd be back.'

'So that you could punch me in the face again?' Piper said, one eyebrow raised.

'Sit,' said Simon, waving us to the side of the tent, where a table and benches had been cobbled together from fresh-hewn wood. 'And eat something. You look like you need it.'

'We didn't come here for a tea party,' said Zoe.

'Speak for yourself,' said Sally. The bench creaked as she slumped down onto it and reached for the food.

Simon left us alone until we'd finished helping ourselves to the flatbread and water on the table. I made myself eat, but I was so tired that my head felt heavy on my neck. I poured a little of the water into my hand and splashed my face.

Simon lowered himself onto the bench next to Piper.

'You know I don't agree with what you did.'

'Say what you mean,' I interrupted. 'Stop edging around it. *What you did*. Why can't you just say it? You would have handed me over to The Confessor. Or just killed me yourself.'

At least Simon looked me straight in the eye. 'Yes. That's what I would have done. That's what I wanted Piper to do.'

'You know it wouldn't have saved the island,' said Piper.

'They'd have taken her, and they'd still have killed the others.'

'Perhaps.' Simon leaned forward, elbows on his knees, and rubbed his face. 'That's what some people believe, anyway, now that they've seen so much of the Council's ruthlessness. Perhaps you'll be able to persuade more people round to your way of thinking, now that you're back.'

'We can worry later about what people think. But there are things you need to know, about the Council's plans for New Hobart. Things that Cass has seen.'

'I'd keep quiet about the seers for now,' Simon said. 'People might accept you back, if I'm seen to endorse you. And bringing Sally was a wise move. But wandering in here, trailing not just Cass but another seer, and an Alpha, isn't going to help. After all that's happened, people need to feel that you're one of us.'

'Don't give me that,' Piper said. 'Zoe's done more for the resistance than almost anyone. And seers are Omegas, just like the rest of us.'

'You know what I mean,' Simon said. His gaze, as he looked me up and down, said enough. I'd seen it before: the appraising way that people would stare at me, once they'd realised that my brand didn't correspond with any visible mutation. The distance that they kept, from then on.

Simon went on. 'And since the island, they've got a better reason than ever to fear both seers and Alphas.' He looked at me again. 'Tell me what happened. How did Kip kill The Confessor?'

I swallowed, and took a breath, but the words didn't come. Piper stepped in, and gave Simon a brief account of what had happened in the silo.

'I should've known you had something to do with that,' Simon said to Piper. 'That'll go a long way in winning people over. They saw what The Confessor did, on the island. If they knew you'd had a part in killing her, they'd forgive you for what you did. They'd even come around to the seer.'

'We don't want their forgiveness,' said Zoe.

She hadn't even been on the island, but I noted how she took on Piper's guilt, and his defiance, as her own.

'You might not want it,' Sally said, 'but that doesn't mean you won't need it. This isn't about your ego. It's about reuniting the resistance.'

'It makes no difference,' Piper interrupted. 'We can't go around proclaiming that we were involved in killing The Confessor. The official story is that only Kip was there. If the Council links her death to Cass, they might decide to take out The Reformer themselves, to get rid of her.'

Simon sighed. 'You're not making it any easier for me to welcome you back.'

'Did you think the job would be easy, when you took over?' Piper said.

'I didn't take over. You left, to chase your seer. Those who remained chose me to lead. I didn't choose this.' He grimaced and rubbed the back of his neck. 'What about the song? Was that you as well? One of my scouts reported a bard in Longlake, singing about the refuges. Warning people not to go.'

'A blind bard? With a younger woman?' I asked.

Simon shook his head. 'A young bard. He was travelling alone, my scout said.'

Piper and I exchanged smiles. The song was already spreading.

'I wouldn't be celebrating too much,' Simon said. 'Every bard who sings it might as well be sticking their head in a noose.'

'Did the scout say anything about bards being caught for it?'

'No. But it's only a matter of time. Word's spreading.'

'That's the point,' I said.

'What news of the ships?' Piper asked him.

'Eight are moored nearby, at deep anchor off the peninsula. But the Council's increased its coast patrols, so we'll have to move the fleet east again. At least four of our ships were seized soon after landing, right by the Miller River. There's a report that *The Caitlin* went down, further north. An unconfirmed sighting of *The Juliet*, much further north – could be that Larson and his crew are still on the move. The rest still unaccounted for.'

'That's good news about the eight, at least. But that wasn't what I meant. What about the ships out west?'

'Nothing.' Simon shook his head. 'It was always a waste of time. I said so back then, too.'

'You've seen Sally's Ark paper yourself,' Piper said. 'You know Elsewhere exists. You were outvoted.'

'We know it existed in the Before – that doesn't mean anything now,' Simon said. 'And I was outvoted because you had the Assembly eating out of your hand.'

'They made a decision.'

'The Assembly's decision didn't seem to matter so much to you in the end, though, did it?'

Piper ignored the jibe. '*The Rosalind* and *The Evelyn* are still out there,' he said.

'We don't even know that – all we know is that they haven't come back. They could've sunk months ago, for all we know – or been picked up by the Council fleet.' Simon paused, and lowered his voice. 'I did send scouts. Not that I held out any hope for Elsewhere – but I could use every ship we've got, not to mention the troops who were manning them. So I sent Hannah, and two scouts. They waited at Cape Bleak for three weeks. No signal fires, and nothing to see but Council ships patrolling. The winter storms were closing in. If the ships were still out there by then, there was no hope for them. I need my troops here, not waiting for ghost ships.'

His voice was grave. I was glad, at least, that he took no pleasure in telling us this.

Piper had closed his eyes against the news, but only for a few seconds. Now he was pursing his lips, eyes on the table in front of him. He was already recalculating, figuring out where to go from here.

'Elsewhere's still the one thing that can offer real change,' I said. I remembered how I'd felt, when I read the mention of *allied nations* in the Ark paper: a sense that the world had stretched, widened. That the blank spaces where our maps had always ended might hold something after all, and that there could be something beyond the Council. Beyond the cycle of violence that pitted us against our twins, and killed both of us.

'I'm telling you now,' said Simon. 'There'll be no more boats sent out while I'm in charge. That's the kind of gamble that you might be able to justify in decent times, but not now, when everything's gone to hell.'

'Isn't that the time that we need it most, though?' I said.

'While you've been preoccupied with your pie-in-the-sky ideas, I've been busy doing the real work of keeping the resistance going. We've been working day and night: organising shelter and rations for all the evacuees. Re-establishing the communications network, and finding new safehouses, now that so many have been raided. Getting warnings to all the people who are at risk, given who's been taken. Monitoring Council troop movements, and keeping track of their fleet, too. We've identified a site in the south-east that might be able to accommodate some of the refugees, and we've got a team out there setting up shelters, to see the most vulnerable through the winter, at least.'

'It's not enough,' I said.

Simon turned to me. His voice was a low roar. 'You have no idea what it takes to keep the resistance together.'

'It has to be done,' I said. 'And I don't doubt that you're doing it well. But it's never going to be enough. It's just rebuilding what we had before. It's more running and hiding. You want to build another hiding spot, only this time near the deadlands? What happens next? Another Council raid, another attack. How can things ever change, if running and hiding is all that we do? What about striking back?'

'How?' Simon threw out his hands. 'We lost half our troops on the island. There might come a time when we can strike back against the Council. But it's not now. Not with our troop numbers slashed, and half our civilians on the run and going hungry.'

'It'll be too late,' I said. 'That's what the Council's counting on: keeping us downtrodden enough that we can't conceive of fighting back.'

'What would you do, to strike back?' Simon said.

'I'd send more troops north, to seek the ships again. I'd outfit new boats, ready to send out as soon as spring comes. But that's not all. I'd free New Hobart.'

CHAPTER 13

Simon slammed his hands onto the table, knocking over one of the water mugs and setting a plate spinning.

'Freeing New Hobart would be a massive undertaking at any time – let alone now, with the whole resistance in disarray. You're talking about open battle. Attacking a tightly guarded town.'

I explained what I had seen: that the town would soon be tanked. Thousands at once, worse even than the insidious expansion that was already taking place in the refuges. I could picture it: Elsa and the children, and all the thousands of others in the walled town. The hubbub of the market square replaced with the sterile hum of the tanks. But Simon addressed Piper instead of me.

'All these mad schemes, the wild-goose chases. The boats out west. Throwing your lot in with the seer. Even that bloody song that the bards are singing. Now this. You could be doing real good, if you'd work with me, instead of chasing mad ideas.'

'One of our *mad ideas* got rid of The Confessor, and her database,' said Piper. 'It's done more strategic good than anything else the resistance has achieved in years.'

'The people coming to me aren't concerned with strategy. They're just trying to survive,' said Simon. 'They're afraid, and hungry.'

'They're right to be afraid,' said Sally. 'The Council wants them all tanked, in the end. Survival isn't going to stop the Council, or keep us out of the tanks. You need to fight back, now more than ever. Throw everything you have into finding the ships, and freeing New Hobart.'

'You've been doing this for long enough to know the responsibilities that I have,' Simon said. 'I need to devote our resources to rebuilding. Re-establishing the safehouses, finding shelter for the evacuees –'

Piper stared unblinkingly into Simon's eyes. 'I protected Cass, at great cost, because of her value to us. If you ignore what Cass is telling you, that sacrifice is in vain.'

I closed my eyes. Piper was doing the same thing that Simon had done – measuring lives in terms of costs, and value. Everything reduced to some kind of calculation.

'It was your sacrifice,' Simon spat, 'not mine. And I won't throw away more lives on the whim of your seer, just to make you feel better about saving her.'

'Then the price we paid on the island is for nothing,' Piper said.

'You don't need to tell me about the price.' The shout burst from Simon like one of Xander's cries. 'I was there. I saw those people killed. But is that even the price you're talking about? Or are you just talking about the cost to yourself – being forced out of leading us?'

'This isn't about me,' Piper said. 'Not at all.'

'Are you so sure?' said Simon.

It was nearing sunrise, and we hadn't slept since the previous dawn. Sally made no complaint, but I saw the slight tremor in her hands as they rested in her lap. Next to her, Xander had fallen asleep with his head on the table.

'You need rest, all of you,' said Simon. 'We'll talk more about this later,' was the only assurance he would give, as he stood and headed for the door.

When he led us through the quarry to our quarters, the resistance soldiers were already awake, fifty or more of them gathered around the campfires. Their conversations stopped, and they turned and watched our progress on the muddy path. Sally, at the front, was greeted with smiles and, from two older men and a woman, salutes. But when their gazes turned to the rest of us, the smiles faded. They stared warily at me and Zoe, leading Xander between us. I looked back to see how they greeted Piper. A few nodded in acknowledgment as he passed, but a tall woman with red hair glared at him with her single eye, and a man leaning on a crutch spat on the ground, muttering something to his companion.

Simon guided us to a tent that had been hastily cleared of its previous occupants' belongings. Before he left, he reached for Piper again and clasped Piper's hand with all three of his own.

'I'm glad you're back,' he said. 'Despite everything.'

As Simon was ducking out of the tent door, I called to him, looking once again at the yellowing skin around his eyes, and his wilting stance.

'What happened to you, since the island?'

He exhaled heavily. 'I took over Piper's job, that's what happened.'

*

We rose before noon, after just a few hours' sleep, though we left Sally and Xander to rest for longer. Back in Simon's tent, with Piper, Zoe, and a handful of Simon's advisors, I began to get some sense of the daily business of rebuilding the resistance. Periodically, the signal whistle would be relayed down into the quarry, announcing the arrival of a scout. Messengers came to Simon with news of raids, of patrol numbers, and of the evacuees from the island still in search of safe haven. A scout from the east reported more expansions at Refuge 14, and of posters in the region announcing another increase in tithes. Another scout from near Wyndham brought rumours of tension within the Council: of more jockeying for power between The General, The Reformer, and The Ringmaster, since The Judge's death. We recounted our own encounter with The Ringmaster, and the news that reached Simon now seemed to accord with what we'd heard. The Ringmaster still commanded huge loyalty amongst the army but was increasingly sidelined in the Council Halls, where The General was ruling, with Zach at her side. But that was as far as our information went – in these days of strict segregation, it was harder and harder to gain any intelligence about the Council beyond the scraps of tavern gossip that filtered down to the Omega townships and settlements.

Throughout the long afternoon of discussions and plans, whenever The Reformer's name was mentioned all eyes in the room would turn to me. Zach was a problem to which my own body held the solution. All day I noticed how Piper and Zoe positioned themselves in front of me, between me and the others, and how Piper's arm never strayed far from his belt, loaded with knives. But hearing the news from the Council, I knew there were threats from which they couldn't protect me. I'd seen for myself how brutal the rivalries in the Council could be. The Judge had lived longer than most. If Zach had powerful enemies at Wyndham, then my death was as likely to come from an assassin's blade to Zach as it was from an ambush at the quarry. My own death might have nothing to do with me.

Over that day and the next, in Simon's crowded tent, I began to understand his exhausted demeanour. Each new report from a scout demanded decisions, and action: a doctor was dispatched to the east, where the newly established camp for evacuees was overrun with dysentery, while five guards were sent to help the camp shift to a spot with a cleaner water source. One of Simon's advisors, Violet, was sent to a camp a day's ride north, to oversee the interrogation of a Council soldier captured near New Hobart.

'Will he be tortured?' I asked Simon.

Sally rolled her eyes. 'This isn't a time for squeamishness,' she said. 'Do you think the Council hesitates to use torture when they need to?'

'And is that our aim, then, to be like them?' I shot back.

Nobody had an answer. And the messengers and reports kept coming, most of them the same: news of families, or sometimes whole settlements, struggling with the onset of winter, after another year of high tithes and land that would yield only meagre crops. More and more of them were turning to the refuges, not knowing, or perhaps not believing, what awaited them there. Others were being burned out of their homes, not by soldiers but by ordinary Alphas, in response to the news of The Judge's death, supposedly at the hands of his Omega twin.

Simon sat at the head of the table, his advisors beside him. He issued orders decisively, and remained calm, but the longer I watched the more he seemed like a man trying to gather water in his arms. And the more it seemed to me that we were all mired in the endless stream of small crises, with no chance to consider any larger strategy. Simon consulted us as he went about the day's business, and his advisors listened avidly to Sally, and even tolerated Piper's views. But when we raised the issue of the ships, or of New Hobart, they brushed us aside, returning to the day's immediate concerns: a new message about a raid on a settlement; the next scout's arrival. Even Piper was less insistent, now, on the subject of the ships. When he pressed Simon to send more scouts north, his voice lacked its usual conviction. I thought of the dark waves that I'd crossed to reach the island, and tried to imagine them whipped by winter storms, let alone the hazards of the ice sheets that lay further north. I looked at the rigid set of Piper's shoulders, his head slightly bowed, and knew that he was thinking of the same thing.

Each night, back in our own tent, I bent over the Ark paper. By now I knew every word by heart, and needn't have bothered with the paper itself. But I clutched the page as I ran over the words again and again, as if that fading sheet of parchment was a map that would help guide my visions to the Ark, or to Elsewhere. But all I could find was my own fear, and the tank water rising over New Hobart. I couldn't make the pieces fit: Elsewhere; the Ark; New Hobart.

'Perhaps the Ark's there – under New Hobart. Maybe it's that simple,' Sally said. 'And that's why the Council seized the town – to get at the Ark.'

I shook my head. 'No. I was in New Hobart for weeks. If the Ark were there, I would have felt it – places are the thing that I usually feel most clearly.' I'd felt the tank rooms under Wyndham, and the caves and tunnels through the mountain. I'd felt the island. 'The Ark isn't in New Hobart,' I said. When I closed my eyes, I saw it again: the defencelessness of Elsa's open mouth, the liquid creeping in, thick and slow, like the probing of an unwanted tongue. The visions came again and again, until my jaw was sore from being clenched so tightly, and I was sweating, even though the ground underneath our tent was hardened with frost. I was so tense that the sounds of my own body felt exaggerated: the passage of air in my nostrils. The sound of skin on skin as I pressed my hands over my eyes and rubbed them.

'It's not finished,' Xander said, reaching for the paper. 'The maze of bones.'

'What are you talking about?' I snapped. 'Say what you mean.' I could hear the glint of hysteria in my own words.

Sally moved between us. 'Don't talk to him that way,' she said, and I knew she was right. I looked at him, mouth opening and closing like a fish. And I, more than anyone, knew that he wasn't trying to be obscure. I knew that his visions had knocked words loose inside his head, and that he was scrambling amongst the wreckage.

'I'm sorry,' I said, and tried to reach for his hand, but Sally blocked my arm, turning her back to me as she soothed Xander.

All night I heard his mutterings and cries, his mangled words being spat from his mouth like broken teeth.

It was my fault, and my future.

*

On the third night, after midnight, Simon yanked open our tent flap.

'You need to come, now,' he said. He waited while we rose and threw on our clothes, his swinging lamp tossing agitated shadows on the walls of the tent. Xander was muttering, halfway between waking and sleep, so we left him to rest.

Outside Simon's tent, a guard was holding a horse, its

grey coat dark with sweat, its hot breath steaming into the night air. When Simon entered the tent ahead of us, the woman inside stood hastily, but Simon gestured for her to sit. There were flecks of mud on her face from riding fast through the wet night. She was closer to Simon's age than Piper's. Her dark hair was bound back tightly and she had the wiry strength of a life lived hard. Her left wrist finished at a stub, rounded like the end of a loaf of bread.

'Tell them, Violet,' Simon said.

Violet raised an eyebrow. She was looking at Piper and Zoe, and at me.

'I've told you already.' Simon pushed his chair and stood. 'They can be trusted.'

She spoke, while Simon paced by the door.

'I've been north, seeing what we could get out of the soldier that Noah's crew captured. He was a courier, heading back to New Hobart from one of the southern garrisons. The message he carried wasn't of particular interest – updates on troop replacements and cargo. But we were able to get more out of him, about New Hobart itself.'

'How?' I interrupted. 'Did you torture him?'

Simon glared at me. 'We have a job to do. Don't tell us how to do it.'

Violet ignored us both. 'He said they've been searching for something,' she said. 'Inside New Hobart. Asking about documents.'

'Nothing else?'

'He didn't know any more than that,' said Violet. 'Said only the senior soldiers were privy to the details. But they've all had the orders: anything old, any papers, to be reported straight away. Twice his squadron was sent out to search, after tip-offs. They found nothing but a secret school – illegal, sure, for Omegas, but usually the Council wouldn't be so zealous about stuff like that. They were told to search the whole place, and all the papers had to be packed up and taken to their HQ.' Violet shrugged. 'He thought it was funny at the time – all the kids' papers with their ABCs scrawled on them, being parcelled up carefully to be examined.' Her face hardened. 'He didn't think it was so funny by the time we'd finished extracting the story from him.'

They all stared at me when I stood.

'Get Xander,' I said to Sally.

Violet rolled her eyes. 'Isn't one seer enough? What's the point of dragging the mad one into it?'

I went to speak, but Simon spoke over me.

'You're dismissed for tonight,' he said to Violet. 'Rest, and we'll talk again tomorrow.'

She glared over her shoulder at Piper as she left. Sally stood too. 'I'll bring Xander,' she said.

I turned to Piper. 'Xander tried to tell us. He told us that it wasn't me they were looking for in New Hobart. *You're not what they're looking for*, he'd said. I thought he'd meant that The Confessor had really been searching for Kip, not me. But that's not what he was saying.'

It's not finished, he'd said. I'd been trying to make the pieces fit, Elsa and the Ark paper and New Hobart, but it was all one piece. And Xander had known all along.

Sally brought Xander in, a blanket draped around his shoulders. Zoe led him to the bench and I knelt beside him.

'What's the *maze of bones*?' I said, trying to keep my voice calm.

He didn't speak. His eyes began their usual surveillance of the ceiling.

'Tell me,' I said.

'I told you already,' he said.

'You did,' I said. 'But we didn't understand. Tell me again.'

'It used to feel different,' he said. 'A quiet space, underground.'

I wanted to prompt him, but I forced myself to wait. His eyes did another lap of the tent's ceiling. Sally's hand, on his shoulder, was tensed.

'Then it got noisy,' he went on. 'People rattling the bones.'

'Is it the Ark?' I said.

'It's just a hole,' he muttered. 'A place where people lost their bones. A maze of bones.'

'But now you can feel noises there? People in it?'

He nodded. 'Sounds in the dark place.'

'Has the Council found it? Do you know where it is?'

He swung his head from side to side. 'It's noisy there now. But they're still looking for pieces. Paper pieces. Word bones, from Before.'

'In New Hobart?' I asked. I remembered what Zoe had told me, the report about papers surfacing in New Hobart years ago, and the Council crushing the resistance cell before anything more could be found. 'Papers from the Ark, like the one that Sally made a copy of – is that what they're searching for there?'

Xander nodded. 'They need them,' he said again. 'It's not finished.'

CHAPTER 14

That was all we could get out of him, but it was enough. When he had descended again into aborted syllables and broken words, I turned to Simon.

'If thousands of people being tanked wasn't enough to get you to free New Hobart, will this make a difference?'

'We had a lead from New Hobart about the Ark, years ago,' he said. 'But it came to nothing. The soldiers got there first, wiped out our whole cell.'

'Whatever there was to be found, it was important to the Council,' I said. 'Important enough for them to move quickly, and to kill for. They're still searching – there's more to be found. And I think Elsa knows something about it.' I thought again of her face as we'd stood in her kitchen, when I'd asked about the resistance. She'd mentioned her dead husband, but she'd never dared to tell me what had happened to him. His story was an intake of breath that had never been exhaled. 'Her husband was killed, and she hinted that it was from asking too many questions. Couldn't he have been involved?'

Piper shook his head. 'We had six people in New Hobart.

I knew all of them myself. None of them was married to the keeper of the holding house. I'd never heard anything to suggest a link to her.'

'It's a bit convenient, isn't it?' said Zoe. 'That the person who might have crucial information for you should just happen to be the person you stayed with there.'

I turned from her to Piper. 'You're the one who's always going on about how important my visions are. What they're worth. Didn't it occur to you that there was a reason that Elsa was the person I went to in New Hobart? That something could have drawn me to her house, even if I wasn't aware of it, the same way I was drawn to the island?'

I'd been wondering about this since Kip's death. I'd been thinking of all the tanks lined up in that chamber I'd discovered under Wyndham. Had I found myself at Kip's tank, of all the tanks in that room, because something had led me there? Had my fear of The Confessor drawn me, unwittingly, to find her twin?

'Whether your friend is involved or not,' said Simon, 'it makes no difference –we can't free the town. That would mean open war, outnumbered and under-resourced.'

'It's already war,' I said. 'Just a slow war, and we're losing. They're looking for something in New Hobart – something important enough for the Council to hold the city all this time. It's something that could help us to find the Ark, or even Elsewhere. It could make all the difference.'

'How?' Simon's voice was weary. 'Even if we could free the town and find the papers, what will some dusty documents offer us? More details of the Before? More taboo machines that we can't understand?'

'You're sounding like The Ringmaster,' I said. 'We can't run from this just because the machines scare us. Zach and The General have been using machines all along. That's always been at the heart of their plans. They've already found the Ark. The papers could lead us there, or to Elsewhere. You want to let the Council find the papers first? The more information they have, the more dangerous they get.'

For an hour, we argued. We kept coming back to the necessity of freeing New Hobart, and the impossibility of doing so. The conversation was a closed loop, like the wall around the town itself.

'If we lost the battle,' Simon said, 'it would be the end of the resistance.'

Sally had been sitting in silence, Xander's hand in hers. She spoke quietly.

'That's all we focus on these days, isn't it? The massacre on the island. Shifting out to the east, like you're doing now. Call it what you like – it's a retreat. But when did we stop thinking about what we're fighting for? We're just running and hiding, trying to forestall the end of the resistance. I understand the fear – I've seen how hard things have got. I know what we're up against. But what if this Ark could really change things? What if we stopped thinking about the end of the resistance, and started thinking about the end of the Council?'

*

Just before dawn, Simon gave the order to strike camp and head for New Hobart. Troops were sent to the woods to retrieve the horses hidden there and to lead them down to the quarry to be loaded with gear. Two guards were being left in the quarry, but tents and gear still needed to be shifted. The white clay clung to everything, including the tents, and the horses slipped on the paths that had become troughs. Twice I tried to help with the loading, but each time I approached, the guards would turn from me, dragging the horses away without a word.

Our group set off before noon, and we rode late into the night. Piper and I were at the front, next to Simon. Behind us rode Sally, holding Xander in front of her, with Zoe beside them, and two of Simon's scouts. After all the time I'd spent travelling with just Kip, or Zoe and Piper, it was a luxury to ride on horseback, with scouts navigating and keeping watch, and others to set up the camp and cook. We travelled in small groups, mainly at night, joining others occasionally when we camped at rendezvous points. But whenever we joined the other troops, I caught them staring at me. I recognised the look; all Omegas were familiar with it. It was the same look that the Alphas gave us: a mixture of fear and disgust. The troops were hostile to Piper and Zoe, too. Once, when we camped for a day in a boulder field, I heard a man scoff as he saw Piper.

'There he goes, with the Alpha and the seer again,' the man said.

A woman joined in. 'More interested in them than in his own kind.'

Zoe had spun around, but Piper gripped her arm and guided her onwards.

'You're going to stand for that?' Zoe said.

'Starting fights with our own troops isn't going to help us free New Hobart,' Piper said. 'And we still have a long way to go.'

Xander began to mutter, echoing the words he'd heard, as if they were bouncing off him. 'Long way,' he said, again and again. 'Long long way.' His hands rose and fell. He was often like this when he sensed that others were angry, and I moved away while Sally pressed his cheeks with both hands and bent her head to his, to talk him down from the precipice of his anxiety. When Sally had managed to calm him, she looked over her shoulder to Piper and spoke in a low voice.

'You need to deal with the troops at some stage. They need to be fighting for you, not against you.'

He gave her a quick smile. 'Let me pick the time,' he said.

*

The resistance might have been hard pressed since the attack on the island, but under Simon's leadership it was still substantial and well-organised.

Within two nights we'd crossed McCarthy's Pass, a narrow gap in the mountain range at the base of the central plains. The night was clear, and from the top of the pass we could look down to the south and see the sea again. We dismounted to let the horses drink from a spring. Piper followed me when I stepped away from the group to stare down at the coast.

'It's always said that everything's broken, since the blast,' he said. 'And we both know there's plenty that's broken enough.'

There were so many different kinds of brokenness to choose from. The broken-down mountains, slumped into heaps of slag and scree. The towns and cities from the Before, the bones of a world. Or the broken bodies he'd seen, too many to count.

'But look at that.' He waved down at the view below us. The rocks of the mountain pass gave way to the hills. Further down, the sea hugged the curves of the shore like a sleeping lover.

He turned to face me. His look was always like this: direct, unabashed. 'It's easy to forget, sometimes, that what's left isn't all ugliness.'

It was impossible to argue with him. Not in front of the ocean, unconcerned with us. And not in front of Piper himself. His eyes, their clear, pale green startling in his dark face. The ledge of his cheekbones, and the clean jut of his jaw. The world had always taught me that we were broken. But when I looked at Piper, I could see no brokenness in him.

He touched my face. I could feel the calluses on his fingers, from handling rabbit snares and knife blades. The softer skin of his palm, yielding when I pressed my face against it. Soft as Kip's cheek.

I jerked backwards.

'What do you want from me?' I said.

'I don't want anything from you.' His eyebrows drew together. 'I see you struggling with your visions. And I know it's not easy for you to see what's become of Xander. I'm only trying to comfort you.'

I didn't know how to say to him that there was no comfort for me. That he had refused the brokenness the world had thrust on him, but I was broken in ways he couldn't understand. That if you cut me open, all that would tumble out would be fire, and visions of Kip in the tanks, and of Kip falling to the silo floor. That there were some things that could not be put right.

I left him on the hillside, amongst the stones of the shattered mountain.

*

It took us a week to get to New Hobart. At first we were travelling through Alpha territory, but Simon's scouts kept us well clear of the Alpha villages and patrols. We moved mainly at night, until we reached the arid plains to the south of New Hobart, where the Alpha settlements withdrew, and we could travel in daylight again. The winds that ripped through these plains were ferocious, leaving my eyes red and my lips dry and chapped. Nothing grew but the wiry, tall grass, and our tracks were blown away as soon as we made them. Winter was beginning to establish its stranglehold on the land now.

When we passed the small town of Twyford, the fires were lit, smoke blurring the sky. In our tent, Xander whimpered with the cold and slept close between Zoe and Piper. It wasn't his moans or muttering that kept me awake, though. It was the thrashing of his mind. Once, when I was a child, an ant had crawled into my ear. For two days all my squirming and poking had not been able to dislodge the ant, and I'd felt it moving, its every twitch, amplified within my head. Being near to Xander was like that, for me.

At noon the next day, Sally shouted Piper's name. She and Xander, sharing a horse, were riding just behind us, a guard at each side. At her shouts we wheeled our horses and rode back to her, but there was no sign of ambush or disaster – only Xander's usual faraway expression, and Sally clutching both of his shoulders from behind.

'Say it again,' she said to Xander. He opened his mouth but no words emerged. Their horse shifted from side to side, as though Xander's unease trickled down to him too.

'Say it again,' repeated Sally. 'Tell Piper what you said to me.'

When Xander still said nothing, Sally turned to Piper.

'Which ships did you send out to search for Elsewhere?' she said.

'*The Evelyn* and *The Rosalind*,' Zoe and Piper said in unison.

Sally smiled, contorting her wrinkles into elaborate new configurations. 'That's what he said. Rosalind.' She grabbed Xander's shoulders once more. 'Tell Piper,' she said. 'Say it again.'

Xander looked impatient, but spoke. 'I already said it. Rosalind. Rosalind's coming back.'

He couldn't be persuaded to say any more, but those words were enough to spur us onwards for the long day's ride. Simon was non-committal, only muttering that he'd reconsider sending more troops to Cape Bleak, in search of the ships, if we managed to free New Hobart. I understood his reluctance. A few stuttered words from Xander didn't seem much, in the face of the ships' long silence, and the winter storms that would be thrashing the sea.

Nonetheless, through all that day, and the next, I held Xander's words as we rode, cupping them in my mind like a bird's egg. *Rosalind's coming back.*

*

The cold was worse when we reached the swamps. If we'd been travelling at a leisurely pace we might have had the luxury of avoiding the worst of the mires, but we had no time to waste, and sometimes spent half a day or more leading our horses through the knee-deep water. Sally never complained, but at night, as we huddled around a fire of half-damp reeds, I could see how she struggled to hold her rations in her hands, which the cold had tied into intractable knots. I saw, too, how Piper's jaw muscles were tensed against his shivering, and how Zoe pulled her sleeves down over her blue-tinged hands.

When we were six miles east of New Hobart, deep in the marshes, Simon ordered the troops to make camp. The swamp was stubborn here, a mess of pits and marsh, held together only by threads and islands of higher land. The water, already iced at the edges, was too deep to wade through, and the reeds grew taller even than Piper. Where trees sprouted in the higher ground, they were contorted by the wind, their branches twisted and arthritic. Smaller trees clung at the edge of the swamp pools, their roots dangling straight into the water. It took us a day of seeking to find the best spot, an acre or two of tussocked island amid the foetid water. A single, circuitous path led there through the miles of swamp. The horses had to be led slowly through the path, testing each hoof as they placed it, and when we were in the camp, they clustered by the reeds and whinnied their suspicion. But the noise was no concern – this wasn't territory for passers by. Any wanderers were more likely to drown in the murky, ice-rimmed water than to stumble across our camp, deep in the reeds.

Messengers and scouts had already been sent out, to muster the surviving members of the resistance. But it would take days, if not weeks, for them to join us. In Simon's tent, we gathered around a map of the region. Rendered down to pen strokes on paper, the town itself was shown, rising on a hill on the plain, now ringed by the Council's wall. A mile or more to the south lay the forest that Kip and I had burned. To the north and west, the plains were broken only by occasional gullies and copses. And to the east, the swamps where our camp perched, islands of mud amongst half-frozen water and reeds.

'Don't get too comfortable,' Simon said to Piper, when he found the three of us surveying the camp. Zoe snorted, looking out over the island of mud and reeds with its few straggling trees. 'I'm sending you and Zoe to watch the town from the south,' Simon went on. 'I've already sent Violet and two of her scouts to watch the northern perimeter. I want troop numbers, and whatever details you can get about the Council's defences. Patrol procedures and routes, and anything else you can gather.'

'Cass is coming with us,' said Piper.

'It's not a holiday,' said Simon. 'I'm sending you and Zoe because you're the best for the task. Cass is safer in the camp.'

'She goes where I go,' said Piper.

I registered Zoe's eye-roll.

'I know New Hobart,' I said. 'I've travelled the plains and the forest more recently than any of you.'

'The forest?' said Zoe. 'You mean what's left of it, since you and Kip burned it down.'

I ignored her. 'You know I'm better than anyone at finding places, sensing things. I'm going with them.'

Simon looked from me to Piper, and back again. 'Fine,' he said. 'But watch her.' He turned away. It wasn't clear whether he was telling them to protect me, or to spy on me.

Either way I was grateful to be leaving. The hostility of the troops had been slightly blunted, less out of trust than familiarity, and the daily exchanges that were unavoidable when camping and travelling together. They spoke to me civilly enough when they needed to ask me to pass a water flask, or to pick the safest route through a patch of swamp. But most of the time they avoided me, and their stares followed me around the camp. I suspected that Simon had noticed it too, and figured that it would improve morale for the three of us to be away from the camp.

We left Sally and Xander with the troops in the swamp.

I would never admit it to the others, but I was as relieved to be away from Xander as I was to be away from the quiet hostility of the troops. Since Xander's words about *The Rosalind*'s return, he'd hardly spoken. But each time his hands twitched, or he spat out half words, I became more aware of the restlessness of my own hands, and of the visions of flame that jostled one another in my crowded mind.

It took hours to negotiate the marshland before Piper, Zoe and I could draw close to New Hobart. When the marshes receded, we were in the forest – or what remained of it. It had been late summer when Kip and I set the place alight; now it was a wasteland of scorched stumps, whittled by flame. The smaller trees were gone altogether and only the trunks of the larger trees were left. I touched one and my hand came away black.

Before the fire, we might have needed a lamp to make our way at night, but in the ruins that Kip and I had made, the moon lit the way through the spindles of tree trunks, their sharpened tips accusing the sky.

Had the whole world looked like this, after the blast? Worse, probably – no trunks would have remained, however charred. Was there a forest, anywhere, that had been spared the flames of the blast? The world had been swept of its growing and living things. I thought of the total bleakness of the deadlands, where nothing grew, even after centuries, and I wondered whether Elsewhere would be any different.

Closer to New Hobart, there were sections of forest that had not burned. Here, with the lights of the town visible just a few miles to the north, we made camp for the night. Piper took the first shift, but I looked toward the town too as I lay down to sleep. It was strange to lie there, seeing the lights on the hill and knowing that Elsa, Nina, and the children were so close. After what I'd foreseen, I couldn't think of them without feeling my heart leap like a startled toad in my chest. Every night, now, in my dreams, Elsa floated in a tank, her mouth slack around the tube that penetrated it. I dreamed, too, of the children crammed together in a larger tank, a tangle of bodies. I could make out some of their faces: Alex, who used to laugh himself breathless when Kip tickled his stomach. Louisa, who followed me everywhere, and who had once fallen asleep on my lap. I'd learnt, then, how the weight of a sleeping child is subtly different from their weight when awake. Now, in my visions, Elsa and the children were all weightless, their hair drifting across their faces.

I woke from the waterlogged dream with a shout.

'You insisted on bringing her,' Zoe hissed at Piper, who was leaning over me to hush me.

I couldn't speak, my mouth clenched shut against the scream that would otherwise break out again. During the dream, one of my sleeping hands had clawed at the earth. I stared at the gouge marks I'd left in the black soil.

'It's not her fault.' Piper's hand was pressed against my shoulder, steadying my shaking as he spoke coolly to Zoe. 'You know that,' he said. 'And we need her.'

'What we don't need,' Zoe said, 'is her bringing a patrol down on us.' She strode away. For three days we watched the town. Each morning, before dawn, we set out from our base in the ruins of the forest and ventured onto the plain. We moved slowly in the deep grass, creeping to the few hillocks and copses that granted us some cover. Around New Hobart, the wall that was being hastily constructed when Kip and I escaped was now a solid structure, stoutly braced with posts. Red-shirts, the Council's soldiers, patrolled the perimeter, and manned the huge gates. We made note of the numbers of patrols, mounted and on foot, and the time of each shift changeover. We counted the wagons that sometimes came and went, escorted by soldiers, on the main road that traced through the eastern swamps toward Wyndham. When a wagon entered the city, we noted the procedure at the gate, observing how many soldiers it took to open the gates, and counting the guards in each of the watchtowers. There were so many of them; each day of watching only confirmed the Council's grip on New Hobart, its wall encircling the town like a strangler's hands.

Only a few miles from where we watched, Elsa, Nina and the children were waiting. Somewhere, too, within those guarded walls, were the papers that held more clues about the Ark, and the secrets that it contained. The soldiers were searching. The tanks were filling. The hours while we watched the town felt too long, and never long enough.

Each morning, not long after dawn, fifty or more Omegas filed out of the eastern gate. Corralled into a tight group by mounted soldiers, they were led to the farmland to the north-east of the city. There they laboured, watched by the soldiers, until they were escorted in again in the evening, along with the barrows of harvested food.

While the farmers worked, the soldiers milled about and talked together. Once, an older Omega stumbled and dropped an armful of marrows that he was loading onto a cart. The soldier driving the wagon turned and whipped him, as casually as a horse flicking its tail at a fly. Without looking back he urged the cart away, leaving the man fallen in the mud, clutching at his face. Even from a distance we could see the blood running off his chin. The other Omegas nearby had turned to look, and one woman moved to help the bleeding man, but a shout from another soldier sent her bending back to her own task.

We noted, too, the new building on the slope of the hill inside the southern wall. Long and low, it stood out against the jumble of old houses around it. There were no windows. If it weren't for what we knew, I might have thought it was a storehouse. As it was, I only had to look at it to feel the tank water rising within.

The Council had occupied New Hobart for just a few months, and the tanks were not an easy thing to build. I'd seen the tank chamber underneath Wyndham, and the complex tracery of wires and pipes and flashing lights that kept those people suspended in their almost-death. I'd felt the elaborate darting of the Electric through the wires. But lately I'd also seen the children's tanked faces in my visions, night after night. They didn't have long.

*

On our third day of watching the town, Zoe came back at a run from her post, a low hill in the marshes with a view towards New Hobart's western gate. Before she could speak she bent over, hands on knees, to reclaim her breath.

'We're not the only ones watching the gate,' said Zoe. 'There are footsteps by the lookout spot. At least four or five people. Fresh prints – since yesterday's rain. Based on how the grass was flattened, I'd say they'd been watching the gate for most of the night.'

'Could it've been Violet and her scouts, coming to our side of town for some reason?'

'Not in identical boots,' she said. 'The prints are all the same. They're Council soldiers, in regulation boots.'

'Why would they be sneaking around at night, watching their own guard posts?'

None of us had any answers.

'The tracks head away from the town,' she said. 'But I lost the trail when they reached the grasslands. And there's not much cover out that far – I couldn't spend too long looking.'

We returned to camp before nightfall so that we wouldn't have to navigate the intricate swamps in the dark. We reported in detail to Simon all that we'd seen, including the signs that somebody else had been watching the town.

'Have Violet's scouts to the north seen any signs of others?' Piper said.

Simon shook his head. 'No. But Crispin did. He and Anna saw something when they were hunting to the west. In the gully with the lone spruce at the crest – two uniformed sentries on duty, and a few soldiers coming and going throughout the night. They seemed to be monitoring New Hobart.'

'It doesn't make sense,' Zoe said. 'Why would the Council be watching New Hobart, when they're the ones holding the town?'

'There isn't any single *Council*, though,' I said. I was remembering what The Ringmaster had said: *You really think we're one big happy family? A Councillor's greatest enemies are those closest to him.* I remembered, too, the last time that we'd caught glimpses of hidden watchers, the night before The Ringmaster had sprung on us. I could feel him, as if his arm was once more around my neck.

'It's The Ringmaster,' I said. 'He's here.'

'You can't know that,' Simon said.

I turned on him. 'Can't? If you weren't so busy telling me what I can't do, you could use my visions to help us. I found the island. I found my way out of the Keeping Rooms. I found The Confessor's machine.'

'Why would he be watching New Hobart?' Simon said impatiently.

'For the same reason we are,' I said, thinking of the disgust in The Ringmaster's face when he'd spoken of the machines. 'He doesn't trust The General or Zach. He wants to know what they're up to, what they're looking for in the town.'

'Discord in the Council is good news for us, in the long term,' said Piper. 'But even if it's The Ringmaster out there, it makes no difference to us now.' He turned to Simon. 'Warn the guards on the camp perimeter, and station sentries by the northern edge of the forest, so we'll know if they head this way.'

I noticed how he threw out the orders, as instinctively as he would throw his daggers. I noted, too, how Simon nodded and obeyed.

CHAPTER 15

From dawn until dark, our camp crawled with the preparations. Near where I stood by Simon's tent, two men without legs were lashing together a ladder. I watched the precision of their hands, binding the struts to the spars. At the camp's edge, under a lopsided tree, a squadron was practising with grappling hooks. They hurled the hooks again and again, climbing the knotted ropes when they gained a purchase. If the attack was to succeed, we needed to penetrate the wall – otherwise we would die in front of it.

Each day more troops arrived, and each day we were disappointed that more had not come. They came on foot, in small groups, or sometimes alone. Some knew how to fight, but had no weapons. Others brought what they could: rusted swords; blunted axes, made for chopping wood, not fighting. They'd come hurriedly, when the messengers had spread the word, but they also bore tales of those who would not come. Too worried, with their families to provide for, and winter upon us. Too scared, after the attack on the island, and with the safehouses being raided. I couldn't blame them.

Some of those who had come were well-trained fighters – those who had survived from the island, and those who worked for the resistance on the mainland. But they were a shadow army, not a standing force. Their experience wasn't in battles. It was in skirmishes with Council patrols, and raids on Alpha villages to snatch Omega babies before they'd been branded. They were used to evading Council soldiers, stealing horses, and attacking supply convoys. More than a century ago, as rumour had it, the Council crushed an Omega uprising in the east. Since then, the only large-scale battle I'd heard of had been on the island, and few enough of our fighters had survived that.

Others who came to the camp were resistance contacts rather than troops. They were untrained in combat, and sometimes unsuited for it. They were loyal to the resistance, and we were thankful that they'd come – but often, at night, I thought of the limbless and the crippled who had shuffled their way to the encampment, and I wondered what we were leading them in to.

*

That night I dreamed I was inside Elsa's holding house again. I walked the long dormitory where the children's beds were pressed up against the wall. Everything was silent. At first I thought the children must be sleeping. But when I bent down to one of the beds, I saw that it was empty. That's when I noticed the thickness of the silence. In all my weeks in the holding house, it had never been silent. In the daytime, the children were noisy in the courtyard or the dining room. Nina was usually banging pots in the kitchen, and Elsa's voice could be heard around a corner, chiding a child about this or that misbehaviour. Even at night there were the sounds of forty sleeping children. The light snores and open-mouthed breathing; the odd cry of one of the younger ones, half-wakened from a dream. There was none of that now. Only a single noise, a dripping sound, a *plink plink plink* coming with eerie regularity from the far end of the dormitory. I moved through the darkness, trailing my hand along the rail of each empty bed. Perhaps there's a leak in the roof, I thought, or a crack in one of the pitchers laid out for the children to wash with each morning. But when I reached the far wall, I could find no puddle on the floor. The noise seemed to be coming from above. I tipped my head back and looked up. I could see it now, the drip, falling from the ceiling. It hadn't far to fall. Each drop landed only a foot below the ceiling, on the surface of the liquid that filled the whole room. From where I stood, looking up, I could see the concentric circles, spreading on the surface with each drop. I opened my mouth to scream, but in the thick fluid the sound was muted, even to my own ears.

When I woke, Piper's hand was on my arm, shaking me. I hadn't been screaming, but the rolled jacket that I used as a pillow was wet with sweat, my blanket rucked around my knees from my flailing.

'They're going to tank the children first,' I said.

'When?'

I shook my head. 'Today. Tomorrow, maybe. I don't know. Soon.' There'd been no mistaking the urgency of the vision. 'We need to attack now.'

'There's sixty troops from the western ranges due any day,' Piper said. 'More still to come from the east, too, if the messengers got through in time.'

'It'll be too late,' I said. 'The kids are being tanked any day now.'

'We won't save them, or anyone else, by leading our troops into a massacre,' said Zoe. 'We only get one go at this. We need whatever the Council's looking for in there. And we need enough troops to give us a chance.'

'What about the children's chance?' I said to Piper. 'You saw what the tank did to Kip, and he was an Alpha. Even if we can free the town eventually, and get them out, they'll never be the same. Don't you want to save them?'

'This has never been about what I want,' he said, and looked away. 'It's about what the resistance needs.'

All morning, as I watched the troops at their training, I could taste the tank liquid at the back of my throat. To distract myself, I asked Zoe to help me to practise fighting again. We didn't speak much while we sparred, except for her instructions: *Lower. You're leaving yourself wide open. When you're in close like that, use your elbow, not your fist.* I was getting faster now, the gap between thought and movement narrowing. The punches and jabs that she'd taught me had grown closer to habit, and while I could never best her, I was able to dodge some of her strikes. Even in the cold, we'd stripped off our coats and jumpers, and my shirt clung to the sweat on my back and my elbows. The training forced me to focus on my body: the strain of my right shoulder, from keeping my knife arm raised before my face; the bruise on my cheek, where Zoe's kick had slipped past my guard. As we circled and jabbed and circled again I had to concentrate on each breath, instead of on my visions of the children.

'We're done here,' she said after an hour or more. 'No sense wearing yourself out.' But before she stepped away, she nodded at me. 'Better,' she said. It was as close to approval as I'd ever had from her.

*

I stood in the entrance of our tent. Nearby, Sally sat on a fallen tree, four soldiers squatting by her feet as she jabbed with a stick at a map spread on the ground. Beyond her, the hobbled horses were feeding noisily on hay fetched by scouts from beyond the swamps. Three armourers were at work, cutting up a felled tree to carve shields. Near the camp's centre, on one of the few flat patches of ground, Piper had joined a squadron in some combat drills. They practised one-on-one, the clatter of sword strikes reminding me of the warning bells that had rung out on the island when the Council's fleet came. Piper was sparring with Violet, Simon's advisor. He had the advantage of height and strength, but she had both arms, and the missing hand on her left arm didn't stop her from wielding a shield, strapped to her forearm. They were well matched; her short-sword was speedy against Piper's longer blade, and her shield blocked some of his parries. His single arm meant he carried no shield, and he had to move quicker than her, and more economically. Each block and turn was precise, and he seemed to pivot on the spot, forcing her to move around him. He pounced only when her more extravagant swipes gave him an opening.

They seemed to alternate in gaining the advantage. Twice Piper's reach allowed his sword to find her neck, where he gave a gentle slap with the flat of his blade; twice Violet's speed allowed her to get beneath his defences and nudge his body with the flat of her own sword. Then the two would step apart briefly, before beginning again. I noticed, though, that while Piper nodded at her each time he conceded a point, and laughed once at his own folly when he over-reached and stumbled, Violet's face was fixed. She launched herself at him ever faster, each time they had stepped apart. Soon enough they were both panting, and the grass around them was a circle trampled free of frost.

Then, when she gained a point, instead of turning her blade she struck home with the edge. Not a real strike, but enough to make him wince, and to sketch a thin line of blood on his shirt. Zoe, who'd been talking with Simon, turned suddenly. I wondered whether she'd felt a jab of pain from Piper's wound, or had just heard his intake of breath.

Piper stepped back from Violet, an eyebrow raised. He didn't look down at the blood, but stayed in the fighting stance that I recognised from my own lessons with Zoe: knees bent, weight lightly on his toes, sword raised.

'You doing the Council's job for them now, Violet?' he said.

'You'd know about that, since the island,' she said.

The two of them were moving in tandem, pivoting slowly around the point where their raised swords almost met.

The others sparring nearby had stopped. Weapons lowered, they watched Piper and Violet.

'You should have handed the seer over,' she said to him.

'What kind of a leader would I have been, if I'd rolled over and given them one of our own?'

Violet came at him again. On the third strike her blade shrieked its way down the length of his, and they were brought close, their swords locked together at the hilts. She aimed a kick at Piper, which he dodged, and while she was off balance, he shoved the sword hilts away, twisting his blade free. Violet's own hilt struck her, and she wiped her face with the shoulder of her shield arm, smearing the blood that ran from the corner of her mouth.

'She isn't one of our own,' she said. 'She's a seer.'

The stares of the crowd shifted to me, and I forced myself to return their gaze.

'Cass is one of us,' said Piper.

Violet moved forward again, her sword darting low. He blocked the strike, and the one that followed.

'Giving her to The Confessor wouldn't have saved the island,' said Piper, each word coming as a grunt as their blades clashed.

'You don't know that,' Violet said. 'And anyway, we've all seen how you look at her. Don't try to tell me you saved her for the good of the resistance.' She swiped low again, and Piper had to step back to dodge the blade that came at his thigh.

Then he pressed forward, striking three times, fast. Violet blocked the strikes, but had to retreat a few steps. Piper advanced, toe-to-toe with her. As she stepped backwards, he hooked his foot behind her heel, so that she fell. When she landed, Piper was over her, knocking her sword from her hand. He knelt above her, planted his knee in her ribs, the tip of his sword at her neck.

For a second I thought he would plunge the blade into her throat. I shouted, my *No* hanging in the frosted air.

He kept his sword where it was, and bent his head close to hers, so she couldn't look away from him as he spoke. 'Even if it had saved the island, if I'd given them Cass and Kip – who would I hand over the next time they come? And the time after that? What happens when it's your husband, or the woman who raised you, or the child you've cared for? And what happens when I've handed all of us over, one by one? What then?'

'You should have been willing to compromise,' Violet shouted. Her hand swept the ground beside her, groping blindly for her weapon. With his own blade, Piper flicked her sword out of reach.

'There is no compromise with the Council,' he said. 'Just surrender in stages. Do you really think they were ever going to just let us keep living peacefully? Maybe once, when they had no alternative. But now they have the tanks, that's their goal: every single one of us, floating. They're not going to stop until that happens. Handing over Cass would only have sped up the process.'

He threw his sword aside. It landed in the mud by my feet. Then he stood. He looked down at Violet, still sprawled on her back.

'I fought on the island too. I bled there, along with you, and I grieve with you for those who died there.' He spoke loudly now, his words for the assembled crowd, not just her. 'I'll fight and bleed again when we go to free New Hobart. But I'd rather die at the wall outside New Hobart than live in a tank.'

He bent, and held out his hand to Violet. For a moment she waited. A narrow streak of blood was running slowly from the corner of her mouth to her chin. Then she took his hand, let him pull her up, and walked away.

Piper turned to the watching troops.

'Does anyone else have anything they want to say to me, about the island?'

Nobody spoke.

'Then let's get back to work,' he said, and picked up his sword. I saw Sally's smile as she watched him stride back to the centre of the sparring ground, the troops moving quickly out of his way.

*

That night, I was woken by a quiet keening in the darkness. It took me a few minutes to realise that it wasn't Xander. He was peacefully asleep, mouth open, lying close to Sally. Next to Sally, Zoe and Piper slept too, the blanket halfway over Zoe's face.

The crying was in my head. And from the wailing I began

to pick out individual voices. I heard the phlegmy gasps of little Alex, and remembered Elsa always swiping at his runny nose with her handkerchief. The high-pitched sobs of little Louisa.

'They're taking them now,' I said, shaking Piper's arm.

Through the hours that followed, I was grateful that he did not speak, or try to tell me that everything would be alright. He sat with me, legs crossed, and when I found myself rocking, or crying out, he did not stare or try to hold me still. He just waited with me, patient as the dark.

The only thing that I could do for the children was to bear witness. I kept my eyes closed and surrendered to the vision. I saw the wagons being hauled down the narrow street, a single lantern swinging from a hook above the driver. I saw the silhouette of the long, low building, blocking out the stars. At the back of one of the wagons I saw the small hands clinging to the gaps between the boards. The cries coming from within weren't loud anymore, as they'd been when the vision first woke me. This wasn't the sound of children calling out expecting to be heard, let alone helped. This was a crying of voices in the dark, of children who knew that nobody would come. And they were right.

CHAPTER 16

The first snow began at dawn, and by the afternoon the tents were already sagging under the weight of it. The swamp made for awkward camping at the best of times. Now, it was a morass of ice and mud, overcrowded and with a chill wind slapping the loose tent flaps. Waste pits had been dug at the eastern edge, but their smell crept across the whole camp.

There were nearly five hundred soldiers gathered here, Simon estimated. It was more than I'd feared, but fewer than we needed.

'It's not enough,' Simon said quietly. 'You've seen our tallies of the Council's soldiers. There's fifteen hundred of them in New Hobart, at least, and heavily armed.'

'There are divisions within the Council,' I said. 'We should be exploiting that.'

'What are you talking about?' Sally said.

'The Ringmaster.'

From the way they reacted, my words might as well have been one of Xander's incoherent outbursts – Zoe was rolling her eyes, Simon shook his head. But I pushed on.

179

'We know he's watching New Hobart. We know he's against the tanks.'

'He's a member of the Council,' said Zoe. 'That's all we need to know.'

'What if we asked him to help us?' I said.

'He wouldn't,' said Piper. 'And we couldn't even ask him without giving away our plans. He might be at odds with Zach and The General, but his loyalty's still with the Alphas, and the Council. He'd warn them, and ruin whatever chance we have.'

I shook my head. 'If he took a stand against Zach and The General, other Alphas would follow him.'

'The General has pretty much the whole Council in her pocket,' Sally said. 'They're not going to follow The Ringmaster into some kind of revolt.'

'I'm not talking about the Council,' I said. 'I mean ordinary Alphas. The soldiers, for one thing. Some of them would follow him. You heard what he said, about how a few of Zach's soldiers had come to him already, scared by the machines they'd witnessed.'

'Why do you think the machines horrify people so much?' said Piper. 'Because of us. Of all the blast's abominations, we're the one they fear most. You think those soldiers would go to battle for us?'

'I think they'd follow The Ringmaster, if he asked them to.' I remembered how he'd stood, undaunted, before Piper's and Zoe's raised knives. He was a man who was used to being obeyed.

So was Piper. He cocked an eyebrow at me now. 'You want to ally yourself to somebody who doesn't see a fundamental problem with tanking, except for the machines they're using to do it? Somebody who'd be thrilled to get rid of us altogether, if he could only do it without using technology? The Ringmaster's not on our side.'

'We need help – we don't get to be fussy about where it comes from,' I said. 'Do you have any better ideas? I know The Ringmaster's motives are hardly pure. But you said it to me only last night: it's not about what we want. It's about what the resistance needs. He could help us to keep the people of New Hobart out of the tanks.'

But Piper talked over me. 'He could, perhaps. But he wouldn't. He'd never go that far. He came to us to exchange information – nothing more. We can't risk blowing the whole attack by trusting him.'

He turned back to the maps, and the conversation continued around me.

'We attack at midnight in five days, at the turn of the moon,' Piper said. 'It'll give us the greatest cover as we approach the town.'

I closed my eyes, and saw nothing but swords and blood.

*

'There aren't enough,' was Simon's constant refrain, whenever we gathered with him in his tent and tallied the daily arrivals.

'There are thousands in New Hobart who would fight along with us,' I said, 'if only we could warn them to be ready.'

'If you've got a bright idea for getting inside those walls, do share,' said Zoe.

'What about the ones who aren't inside the walls?' I said, thinking of the workers who we'd seen filing out of New Hobart each day.

'You've seen them,' Piper said. 'They're surrounded by

the soldiers all day. There's no chance of getting close enough to speak to them.'

It was true enough. Only two days earlier, we'd watched the workers filing through the gate. Most of the harvesting was complete, and the remainder was overdue. The workers had been digging with bare hands in the frozen ground. It made for slow work. The soldiers had looked relaxed enough, chewing tobacco and chatting amongst themselves as they patrolled the perimeter of the fields, but at one point they'd converged with their whips on the slowest of the Omegas digging potatoes.

'The fields are only guarded in the day though,' I said.

'What are you getting at?' Sally asked.

'We could sneak into the fields at night and leave them a message. Tell them to be ready to fight.'

'Fight with what?' said Piper. 'The Council will have long since taken any weapons from them. They've not even given them scythes for harvesting. And we can't spare weapons, even if we could smuggle them in.'

'There are still ways they could be helpful, if we could warn them about the attack. Maiming the soldiers' horses, creating diversions. Starting fires at the wall. Arming themselves with whatever clubs and kitchen knives they can muster. They'll help, if we can find a way to leave them a message in the fields.'

'On the off chance that someone sees it?' It was Simon's turn to sound sceptical. 'Hell on earth, Cass. A lot of them can't even read.'

'True enough,' I said. 'But if they see a message, they'll find a way to show someone who can.'

'And what if it's a soldier who finds it, instead of one of the Omegas?'

'We watched the soldiers for days. Did you ever see them

getting their hands dirty out there? If we hid it well enough, nobody would find it but the workers.'

'We don't know who those workers are. What if they turn us in?' Simon shook his head. 'It only takes one of them to tell the soldiers, and it's all over. Just one of the workers has to be too scared – or someone angling for favour from the soldiers.'

'Before they took the children, I'd have agreed,' Sally said. 'But not now. Cass is right. They've seen the children taken. They must know by now how desperate their situation is.'

'It's still a risk,' Piper said.

I met his gaze. 'Is there anything we've done lately that hasn't been a risk?'

*

We reached the edge of the charred forest as night fell. In the plains beyond, outside the town's walls, only a few of the vegetable fields remained to be harvested. Rows of pumpkins were topped with a thin layer of snow.

Simon had found paper and ink for us, but we'd feared that any words we tucked amongst the crops would bleed away in the snow. In the end, we decided to be even more direct. And so we found ourselves squatting in the dark, only a few hundred yards from the sentries on the walls, carving our message into the underside of the pumpkins.

We'd crawled on our bellies through the snow, moving so slowly that the cold began to feel like a more acute threat than the sentries. The clouds were thick, covering the waning moon. In all our days of watching New Hobart, we'd never been this close to the town. My clothes were soaked, chafing my chilled skin as I crawled. I gave up trying to repress the shaking. We edged forward, only a yard at a time. When a patrol passed the eastern section of the walls, we stopped entirely, faces pressed to the ground while the soldiers made their way around the wall's perimeter. The sound of hoofs on the iced ground, the heavy jangling weapons, seemed very close. When they rode past the eastern gate we could hear the calls of greeting from the watchtower.

By the time we arrived in the pumpkin field, my hands were so cold that I dropped my knife twice as I began carving.

We'd agreed the exact wording – the priority was to make the message short and clear. Each of us had a sentence to write, as many times as we could. Piper's: *Soon they'll take you all, like the children.* Zoe's: *To a prison, worse than death.* We'd decided against trying to explain the tanks – they were hard enough to describe at the best of times, let alone to inscribe on the underside of a pumpkin in the freezing dark. My sentence: *We attack at new moon, midnight – be ready.* And each of us added the Omega symbol that I wore on my forehead, and that had been hoisted on the flag above the island before the massacre: Ω. Even an Omega who had never learned to read wouldn't mistake the sign that was scorched into their own flesh.

Each letter was a struggle. My blade skidded from the curved skin of the pumpkin. The darkness that shielded us from the sentries' view made it hard to see what we were doing, so we were working as much by feel as by sight. On my first pumpkin I started too large, so that by the end of my sentence I had to cram the letters in, tiny scratches on the pumpkin's flesh. The second one was easier – I'd learned how to angle my knife so that it cut smoothly into the toughened surface. The words took shape beneath my shaking fingers.

On the third pumpkin, I threw my head back and shudders escaped me.

'Are you OK?' Piper had whipped around to see what the sound was. I pressed my hand over my own mouth but my laughter still escaped in quiet gasps.

'It's so absurd. The whole thing. For crying out loud: pumpkins.' I struggled for air. A tear was tickling the corner of my eye. It felt warm on my frozen face. 'I thought Leonard and Eva's song was a strange weapon, but this tops even that. This is our revolution – the pumpkin revolution.'

He grinned. 'Not exactly the stuff of legend, is it?' he whispered. 'Nobody's going to write a song about this. Even Leonard couldn't make this sound good.'

'We're not doing it for the glamour,' said Zoe. But she was grinning, too. We all were, as we knelt in the snow, the shrinking moon above us counting down the hours until the attack.

*

We camped the rest of the night in the forest, and came back at dawn to watch the workers being led through the gate. From where we crouched, behind a tussock in the swamp to the east of the fields, we could see that the fresh snowfall had covered our trails from the night before. But the crops, too, were veiled with snow, our painstaking messages buried under inches of whiteness.

For the whole morning, the workers came nowhere near the pumpkins. The soldiers led them to the next field, and we watched them work for hours, on their hands and knees amongst rows of uprooted carrots and parsnips.

We didn't know how long our messages would last, or whether the pumpkin flesh might already be healing over our whittled words. If they weren't harvested soon, it would be too late to matter – there were only three more days before the new moon anyway.

At noon the gates opened again, and two soldiers drove out on an empty wagon. When it halted at the fields, the soldiers began moving the workers, with shouts and blows, across to the pumpkin field. Zoe nudged me, and the three of us edged forward, peering through the grass.

It took an hour or more for the Omegas to work their way to the corner of the field where we had inscribed our messages. Two women were making their way along the row towards the pumpkins we'd marked. The women had been allowed no scythes or knives, instead having to wrench each frozen stem free from the vine. It was heavy work; one woman had an arm that ended at the elbow; the other woman was a dwarf, the larger pumpkins reaching above her waist. A soldier stood ten yards from them, stamping his feet from time to time to shake loose the snow from his boots. As the women freed the pumpkins, they passed them to a tall Omega who carried them to where another soldier waited, leaning against the wagon into which the pumpkins were loaded.

The dwarf woman paused in her tussle with one of the pumpkins. Beside me, I heard Zoe's breath halt. Then the woman heaved again, and the stem snapped. She tossed the pumpkin aside to wait for the tall man's return. At the next pumpkin, she took longer, bending low as she grappled to twist and break the stem. Hundreds of yards away, through the long grass and the falling snow, I couldn't see clearly what she was doing. Did she crouch that way just to gain a purchase on the stubborn vegetable as she wrenched it loose, or had her fingers traced the message? When the stem was broken and she hauled the pumpkin into her arms, she didn't drop it on the ground this time but held it for a few seconds as the man approached. He leaned down to her as he took it from her hands. If she spoke to him, we had no way of knowing. He gave no sign of it, but when he walked to the wagon I noticed that he placed the pumpkin carefully, the right way up, on the side of the cart furthest from the soldier.

We scanned their every movement while they emptied the corner of the field. Each time one of the women took a while freeing a pumpkin, I imagined her stealing glances at the messages we'd carved. Once, the dwarf woman called the taller woman across to help her. It might have been because the pumpkin she was lifting was larger than the others, but I wanted to believe that she was whispering to her companion. That our carved words were spreading. Either way, the soldier nearby gave a shout when he saw that the women had drawn close, and they sprang back to their allotted places in the row of workers.

The last of the pumpkins were harvested in the dark. Snow was mounting on the vegetables stacked in the wagon as it was towed back through the gates.

'Even if they haven't seen the messages yet,' I said, 'there's a chance they could still be seen, when they unload them, or store them.'

'A chance they could be seen by the soldiers, too,' said Zoe.

The gate was drawn closed again. We could hear the distant thud of the wooden crossbeam being dropped, as final as an executioner's axe hitting the block.

CHAPTER 17

Back in the camp in the marshes, I dreamed of blood. A flood of it rose over New Hobart like the tank water had risen in all my earlier visions. Elsa was there, sinking beneath the red tide. When she was fully submerged, she opened her eyes to stare at me. She opened her mouth. Nothing emerged but bubbles.

When I woke, long before midnight, Piper and Zoe were sleeping back-to-back. Zoe was facing me, her mouth open, and her slumbering face looking younger and less guarded than her prickly daytime self. On the far side of Piper lay Xander. Sally was taking the lookout shift that night, and without her Xander slept restlessly, half-formed words tipping from his mouth each time he rolled over.

I crept from the tent, moving nearly as slowly as we had in the pumpkin field. Outside, the snow had added another layer of silence to the sleeping camp. To the west was the single path of reeds that was the only way out of our camp. Halfway along it, I knew, was the sentry post where Sally was on lookout. Beyond her, in the swamp, more lookouts were stationed. I headed to the far side of the camp, where

189

the reeds were deepest, and crouched to assess the water's icy crust. When I prodded it with a foot, the ice creaked. It wouldn't hold my weight, so I braced myself to crack the ice and swim. It was only a hundred yards to the next island of reeds, but the cold would be more of a risk than the distance.

'If you don't drown yourself, you'll freeze to death.'

The shock of the whispered voice sent my foot jerking through the ice, and I had to throw myself backwards to avoid falling in. The cold of the water forced a sharp intake of breath from me.

'I wondered if you'd go to him tonight.' Sally stepped from amidst the reeds.

'What are you talking about?' I said. 'I just need a walk, and some time alone.'

She sighed. 'Haven't you figured out yet that I don't have time to play games? Why do you think I volunteered for the lookout shifts these last few days? I've been watching you ever since you raised the question of The Ringmaster, and got shut down.'

Silent, I bent to wring the water from my soaked trouser leg, avoiding Sally's eyes.

'Can you really think a Councillor would help us?' she said.

'He wants to stop the tanks,' I said. 'I know that.'

'Enough to take up arms against his own people? Enough to start a war?'

It was strange to hear talk of war in her breathy, whispered voice.

I wished that I could answer her with any certainty. 'I think he's a man of principle, in his own way. But his principles aren't the same as ours. He believes in the taboo, and wanting to protect Alphas.'

'It's a hell of a leap from that to attacking the Council. And a hell of a gamble, to tip him off before we attack. Your little excursion tonight could have cost us everything.'

'I know,' I said. 'But I can't see any other way.' I looked down at my hands, and remembered the blood that I'd seen rising over New Hobart in my visions. 'If we gave him the chance – if we asked him – he could help us.'

'Perhaps you're right,' she said. 'But Piper and Zoe will never take that risk. They'll never let you try.'

'Can't you try to persuade them?'

'Not even I could do that,' she said. 'Piper and Zoe have their own principles. Simon too. They'd never turn to a Councillor for help.'

I knew that she was right. I exhaled, slowly, and waited for her to call the guards, or Piper. I knew that I wouldn't fight Sally. And even if I could bring myself to, it would only take a single shout to rouse the camp and bring the troops down on me.

She stepped back. 'I've tethered a horse to the roots of the big mangrove, just beyond where the path meets the next bank of solid ground. You'll have to skirt the watchmen on the outer perimeter. Have the horse back by dawn, when my shift ends.'

For a few seconds we stared at each other. She didn't smile, but she gave a small nod. 'Hurry,' she said.

'What about your own principles?' I said.

She shrugged. 'If I ever had principles, it was too long ago for me to remember.' She kept her voice low. 'I've never seen The Ringmaster. I don't know about him, or what he believes. But I know about fighting and campaigns. And I don't think we can win the battle like this.' She waved an arm back at the camp and the line of tents that slumped in the snow. 'There're too few of us, and too many of them.

I'm old, Cass. I don't care if I die. But I want Piper and Zoe to have a chance. Xander too. So I'm willing to do what Piper won't.'

I reached for her hand, but she brushed me off.

'Hurry,' she said again. It was the first time I'd ever heard her sound afraid.

*

The moon was almost at its thinnest, and the night nearly black. I had to lead the horse through the swamp, wading waist-deep when I left the paths to avoid the outer perimeter of our guards. As soon as the ground was solid enough, I rode, shivering with cold in my wet trousers. A light snow was still falling – enough, I hoped, to cover my prints if anyone noticed my absence and came after me. I had to skirt a long way west to keep a safe distance from New Hobart itself, and the dark and the snow conspired against me to make it hard to find the gully. In the end, instead of scanning the blurred horizon, I closed my eyes and let my mind grope towards The Ringmaster. I concentrated on what I knew of him: the memory of his breath on my neck; his voice when he'd ordered Zoe and Piper to stand down.

It was hours before I spotted the lone spruce tree. As I neared the mouth of the gully, it wasn't only the darkness that slowed my progress. I moved hesitantly, aware that at any moment The Ringmaster's sentries would see me, and that swords would spring out of the night. Ever since I left the Keeping Rooms, I'd been doing my utmost to avoid being taken by Council soldiers. Now I was seeking them out. I was undefended, Piper and Zoe miles away, on the other side of New Hobart. After all this time spent together, their absence now was like the snow, making the world unfamiliar.

I pushed onwards, the horse picking its way through the deepening snow. The Ringmaster had assured me that I was no use to him as a hostage, now that The General was the main force behind the Council. But he could change his mind. I might not be enough to stop the tanks, but handing me over to Zach would still gain him some leverage. Each step I took now might be leading me back to the Keeping Rooms, or worse.

When had the decision been made, that had led me here? It wasn't when I'd crept away from Zoe, Piper and Xander sleeping in the tent, or even when we'd decided to try to free New Hobart. It went further back. To the island, and the massacre there. Or to the tank room underneath Wyndham, when I'd chosen to free Kip, and we'd set out together.

Further back still: to Zach, and the day he'd succeeded in having me sent away, the brand still a fresh wound on my forehead. That day, the first that we'd been separated, had set us both on our paths. There was no going back. Zach had shed me, like his old name, to become The Reformer, and conjure his dark fantasy of the tanks. All that I could do was ride onward, into the thickening dark, and do whatever I could to stop him.

A shout came from ahead, and then it all happened quickly. Soldiers converged, stepping out of the darkness. A ring of raised swords. If I'd moved a foot in any direction I'd have been skewered.

'I'm here alone,' I shouted, throwing up my hands. 'I need to see The Ringmaster.'

One of them grabbed my bridle, and another half dragged me from the horse. My dagger was ripped from my belt. A soldier raised his lamp close to my face to inspect my brand. 'It's one of them,' he said, his face so close that I could see the patch of stubble on his jaw that his razor had missed when he shaved. 'Might be the seer – can't see anything else wrong with her.' As he patted me down for other weapons, his hands lingered on my body.

'I don't think my breasts are a threat to your boss, do you?' I said quietly.

One of his companions snickered. The man said nothing, but he moved his hands on, rubbing them down the outside of my arms, and kneeling to pat down my legs.

'Stand down,' said The Ringmaster. He was panting as he ran up the gully. His black jacket had a fur lined hood, so that it was hard to tell where his curls ended and the fur began.

The swords lowered.

'Bring her in,' he said. 'But double the guard on the perimeter. Make sure she came alone.'

He didn't wait for my reaction, just turned and led the way down into the gully. I followed him, a soldier at each side, while the third dropped back, still holding my horse.

I'd thought it was dark before, but as we descended, the gully cloaked us in a second layer of darkness. The tents were pitched at the very base, shielded by the growth over-hanging the cliffs on each side. Horses were tethered in a row by the largest tent, stamping and whinnying as soldiers rushed past us, carrying lamps.

The Ringmaster threw back the flap of the central tent and strode in. 'Leave us,' he said to the soldiers, who stepped back into the night.

He might have been camping, but the arrangement bore no relation to the makeshift camps I'd occupied for the last few months, or the sagging tent-city that housed the resist-ance troops in the swamp. The Ringmaster's tent was thick white canvas, tall enough that he could stand upright. A blanket of fur covered the raised bed in the corner, and close to the entrance stood a table and chairs. A lamp was mounted on the pole in the centre of the tent, throwing warped and darting shadows on the canvas.

He pushed back his hood. 'Do your resistance companions know you're here?'

I shook my head.

'Sit,' he said. I remained standing, but he sat, and leaned back in his chair to stare at me. 'It's dangerous for you to be travelling alone. Don't you know how many people are searching for you?'

'Don't patronise me,' I said. 'I know exactly who's searching for me, and why. But this was the only way. Why are you watching New Hobart?'

'The same reason you are. Your brother and The General are interested in this place. That means I am too.'

I made an effort not to quail under his stare.

'I knew you'd change your mind,' he went on. 'What information do you have for me?'

'I haven't changed my mind,' I said. 'I've come to give you a chance. If you really want to stop the tanks, I need your soldiers and their swords. I need your army.'

This time he laughed.

'You're offering me nothing, and asking for something you know I can't possibly give.'

'I'm not offering you nothing,' I said. 'I have information for you. We're going to attack the town.'

'That's madness.' He picked up a jug and poured a glass of wine for himself.

'Not if we have your help.' I took a step closer to him. 'I know you have soldiers loyal to you. If we fought together, we could succeed.'

'Half the army or more is loyal to me,' he said. 'Your

brother and The General are too caught up with their personal projects to stay in touch with the people on the ground. But being loyal to me doesn't mean my men would fight alongside Omegas, for an Omega cause. You ask too much of them. And of me.'

'I don't want to ally myself with you any more than you do with us.' I hadn't meant for the disgust to be so audible in my words. I tried to moderate my voice. 'You know they've already tanked the children?'

'That doesn't surprise me,' he said. 'That's always been their strategy, thinking in the long term. Stop the Omegas at the source. You should hear the way they talk. *Less resource intensive*, The General said to me, if they're tanked as infants. I don't think they grow once they're in the tanks, you see. So they stay small forever. Cheaper to feed. Take up less space.' He grimaced as he spoke, spitting out the words.

'How can you have heard them say things like that, and not want to stop them?'

'You're asking me to start a war. To set different factions of the army fighting against each other.'

'I'm asking you to stop an atrocity.'

That wasn't entirely honest. An atrocity was unavoidable. If we fought to free New Hobart, many would die, and their twins with them. I was choosing those deaths over the endless not-quite-death of the tanks that would otherwise await the town's inhabitants. I couldn't remember a time when decisions had seemed uncomplicated.

'You wanted information,' I said. 'You wanted my help. I'm giving you this: we attack in three days' time – at midnight, on the new moon.'

It was in his hands now. This information could see us all killed, if he decided to betray me. I thought of how Leonard had reacted when we'd told him about the tanks and the refuges. We hadn't asked for his help – we hadn't needed to. We'd given him the information, and that had become an imperative. And I thought of Kip, and how his eyes had met mine through the glass of the tank. He had asked nothing of me. The knowledge that he was there, trapped, conscious, was enough. I knew that sometimes a moment could become a promise.

'It's a fool's errand,' The Ringmaster said. 'Even if I wanted to help you, there's not enough time to prepare. The soldiers in New Hobart are loyal to The General. I'd have to muster my soldiers from further north. And for what? For an attack that can never succeed.'

'We don't have any choice. Nor do you. You can't step away now as if it's nothing to do with you.'

He raised his hands. 'It's too soon. What kind of army can you have mustered, since the island?'

'Any later is too late,' I said. 'You know that. They've taken the children. Soon they'll take the others. And you're going to sit back and watch us try. If we succeed, you'll be glad, and you'll use it to help you in your manoeuvring against Zach and The General. And if we fail, you'll wash your hands of it.'

'If you already have me so well figured out, what did you hope to achieve by coming here?'

I looked at his pale face, his hand tight around the stem of the wine glass. 'Why are you so afraid of us?' I said. 'When you first came to me, I'd hoped it might be compassion that made you want to stop the tanks. But it's fear. You say you want to uphold the taboo. But your fear of the taboo is just fear of us. We're what the machines wrought. We're what you're afraid of. But you can't fight the machines unless you fight alongside us.'

'You don't know anything about me,' he said. He pushed

the wine away so hard that it spilled. I watched the red trickle down the stem of the glass and pool on the table.

'What did we ever do to you?'

He stared at me in silence for several moments. He wore a knife in a scabbard at his belt. Have I pushed him too far? I wondered. He could kill me in an instant. His soldiers would drag my body away, and he wouldn't even need to clean up the mess. I could see it unfolding. But it was less vivid than the other images that stalked my vision: the tanks waiting to swallow the whole of New Hobart; the battle; the ring of blood around the town, from our futile attempt to free it.

'I had a wife.' The Ringmaster's voice jolted me from my thoughts. 'We got married young. We were going to have a child.'

'Children,' I said.

'Call it what you like.' He lifted his glass again, avoiding my eyes as he drank. 'For nine months we watched Gemma's belly grow. I left the army, started working for a Councillor, because I didn't want to be away so often. I wanted to see my child grow up.

'When Gemma went into labour, the Alpha came first. She was beautiful. Perfect. I got to hold her, while we were waiting for the Omega. But it couldn't come out. It got stuck.' He paused for a moment. 'We had the midwife there. We did everything we could. But its head was deformed.' He looked down, his mouth distorted, as though the memory were a bitter taste on his tongue. 'There were two heads, maybe, the midwife thought. Anyway, it wouldn't come.

'My wife told me to get the doctor to cut it out of her, to try to at least save the baby. But I couldn't do it. I should have done. It was stupid of me. As it was, I lost them both.'

For a second, I thought he meant both twins. That he was at least acknowledging that he'd lost his Omega child too. But he went on.

'My baby girl first. And then my wife too, within a day and a half. The other baby was stuck in her, dead, and Gemma got sicker and sicker. She went grey. Her fever was so high that she was half-crazed. And the whole time she was asking about the baby, our little girl. I didn't have the heart to tell her it was wrapped up, on a chair in the kitchen, dead.' He looked up at me. 'If anyone tells you they don't fear Omegas, they're lying. You are the curse that the blast left us with. You're the burden that the innocent have to bear.'

'Your son,' I said. 'Wasn't he just as innocent as your daughter? And the children of New Hobart – weren't they innocent too?'

'The Omega baby killed my whole family.'

'No. He died, and they died too. And it was terrible, and cruel, for all of them. But when your wife died, her Omega twin died as well – and that's not her fault either. If you turn tragedies like that into a reason for hating all Omegas, we end up with people like Zach and The General arguing that we should all be tanked.'

He continued as if I hadn't spoken. 'After she died, they cut it out of her. I asked them to.' He looked up at me. 'I wanted to see it for myself.'

'He was your son.'

'You think that's why I wanted to see it?' He shook his head slowly. 'I wanted to see the thing that had killed her. Not two heads, or not quite. One huge head, with a second face bulging out the side of it.' Disgust contorted his face. 'I told the midwife to get rid of it. I didn't want it to be buried with my wife and daughter.'

'He was your son,' I said.

'You think if you keep saying that, it will somehow make it mean something?'

'And do you think if you keep denying it, ignoring it, it will make it untrue?'

He stood. 'I can't help you free New Hobart. Even if I wanted to, I couldn't do it in time.'

'At least tell me this,' I said. 'What do you know about the Ark, or Elsewhere?'

'Nothing,' he said. I scanned his face, and could find no lie there. 'Nothing but conversations that stop when I enter the room. This isn't something they discuss openly, in the Council Halls. I've heard whispers of an Ark. I know it's part of their plan, but I don't know how it all fits together. And I know it's something to do with what they're searching for in New Hobart.'

'If we free New Hobart, I can help you find it. We can find the Ark. We can change everything.'

'Do you believe that?' he said.

I stood and pushed back the tent flap. The canvas was heavy with ice.

'You can't change what happened to your wife and your children,' I said. 'But you can change what happens now. Whether you sit back and let the tanks come, and let Zach and The General find what they're looking for in New Hobart. Or whether you make a change.'

He stood outside the tent, watching as I began to walk up the gully, ignoring the soldiers who turned to watch me go.

'I can't help you,' he called after me.

'Midnight, on the new moon,' I said again. It felt just as futile and absurd as our carving of the messages on the pumpkins. If The Ringmaster warned the Council, our attack was doomed before it began. But it was all I could do, and so I did it. I'd seen the blood and the tanks that were New Hobart's future. I gave The Ringmaster those five words, because they were all that I had to offer. And because if I wanted the Alphas to recognise our humanity, I had to take a gamble that somewhere within The Ringmaster was some humanity too.

At the head of the gully, a sentry led my horse to me. He wouldn't give me my knife until I was mounted, and then he handed it to me carefully, holding it by the blade, so that our hands didn't touch.

By the time I led the horse along the tangle of paths through the swamp, it was nearly dawn. I was exhausted, and the horse was quivering with cold as we waded through the iced water to avoid Simon's sentries in the outer marshes. When I reached the final path to the camp, the water deep on each side, Sally was waiting.

'Will he help us?' she said.

I shook my head. 'We had to try,' I said as I handed her the reins.

She said nothing, but as I slunk back into the tent where the others slept, oblivious, I was glad that Sally knew what I had done. If I'd just betrayed the resistance, at least Sally and I were bound together in this. My betrayal was her betrayal, my hope her hope.

CHAPTER 18

For those final three days, my mind was with The Ringmaster. While weapons were sharpened and distributed in the snow-bound camp, I was picturing him, in his comfortable tent, and wondering whether he would betray our plans to the Council. While Simon and Piper drilled the troops, and Sally went over the plan of attack with them, I waited and waited for some sign from The Ringmaster. If he'd moved quickly enough, there might be time for him to bring soldiers to us before we marched on the town. I watched the horizon to the north and the west. Sally kept her distance from me, but on the last day she caught me alone, staring beyond the ring of reeds that encircled the camp.

'No messengers? Nothing?' she said.

'Nothing.' I could feel no hint of reinforcements, or of The Ringmaster's presence. Nothing was visible on the horizon but the charred bones of what had been the forest. Tomorrow we would attack, and we would be doing it alone.

I had seen the blast scorch the world, a thousand times or more, but the battle scenes in my recent visions were so intimate that they affected me differently. I saw a sword hilt breaking a jawbone. An arrow striking a chest with such force that the tip emerged at the back. A death was a personal thing – it felt indecent to have seen what I had. In the camp, as I watched our troops adjusting their bows, and fixing their improvised shields, I had trouble meeting their eyes. I wanted to allow them the privacy of their own blood.

Piper and Simon kept them busy. They ran drills at night now, as well as in the day, to prepare for the midnight attack. The troops responded efficiently to Piper's and Simon's shouted orders, and when I watched them practise they were grim but focused. But we couldn't keep them occupied every moment, and amongst the rows of leaking tents, unease was growing. I overheard complaints about the rations, and the allocation of weapons. Fear had infested the camp like lice. I'd heard what they were muttering, as they clustered around the fires with their hands tucked into their armpits for warmth, and their shoulders hunched against the wind. *A fool's errand*. The same words that The Ringmaster had used.

'We can't win like this,' said Simon, the night before the attack, when we were gathered in his tent. 'Not if they go into battle already convinced of our defeat.'

I had no answer for him that would not be a lie. Nobody knew better than I that we couldn't expect to succeed. I'd seen the blood and the blades.

*

Right up until the day of the attack, I was still arguing with Piper and Zoe about whether I would join the battle. Piper was adamant: 'It's mad,' he said. 'We haven't kept you safe for all this time only to risk you now.'

The three of us were walking towards Simon's tent. I was almost running, to keep pace with Piper and Zoe's long strides. 'Kept me safe for what?' I said. 'If we lose tonight, there isn't anything else to be done. It'll all be over. We need to throw everything we have into this attack. I should be there. If I have a vision, it could help.'

'There'll be enough screaming and weeping without you having your visions,' Zoe said.

'I could see something that would help in the battle.'

I didn't want to fight – I wasn't stupid. I'd seen the battle on the island, and I would never forget the smell of blood, and the sound of broken teeth spraying on flag-stones. I'd learnt, on the island, that the body's wholeness is an illusion that a sword quickly shattered. I had seen the Council soldiers fight, and I knew that my knife and my lessons from Zoe would count for little, in the brute chaos of a battle.

But it was the battle on the island that made me sure I had to join. I couldn't hide, once again, while other people did the fighting. The dead who I carried were already too many – I could tolerate no more. It was selfishness, not martyrdom. I was afraid of fighting – but I was more afraid of hiding, and of seeing the dead mount up in my absence. Of being left behind with the burden of the ghosts.

I didn't try to explain that to Piper and Zoe.

'If the Council soldiers know I'm there, in the thick of the fighting, it might force them to hold back,' I said. 'They'll have orders from Zach not to harm me. He'll protect himself, as always. It made a difference on the island, and I wasn't even fighting there.'

'They won't hold back,' Zoe said. 'Not if New Hobart's as important to them as we think. You heard what The Ringmaster said: The General's the real power now, not Zach. If she has to put him at risk, to protect her plans, she won't hesitate.'

A dark-haired woman interrupted, stepping in front of us and blocking the path. After days of footfalls from hundreds of soldiers, the path had become a furrow of half-frozen mud.

'If you can see the future,' she said, 'then you can tell us how it's going to go tonight.'

'That's not how it works,' I said.

She made no move to step aside.

I couldn't tell her what I'd seen. Her death would come soon enough – I couldn't bear to be the one to hand it to her, there, on the muddy path. I stepped around her, Piper and Zoe flanking me.

'Tell me,' she called after me, as I hurried away. It wasn't just the ice-slickened mud that made me stumble. It was what I'd seen, slipping in between my eyes and the world. All the blood, unforgiving on the snow.

In the end, it was that woman who persuaded them to let me fight. Her and the others who gathered around me, each time I ventured out of our tent. Most of them kept their distance, looking at me with the mixture of unease and disgust that I'd become used to. But they all had the same question: *Tell us what happens. Tell us how it will be.*

'You need me to fight,' I said, as soon as we'd regained the cover of Simon's tent.

'We've talked about this,' said Zoe. 'It's not worth the risk.'

'It's not about me,' I said. 'It's about them.' I gestured at the tent door. 'They know that I can see what's coming. And they need to believe that there's at least a chance of victory. And they won't, if they see me staying back.'

'They might believe in your visions, but that doesn't mean they'll rally behind you,' Piper said. 'They don't trust you. You know what people are like with seers. You heard what Violet said just the other day.'

Sally was looking at me. 'She's right,' she said. 'It's because they don't trust her that they'll follow her. They'd never believe that she'd go into a battle that she didn't know we were going to win.'

'I have to be there,' I said. 'Right at the front, where they can see me.'

So it was decided. I'm glad, I told myself, and it was true. But my lungs strained at each breath, a pair of creaking bellows, and sweat itched where my woollen jumper touched the back of my neck. It wasn't just the fear of battle, though there was plenty of that. It was the knowledge, hard and certain in my stomach, that my presence at the battle was to be a lure. A false assurance to our troops that victory was possible.

*

At sunset on the night of the battle, Sally and Xander sat alone amidst what was left of the dismantled camp. We were leaving them there, along with the handful of troops who were unable to fight.

'Where will you go, if we don't free the town?' I said.

'Will it make any difference where we go?' she said. 'I'll do my best to keep Xander safe. Maybe we'll make it as far as the Sunken Shore. But you and I both know there's not much chance for any of us if we don't win. You heard what Piper said to me, when we were in my house: the soldiers will come for me there, eventually.'

I knelt next to Xander, but he wouldn't look at me. He sat with his knees drawn up before him. One of his hands tapped out a silent message on his shoe.

'We're going to try to find the papers,' I said to him. 'The papers that you told us about, from the maze of bones.'

He nodded, and then the nod spread to his whole body, until he was rocking backwards and forwards. 'Find the papers. Find the papers,' he said. There was no way of knowing whether it was an order, or an echo. When I walked away he was still rocking.

In the last few weeks, time had seemed to run away from us. Not enough time to gather troops, or to drill them; not enough time to warn the people of New Hobart; and always the fear that we might be too late, and that the tanks would consume them before we could free them. That the Ark papers would be found before we could enter the town. Now, as we waited in the darkness, time was a landslide on a scree slope, gathering speed, and taking us all with it.

I knew I would fight and not turn back. But as I stood next to Piper and Zoe, the troops gathered behind us, my body was undergoing its own quiet revolt. A shaking had begun in my damp feet, and now spread through me, my whole body resonating like a struck bell.

The armourers had given me a short-sword and a wooden shield. I clutched the sword now in my sweaty hand. I would have been more comfortable with my knife, its leather-wrapped handle that had moulded to my own grip, but Piper had insisted. 'By the time anyone gets close enough for you to use that, you'll be dead,' he said. 'You need range, and heft.'

'I don't know how to fight with this,' I said.

'It's not as if you're an expert with the knife,' Zoe said. 'Anyway, you're not going to be trying to fight. All you need to do is be seen, and not get killed. Keep your shield above you in the charge – that's when they'll use their archers. And stay close.'

I kept my old knife with me as well. In the hours of walking from the camp to the edge of the forest, the silent troops massed behind us, I'd been comforted to feel its familiar weight at my belt.

Zoe and Piper had been given swords, too. I picked up Zoe's to test its weight – it was so heavy that I needed both hands to hold it.

'This isn't a game,' she said, snatching it back from me and turning away.

She stood at my left, now, her eyes fixed on the blade as she passed the sword from hand to hand. Piper was at my right. He, too, carried a long-sword, but he also wore his usual row of throwing knives in the back of his belt. Behind us, the soldiers were gathered – more than five hundred, at the final tally. Leaving the camp had, alone, taken hours; the swampland didn't permit an orderly march, and instead the troops had to straggle their way, single file, along the few strips of land that emerged from the icy pits. The horses were led, one by one, along the narrow, tussocked paths; they kept their heads low and their nostrils wide, sniffing at the edges of the trail. Only once we reached the forest could the troops mass properly. Now they waited, row upon row. A few wore the blue uniforms of the island's guards, but more were wrapped in their own winter clothes, ragged and patched. Their faces were muffled against the snow. Nobody spoke. I looked away from them to the frozen trees around us. The icicles, stiff as the fingers of corpses. Everything seemed sharpened, as if I were seeing it for the first time.

I thought of the Ark papers that were hidden somewhere within the walls. And I thought again of those small hands clinging to the boards of the nailed-shut wagon. We were already too late to keep the children from the tanks. I thought, too, of Elsa and Nina, waiting within the walls. What we were about to do might make no difference to their fate – my dreams had shown me too much blood for me to have any faith that tonight's attack could free the town. Perhaps that was the only difference we could make: that if the people in New Hobart went to the tanks, they would at least go knowing that we had fought for them.

I'd felt the troops staring at me as I walked to my place with Piper and Zoe. My whole body was a trap, to lure these people into a battle that could not be won.

I turned to Piper.

'I'm lying to them,' I whispered haltingly, my breath uneven.

He shook his head, keeping his voice low. 'You're giving them hope.'

'It's the same thing,' I said. It was the first time I'd spoken so bluntly about what I'd seen. 'There isn't any hope. There're too many Council soldiers. In my visions, there's too much blood.'

'No,' he said. He bent slightly, so that his face was close to mine. In the night air, the steam of his breath hung white. 'You're fighting, even though you've seen us lose. You've known all along, and you're still standing here, ready to fight. That's hope, right there.'

There was no time to say anything else. The troops were gathered in the expectant dark. They were watching Simon, waiting for him to step forward and address them. But Simon turned to Piper.

'You were always better at this than me,' he said.

'You're their leader now,' Piper said quietly.

The older man shook his head. 'I'm in charge of them. That's not the same thing. They'll do what I tell them to, sure enough. But I haven't led them. Not since I brought you out to the island, all those years ago. You lead them, Piper.'

He put a hand on Piper's arm. They exchanged a long look. Then Simon raised his arm to his head, in a small salute. The troops whispered, and shifted to see more clearly, as Simon stepped back.

When Piper moved forward to address them, the whispers stopped.

'Our Omega brothers and sisters are waiting for us, in New Hobart,' he said, his voice cutting through the dark air. 'I can't promise you that we will free them. But the alternative is to wait, while the Council steals from us more and more lives. They'll see us all tanked, if we don't stand against them. After centuries of Alpha oppression, there is no place, anymore, for Omegas in this world, except the one we begin to build here, tonight. It may be that we build it with our own blood – but the tanks are worse than death.'

He turned his head, unhurried, to survey the entire mass of troops before him. 'The Council underestimated us,' he announced, his voice loud and clear. 'Just as they always have done. They thought we would be crushed – that year after year of tithes and beatings and hunger would leave us broken, and ready to submit to new horrors. To go meekly to the tanks. They were wrong.

'Because they don't allow us to marry, they think we don't weep when our wives or husbands are beaten, or killed. Because we can't bear children, they think we don't mourn when they take the children we have raised. Because they see no value in our lives, they don't believe that we will fight for those lives, and for one another. Tonight we show them that our lives are our own, and that we are more human than they can ever know. Tonight we say *enough*. Tonight we say *no more*.'

I felt the ground shake, as hundreds of staffs and axes beat the earth in time with Piper's final words. *No more*.

CHAPTER 19

We carried no torches – darkness was our ally. Piper gave the signal, his sword raised high and then sweeping down. He stood so close to me that I could hear the blade slice the air. The advance began, as quietly as five hundred armed troops could manage, to the northernmost edge of the charred forest. At another signal from Piper, the advance troops slipped from the woods. Surprise was our only advantage, so we held off on the main charge as long as possible. For now, it was just six pairs of assassins, hand-selected by Simon and Piper, loping up the plain toward the town with knives destined for the throats of the patrols circling the city.

The night quickly swallowed the assassins as they moved over the plain in a crouching run. We'd watched the town for long enough to know that there would be three patrols orbiting the walls at any time, but we also knew that the patrols were complacent. The sentries in the four gatetowers looked mainly inward, at the captive town itself. If they were expecting any trouble, it wasn't from outside.

One of the patrols was within our sight, a torch tracing

their journey around the town's southern edge. There would be at least three riders, their leader carrying the torch. When a shout came from further west, the torch swung around – but the noise cut off, stopping so swiftly that I wondered if it had, after all, been just a crow's hacking call. There was a moment's stillness, before the torch resumed its route around the wall. Then came another sound, a shorter yell this time, and two clashes of steel. The torch dropped, bounced once, and was extinguished in the snow. I could hear, away to the east, the distant noise of a horse bolting. Silence returned – but this wasn't ordinary silence. Knowing what was happening on the plain, the silence felt stifling, a blanket thrown over the night.

The next signal came from the assassins: a flash of light at the base of the wall, halfway between the northern and western gates. They had carried oil and matches, to get the fire started quickly. Ideally it would weaken the wall; at least it would be a diversion while we charged from the south.

Once more, Piper's sword was raised, and then lowered. We began to run. There was the noise of five hundred people's footsteps, stumbling on the uneven ground. Panting breaths, in lungs tightened by waiting in the cold, and by fear. Scabbards knocking against legs; knives jangling.

The Council's soldiers hadn't been forewarned. My journey to meet The Ringmaster hadn't won his help, but at least he hadn't betrayed us. There was no ambush, no phalanx of soldiers pouring from the gates to meet us. The first cries of warning came when we were halfway across the open plain between the forest and the town. Shouts and cries spread from gate to gate, and there was a scrambling of lights within the walls as the warning was sounded.

The arrows came first, when we were a few hundred yards from the walls. One landed just to my left, ploughing a ditch two feet long in the ground. I kept my shield over my head, but there weren't enough shields for everyone, and not all our troops had two arms to carry them. Beside me Piper carried only his sword, and so did Zoe, to keep her left arm free for her throwing knives. In the near total darkness, there was no kidding ourselves that we might dodge the arrows – they sprang from the dark above us, as if the night sky itself were suddenly sharpened. The archers made it clear, right away, that the Council soldiers weren't holding back, as they had on the island. If they knew Zach's twin was part of the attack, it wasn't stopping them. I wondered if The General ordered that no concessions to Zach's safety should be made, and if this was a sign of his waning power. But all speculation was ended by the scream that went up behind me, the sound of an arrow finding its mark. I turned, but the fallen man had been overtaken by our oncoming troops, his scream already half drowned in blood, a gurgle of sodden lungs.

The southern gates opened, spilling light as well as the Council soldiers in their red tunics. The mounted soldiers came first, four abreast. They carried torches, as well as weapons, so that the flames flashed off the blades, and off the eyes of the horses.

Back in Simon's tent at the encampment, when we'd planned the attack, it had seemed straightforward: arrows and crosses marked on a map. The best vantage point for our archers to plant themselves, to provide cover for the runners with grappling irons and ladders for the wall. The routes where our two mounted squadrons would flank the town and lay siege to the northern wall where the assassins had begun the fire. Four squadrons to charge at the eastern gate, where the sentry tower was flimsiest. On Simon's map, everything had been neat and contained. As soon as the battle began, that neatness was lost in blows and blood. On the island, I had watched most of the battle from the window of a locked room in the fort; I thought I'd witnessed what fighting was. I realised, now, how wrong I had been, and what difference a few hundred yards could make. In the midst of the battle, now, I had no sense of strategy, or of the overall shape of the battle. I could see only what was happening immediately in front of me. My instructions were to stay close to Zoe and Piper as they led the attack on the eastern gate, but I quickly lost any sense of our destination. Everything was too fast, the whole world accelerating. The horses' hoofs set the ground beneath us trembling. A mounted soldier thrust a blade downwards at Zoe, and she dived to the side. I ducked to avoid a sword that swung by my head, as Piper exchanged blows with another soldier to my right. Zoe had regained her feet when I next looked, and when the rider blocked her strike, she slipped under his sword and severed the girth. Her blade nicked the horse's belly too, and blood dropped to the snow as the saddle slid down the far side, taking the soldier with it, so that he fell almost on top of me. He scrambled up, but had dropped his sword in the fall. When he bent to retrieve it, I stamped my foot on the hilt, pressing it into the snow.

The fallen soldier looked up from where he crouched. Now I should kill him. I knew that, and my hands tightened on my sword hilt. But before I could raise my blade, Zoe had dodged around the flailing horse and sunk her blade into the man's stomach. She had to shove the sword again to dislodge him. His blood left her blade blackened as he slid backwards off it to the ground.

Next to me, Piper had fought free of his opponent, but another horse came straight at him. He stepped aside at

Francesca Haig

the last moment, aiming a low slash at the horse's legs. It was a terrible sight – one of the legs seemed to have gained an extra joint, a bend where none should be. The horse went down screaming, and the soldier jumped clear just in time to avoid being crushed as his mount rolled to its side, knocking me down as it went.

Piper and Zoe were fighting above me, each hand to hand with a Council soldier. Beside me, on the ground, the horse tried to right itself on its broken legs. Its nostrils flared, wide as overripe lilics. Its eyes had rolled so far back that all I could see was the white, marbled with red veins. When the horse screamed, the noise was somehow more human than half the sounds of the battle around me. One of its legs was pierced by its own bone, a spar of white thrust through the blood-matted hair.

I pulled my knife from my belt, reached up to the horse's thrashing head, and slit its throat. The blood emptied itself onto my hand, surprising me with its heat. Its force, too. It didn't run but spurted, spraying up my arm. The snow beneath it melted, the blood soaking into the iced earth. Then it was finished.

The horse died a single death. I felt it, the simplicity of it – no answering echo of death from a twin. For something so blood-soaked, it felt clean. I scrambled to my feet.

The first wave of Council riders had broken through the front lines of our advance, but to the west I caught sight of ladders against the walls, and figures were scrambling up them. I had no time to see whether the climbers reached the top; the Council's foot soldiers, carrying shields as well as swords, were swarming into the gaps created by their riders in our front line. I'd lost my shield, and I didn't even remember where, or how. I stuck close to Piper and Zoe, staying out of the way when I could, and swinging my sword

217

in wide slashes whenever a soldier drew too near. Any time a soldier bore down on me hard, Piper or Zoe stepped in to fight them off.

The few times my sword hit flesh, I had to quash nausea. But that didn't stop me. I didn't deal any killing blows, but only through inexperience, rather than reluctance. Nonetheless I made several strikes, and my blade was beaded with blood before long. I'd been the cause of so many deaths already that it didn't feel strange to see the blood on my own weapon, finally, a tangible proof of what I'd already done so many times.

All our effort seemed to make little difference. The three of us had gained some ground, but from what glances I was able to snatch it was clear that our troops were being overrun. The Council's soldiers were still pouring from the southern gate, and our troops with ladders had been surrounded, trapped against the wall. Further west, where our first wave of troops had tried to set fires along the wall, the damp had repelled them, and only two of the fires remained lit. Scanning the wall, I could see no breaks yet in the structure, and the gates themselves remained tightly defended.

As we gained a little ground we could see better, the torches and fires along the wall throwing flashes of light. But the closer we were to the walls, the more deadly were the arrows. When we were in close combat with the Council's soldiers, the archers held back, but as soon as we had a moment's respite, the arrows found us again. They didn't fall from above – falling is too airy a word. They stabbed down, forceful as a horse's kick. Forceful enough to bury themselves inches deep in the earth. Twice arrows passed so close that I felt the chill air warmed by their passing. A third arrow struck Piper in the leg, but my

Francesca Haig

warning cry came in time for him to leap aside, so that the arrow's head glanced along his flesh, rather than tearing through it. Time had become blurred, and when I wiped my face my hand came away dark and wet, but I couldn't tell whether it was my own blood or someone else's. Several times, I staggered over bodies on the ground, lying in postures that announced themselves as lifeless. A head thrown back at an angle that no intact neck would allow; a knee that bent backwards instead of forwards. There was no light from the moon to cast shadows, only the glow of the distant fires at the wall. But the fallen bodies made their own shadows, bloodstains black in the snow.

Piper retrieved his knife from the neck of a dead soldier a few yards away. There was a boulder, dusted with snow, and we crouched in its shelter for a moment.

'There should be more Council soldiers,' said Piper, looking around. 'By our tally they should have upwards of fifteen hundred in there. Where are they?'

'I think we have enough to be going on with,' said Zoe. She wiped each side of her sword on the snow, leaving two smears of blood.

We hunched as we ran, flinching from the sounds of arrows overhead, to rejoin Simon, who was sheltering in a shallow ditch barely fifty yards from the southern gate. Ten or more of our troops were there with him. One man swore as he spat two broken teeth out into the snow. A woman with a gash on her calf was binding it tightly with a strip of cloth, her teeth clenched over her bottom lip as if she could bite back the pain.

Simon spoke quickly.

'Violet's squadron have got the ladders up twice, and been repelled both times. I've drawn Charlie's men back from the western side – that's too heavily fortified, and the

219

fires aren't taking. They're going to join Violet for another push at the south, where the watchtowers are furthest apart, and the fire's damaged the wall.'

'And Derek?' Piper said.

Simon wiped a hand down his face, and gave his head a quick shake. 'Killed at the wall, with all his men – though they managed to get some fires started first.' Simon's sword hand was bruised and swollen, the skin purple and stretched too tightly on the fattened flesh.

'Derek's squadron didn't light that,' said Piper, pointing up at the town. From its centre, high above the walls, a plume of smoke was unfurling into the sky.

'Something's going on inside,' said Simon. Despite the streak of blood on his cheek, and his bruised hand, he looked more animated than I'd seen him since the island. 'The harvesters must have got the message. They're joining in.'

'It explains why the Council haven't unleashed their full numbers out here,' Zoe said. 'But the Omegas in there can only do so much. They won't even have proper weapons.'

She was right. I pictured New Hobart's residents, armed with pokers or cooking knives, pitted against the broadswords of trained soldiers.

'We need to get in there before they're all killed,' I said. My voice came out higher than I'd intended.

'What do you think we're trying to do?' said Zoe.

Piper looked behind him, surveying the plain between the town and the burnt forest. Most of our troops had hunkered down now in whatever sparse shelter they could find. Some were huddled behind the bodies of horses or soldiers, peering up at the walled city above us. The Council soldiers, too, had regrouped, drawing back to the gates, though some fighting was still visible near the western gate.

'We need to make a push on the southern gate, while

their soldiers are distracted by what's going on inside the walls. Bring the archers forward to those boulders to cover us.' Piper gestured at a cluster of low boulders on the plain, a little to our west. 'Pull back the troops from the eastern wall too – we'll need them all.'

This was it, then. The final push. Within the walls, the people of New Hobart would be fighting, and dying. On the plain below us were the broken bodies of our troops, and of the Council soldiers. Their twins, wherever they were, would never wake today. The carrion birds were coming with the dawn.

Under Simon's and Piper's directions, our surviving troops began to mass on a small hillock just south of the wall. Some arrows still reached us there, but I'd found that if I concentrated, I could usually sense their approach before we heard the sound, giving us a few extra seconds to scurry aside. Even those troops who had glared at me in the camp obeyed me now when I shouted my warnings.

It took half an hour for our troops to muster for the final assault. A small force of soldiers rode out of the town and tried to cut off one of our squadrons before it could join the main group, but the icy ground was treacherous for the horses and there were four axemen in the squadron who managed to hold them off long enough for the group to reach the shelter of the hill.

'How many of us are left?' I said to Piper.

He scanned the gathered troops. 'More than half.'

Neither of us had to say it. *Not enough*. But we'd fought better than I would have dared to imagine. Already we'd lasted longer than my worst fears had predicted. Perhaps Piper had been right: our troops had needed to believe that winning was possible. It had made a difference. The axemen who I'd just watched, holding ten mounted soldiers at bay, had been different from the downcast troops at the encampment the day before. And those within the town had not only received our message, but they'd answered it and fought with us. It might not be enough to save any of us. But Piper had been right – there was some hope in this day, even amongst the blood.

We formed into rough lines, and again Piper, Zoe, and I were at the front. When Piper gave the shout to charge, we left the cover of the hillock and ran. Time, which had been running so speedily, now seemed very slow. I had time to hear everything: my own noisy breath. The knives tucked in Piper's belt striking one another as he ran beside me. The sound of the soft new snow giving way underfoot, and the crunch of the icy layer beneath.

I called out a warning when I felt the arrows coming, but here we had no shelter, and running as a pack meant there was no room to dodge. A woman to my left went down with an arrow to the face. The sound of the impact wasn't fleshy – it was a bone-crunch, like an axe into wood. There were shouts from behind me, too, as others were struck.

The arrows only relented when the first Council soldiers reached us, a hundred yards from the wall. After the spread-out clashes on the plain, here the fighting was cramped. Twice I had to duck to avoid the swords of our own troops. Piper and Zoe were fighting back-to-back. Between them, there were no spare movements; each sword thrust or elbow jab was precise and intentional. Everything that they touched bled.

'Stay close,' Piper grunted, glancing at me from the corner of his eye while he exchanged blows with a tall soldier.

I stayed as near to Piper and Zoe as I could, striking only

when I had a clear chance and wouldn't get in their way. But after several minutes, one of the Council soldiers had gained on Zoe, pushing her back so that she stumbled into Piper. She landed on her back, and managed to keep her sword in hand, but the soldier made the most of the fall and kicked out, hard, at her jaw. Her head was thrown back with the force of it, her neck exposed. When the soldier drew back his sword, I swung at the back of his head.

I'd travelled too long with hunters to be squeamish. I'd plucked pigeons and skinned rabbits and picked through the carcasses for anything edible, kidneys and liver and all. In the attack on the island I'd seen people killed, and smelled the rich iron whiff of blood. But this was different. I felt the resistance of the skin, and its giving way, and finally the jar of the blade lodging in bone.

I heard three screams: the dying man's. His twin's, in my mind. And my own, lasting longer than either of the others.

CHAPTER 20

I pulled back my blade. The man fell as if my sword had been a hook on which his body hung.

Something broke in me. All the visions I'd had over the past few months were knocked loose, to rattle at random through my mind. The blast. Rows of tanks, now full of fire. The island's crater, full of blood. The blast.

Piper grabbed me, shook me until I had to stop the scream to draw breath.

'Concentrate on staying alive,' he said, then shoved me to the side as another soldier came at him. I staggered back, sword shaking as I held it out before me.

I had already been responsible for more deaths than I knew. But this was new. The swing of my arms and the steel of my sword had put an end to that man. It was final, and absolute, and as intimate as a kiss. It could never be undone. His twin, wherever she was, had died too, without even knowing why.

'Pull yourself together,' Zoe shouted at me. I looked up. She was standing again, blood running from her mouth where the soldier had kicked her. Her shirt was sprayed with blood. At the collar it had stiffened, standing out from her neck at a strange angle. Even her teeth, as she shouted at me, had flecks of blood on them. Could she taste it? I wondered. What had happened to us? I used to work in the fields, and grow things. Now, on this icy plain, I was a harvester of blood.

'Pull yourself together,' she shouted again. I breathed out, and in again. Somehow my sword was still in my hands.

I looked up. We were making no progress. The front line of our final charge had already broken, the soldiers driving us further from the wall. Simon and a cluster of his troops had gained a little ground, but not enough. They were cut off now, and surrounded by Council soldiers. They reminded me of the islands of the Sunken Shore, being gradually swallowed by the hungry tide. Simon fought with two swords, and a knife in his third hand. Nobody got past him. But two of the Omegas next to him had already fallen, and the soldiers were closing ever tighter around him.

Perhaps I felt the riders coming – perhaps that's what led me to turn east, to the road, just as Piper gave the shout to push forward once again. I almost fell as I turned to look, everyone around me running. Piper saw me looking, and turned too.

There were hundreds of them, devouring the horizon with their galloping hoofs. Mounted soldiers in their red tunics, leaving the sunrise behind them as they raced toward the town. They would be on top of us in minutes.

We were outnumbered – five to one, at least. Whatever hope our makeshift army had been able to muster, it was finished now. This was where my visions of blood on snow had been leading. This was how it would end.

I thought of Zach, and wondered if he felt his death approaching. When I pictured him, it was his face as a child that I saw. His wary eyes, watching everything I did. The way he'd cover his face with his arm when sleeping, as if hiding his dreams from the night's gaze. It had been years since Zach and I had shared anything, but as the soldiers rode closer I thought of him, and it was easier, somehow, knowing that we would at least share our deaths.

I heard Piper swear, and Zoe call back to him, and her voice stop mid-shout as she saw the soldiers coming. And I was sorry that this would be their end, too. At least, I thought, they were near each other. It seemed right that they would lie together at the end, their blood mixed.

The Council soldiers at the gate were calling out too, a whoop of relief and renewed vigour. When I heard their shouts, I realised how close we had come. They'd been afraid. We might have taken the town after all. It was luck, in the end, that had turned the battle against us. A messenger who managed to slip out, past our archers. Or perhaps reinforcements had been due anyway, in preparation for the tanking of the townsfolk. On such small things, so many lives would turn. We might have freed the town. Now we could not.

I hoped it would be quick. No torture, and no tank.

I saw that Piper had turned to watch me. He had planted his sword in the ground before him, and instead held one of his small knives in his hand. It was pointing at me, not the oncoming riders.

I knew that he would do it, if the soldiers reached us. I wasn't surprised, or even afraid. The sudden steel of the knife in the throat – a gush of hot blood. An act of mercy, like my knife in the horse's neck. Better than the cell and the tanks. He saw me looking, and he made no pretence, didn't move to hide his knife, or avert his gaze. I gave him a slow nod. I didn't have it in me to smile, but it was as close to a thanks as I could muster. Kip had given me his death, for my life. Piper would give me my death, and I would be grateful, in the end.

The soldiers at the gate held back now. There was no rush – soon enough we would be trapped between them and the reinforcements, pounding up the eastern road. The percussion of hoofs made the frozen earth shift underfoot. They were only a hundred yards away now. Piper was watching me, Zoe watching him. I closed my eyes.

But the noises that reached me were wrong. I felt as though sound had come unmoored. The cries and shouts were coming from the wrong place: from our right, at the eastern gate of the town.

The riders had not left the road to charge to where we clustered at the south of the wall. Instead, they'd stayed on course for the eastern gate. From within the mass of riders, a row of bows was raised. The first arrows fell on the sentry tower at the eastern gate. Then the riders caught up with the arrows, and grappling irons were hurled over the gate itself. The gate was lightly manned; most of the occupying soldiers were at the southern gate, holding us off. Already the arriving fighters had thrown a ladder against the eastern watchtower.

I saw him then: The Ringmaster, at the centre of the mounted mass of soldiers. He carried a sword, but was busy directing his soldiers, shouting and pointing, bending sometimes to confer with those around him.

Part of the eastern gate was aflame. More arrows buried themselves in the watchtower. There was a scream, and a body dropped from the tower, lodging on the top of the smouldering gate. With a shriek of ripping wood, the gate was breached, grappling irons hauling the spars from the frame. The Ringmaster's army had the numbers to keep the Council troops at bay while they prised the gate apart. Already, the new attackers were streaming into the town. There was no way that New Hobart could withstand this onslaught.

The soldiers facing us had realised they were about to be trapped between The Ringmaster's forces and ours. A squadron of his soldiers had already veered away from the fallen gate and were galloping in formation along the wall towards us. They wore the same red uniform as the Council's soldiers, but didn't hesitate to ride them down. There were cries for the Council soldiers on the plain to retreat and regroup. But there was nowhere for them to retreat to. The eastern gate was down, and our forces, though depleted, were still pushing in from the south and west. More of The Ringmaster's troops were pouring onto the plain from the east. Now that they were closer, I could see that they each wore a strip of black cloth bound around the forehead, to distinguish them from the soldiers they were facing. Everywhere I looked, the black-handed soldiers outnumbered the others.

Once they'd taken the eastern gate, the town fell quickly. More smoke rose from within the walls. The southern gate, closest to us, was forced open from within, and it was The Ringmaster's troops who stormed their way through the fighting at the base of the watchtower and rushed out of the gate. I heard shouts from within the walls, and imagined the confusion of the townsfolk, faced with these new arrivals who still wore the Council's red tunics but who were fighting alongside them to free the town.

Something pale swung from the eastern watchtower. At first I thought it might be another body, slumped over the railing. But the wind gusted and the pale object lifted, flapped twice, and then unfurled. I could see the silhouette of a hunchbacked woman, raising the flag to the wind. It was the Omega insignia, painted on a sheet.

The Council had branded it on our foreheads. Now, it hung from the tower, above the smoke and blood. The town had fallen.

Out on the plain, the remaining Council soldiers were fighting with the frenzied energy of those who knew they could not win. Next to me, Zoe struggled hand-to-hand with a bearded man. Beside her was Piper, holding off a soldier who was already bleeding from a slash to the head. Piper dodged beneath the blow of a second soldier, a woman bearing an axe. When she saw me standing behind him, she came straight at me, axe raised. She looked as scared as I was, her eyes open too wide, white showing all around the pupils, like those of the horse I had killed. Had that been only hours before? Time had slowed until it was something I waded through, like the bloodied snow.

I raised my sword and braced myself. I blocked the first swing. When she came at me again, the impact knocked the sword from my hands. She raised the axe once more. Everything in the frost-tipped morning suddenly seemed very bright. *Zach*, I thought. *What have I done to you? What have you done to us?*

CHAPTER 21

My first thought on waking was that I must be back in the deadlands – my vision had the same cloudiness as in those weeks of watering eyes and ash-laden winds. Then I saw that I was indoors, and there was no ash, only a blurriness that pulsed slightly, the room around me sharpening, then slipping back into haze, keeping time with the throbbing lump at the back of my head.

It took a while for me to distinguish between the different pains in my body. The surface pain of the grazes and scrapes on my knuckles and knees. The tightness at the side of my head, the swollen skin amplifying my pulse so that each beat became a wince. And the one pain around which the others orbited: my right forearm.

'She's awake.' Zoe's voice.

Piper walked towards me. He was limping heavily.

'You hurt your leg?'

'No.' He gestured at Zoe. She was still sitting, and as my vision began to clear I could make out a bandage around her right thigh. Blood had seeped through it, carving a red smile in the white cloth.

231

'It's a clean cut, and it's been stitched. It'll heal quickly,' she said.

'What about your head?' Piper asked me.

I lifted my good arm to touch the lump, which felt hard and hot. My hand came away clean of blood. But when I tried to lift my other arm, there was a pain that didn't limit itself to the wrist but darted through my body, and brought me to the brink of vomiting. The wrist had swollen, thickening to twice its normal width. I tried to move my fingers, but they ignored me.

'What happened?'

'It's broken,' Piper said.

'Not that. What happened at the end of the battle?'

'We're in New Hobart,' he said.

'Us and The Ringmaster,' said Zoe pointedly.

'We can talk about that later,' Piper said. 'We need to reset the bone, straighten it before the swelling gets worse, and get it in a splint.'

'You can't do it yourselves,' I said.

'You see any doctors around here?' Zoe waved her arm at the room around us. It was small and half in darkness. The shutter on the window had been smashed, the broken spars casting uneven lines of shadow across the floor. The door to the next room was burnt away, nothing remaining but a strip of wood next to the hinges. Through the door I could see a pile of broken chairs, stacked haphazardly. I was on a bare mattress. Another mattress lay against the opposite wall, beside a jug of water.

Zoe took the edge of the sheet from the other mattress and began to rip it into strips. The noise reminded me of the tearing of arrows through the air. I tried to sit up, and the pain flooded my arm again.

Somewhere in Wyndham, or wherever he was, Zach was

feeling the same pain. Once, when we were eight or nine, he'd cut his foot open on some broken glass in the river. I'd been sitting alone on the doorstep peeling parsnips when the pain came. I'd looked down at my foot. There was nothing to see: no blood, no wound, nothing at all to explain the slicing pain that had made me cry out and drop the vegetables to the ground. For a moment I'd thought I must have been bitten by a spider or a fire ant. But as I examined my intact foot, crying, I realised it must be Zach. Soon he came limping up to the house, leaving red footsteps in the dirt. His foot was opened from instep to heel, a cut so deep that it had to be stitched. I limped for days, he for weeks.

Now, as Piper whittled a chair-leg into a splint, and Zoe prepared the bandages, it was comforting to know that Zach would be feeling my pain too. Was it that I wanted him to suffer? Or because he would share my pain, understand it? Both, perhaps.

I couldn't help but cry out when Zoe braced her foot against the table and pulled my arm straight. Piper was holding me still, and I turned my head into his neck so I didn't have to watch what Zoe was doing. When she began, Piper's grip tightened against me as I tried to shy away from my own arm. There was a grinding of bones.

Then it was over. Not the pain, which continued, but the dragging of bone on bone. My body slackened onto Piper's chest. I could feel my sweat, greasing both our skin.

Zoe was busy, strapping the wooden splint tightly to my arm.

'You'll need to keep it still, and raised if you can,' Piper said. 'When Zoe broke her wrist as a kid, she made it worse by refusing to rest properly after Sally set it for her.'

'Did it keep hurting for long, after it was set?'

I'd asked Zoe, but they both answered. 'Yes.'

'Done,' said Zoe, tying the bandage tightly.

Piper lowered me so that I was lying down again. He placed a folded blanket under my arm, to prop it higher. He moved me as carefully as a person carrying a butterfly in cupped hands. I thought of how his knife had been trained on me when our defeat had seemed certain. I said nothing of it to him. We both knew there was no less tenderness in that poised knife blade than there was in this holding.

'You should rest,' he said.

'Tell me what happened.'

'You saw almost all of it,' Zoe said. 'The Ringmaster and his soldiers tore through the eastern gate in no time. There was some confusion, inside, from the Omegas of the town, but they worked it out soon enough. The Council soldiers fighting us were outnumbered.'

'What happened to them?'

'They refused to surrender,' Piper said. 'Most of them were killed.'

I didn't realise that I'd winced, until Zoe rolled her eyes. 'Don't act precious about it,' said Zoe. 'You were out there yourself, swinging a sword around. You knew what it meant, when we decided to free the town.'

As if I could forget. I could still feel the sensation of killing that man. The feeling of blade wedged into bone. The double scream of him and his twin, in different octaves of terror.

Piper went on. 'Some fled north. We didn't pursue them. A few gave themselves up, at the end. We still haven't decided what to do with them.'

'You say that as though it's up to us,' Zoe said. 'The Ringmaster's soldiers are guarding them. You really think he's going to ask for our opinion?'

'We did it, though,' I said. 'We freed New Hobart.'

'It's under the rule of a different Councillor, at least,' said Zoe.

I closed my eyes again. Or, rather, they closed themselves. Unconsciousness was claiming me again.

'Find Elsa,' I tried to say, but my lips wouldn't obey me, and I slipped into silence.

*

I was thirsty, and stuck amidst dreams of flame. Somewhere nearby, I heard The Ringmaster's voice.

'But she's going to live?' he said.

'If you let her rest,' Zoe snapped. Somebody wiped my face with a cloth, and I turned to press my skin against its coolness.

'Why's she so pale?' The Ringmaster asked.

The flames rose again, and I heard nothing more.

When I woke there was no sign of him, or Piper. Only Zoe, asleep on the floor by my mattress. I didn't know how long I'd been asleep for, but the blood that had been scarlet on her bandaged leg was now dried and black.

She woke when Piper came in. When he'd strapped my broken arm into a sling, made of torn sheets, I managed to eat a little of the bread that he'd brought with him. Standing was difficult, and my whole body moved awkwardly around the pivot of pain that was my bound arm. I had to lean on Piper's shoulder as I followed him and Zoe into the next room. Beyond the stack of smashed chairs, the room opened up into a large hall. A circle of intact chairs was laid out in the centre, where The Ringmaster was waiting, with Sally, Xander, Simon, and an older woman. I'd not met her before, but I recognised her short hair and the hump on her back.

It was she who'd unfurled the makeshift flag from the eastern tower, towards the end of the battle.

'This is June,' said Piper. 'She led the uprising inside the town.'

She glanced at my arm, the splint protruding from the bandage at my elbow. 'I won't shake your hand, then,' she said.

'And of course you remember The Ringmaster,' said Zoe. Her words were sharpened.

'You'd all be dead, or tanked, by now, if she hadn't gone to him,' Sally said.

'You lied to us,' Zoe said.

'If I'd told you I was meeting him that night, you wouldn't have let me go. We wouldn't have been able to free the town.'

'Is it free?' said Zoe. 'I still see Council soldiers patrolling the gates.'

'I've told you,' said The Ringmaster. 'They work for me, not the Council. And if it weren't for them, the Council could retake this town any time they wanted.'

He sat apart from the others. There was a cut on his cheek, already healing. Simon, opposite me, had his left arm in a sling, and a bruise at the corner of his mouth.

'What is this place?' I asked, looking around. It was big – too big to be a house. This room alone was bigger than the children's dormitory in Elsa's holding house.

'It's the Tithe Collector's office,' The Ringmaster said.

'It doesn't help with the morale in the town,' June said. 'You setting yourselves up here, where the Council used to make us queue to deliver our tithes. That and taking down the flag.'

'This place was empty,' The Ringmaster said. 'What would they prefer? That we turn someone out of their home and base ourselves there? As for the flag, you can't expect my troops to be happy about working night and day under an Omega flag, when it was them who freed the town.'

'We freed it together,' I said. 'If we hadn't attacked, you and your soldiers would have done nothing to free New Hobart.' I turned to June. 'When we left the warnings for you, we never hoped that you'd manage to do so much. How did you do it? Had you hidden weapons?'

'A few, but not enough,' she said. 'They were thorough, in the weeks after they sealed the city. There were searches and raids, and rewards if people turned each other in for concealing contraband. They had us pretty well disarmed. Not to mention afraid.

'It was the pumpkins that gave us the idea,' she went on. 'You'd already used the food against them once – we just did it again. They had us cooking for them, you see. They were stupid to trust us, especially after they'd taken the children. I even heard two of them talking, when the gate shifts changed over, the day after they'd taken the kids away. *Expecting trouble tonight, after yesterday?* one of them said to the soldier coming off shift. His friend just shrugged, said, *Why? It's not as if it's even their kids.*'

I was watching The Ringmaster. His face was expressionless.

'They took all the children under ten,' June went on. 'They cleared out the holding houses, and I saw the soldiers dragging my neighbour's adopted children away, kicking and screaming.' Her face hardened. 'So when we got your message, we were ready to act. There's belladonna, climbing up the embankment behind the market square. And hemlock, in the ditches by the wall. Four of us sneaked out after the curfew, to pick as much as we could. Even then, we couldn't poison all the soldiers. The first shift was already getting sick not long after sunset, before the next shift came in to the mess hall. Some of them died. A lot more were collapsing. They realised pretty quickly what we'd done. Had already whipped three of the cooks by the time the attack started. It would have got ugly, in here, if you hadn't attacked when you said you would.'

It was already ugly, I thought, picturing the slow deaths of the poisoned soldiers. But I had no right to judge June for it. The people of New Hobart had done what we asked, more successfully than I could have imagined.

June turned to face The Ringmaster. 'But we didn't risk everything just to find ourselves under a new occupying force.'

The Ringmaster stood. 'You're not the only one who risked everything. I've given up my seat on the Council. My soldiers have risked their lives to defend you. Your rag-tag army of Omegas was on the brink of being massacred when we arrived. If you think your forces are capable of withstanding a Council attack on New Hobart, I invite you to take over the defence of the town. Until then, be grateful.'

'Grateful?' spat Zoe.

'I don't relish working with you any more than you do with me,' he said quietly. 'We all want to stop the machines. I don't wish harm on you people. Not like The Reformer or The General. I just want to manage the situation, to avoid another catastrophe like the blast.'

'*Manage the situation*,' I said. 'All of us in refuges, eventually – that's what you mean, isn't it? Locked out of sight, in work camps, where we can't be seen, let alone have lives of our own.'

At my raised voice, Xander began rocking backwards and forwards, hands pressed over his ears.

The Ringmaster ignored him. 'It would mean security and stability, for Omegas as well as Alphas,' he said. 'And it's better than what your twin is proposing.'

'They're not our choices,' shouted Piper. 'We don't have to choose between you and him, or The General . . .'

'We're wasting time,' Sally interrupted. 'This isn't going to help us. We fought together, and we won. That's more than we expected. We've kept this town from the tanks. But it's only the beginning. If we bicker, we'll just make it easier for the Council to fight back.' She turned to The Ringmaster. 'How much of the army do you command, and will they stay loyal to you?'

If he was taken aback at having to answer to an old woman in a threadbare shawl, he didn't show it.

'I'd say perhaps half the army will follow me, if it comes to that,' he said. 'The Reformer and The General have been so seduced by the machines, they've underestimated what the taboo means to most people. I've had defectors coming to me, ever since the first rumours about the machines began to spread. Most of those who aren't already here have left Wyndham, to muster to the west, inland of Sebald's Bay.'

June stood. 'My people aren't happy that there are still soldiers manning the walls, whether they call themselves Council soldiers or not. If it were up to us, we'd tear the walls down.'

'And make the town completely vulnerable to the Council's attack,' said Piper. 'If we can use them defensively, they stay. But I want Omega patrols out there as well.'

'My soldiers won't stand for that,' The Ringmaster said. 'It was hard enough persuading them to fight against the Council. But asking them to work directly with Omegas is too much. And it won't help any of us if the soldiers start picking fights.'

'Then make sure they don't,' I said. 'Work it out.' I stood, but had to steady myself on the back of my chair. 'Draw up a roster so that Omega patrols can take turns. Or have your men patrol the walls, and ours manning the gates. Just work it out.'

I stepped closer to The Ringmaster. 'Do you have ships?'

'What are you talking about? How are ships going to help us to hold New Hobart, or to tackle the tanks?'

'We're looking for Elsewhere,' I said. 'You're right – it will be next to impossible to win here. And if the only way we can do it is with battles, then ultimately nobody wins. But there might be an alternative. Somewhere where things are different. Somewhere that could help us, or at least offer a real haven.'

'Right now,' said The Ringmaster, 'The Reformer and The General will be massing their troops. Working out how best to rout us. Who next to tank. Which settlement to target when they make reprisals – which you know they'll do. If you focus on sailing away and looking for Elsewhere, people will see it as a betrayal.'

There was a long silence before I spoke. 'Everything we do through force is just stalling,' I said. 'Nothing lasting can come from it – only more death. We fought this battle because we had to. But already, there will be Alphas mourning those who died here, and turning against us more than ever. We did what was necessary, and we may have to do it again. But it's not the answer. We can't kill our way to a lasting peace. That's not how killing works.'

'She's right,' Piper said. 'We need to seize this chance. Not just to recruit more Omegas to the resistance, but also to renew the search for the ships. The Council's attention will be here, and not on the coast. We could fit out new ships, if we act quickly. Push further north, past the ice channel –'

'Don't start this again,' interrupted Simon. 'The ships are gone. If the Council's fleet didn't finish them off, the winter storms will have. My scouts waited at Cape Bleak as long as they could, Piper. There's no chance for the ships – not this far into winter. You've always clung to the idea of Elsewhere. It's just a way of avoiding the real problems of here and now.'

Piper spoke over him, to The Ringmaster.

'Two of our ships sailed north-west more than four months ago. If they have the good sense to scout the island before landing, and not sail right into the Council's arms, then they'll come to the mainland instead. We need to have scouts posted on Cape Bleak.'

The Ringmaster shook his head. 'Whose scouts? Have you got the soldiers to spare? Cape Bleak wouldn't just mean getting safely out of here – it'd mean getting through hundreds of miles of densely populated Alpha territory. There's a Council garrison between here and there that's half the size of Wyndham.'

'What would you do instead?' I said. 'We need to push for real change, not just more battles.'

'Real change is what I'm talking about,' he said. 'Change that we can actually achieve, instead of some pipe dream. We're in a position to negotiate with the Council now – to use this victory to push for Council reform. Challenge The General for control of the Council. There are others in the Council who'd support me. It could be a new Council of moderates, more sympathetic to Omegas. We'd uphold the taboo. Stop the tanks. Bring tithes back to reasonable levels. Isn't that what you want?'

'Sympathetic to Omegas,' Piper said. 'But still ruling over us. Reasonable tithes? Why should we be paying the Council anything? We didn't pay tithes on the island.'

'There isn't any island,' said The Ringmaster. 'Not anymore. I'm not committing more men to some wild-goose chase for Elsewhere. I'm here to stop the machines, to try to bring the Council back into safe hands. That's all.'

'Safe hands?' said Zoe. 'Your hands, you mean.'

'Would you prefer that The Reformer and The General stay in power? Because without me, that's what will happen.'

'We can't waste time arguing about this,' I said. 'We need to think beyond swords and battles and blood. If the ships make it back to the mainland, we need to find them before the Council does. And we should be searching already for the papers that the Council was looking for.'

'They were looking for some papers alright,' said June. She gave a tired laugh. Everyone turned to look at her. 'There's not a recipe or a love letter in New Hobart that they didn't confiscate, these last months. Took apart all the traders' shops down at the market, too. Dug up half the road outside the baker's place, when somebody gave them a lead about something buried there.' Her smile faded. 'I shouldn't laugh about it. They roughed up a few people pretty badly when they thought they were holding something back. But they've been searching for months. Offered rewards, too. If people weren't going to hand them over for the gold the Council was offering, in these lean times, how are you going to find them?'

'I need to talk to Elsa, from the holding house. And I need to see the tanks, so we can start working out whether it's safe to take the children out.'

A silence settled over the room.

'What?' I said. 'What haven't you told me?'

Piper stood. 'I'll take you to the tanks. Elsa's there already.'

CHAPTER 22

The snow had drained most of the colour from the streets. Black wooden beams, white snow, black mud. Many houses bore damage from the battle, or from the months of occupation. A few were completely burnt out; on others, the doors or shutters were broken, or hastily mended. Those people we passed in the street looked thin, and some wore bloodied bandages. I walked slowly, my arm jarring with each step, despite the sling. A blind man came the other way, his cane scraping to and fro on the icy paving stones. He stumbled where a burnt door had fallen on the road. Piper took his arm and helped him over the obstacle. 'Used to get around here just fine,' the man said. 'It's all changed.' It was true – I would barely have recognised New Hobart from my time there months ago.

A corner of the new building had been damaged when one of the fires lit against the wall had spread. A black scorch mark climbed towards the roof. The door was broken in, and snow had blown through the open doorway.

I followed Piper inside, but stopped after a few steps. The door behind me admitted the only light in the long room, and it was reflected in the curve of huge tanks lining the space. Everything else was darkness.

There should have been rows of lights, flashing green above the tanks. And there should have been a low hum, the snoring of the machines. Instead, there was only a waterlogged silence, so heavy that I couldn't follow Piper any further. I stood, stranded by the door.

Elsa stepped out from behind one of the tanks, brandishing a kitchen knife. When she saw Piper, she tossed it to the floor.

'I already told you, and your soldiers. I don't need help. I'll do it myself.'

Her disembodied face had drifted before me in so many visions that it was a shock to see her like this: solid, with dirty hands and a rag tying her hair back, and a bruise swelling one eye closed. She looked older than I'd remembered, her hair greyer and her posture more slumped.

I called her name. She squinted at me, against the light from the doorway behind me. Then she ran, uneven on her bowed legs, and grabbed me to her. She pressed me to her chest so tightly that I was sure I must have had the imprint of her shirt buttons on my cheek. I cried out as my splinted arm was crushed, and she released me.

'Where's Kip?' she said.

'He's dead.' It still shocked me to say it out loud. But there was no time to dwell on it. Not with the silent tanks waiting behind Elsa.

'What happened?' I said.

She pursed her lips. 'Looks like we both have stories to tell. And no happy endings, either.' She moved her hands to my face, and for a moment she smiled so widely that her uninjured eye was nearly as closed as the swollen one. 'But it's good to see you, girl.'

The smile was gone. She took my good arm and led me deeper into the room, to where Piper stood. I could see the tanks clearly now. They were the same height as those I'd seen before, reaching a few feet above my head, but each one was fifteen feet wide. I thought of what The Confessor had said to me in the silo: *our recent experiments in mass tanks.* They filled the room, two rows of huge vats. Enough, I figured, to tank the whole town, eventually. For now, all but the nearest three tanks were empty, encasing nothing but air.

The tank closest to us had been drained. A few inches of fluid pooled at its base, around the open plug set into the floor. A rope ladder, tied to the gangway above, stuck to the tank's damp side before coiling in the liquid at the bottom.

I stepped further into the room, gripping Elsa's arm more tightly.

The next tank was full of liquid. But the children's bodies didn't float, like the Omegas in tanks I'd seen before. They were piled at the base of the tank, six deep. The tubes that had pierced their mouths and wrists still stretched out of the liquid's surface, but they were tangled, and some had pulled loose and dangled at large in the fluid. The surface of the liquid was utterly still; it didn't vibrate with the orderly hum of the Electric. And without the Electric, each tank had become nothing more than a glass crypt. The children were all drowned.

'The fire didn't do this,' I said.

I knew, before Piper spoke, what he would say.

'Half the machines had been smashed,' Piper said, 'and the wires cut.' I looked where he was pointing. At the far end of the room, a huge metal box had been pulled open, its wire innards exposed and slashed. The pipes that ran from the wall to the tanks, and along the ceiling above them, had been shattered, too. One of the pipes was leaking, liquid dripping to the ground.

'I sent men here as soon as the town was secured,' Piper went on. 'They found it like this. The Council's soldiers must've done it as soon as they realised they were under attack. They must have had orders not to let the machines fall into our hands.'

Elsa interrupted him. 'That's not why they did it. That might have been part of it, sure. But you know as well as I do that this was a punishment.' She looked back at the tanks. 'They broke the machines and they let the children drown, because we fought back.'

I couldn't look away from the slumped bodies. It was hard to differentiate individual children amongst the mass of limbs. Most of their eyes were open, their mouths wide in underwater screams. I couldn't bear to think about their final minutes, but I couldn't look away. What price had we paid, to free New Hobart? But we hadn't paid the price. These children had.

'I found the way to open the plug and drain the first tank,' Elsa said. Her sleeve on my arm was wet. I looked down at her. Her whole shirt was soaked, and her trousers, too, were wet to the knees. She led me to the far end of the room. There, laid out on a sheet, were the bodies she had pulled from the first tank. They lay there, drenched, like seaweed dumped on a beach by the sea.

'I've got the first twelve kids out,' she said. 'But I've got more work to do. There are sixty kids or more in here.'

And sixty more again, in Alpha homes, where parents would have gone to wake their children the morning after the battle and found them in their beds, blue-lipped and drowned in air.

Zach had done this. Sickness twisted my guts, bile rising at the back of my throat. When I was a child, and had hidden my visions so that Zach and I could not be split, he had outwitted me by declaring himself the Omega. He'd known me well, my clever brother: I protected him, and took the branding and exile that I could not bear to see inflicted on him. Even back then, he'd been willing to risk hurting himself in order to be rid of me. Ordering the killing of the children, even knowing that Alpha children would die too, was the same gesture, on a grand scale. His declaration, and The General's, that no cost was too great to be rid of us.

In the end, I persuaded Elsa to accept help. She was soaking and exhausted, though she wouldn't admit it. Piper fetched Zoe and Crispin, the dwarf who had been on the lookout when we'd first reunited with the resistance at the quarry. Elsa would let nobody but her lay out the bodies, but she allowed the others to take on the task of hauling the children from the tanks. She showed Piper the lever she had found in front of each tank, to open the plug at the base. As the liquid drained away, circling the plug, the mounded bodies shifted and stirred in a grotesque parody of life. The first time it happened, Crispin vomited quietly behind one of the tanks.

Nobody spoke. It wasn't just the horror of the dead children - it was the machines themselves. I watched how Piper moved warily amongst the tanks, and saw how Zoe flinched when her arm brushed one of the inert pipes, as though it were hot. I'd spent years under the electric lights of the Keeping Rooms, and had seen tank rooms before, as well as The Confessor's database. But the others navigated the room as if each pipe and wire was a snare, ready to entangle them. Everything in this room was taboo. Crispin stared at the machines the same way that Alphas stared at us: as if the machines carried the taint of the blast itself.

When each tank was drained, Zoe and Crispin climbed down the rope ladder and disentangled the bodies. I watched how carefully they both stepped, to avoid standing on the children, and how gently they slipped the tubes from the open mouths, and from the wrists, before climbing the ladder to hand their sodden burdens to Piper, waiting on the gangway. He passed each body down from the gangway to Elsa.

I had seen the world burn, and I'd seen flesh slashed in the battle only days before. But there had been no horrors in my life to equal that day, in the half-dark room, seeing the small bodies dredged from the tanks, or watching Elsa stroke their hair from their faces and straighten their stiffening limbs. She tried to close their eyes, but they had stared too long at death and their eyelids would not be moved.

Piper had ordered soldiers to fetch more sheets and blankets from the holding house, and I helped Elsa shroud the children. It was hardest when I recognised the faces. Not all the children were from Elsa's holding house, but many were. When it was Louisa who was laid before me, I saw that her mouth was open. I couldn't stop looking at her small teeth, and the gaps between them. Of all the things I saw that day, it was the sight of those little white teeth that made me turn away.

We worked in silence, because the words had not been made that could encompass what we did. Sometimes Elsa cried, in silence too. When we were finished, we shifted the shrouded bodies to the doorway. Elsa carried the older children and I, with one arm in the sling, took the babies and toddlers. Wrapped, the smallest child I carried that day was barely bigger than a loaf of bread. But even the infants felt heavier than they ought to have done, their tiny lungs and stomachs awash with liquid.

Only when all the wrapped bodies were laid out by the door did Elsa and I talk. Zoe and Crispin had gone back to the Tithe Collector's office, and Piper was outside, speaking to another soldier about sending a cart for the bodies. My arm was aching, and I could see that Elsa was exhausted, and I was tempted to wait another day before I burdened her with my news. But I'd learned better than to count on more days, and there were things that we both needed to know.

It took a long time to unravel the weeks and months since I'd last seen her. I told her about what had happened on the island, and she nodded.

'Usually we heard nothing about what was going on outside, but the soldiers here were keen enough to spread that news. Before then, I'd been hoping you'd found your way to the island. Then, when the news came in, I was praying that you hadn't.'

When I told her who my twin was, I was watching her face. She looked back at me, examining my face carefully, as if reassuring herself that I was still the same person. Then she gave my hand a squeeze.

'It doesn't change who you are,' she said.

I wished it were true. But Zach had changed who I was. He, and all that he had done, had shaped me, as much as I had shaped him. One of us was the blade, the other the whetstone.

I kept hold of her hand while I explained what we had learned about the tanks, and Zach's plans for them.

'I'm not stupid,' she said, her voice low. 'I knew it was bad, when they took the kids. But this place, and what you've told me – it's worse even than I feared.'

'You tried to stop them, when they came for the children?' I said.

Elsa turned her face to me, raising the eyebrow above her blackened eye. 'What do you think?'

'And Nina?' I asked.

She looked down. 'She was hurt worse than me, when we tried to stop them taking the kids. Took a blow to the head, and then blood started coming out of her ears.' She took a slow breath. 'She died two days later.'

We sat together, the shrouded children laid out in rows at our feet.

'Maybe they didn't suffer,' I said.

Elsa reached for my hand again. 'When you and Kip first came here, I understood why you had to lie to me about your names, and where you'd been. But you don't need to lie to me now. I'm too old for it. There's no time for it anymore.'

*

We were watching the troops load the children's bodies onto wagons when Piper's name was shouted from up the hill, and then mine. Zoe rounded the corner, running. She was sweating, and her haste had reopened the wound on her thigh; fresh blood seeped through the leg of her trousers.

'A messenger, from the Council,' she said. 'He came alone, ten minutes ago, to the eastern gate.'

Elsa squeezed me again, hard, before we left, and I told her I'd return soon. Piper, Zoe and I rushed together through the town, as fast as her injured leg and my broken arm would allow.

'It's your brother.' The Ringmaster stood when we entered the tithe collector's office. 'Sent a message: he wants to talk.'

250

'He's coming here?'

'Him and The General. They're to the east, with a squadron. The messenger asked us to meet them in the middle, on the eastern road.'

'All of us?'

'You want to see your twin alone?' The Ringmaster was watching my face. Suspicion coated everything in this room. It lay thicker than the snow outside.

I shook my head. 'I don't want to see him.' My hands were still sticky with the tank fluid that had dripped from the hair of the dead children. It was Zach and The General who had given those orders. Their decision to have the children taken and tanked. Their decision to have them drowned in the dark.

'We're all angry about the children,' The Ringmaster said. 'But we need to meet both of them, and make the most of this opportunity. They know how much of the army has defected to me. This is our strongest chance to negotiate.'

I shook my head. 'They haven't come to negotiate,' I said.

'How do you know?' Sally said. 'Have you seen it in your visions?'

I shook my head. 'No. But I know Zach.' I had seen his ruthlessness. The same ruthlessness that had led him to risk everything, as a child, in order to expose me as the Omega, and that now led to those mounds of sodden bodies in the tanks. So much had changed since then, and so little. 'I know what he is,' I said, 'because I made him what he is.'

They'd been The Confessor's words to Kip, in the silo: *You did this to me. You made me what I am.* I saw how our childhood had formed him. It wasn't a question of blame, now – only of knowledge.

We rode out to meet them when the sun was at its highest. Twenty soldiers accompanied us – ten of The Ringmaster's troops, and ten of Simon's. At the front rode the five of us: me, Piper, Zoe, Simon, and The Ringmaster. Half an hour's ride from New Hobart, we saw them coming the other way: twenty or more riders.

Zach rode at the front. Even from a distance, I could see the sharp line of his jaw, and the way he moved his head: sudden, jerky movements, between the long stillnesses of his stares.

The sun glared off the snow. I squinted at the outline of that man, my twin. He was pale, and the cold had daubed his cheeks with red. I saw how he held his right arm gingerly, and I glanced down at my own arm, still in its sling. If I were to squeeze my own swollen flesh, I would see him flinch.

The woman who rode next to him was the only other person who didn't wear a soldier's red tunic. The eyes of all the other soldiers were trained on her alone. The General. Zach glanced several times at her as they rode, but she ignored him entirely. Her angular features were emphasised by her hair, pulled back tightly from her head. She rode very upright, eyes fixed on us.

When she raised her hand, the soldiers beside them halted. She and Zach rode the final few yards, to draw up in the middle of the open space between the two groups. She didn't look at me, deliberately, but focused only on my companions.

'It's quite the alliance,' she said. 'A disgraced resistance leader, rejected by his own Assembly. An Alpha, lowering herself to live amongst Omegas. And a Councillor who's been cast out of the Council.'

'Spare us your speechifying,' said Piper.

She ignored him and turned to face me. 'And you. A seer, whose visions seem to lead the resistance from one massacre to another.'

'We freed New Hobart,' Piper said. 'We couldn't have done it without Cass.'

Zach interrupted him. 'You couldn't have done it without The Ringmaster, not Cass. And it cost you half your troops.' He stared from Piper to me, and back again. 'Things haven't been going so well for you, have they, since she came along? You lost the island. You lost your position. Your numbers have been slashed. Haven't you worked it out yet?' He leaned forward, dropping his voice to a confidential whisper. 'She's poison. She always has been.'

I spoke over him. 'You can call me what you like,' I said. 'But you're afraid of me. You always have been.'

His voice was a lash, quick and furious. 'Be careful how you speak to me,' he said. 'I have something of yours.'

The General interrupted him. 'Fascinating as this is, we didn't come here so that you and your twin could hash out the intricacies of your relationship.'

'She's right,' said The Ringmaster. 'We need to talk about where we go from here.'

'There isn't any *we*,' The General said. 'You took New Hobart. You might even be able to hold it. It's a delay, no more than that. Just like destroying the database was. There are other settlements, other towns.'

'You can't stop us,' Zach put in. 'All you've done is pointlessly sacrifice lives by pushing us to battle. Everything I've been working towards is about saving lives.'

'Saving Alpha lives,' I said, 'by putting us in tanks. That's worse than death, and you know it.' I knew the tanks for what they were: a dying that goes on forever. 'And how can you even talk about saving lives, after what you did to the children?'

The General smiled, but her eyes didn't move. Just her mouth, a curve as precise as a dagger's edge. 'Since we weren't in New Hobart to welcome you in person, we wanted to make sure our soldiers left you a gift.'

She turned to The Ringmaster. 'You know you can't return to Wyndham now. Your days on the Council are finished.'

'They were finished long ago,' said The Ringmaster. 'How long has it been, really, since anyone other than you two wielded any real power?'

'And you think you can seize that power now?' She laughed at him. 'Just because a bunch of disaffected soldiers are running to you, because their superstitions are larger than their ambitions? You really think they're going to stick with you, if this uprising continues?'

'They can see what you're doing is wrong,' I said.

Zach shook his head. 'You're as naïve as ever, Cass. It's not compassion that's driven them to The Ringmaster, any more than it's compassion that drives him. It's fear. The taboo. They don't have the intelligence to see what technology could offer us.

'Their fear's nothing that education won't remedy. I've seen it myself, with the people we recruited to work on the tanks. Every one of them was hesitant, at first. But when they understand what I can offer them – a world in which they never have to worry about their twin again – they see the benefits. Nothing dissolves fear as quickly as self-interest.

'And what are you offering them, as an alternative?' He looked at me as though I were a foolish child. 'I can offer a future free of the twinning,' he went on. 'You're offering war. Thousands will die, Alphas and Omegas alike. And even if you were to win, what then? No progress. The fatal bond still there, a burden to everyone. Our lives still won't be our own. Do you really think people will follow you, once they understand that?'

'If you think your position is so unassailable, why did you call this meeting?' The Ringmaster said. 'You're running scared. We've taken back New Hobart, and you realise it's time to start negotiating.'

'You can't negotiate with Omegas,' The General said. 'They're not capable of it.' She waved an arm towards me, Simon and Piper. 'It's always been the problem with you people. It's because you can't breed. You're not fit to parent, so you don't have the responsibility of future generations to consider, like we do. It's why you're fundamentally short-sighted.'

'Not fit to parent?' I said. I was picturing Elsa, the soft-ness of her hands as she smoothed back the hair of the dead children. And Nina, who had died to protect children who had been brought to the holding house by strangers. 'How can you sit there and say that to me, after what you did to the children? Even before then – you Alphas are the ones who send half your children away, not us. We take them, and care for them, and do our best to protect them from you.'

The Ringmaster spoke over me. 'This isn't the time for sniping at one another. We all want to avoid civil war, so let's discuss our demands. A guarantee that the Council will uphold the taboo, as a first step.'

'Your demands?' The General said. 'You want to nego-tiate?' She nodded slowly. 'Fine. I brought you something. Another gift, if you like. Something to open negotiations. I thought you might like to see it.'

Without turning, she raised a finger, gesturing at Zach. He turned back to where their soldiers waited, and ushered two of them forward. As they obeyed, I saw that they carried a wooden chest, slung between the two horses.

Zach dismounted and handed his reins to one of the soldiers. While they lowered the trunk, Zach steadied it with his left hand. Something rattled within as it was settled on the ground. The soldiers moved back, taking Zach's horse with them.

'Open it,' he said to me. 'Go on.'

'You open it,' I said.

Zach looked up and smiled. He seemed unconcerned by the fact that we were still mounted, and that he stood alone on the ground before us. He stepped forward, and heaved open the lid.

For a moment I thought they were human heads. They were about the right size and shape. Then the smell reached me, incongruous in the snow-laden air. It took me straight back to the island, where the air had a constant bass note of salt. I leaned forward over my horse's neck, to peer more closely at the two shapes within the chest. They were some kind of wooden sculptures. When Zach lifted one out I saw that it was a carving of a woman's head, with long curls of hair tracing their way down over her shoulders. The wood was bleached with age. Time had blunted the features of her face – her nose was eroded to almost nothing. Only at the neck was the colour different: axe strokes had left sharp lines, exposing the darker wood within.

I turned to Piper. For several seconds, he closed his eyes. When he opened them again, he looked once more at the carved head, then back at The General.

'Where did you get them?' he said quietly.

'It doesn't make a difference,' she said.

'What are they?'

I'd whispered it to Piper, but Zach turned, pulling the

second sculpture from the chest and throwing it to the ground in front of me. My horse snorted and jerked backwards a few steps. The wooden head rocked from side to side several times before settling in the shallow snow. It lay face up, staring blindly at the white sky.

'The figureheads from *The Rosalind* and *The Evelyn*,' said The General. 'Your precious ships.'

CHAPTER 23

'This proves nothing,' Zoe said. 'The crews could have landed safely, left the ships moored.'

'Would you prefer it if I brought you the head of your friend Hobb?' The General said. I saw Piper's hand tighten on his reins.

The General went on. 'They were on their way back to the island, when our patrol ships chased them down on the open sea.'

'Where are the crews?' Simon said. 'Hobb and the others?'

'Tanked,' said The General. She tossed the syllable down, as casual and dismissive as a cough. 'But not before we got information out of them,' she added. 'We know what they were looking for.'

Zach came forward, stepping carelessly over the fallen figureheads, to stand right in front of me. 'You made the mistake of thinking we wouldn't find you on the island. You've seen what we did to the children. See this, now, and remember. There is nowhere, not in the furthest oceans, where we won't track you down. There is no place on this earth where you will be free of us.'

The General looked down at him, and gave him a slight nod. He walked back to where the soldiers waited, and swung himself into the saddle.

'Did you think I was going to come here, cowed,' The General said, 'just because you've managed to claw back this hole of a town? Did you think I was going to apologise, and we were going to have a nice chat about how we're going to do things your way from now on?'

She turned her horse. 'You can't stop us. You can't even begin to know what we can do.' She began to ride away.

I started my own horse forwards. Piper grabbed at my reins, jerking my mount backwards. As my horse skittered on the spot, I called after Zach. The General and the soldiers turned too, but I looked only at Zach.

'What you just said: *There's no place on this earth where you will be free of us.* The same goes for you,' I said. 'All of this – the violence, the scheming. It's all because you and your kind are so afraid to acknowledge that we're the same as you. More than that: we're part of you.'

The General raised an eyebrow. 'You're a side effect of us. Nothing more.'

She rode off. Zach stared at me for a moment then wheeled his horse around and followed The General down the road. The trunk was left open and empty on the ground, the figureheads abandoned where they lay, as the snow began to fall once more.

*

Once we had handed our horses over to the soldiers at the gate, I went straight to Elsa's.

'We should've gone back with the others,' Zoe said as

she followed me up the street towards the holding house. 'We need to talk about what the Council's next move will be – and where we go from here. And it's not safe for you to wander around alone.'

'Go back if you want,' I said. 'But there's nothing to say. Zach and The General want us frightened and bickering. They want to scare us off searching for Elsewhere, and for the Ark papers. They want to make us doubt ourselves. I won't do it.'

We turned the corner into Elsa's street. There were footprints in the snow, but we saw nobody. A shutter slammed closed as we passed a narrow house on the left.

The holding house, the largest building on the street, was still standing, but the front door was gone, and the shutters smashed. Zoe waited by the door, keeping watch as I stepped inside.

I walked down the corridor, calling Elsa's name. I found her in the kitchen, on her hands and knees, sorting fragments of crockery.

'They smashed the place up, when we tried to stop them taking the kids,' Elsa said. 'I haven't had a chance to clean up yet, what with everything that's happened.'

Beyond her I could see the courtyard, a boneyard of broken wood: slats of shutters, and crippled chairs and tables. On one side, furniture had been thrown into a pile and set alight, leaving a mound of blackened wood spars, topped with snow. A fire had etched blackness up one wall and across half the ceiling.

'You've done enough today,' I said to Elsa. 'Leave this.' I waved my hand at the wreckage of the kitchen. 'You need to rest.'

'Better to be busy,' she said, not looking at me.

I thought of what she'd said to me a few hours ago, about

lies: *there's no time for it anymore.* I didn't waste time with preliminaries.

'Your husband – you never told me how he died.'

She stood, slowly, her hands pressing the small of her back like a pregnant woman.

'It was too dangerous to talk about,' she said. 'I had the children to think of.'

Still avoiding my eyes, she began sweeping the smashed crockery into a pile. The pottery pieces scratched loudly against the flagstones. Occasionally she found a bowl or mug that was chipped but otherwise intact, and would bend to retrieve it and set it carefully aside.

'Who are you saving that for?' I said, taking a dented mug from her hands. 'They're not coming back.'

'There will always be more children,' she said, resuming her sweeping.

'You think the Alphas will bring them here, now? It's a war, Elsa. They're all going to be tanked, from birth, if we can't defeat the Council.'

No sound but the crunch of broken pottery and the broom's scraping.

'You never told me the truth about your husband, because you didn't want to endanger the children. Look around you.' I gestured at the empty courtyard; the shutters pulled off their hinges. 'There are no children. They drowned them all. There's nobody left to protect.'

She let the broom drop. The handle clattered on the flagstones as she stared at me.

'They took him,' she said. After all the day's crying, her voice was as rough as the scrape of the broken plates on the floor. 'You've guessed that much already. They came at night, four years ago. They took Joe, and then they turned the house upside down, ripped the whole place to pieces

– slit open every mattress in the kids' dormitory. Emptied every pot in the kitchen.'

'Did they find what they were looking for?'

'If they did, I didn't see it,' she said. 'They just left. Never said a word to me, even when I was screaming at them to tell me what was going on, where they'd taken him, and why.' She sniffed. 'It's funny what sticks in your mind. What you remember. When I think about that night, I always remember how it was my screaming that scared the children. They were used to seeing soldiers roughing people up – even back then, the kids knew not to expect any different from a red-shirt. It was me losing it that frightened them. Nina did her best to keep them calm, but I set them off.' She looked down into her lap, where her hands were rubbing at each other.

'It was the soldiers' fault, not yours,' I said. 'They'd taken your husband, and smashed up your home.'

'I know that.' She looked up. 'And I knew as soon as they took Joe that they'd kill him. And they did.'

'How do you know?'

'I waited for weeks for news of him. Even went to the tithe collector's office, to ask after him. The soldiers wouldn't so much as let me up the steps. Wouldn't tell me a thing. In the end I left the children with Nina and went to Joe's twin's village. It's down near the coast, a long way west. It took me three weeks of walking. And it's all Alpha country out that way, so it wasn't easy. Forget about begging a bed for a night, even in a barn. More than once I had to hightail out of a village with stones coming after me. But you know me.' She laughed. It was hard to tell the noise from a sob. 'I don't give up easily.'

I tried to imagine how it must have been for her, walking into an Alpha village on her crooked legs, demanding answers.

'I'd never met his twin, of course – all I had was her name and the name of the village she and Joe were born in. Didn't even know if she'd still be there.' She looked out the window. 'Well, she was – but six feet under the village green. Flowers planted on the grave; a nice headstone and everything.'

She had never been given her own husband's body back to bury. I thought of Kip again, his body on the silo floor.

'The people in his village just wanted me gone – but I made a nuisance of myself, hung around the outskirts, trying to get somebody to talk to me. Some were threatening to call the soldiers to get me to clear off, but in the end I guess they figured it was easier just to tell me what I needed to know. She'd died a month before, they said. As close as I could figure it, it was a few days after they took him.' She fell silent. Her lips were pressed tightly together, her chin betraying the slightest quiver.

'It wasn't quick.' Her voice had dropped low, each word pulled from her mouth like a tooth. 'That's what they said: that she started screaming, and didn't stop for two days.' She looked up at me. 'Joe made a lot of mistakes, but he didn't deserve what they did to him.'

For a while we just sat there, looking out at the courtyard with its assemblage of broken furniture.

'Do you know what they were looking for?' I said. 'Did you ever hear anything about Elsewhere, or a place called the Ark?'

'No.' She shrugged. 'He never talked much about the stuff he traded in,' she said. 'I didn't want to know, to be honest – I was happy enough to look the other way. And it's not as though I didn't have plenty on my hands, with the kids to take care of. He traded on the black market, sure, and he dealt in some relics and dodgy stuff. But he wasn't stupid. Any machines, anything with wires, he knew it was more trouble than it was worth. That stuff freaked him out, to be honest – and I wouldn't have let him bring it near the house. The bits and pieces from the Before that he traded were just tat – papers, broken crockery. Bits of metal. The kind of thing that's a bit of a curiosity to most people. Half of it, to tell you the truth, wasn't even from the Before. One summer he and his mate Greg did a roaring trade in a load of pottery that they said was taboo. It was just some fancy stuff they'd nicked from the back of an Alpha cart, then chipped and soaked in tea and dirt until it looked ancient. People liked a bit of that: something exotic, a bit dangerous.' She gave a bleak smile. 'He wasn't one to look for trouble, my Joe. He was too lazy for that. He was only interested in little odds and ends – stuff he could sell quickly, bring in a few easy coins, a bit extra that the tithe collector wouldn't know about.'

'He wouldn't be the first person to trade in taboo stuff, or to dodge tithes,' I said. 'That's not enough to explain why they'd kill him. Or torture him for days.'

At the word *torture* Elsa flinched as though she'd been struck.

I pushed on. 'You never saw the things he traded?'

She shook her head. 'I didn't want anything shady here – not with the kids around. He kept his work stuff in his storehouse by the market, anyway. Slept there, too, often enough – I didn't like him being around the kids when he'd been drinking.'

'The storehouse,' I said, 'is it still there?'

'Don't be stupid. The day after they took him, it was burned down – took out the back of the bakery too. It was no accident, of course – Greg saw Council soldiers clearing it out before dawn, taking away everything in it.

'I kept waiting for them to come for me, after that,' she said. 'But for once it worked in our favour, the fact that they don't acknowledge Omega marriages. They knew he worked here sometimes, or they wouldn't've searched the place like they did. But because he had his storehouse, down at the market, they thought he lived there. And because they think of us as not much more than animals, they never figured we were married.'

She fell silent again.

'Tell me what they were looking for,' I said. 'Please.'

'I've already told you,' she snapped. 'He never told me any details about that stuff.'

'That doesn't mean you don't know.'

I'd never seen Elsa look like this before. I was used to seeing her striding around, badgering Nina about the shopping list at the same time as braiding a child's hair. But now she was deflated, shoulders folded inwards. Her eyes were unfocussed, her lips pinched.

'I've kept quiet about this for four years.' She was whispering, even though we were alone in the kitchen. 'I saw what they did to Joe. Now I've seen what they did to the children.'

'I'm not going to tell you that you shouldn't be afraid,' I said. 'You're right to be afraid. I saw what you saw – I helped you pull the children from the tanks. We both know what the Council's capable of. But that's why you have to tell me.' I took her hand. 'If we don't find what they're looking for, we can't stop them. There'll be more tanks, and more killings. Until we're all tanked.' No more children in the holding house dormitory, no more voices in the courtyard. Just the silence of the tanks, and the children floating.

She was motionless, as if the tanks had come for her already.

'Do you know what Joe was hiding?' I said.

'Not what,' Elsa said. She straightened her shoulders and wiped her hands on her apron. 'But I think I know where.'

CHAPTER 24

She sat heavily on the bench. 'Just before they came for him, he was in a bad mood, but that wasn't unusual. He'd come across a stash of stuff the week before. Bought it, found it, or nicked it – he didn't say, and I didn't ask. He'd thought at first he was on to a good thing – thought it might be worth something for a change. But then he said it turned out to be nothing – just papers. Hard to sell, at least to Omegas. He couldn't read, himself – like most of us. I tried to teach him a bit, but he was never patient enough. Once, he might have tried to sell the papers to Alphas – they're just as curious about the Before as we are. He used to have a few Alpha contacts who traded with him from time to time. But it'd been years since he'd dealt with any of them. Since the drought years, and all the new Council reforms, you couldn't trust them not to turn you in for breaking the taboo. So he was having trouble shifting these papers. That's all I knew.'

'You never saw them?'

'I told you. I'd never have let him bring something like that into this house. At first, I thought the papers must've been in the storehouse. Thought the Council must have got them, before they burned it. But then I learned that they'd tortured him. And I remembered how they turned this place inside out. So I thought of the Kissing Tree.'

I looked at her blankly.

'He found it when he was a teenager,' she went on. 'We used to go there when we first met. I was living in a boarding house. Joe had the storehouse, but Greg was always hanging about there, under our feet. There wasn't ever much privacy. So he used to take me to the Kissing Tree.

'It's a huge tree, and hollow on the inside. Somewhere private, and out of the weather, at least.' She didn't look embarrassed – instead, for the first time since I'd returned to New Hobart, she gave her old grin. 'Joe even put up a little shelf. We used to keep candles there, and matches, a blanket. Even after we were married and I'd taken over running this place, we went there sometimes. Used to take a bit of a picnic, grab a moment away from the kids.' She exhaled slowly, making her way back through the years that had passed since then. 'We hadn't been there for ages, when they took him. Years and years. But it was our secret, that place. Just the two of us knew about it. And I know he used to keep stuff there sometimes, if he had something that he didn't want the Council patrols to get wind of. Or sometimes if he didn't want to give Greg a cut of something.'

'Where is it?'

'In the forest, south of here.'

I sat down beside her on the bench, head down, picturing those blackened stumps.

'Don't take it so hard,' Elsa said. 'You didn't burn the whole forest down. And even if the tree's gone, I don't even know for sure that there was anything hidden there.'

'You never checked?' I said.

'Haven't you been listening to me?' Elsa said. 'I saw them take him, and I found out what they did to him.' She shook her head slowly. 'The only reason I'd ever have gone within a mile of that place would be to burn the tree down myself, and anything in it.'

*

Zoe was still waiting outside, and she came with us to the tithe collector's office, to tell Piper and the others. They insisted that we take a small guard of resistance soldiers with us to the forest. There'd been no sign, yet, of Council troops massing close to the town, but we were taking no chances. At the southern gate, on The Ringmaster's orders, the soldiers issued us with horses. Zoe had to help me mount, and I braced my broken arm against my ribs, but couldn't stop my sharp intake of breath as she boosted me into the saddle. Elsa had never ridden before, so she sat behind me, clutching me tightly around the waist.

It had been three days since the battle, and our troops had gathered the bodies from where they'd fallen, but the earth was frozen solid and refused our dead, and there was no time for burials, anyway. When we rounded the hillock behind which we'd sheltered during the attack, I saw the mound of bodies, horses and humans alike. The snow was a map of death, red streaks showing where the carcasses had been dragged. Our soldiers had tried to burn the bodies, but the snow and the wet wood had hindered the flames, and most of the corpses were still whole. The snow had stopped them from rotting, I guessed, as well as burning - there was none of the rancid scent of decay. Instead, just the raw tang of blood, overlaid with the richness of charred flesh. Near the edge of the piled bodies, a fox, emboldened by its feast, stood watching us. He was not twenty feet from where our horses passed. I tried not to look at his red muzzle.

'Simon ordered the bodies dragged there,' said Zoe. 'It was the best option. Apart from anything else, it'll make it harder for the Council to use the hillock for cover if they mount an attack.'

All I could think of were Zach's words: *What are you offering them? You're offering war. Thousands will die.*

I couldn't see any of the white-shrouded bodies that Elsa and I had prepared. 'What about the children?' I said.

'They'll be burned,' said Zoe. 'The Ringmaster wanted them brought out here with the others. Said it was a waste of time, and oil, to burn the bodies properly. But Piper argued with him. He's got troops building pyres now, just inside the northern wall.'

Piper had saved my life many times, but I had never been as grateful as I was for this gesture.

As we rode on, I stopped myself from staring back at the unburied dead, but the snow beneath us on the plain continued to testify to what had passed there. A spray of blood, next to a broken sword. A boot lying empty. Elsa grabbed my waist more tightly when our horse skidded on a patch of red-edged ice.

It was a relief when the first of the burnt trunks began to pierce the snow.

'Nobody's going to be coming here for a picnic for a long time,' said Elsa, as we crossed the threshold of what had been the forest. 'The two of you really did a job on this place.'

The forest was only the beginning of the charred trail that I had left on the world. Now there were the half-burnt bodies, too, as well as those killed on the island. I wondered whether the Council soldiers had buried them, after the massacre, or if the dead still lay in the courtyard, baring their bones to the sky.

There were the bodies of the children, too, wrapped in white and stacked in the wagons like candles in a drawer. My twin had done this, not me. But they were bound to me now, as inexorably as he was. Perhaps Zach had been right when he'd said, on the road, that I was poison. It was hard to argue with the bodies that I had left behind me. I was a walking emissary of the deadlands, spreading ash wherever I went.

Elsa's breath was warm on my ear as she continued. 'When the forest was burning, even with the wind blowing from the north, we could hardly breathe for days – the smoke was so thick. But it slowed them down, all right. Between that and the protest at the market, we had the diversion we needed to get a few more people out of the town. At least a few that I knew of, wanted by the Council for various things, managed to get out when it all kicked off.' She leaned the side of her face into my back. 'When I saw the fire, I knew it was you and Kip.'

It took us a long time to find the tree. Elsa directed us straight to the forest's eastern flank, but the years and the fire had changed the place so much that she couldn't recognise the usual landmarks. We dismounted, leaving the horses with the guards, and wandered together amongst the black stumps and the few trees that had withstood the flames.

Elsa found it in the end. Before the fire, when the smaller trees around it were still standing, the Kissing Tree would have been less distinctive. Now it stood almost alone, the largest tree within sight. Like the trees that had surrounded it, the top of the tree had burned away, but its thick trunk wasn't so easily purged. We approached it, while the guards fanned out to form a loose circle around us, backs to us as they surveyed the area.

The trunk's surface was scorched, split into charcoal scales. The fire had stripped the tree's height, but not its width – the three of us, holding hands, couldn't have encircled it. At its base, the sides didn't meet – there was a gap, just a few feet wide and almost as tall. The trunk was a cloak falling open at the front, revealing the hollow within. Once, this would have provided a cave-like shelter, big enough for two people to lie in, if they curled close to each other. Now everything from six feet up was gone, and the tree's cave was roofless, a ringed space open to the snow.

'I'm sorry,' I said.

'They tortured my husband, Cass, and killed him. They drowned all my children, and killed Nina.' She gave a shrug and a small shake of her head. 'There's nothing a burnt-down tree can do to hurt me.'

Zoe dropped to all fours and peered through the gap in the tree. She crawled inside, and took several minutes there, craning around to survey the whole space. 'If Joe left anything in the tree itself, it's not here now, thanks to your stunt with the fire,' she called. She backed out and stood, dusting her knees. 'If he'd left something on the shelf, it's gone now. No sign of the shelf at all. The whole trunk's charred, inside and out.'

'So we dig,' I said. I dropped to my knees. I could use only my left arm. The snow and the top layer of dirt shifted easily, but within an inch or two my fingernails were snagging on frozen ground.

Elsa sighed as she knelt next to me. 'Joe was too lazy to bury anything properly. If there's anything here, at least it won't be buried deep.'

Zoe came to my other side, and the three of us dug

together. The gap was too narrow, and we got in one another's way, and the icy soil was tight-packed. After the first few minutes my left hand was so chilled that I couldn't feel my fingers anymore. It took us nearly an hour to clear a hole two feet deep and about as wide.

My chilled fingertips didn't feel the trunk when at last we reached it, but I heard the different sound that our scraping made. The shriek of our nails on rusted tin.

When we finally dug it free, it took all three of us to manoeuvre the trunk out of the hole. It was big – at least three feet wide, and two feet deep – and so heavy that I feared the contents must be totally waterlogged. The metal had lost any polished smoothness that it might once have had – it was furred with rust, an ochre and green patina that rasped beneath our fingers when we brushed the last twigs and dirt from the top. There was no lock, but rust had sealed the lid closed. It took Zoe a few minutes of levering with a knife, and one well-aimed kick, before the lid sprung open an inch.

I rocked back on my heels, and pulled Zoe back with me. 'Let Elsa look first,' I said.

'Don't worry,' Elsa said. 'I'm not expecting any love letters. I know my Joe – this'll be a stash of contraband, and nothing to do with me.'

The top of the trunk was clear of soil now, but she brushed it once again, more slowly this time. Then she lifted back the lid, which grated all the way, a husky sigh.

The trunk was crammed full of papers. The stacks of loose pages had merged together with mildew and age. I wondered if that was why I hadn't sensed the trunk beneath us, while we were digging – whether the mildew, rust and water had consumed it so completely that it felt indistinguishable from the earth around it.

Elsa peeled off a page from the top. Damp had thickened it so that it crackled when it bent.

She read out loud, speaking haltingly as she navigated the unfamiliar words. '*Yr. 1, Oct 23rd. Memorandum (14b) for Ark Interim Government: Security Protocols.*'

'Hell on earth,' said Zoe. 'We need to get a cart out here, and take this stuff back to Piper. Now.'

CHAPTER 25

We sent one of the guards back to the town for a cart. It was dark by the time we'd hauled the chest back to New Hobart and unloaded it at the tithe collector's office. Concealing our find from The Ringmaster wasn't an option – his soldiers were amongst the troops with us in the forest, and manning the gates of the town. But when we were all gathered in the meeting room, I saw how his top lip crept up in distaste when I opened the chest.

'I don't even want to touch this stuff,' he said, holding back slightly as the rest of us drew closer to the trunk.

'Elsa's husband didn't die from touching these papers,' I said. 'He died because your Council had him tortured to death. If you don't want to know what's in here, then stay out of our way.'

Piper lifted out the top sheet, and read it out loud. He had to pause over some of the strange words, and at sections when the paper had succumbed to mould, or simply crumbled away.

Yr. 1, Nov. 24th. MEMORANDUM (14b) FOR ARK INTERIM GOVERNMENT: SECURITY PROTOCOLS

. . . and preserving the security of the Ark remains our first priority. However, the condition of survivors on the surface (particularly the percentage of survivors whose retinal damage has left them effectively blind [> 65% – see report from Expedition 2]), allows us to conclude that the current security measures are adequate . . .

'It can't be real,' The Ringmaster said. We'd told him about Sally's Ark paper, but I understood his incredulity. Our whole world was built on the ashes of the Before. It seemed inconceivable that any part of The Before could have survived the blast, even if only for a while.

'How the hell did Joe get hold of all of this?' Zoe said, crouching by the trunk and lifting out more of the papers. 'He wasn't any kind of explorer, by the sounds of it. Not exactly the type to discover this Ark himself.'

'He never went further than the market towns within a few days' travel of here,' Elsa said. 'Not in the twenty years I knew him.'

Piper shrugged. 'Someone got those papers out of the Ark. Whoever stumbled upon the Ark first – perhaps even before the Council found it. Somewhere along the way these papers got lost, or stolen. They probably changed hands - who knows how many times, or whether the people who had the papers could even read them. Until finally they ended up with a low-level chancer like Joe. My guess is he had no idea what he'd stumbled onto.'

'He must've shown some of the papers to someone,' I said, 'when he was trying to fence the stuff. Someone who realised their importance – and they told the Council.'

'It doesn't matter how he found it, or how he was discovered,' The Ringmaster said. He had stepped further from the chest. 'What good can come of it? What good ever came out of the Before? The one thing that we know for certain about these people is that they, and their machines, destroyed the world. They brought about all of this.' His sweeping arm might have been intended to indicate the broken world beyond the walls. The rubble fields, the wreckage of taboo towns. The deadlands to the east. But we all knew what he really meant, when he spoke about the blighted world: us.

He went on: 'I freed this town because I wanted to uphold the taboo and stop the machines from being resurrected. What can this Ark offer us apart from more machines?'

'You're scared,' said Piper. 'Too afraid of the machines to think of what it could mean to us, if we find the Ark.'

'I am scared,' The Ringmaster said. He looked around at us all, one by one. 'If you knew what I knew, you'd be scared too. You should be grateful for the taboo. We all should. If your twin didn't have some idea of how much people feared the machines, he'd have done more than build the tanks. Even when I first met him, when he'd just come to Wyndham and hadn't even called himself The Reformer yet, he was already talking about some of the things they used to have, in the Before – machines and weapons that you can't even begin to imagine. He's always been curious about the Before. Think what you're doing, when you want to start poking around amongst this taboo stuff. If it weren't for the taboo, The Reformer's soldiers would've come after you in vehicles without horses, and a hundred times faster. They'd have overrun us at New Hobart with weapons that can kill a squadron of men half a mile away. You think he hasn't done his best to find these things out, and recreate them? Most of it he can't build again; it was all destroyed. The relics he's tracked down are incomplete. He used to talk a lot about fuel, and other materials he couldn't get hold of. But he knows such difficulties aren't the only obstacle. It's the taboo. If he came out of Wyndham tomorrow riding on some kind of electrical carriage, he'd be lynched. People wouldn't stand for it – the fear of the machines is too strong.' I remembered how Piper had paled when he stood in the shadow of the tanks; how even Zoe had moved warily around the hanging wires and the pipes. 'Knowing about the tanks is what's driven half the army over to me,' The Ringmaster said. 'People won't stand for the machines, not yet – and harnessing that fear is the only thing that gives us a chance to stand against your twin and The General.'

'You're right that the machines are dangerous,' I said. 'But it's more dangerous to ignore this. The Council wouldn't have cracked down so hard on Joe if they didn't have some idea of the significance of the papers. Xander said that there are people in the Ark again, wherever it is. I'd bet my life that Zach and The General have found the Ark, probably long ago. The papers in the trunk would be only a fraction of what the Ark must've held, and they're important enough to keep the Council searching.' I waved at the trunk that sat open before me. 'There could be maps of Elsewhere, in here, or of the Ark itself. Designs for weapons, maybe, or machines and medicines that could help Omegas. Who knows what else.'

'Exactly.' The Ringmaster spoke over me. 'You're messing with things that you can't understand.'

'She understands more than you know,' growled Sally. 'And you'd understand more if you let her speak.'

I tried to give my words the same certainty that I'd always

envied in Piper and Zoe. 'We can't stop Zach and The General unless we know what they're doing,' I said.

'I'm the one whose troops are standing between this town and certain defeat,' he said. My voice had been rising as we argued; his remained low and steady. It was more menacing than if he'd shouted. 'Without my soldiers, you'd be overrun in no time. Tanked, by the same machines that you want to seek out. The soldiers have followed me because they know I'm making a stand to protect them against the machines. If I betray that trust, we lose their loyalty, and New Hobart will fall.'

'There could be knowledge in this trunk that could change everything,' I said. 'Not just the kind of change you're used to thinking of, like a different ruler for the Council, or even a more merciful system of refuges and tithes. I mean real change. A chance to find out what the Before really was, and what they could do. Whether Elsewhere exists, and whether they do things differently there. The kind of thing that could change everything, forever. The kind of change that might have saved your wife, and your children.'

He stepped forward, and grabbed my wrist. 'Nothing's going to save them. How dare you even bring them into it?'

Piper and Zoe had both sprung forward, and I heard knives drawn, a sound like flints being struck. I kept my eyes fixed on The Ringmaster's. I was thinking of Elsa's words, in the holding house kitchen: *there will be more children.*

'You're right,' I said. 'Nothing can save them. But there are other wives, other husbands. Other children, not born yet. The question is whether you're too afraid of knowledge to give them a chance of a different world.'

For a long time he kept holding my wrist. Then, with a shove, he pushed me away.

'Take the papers. Search them. But I expect a full report of everything that you find.'

*

. . . Now we have reached Yr. 20, there can be no more deluding ourselves. The Ark's stated aim, prior to the detonations, of gathering the most distinguished in their respective fields, has inevitably resulted in a population of advanced age. There are now 1,280 people inside the Ark, of whom fewer than 20% are of breeding age. Since the detonations, there have been only 348 births, more than 70% of which occurred in the first decade. It is self-evident that there is no viable breeding population within the Ark. While our supplies will last for many further decades, and the nuclear power cells will outlast us all, the psychological effects of continued subterranean life are continuing to manifest in increasingly troubling ways. What, then, is the purpose in preserving the Ark's isolation from the surface, if the protected population cannot even offer any realistic prospect of perpetuating human existence?

was at its inception intended to be for the preservation of all people, not to provide a shelter for a privileged few. Even now, electricity for the Pandora Project is preserved at the expense of all other priorities. We, the undersigned, reiterate our hope that the Interim Government will re-focus its priorities on the pressing needs of the survivors outside the Ark, and indeed those within it, rather than continuing to prioritise the . . .

*

We had the trunk hauled to Elsa's place, where I could work in peace, and away from the constant interruptions of the tithe collector's office, where sentries and couriers came and went both day and night. I was glad, too, to be back with Elsa, although Piper and Zoe insisted on posting a sentry at the holding house door, and another in the alley behind the courtyard. I didn't object – I was just relieved to be away from the tithe collector's office, and the web of allegiances and suspicions that filled those oversized rooms. Simon, Piper, Sally, and The Ringmaster presided there, interviewing scouts, defusing disputes between their troops, and arguing over our next steps. And even in the hubbub of the meeting room, I was aware that The Ringmaster watched me constantly.

It was a respite, too, to be away from the mutterings of Xander. He never troubled me deliberately – indeed, he showed little interest in anyone but Sally – but when he drooled, or babbled about *The Rosalind* coming back, I found myself scrutinising my own hands for signs of his twitching movements. I noticed that Zoe, too, avoided him, and I couldn't bring myself to blame her, knowing how I flinched from him too.

At the holding house I moved into the dormitory, where there was room to spread out the documents, and attempted to arrange them into some kind of order. I started by laying the papers out on the empty beds; soon the floor too was claimed, the documents covering every surface as if the snow from the courtyard had crept inside. I kept one bed clear, for sleeping in, but had to pick my way to it through an obstacle course of papers. My arm still bound in a sling, I spent my days and most of my nights squatting on the floor, bent over the pages.

Elsa came to the dormitory when her work at reassembling

the holding house permitted, and sat with me for a while as I read. She'd never been to school, and although over the years she'd taught herself the basics of reading, it was a painstaking process for her. These papers made reading doubly difficult: each word had to be extricated from the mess of mould and holes, so that it was a process of piecing together rather than reading. After a few initial attempts to read them, she stopped trying. She still came to sit with me, though. She would take up one of the stacks of paper, coax apart the mildewed pages, and then hold them on her lap. Always she'd been brisk and busy when children had filled the holding house. But in the paper-strewn dormitory she was still. Her hands, red and scratched from scrubbing and sweeping the trashed building, were motionless for once, as she held the papers that had led Joe to his death.

While she sat with me, I worked in silence. The things that we had in common – the children, Nina, and Kip – were also the things that we couldn't bear to discuss. But we'd learned to navigate each other's silences, and there was a comfort in those quiet hours together in the dormitory, or the meals eaten in the cold kitchen.

Most of the time, though, I was alone, with the papers and my visions for company. It was the variety of the documents that made them so frustrating. Sometimes I was able to piece together a few fragments that seemed to belong together, even if they weren't consecutive pages. But more often the pages seemed to be gathered from completely unrelated documents. Some were ripped in half, while others had succumbed to damp, the creeping black mould hard to distinguish from the writing itself. On the island, I'd seen the children work at untangling fishing nets. The process of salvaging the words from the damaged papers felt the same: a disentangling. Even amongst those that were intact, there were often words, or whole passages, that I couldn't understand. But I could figure out enough to sort them roughly into different piles. Many were labelled *report* or *memorandum*, *appendix* or sometimes *briefing paper*, and used the same dry, convoluted language as the document that Sally had found all those decades ago. Many others, page after page, were simply lists of numbers, or diagrams that I couldn't decipher.

Even the paper itself was unfamiliar. Except where the mildew had furred it, it was very smooth under my touch, and so thin the writing on the other side was visible when I held it up to the light. The pages left a fine dust on my fingers, and some of them disintegrated in my hands. Those that looked on the point of falling apart I had to transcribe anew, even the columns of numbers and symbols that meant nothing to me. It was clumsy work, with my left hand.

A few of the papers were dated. Whatever the date had been before the blast had been rendered irrelevant, along with everything else. These papers started at Year 1, and the latest date that I found was Year 58. But even amongst those that were undated, it was often possible to trace the trajectory of the years by the form the documents took. The earliest were printed, the letters smaller and more uniform than any printing I'd seen before. But no documents dated Year 43 or after were printed – from then on, the people of the Ark had reverted to handwriting. Often, papers had been reused, the margins and spaces in the earlier printed documents crammed with added writing, hand-written letters and numbers jostling one another all the way to the edge of the page. Each page told a double story.

*

Yr. 38, March 12. MEMORANDUM (18b): RE. PROLIFERATION OF TWINS (TOPSIDE).

Amongst survivors Topside, anecdotal reports of infertility (or of non-viable births) remain high, and expeditions (see Appendix 6) have gathered evidence of the high rates of miscarriage, stillbirth, or of non-viable infants dying shortly after birth. However, Expeditions 48-9 reported higher rates of successful births, marked by a sudden prevalence of twins (fraternal, XX/XY). The significant aspect of this new phenomenon is the rise in healthy infants, though not uniformly

in each case witnessed by the expeditions (and in 17 further cases reported to them, but unconfirmed) one primary twin is produced, free of any mutations, while the secondary twin manifests the mutation in a more severe form

econdary twins the deformations were all ranked at category 7 or above. Examples noted by Expedition 49 included: polymelia; amelia; polydactyly; syndactyly (in many cases, the twins presented with both [polysyndactyly]); gonadal dysgenesis; achondroplasia; neurofibromat

reported that the primary twin is not only entirely free of deformations, but performing better than the median on all indicators (strength; lung-capacity; resistance to viral & bacterial infections). These

are the most viable subjects yet produced – the
regrettable side effect of the secondary twins
notwithstanding.

can arguably be characterised as a drastic
genetic response, essentially compensatory in nature, to
the sustained exposure to residual radiation

by which, in order to create
a viable subject (the primary twin), the mutations are
effectively displaced onto the secondary twin, who may
be viewed as an unfortunate (but necessary)
epiphenomenon.

*

After four days, Sally brought Xander to the holding house, to see if he could tell us anything about the documents. We guided him slowly through the dormitory, the floor paved with stacks of papers. In the centre of the room, he looked around him and nodded.

'It smells like the maze of bones,' he said.

'The Ark?' Sally prompted him.

'I told you they were looking,' he said.

'And this is it?' I said. 'This is what they were looking for?' I gestured at the pages, yellowed like old teeth.

But he only said again: 'It's not finished.'

'What's not finished?' I said, taking both of his hands. 'Which of these papers is the one we need?'

Xander sniffed, scrunching his face into a grimace.

'Smells like the maze of bones,' he said. He lifted one elbow high, tucking his face into his shoulder, while the other arm jerked from side to side, as if keeping something at bay. As he spun towards Sally, his foot swiped the nearest pile of papers, sending them skidding under a bed. We had to drag him from the room before he damaged any more. Even as Sally was helping him across the courtyard I could hear him shouting. *Maze of bones. Forever fire.*

It took me more than an hour to reassemble the papers that he had kicked. When I finally slept, amidst my visions of the blast and of Kip's floating body, I dreamed of the crackle of paper, and the scent of mildew and ink.

*

. . . *clearly cannot be considered a localised phenomenon. This is consistent with the reports of the most recent expeditions (40 & 41) which observed the proliferation of twins as far east as*

Note 5: The improved health of the primary babies does not mean that we should be complacent – high infant mortality rates are still prevalent Topside. Interviews with Topside survivors report several instances in which even the primary twins who had appeared in good health have died suddenly. Given that these reported deaths were concurrent with the death of the secondary twins, who had previously been unwell, the most likely cause is some environmental factor, or an (as yet unidentified) acute virus. However, these reports are based on a sample size that is statistically insignificant. . . the taskforce remains confident that subsequent monitoring will show that the proliferation of multiple births will lead to an increase in both the (viable) population and life expectancy . . .

*

Every few days Piper came for me. 'It's not healthy,' he said, 'just locking yourself away here.' He dragged me out for walks to the tithe collector's office, or around the town, and questioned me about everything I'd found in the papers.

The streets of New Hobart had resumed a kind of normality. The broken shutters had been taken down, the windows nailed shut with rough-hewn planks to keep out the snow. The bakery had reopened, and a few stallholders once again traded in the market square. But it was a strange kind of freedom that we'd won for the town. The Council soldiers had been cast out, but The Ringmaster's troops wore the same uniform, and still patrolled the walls.

Patrols of Omegas now joined them, taking shifts on the town's defences. Simon's troops had been boosted by new Omega recruits from within the town. But the Alpha and Omega patrols bickered over shifts and duties. On one of our evening walks, Piper had stopped by the eastern gate to speak to some Omega troops who had just come in from a patrol. Waiting for him, I overheard one of The Ringmaster's soldiers mocking the legless archer who was replacing her in the sentry tower for the next shift.

'What are you going to do if the wall gets breached?' the departing sentry said to him, as she watched him haul himself up the ladder to the tower. 'Drag yourself into battle against mounted troops?'

The Omega didn't reply, and kept hoisting himself up the wooden struts, bow slung over his shoulder.

There'd also been scuffles and brawls between The Ringmaster's soldiers and the residents they were supposed to be protecting. There were arguments, for instance, because The Ringmaster had wanted to maintain the identity papers. Piper told me that a large group of residents had gathered on the steps of the tithe collector's office and fed their papers to a bonfire. The remnants of the fire were still there the next day, a black smudge on the snow.

The town's residents were free to come and go now. Many took what they could carry and headed east. Hundreds so far, Piper said, and probably more who'd leave if they had anywhere to go, and if the winter were less harsh. I couldn't blame them for leaving. We all knew a counter-attack was likely. Our scouts and lookouts were already reporting Council troops gathering, only miles from the walls. They hadn't encircled the town – and The Ringmaster was confident that he could match the Council's numbers if it came to another battle, or an outright siege. But it never did. The Council's soldiers simply watched and waited.

Within the town all the soldiers were on edge, Alpha and Omega alike. Without the urgency of battle, this was what they were left with: patrolling in the wind and snow. Poor rations, since traders were still avoiding New Hobart and the early snow had damaged the winter crops. It was a ruthless winter, and fuel for fires was scarce. The nearest stretches of the forest had been burnt, and many townsfolk were reluctant to venture far from the walls, with the Council's soldiers gathering. In the streets, Piper and I passed people bent under loads of wood salvaged from destroyed buildings. Many of the residents were injured from fighting in the battle; all were thin, their winter clothes not disguising bony wrists and gaunt faces. I was reminded, again and again, of Zach's words: *What are you offering them?* I'd thought that the battle, and the pyre of half-burnt bodies, was as bad as it would get. But this had its own horrors, the drawn-out drabness of war when the fighting had paused.

There were a few moments, though, that pierced the bleakness of those weeks. Once, walking with Piper past the burnt-out space where a house used to stand, we saw three Omega teenagers kicking a ball to one another. When the ball rolled close to the fence, one of The Ringmaster's younger soldiers kicked it back to them, and ended up joining their game. Within a few minutes his squadron leader had called him, and the soldier didn't look back as he jogged away, but I saw how he raised his hand over his shoulder as he ran, in a careless farewell gesture. Another day, outside the farrier's barn where the patrol horses were re-shod, we saw an Omega soldier helping to catch a horse that had bolted. When he passed the reins back to the Alpha soldier, the man took them without flinching, and they rolled their eyes together as they muttered about the farrier's clumsy apprentice who had startled the horse. It was hardly reconciliation – just a few words exchanged in the snowy street, and over in moments. But small interactions like that gave me as much hope as anything we'd achieved in the battle.

But these moments alone would not be enough – not with the Council and its machines massing against us. Elsewhere and the Ark were still our greatest hopes. 'We should be sending more scouts back to the coast,' I said, again and again, when I joined the others in their discussions in the tithe collector's office. 'We should be fitting out some more ships, to seek out Elsewhere.'

'We're fully stretched as it is,' said The Ringmaster. 'Not just defending this town – there've been skirmishes from Wyndham to the coast. Every garrison that's declared itself loyal to me is having to fend off the Council's soldiers.'

I looked to Piper to back me up, but he looked away. Even he had become silent on the topic of Elsewhere, since Zach had tossed the beheaded figureheads at our feet.

When I pressed him, Piper shook his head. 'If Elsewhere's

out there, the Ark's our best chance at some real information. Even if we had the resources right now, I can't send more boats out there, blindly.' He looked down at his hand. 'I've sent enough of my people to their deaths,' he said, 'on sea and on land.'

When Xander began to mutter again about *The Rosalind* coming home, we hadn't the heart to tell him what we knew.

*

Yr 49, Nov. 23. LOGISTICAL BRIEFING

Damp has now penetrated Section B, and is affecting both wiring and ventilation. Maintenance team to attempt re-sealing around ventilation ducts, but Walsh says the subsidence in Section A caused by the detonations rules out any access to s

Surface Expedition 61: radiation readings unchanged. Still consistently higher to the east (from Camp 3 onwards). No survivors seen past camp 5.

The psychiatric ward (Section F) is increasingly difficult to manage now that Valium is in short supply. At least half of the patients should be housed in the secure unit (D) but since the generator failure in Section D, this isn't an option. Still awaiting response from Interim Govt. re our repeated requests to divert some auxiliary power from Pandora Project (not just for lighting but also fridges – food now stored in pathology fridge along with . . .

CHAPTER 26

Zoe, Piper, Simon, and The Ringmaster were gathered in the dormitory. I was used to seeing them holding court in the tithe collector's office. Here, perched on the children's creaking beds, amidst the piles of papers, they looked incongruous. Only The Ringmaster refused to sit, standing at the foot of one of the beds, arms crossed over his chest.

It had taken me three weeks to finish reading and sorting the papers. There was still a lump in my forearm, and I couldn't put weight on my wrist without a jab of pain, but I'd stopped using the splint, and could use my hand well enough.

'This one is the first mention of the twins,' I said.

Piper took the sheet that I'd passed him, and read out loud.

Yr. 38, March 12. (18b): RE. PROLIFERATION OF TWINS (TOPSIDE).

'*Topside?*' He looked up at me.

'That's here.' I gestured at the window. 'Above ground,

I mean. In the earlier papers, they call it *the surface*. But later it seems just to become *Topside*.'

'That's us, isn't it,' Piper said, his finger holding his place on the page. 'When they talk about *secondary twins*. That's the Omegas.'

I watched them as they read about the first appearance of the Omegas:

Examples noted by Expedition 49 included: polymelia; amelia; polydactyly; syndactyly (in many cases, the twins presented with both [polysyndactyly]); gonadal dysgenesis; achondroplasia; neurofibromat . . .

It was as though the mutations were so horrifying that they couldn't be contained by ordinary words, and the writer had needed a whole new language to describe them. I watched Piper as he read, and wondered which of those garbled terms, if any, referred to his single arm. Or to my seer's mind, jerking backwards and forwards through time.

Piper's and Zoe's heads were bent at the same angle, their eyes moving in unison as they scanned each line.

. . . a drastic genetic response, essentially compensatory in nature, to the sustained exposure to residual radiation . . . by which in order to create a viable subject (the primary twin), the mutations are effectively displaced onto the secondary twin, who may be viewed as an unfortunate (but necessary) epiphenomenon.

'I don't know what half of that means,' Zoe said. 'More than half of it. *Genetic? Epiphenomenon?*'

'Me either,' said Piper. 'But it seems to be the same thing we've always thought, doesn't it? That we evolved this way so that the species could survive. That we Omegas carry the burden of the mutations, from the blast.'

I nodded. I was remembering The General's words to us during our meeting on the road, just a few weeks earlier: *You're a side effect of us. Nothing more.* Had she read these same papers, or similar ones?

'This is the bit you really need to see,' I said, picking up a page from the far end of the bed. It was delicate, a lacework of paper and holes. Instead of passing it to them, I read it out loud.

Yr. 46, Dec. 14. BRIEFING PAPER RE. TOPSIDE TWINS: TREATMENT OPTIONS

The ongoing study into the continued simultaneous twin deaths observed Topside confirms a link that goes beyond any existing understanding of twins (either dizygotic or monozygotic). While the mechanism for this link remains unclear, we have been able to establish that the twinning itself is susceptible to treatment. With the correct medical regime (see Appendix B for medication list) for primary twins, the twinning should be reversible in future generations. This treatment, in conjunction . . .

Piper interrupted me. 'The medicines that they mention – the list,' he said. 'Was that in the trunk?'

I shook my head. 'If it once was, it's gone now. It could be in the Ark – or destroyed altogether.'

'And there's nothing more on that page?'

'Nothing.' The writing petered out, overtaken by mould. I looked up, to see whether the convoluted words had managed to communicate their meaning. The silence in the room was loaded, heavy with more than dust.

Zoe spoke first. 'No wonder they killed Joe. Bloody hell. A way to undo the twinning.'

They were all standing now. Zoe's hand was squeezing Piper's shoulder. Simon was slowly shaking his head, a smile spreading on his face. The Ringmaster's eyes were narrowed, his brows drawn together.

'It's not as straightforward as that,' I said. They should have known that there were no simple solutions in our blast-warped world. 'Listen.' I read on.

However, in consultation with the Interim Government's Surface Directives group (see Appendix A), the taskforce has debated the advisability of this treatment programme, given that while the resulting subjects will not be twinned, they will nonetheless continue to manifest mutations. The treatment that brings about the cessation of the twinning is likely to mitigate the worst of the mutations, meaning that the subsequent (untwinned) subjects should demonstrate fewer of the most adverse mutations currently present in the Secondary twins. Nonetheless, our modelling suggests that mutations are likely to be pervasive.

One argument cited in favour of the treatment is the fact that autopsies have shown that the mutations in Secondary twins included (in all cases) a complete malfunction of the internal reproductive system – an obvious obstacle to repopulation. However, some in the Surface Directives group maintained that this is a pragmatic evolutionary limiting of the mutations.

'*A pragmatic evolutionary limiting of the mutations,*' Piper echoed. 'Sounds like they were glad, some of them, that we can't breed. It's the Alphas all over again, isn't it – seeing us as something degraded, less than human.'

I nodded. 'That's why they argue about undoing the bond – because it would put an end to Alphas, as well as Omegas. They say that there'd still be deformities. In everyone, by the sound of it. But not as serious as those we have now.'

'And Omegas would be able to breed, if they have this medicine?' Zoe said.

'There wouldn't be any Omegas,' I said. 'No Alphas, either. Just people.'

'But all with mutations,' The Ringmaster said. 'All of them?'

I nodded. 'That's what it says.'

'And the Ark people chose to risk the whole species dying out,' said Piper, 'rather than to see it continue with mutations.'

He was looking at The Ringmaster, as if daring him to defend the Ark-dwellers' decision. The Ringmaster met his gaze, but remained silent.

'It only talks about future generations,' Zoe said, gingerly taking the paper from me to read it for herself. 'There's nothing about undoing the bond, or fixing the infertility, for twins already born?'

'No.' I looked at her. If there had been a way to sever the bond between her and Piper, would she choose to?

Piper interrupted my thoughts. 'So was that it? They knew how to fix the twinning, but they couldn't agree to do it?'

'Getting consensus wasn't the only problem,' I said. 'There were other reasons, too.' I picked up the next page and passed it to Zoe. She read aloud:

The proposed treatment itself is not innately complex, but implementation presents some significant issues, exacerbated by the scattered population of Topside survivors.

These issues include the supply, storage and distribution of the drugs. Our projections show that current stores in the Ark should produce enough of the compound for >5,000 patients (allowing for proposed treatment schedule of 3 doses each, as per Fegan and Blair's findings). However, the drug requires refrigeration and

main obstacle to implementing the mass treatment regime remains the growth in technophobic sentiment that has been witnessed Topside. Outside the Ark itself, the technology that survived the blast has been systematically destroyed. Several expeditions have reported hostile responses to medical testing, with equipment seized and destroyed on 3 occasions. Two of the latest expedition teams have not returned. Given the multiple innate risks of the outside environment, it would be premature to attribute their disappearance to the violent purges of technology that have been witnessed Topside. Nonetheless, this remains a pressing and valid concern.

'That's the taboo,' I said. 'The survivors turning against the machines.'

'You can hardly blame them for it,' said The Ringmaster. 'They'd had to live with the consequences of the blast.'

'Not only that,' I said. 'They had another good reason to be afraid of the Ark dwellers and their machines.'

I moved to the next bed, where I'd laid out a trail of papers, all covered by the same handwriting. The writer had been messy – his handwriting itself had presented almost as much of a challenge as the damp, crumbling paper.

'These pages are all written by the same person. *Professor Heaton*, it says here. And he talks about how they actually did their experiments.'

*Thanks to the work of Professors Fegan and Blair, there is
still a chance for the Ark project to prove its worth. We
have it within our power to repair the twinning process that
is now near-universal on the surface. Blair and Fegan's
results consistently show that this treatment would, with
careful management of our existing resources, be
achievable (at least for the region immediately surrounding
the Ark), and should significantly reduce mortality rates and
rates of severe disability for subsequent generations.*

*The manner in which this research was conducted
(regarding which I have already registered my objections,
both in person and through the official grievance
procedures) is an issue for another time. Notwithstanding
these ethical concerns, the results of the study are now
available to us and it would be foolhardy in the extreme
to fail to act upon them.*

'What does he mean, *the manner in which this research
was conducted*?' said Zoe.

'Here,' I said, passing her the next sheet.

Piper leaned close over her shoulder as they read.

*Of the many issues relating to Fegan and Blair's research,
the use of non-consenting subjects from Topside has
been the most egregious ethical breach. Given the
exhaustive security protocols surrounding entry and exit
from the Ark, the admission of these experimental
subjects to the Ark could not have occurred without
approval from the highest level, meaning that not only
those directly involved in the project, but also the Interim
Government itself, are complicit in what is not merely an
ethical failure, but (given the high mortality rate of the
subjects) an appalling crime.*

'So they took people from Topside and experimented on them,' Piper said. 'Killed some, or all, of them.' When he was angry like this, I was reminded of how intimidating he could be. It wasn't only his height, or the bulk of him. It was lack of doubt in his green eyes. The absolute sureness of his fury.

'And all the time they were doing it, we were still the ones they were afraid of,' I said. 'Locking themselves away, worried about their *security protocols* to protect themselves from us.' My truncated, bleak laugh echoed in the dormitory.

Despite my misgivings about the research undertaken on the twins, I had nonetheless hoped that the ends would justify the extraordinary means. However, if the results of that study are to remain academic, simply to satisfy the curiosity of those within the Ark (or to be preserved exclusively for our own potential future use) then there can be no possible justification. I urge you, as a representative of the Interim Government, to reconsider this decision, and to implement the treatment that could dramatically improve the lives of the Topside survivors, as well as giving them the best chance of repopulation.

This is not the first time I have asked the Interim Government to reconsider their attitude to the Topside survivors, and nor am I the only Ark citizen to express concern on this issue. If the resources (principally, the power generators) currently devoted to the Pandora Project were diverted to the mass treatment of survivors Topside, we could expect to see results by the next generation.

I watched the lines between Piper's eyebrows deepen as he concentrated; the way Zoe bit at her bottom lip as she deciphered the words. They were so alike, and so oblivious to it.

'They didn't do it,' I said, 'because they didn't think it was important enough. Because they were too busy focusing on themselves, and too scared of the survivors on the surface. And things had started to fall apart for them, down there.'

I led them to a trail of papers that stretched to the far wall. These sheets, crowded with crabbed letters filling every inch, traced the final years of the Ark. It wasn't only the change from print to handwriting, or the crowded reuse of paper, that marked these documents as later. The changes in the language were just as telling.

'The earlier documents are all stiff, formal,' I explained. '*Memorandum* this and *postulate* that. Nothing like the way people actually talk to one another. Some of the papers stay like that – the technical ones, especially. But in most of the others, the language changes. It starts to get scrappy. Desperate. Look.'

I passed Piper a handful of the later sheets, criss-crossed with the scrawled notes. The reports became starker, and more curt, as if the language itself had been burnt away.

Springfield baby born – male, healthy, 7lb6oz – but mother can't (won't?) breastfeed.

Lights failing on F. Wing – all remaining residents to temp. accomm. in B. Wing. Electrical curfew 1800h-0600h for all citizens (excluding Section A [Pandora Project] and Mess Hall fridges).

'Do you expect me to feel sorry for these people?' Zoe said. 'They chose. They sealed themselves away in comfort, more or less, while the world above them burned. They didn't help the survivors on the surface. They just studied them, like a kid catching ants in a jar.'

'I know,' I said. 'I'm not saying they were good people.

I'm just trying to show you what happened – how things went wrong down there. More and more of them started to go mad, I think, from being underground for so long. Listen:'

> *Sector F now sealed, to contain those patients whose instability can no longer be managed, and who present an acute security risk to the rest of the Ark population. The quadrant has been stripped of all weapons, but the Interim Govt has generously outfitted the quadrant with food, and the water supplies remain connected. Electricity (excluding ventilation) has been disconnected, to prioritise the needs of the rest of the population.*
>
> *Surface release was considered but was not a viable option, given security concerns should they interact with Topside survivors.*
>
> *All doors and hatches have been permanently sealed. Given the acute nature of their condition, it is not expected that their containment will be prolonged.*

'They hide everything in this language, don't they,' I said. '*Residents* – prisoners, that's what they mean. *Not expected that their containment will be prolonged.* They'll all be dead soon, that means – they were expecting the mad ones to kill themselves, or one another.'

'You think they're the only ones who hide stuff behind soft language?' Piper said. 'They still do it today, the Alphas. Think of the *refuges*.'

It's not just the Alphas, I thought, remembering all the times I'd taken shelter in the gap between word and thing. I'd done it when I told Piper and Zoe about Kip's death. *He's gone*, I'd said. Those words contained nothing of the truth of that moment, or of his death. They were clean, neat. There'd been nothing neat about how he'd lain on the concrete floor, his body broken as irrevocably as an egg. Words were bloodless symbols we relied on to keep the world at bay. When Simon's scouts had ridden out to muster troops for the battle at New Hobart, they would have carried a message: battle; freedom; uprising. Nothing about swords swiping at guts, or piles of bodies half-charred in the snow.

'We're nothing like the Ark people,' Zoe said. 'They buried these people alive, the ones they locked in Section F. Either they ripped one another to pieces, or they starved, if they survived long enough.'

'They were all buried alive,' I said. 'Not just the mad ones who they locked up. Everyone in the Ark, in the end: trapped underground. Running out of light, then food.'

'It still would have been better than being on the surface,' Piper said. 'The survivors there didn't just have the blast to cope with. They had the Long Winter, and all the bleak years afterwards.'

He was right. And because there was no Ark for those people, and no records, we would never know what it was like for them, in those first decades on the surface. Over the years, I'd heard bards sing a handful of songs of the Long Winter. They'd sung of radiation that scrambled babies in the womb. There were stories of infants born without nostrils or a mouth, unable to breathe, meeting their death at the moment of their birth. Children who were melted masses of flesh and half-formed bones. The body as a puzzle that couldn't be solved. But we would never know the full horror of that time. Even the stories that came down to us were as twisted as the babies who'd been born in those years.

'Why did they stay down in the Ark so long?' Simon said. 'More than fifty years, if those dates are right. After a few decades the radiation wasn't so bad. Their own reports say so. I'm not saying it was a picnic up here, but things were growing again. The survivors were managing to breed. Those people could've come out.'

'It wasn't the world on the surface they were frightened of,' said Piper. 'It wasn't even the radiation. It was us.' He looked at his own left shoulder, from which no arm grew. 'You've heard what the Alphas call us, and they're used to us.'

I'd heard the catcalls, even within the walls of New Hobart in the last few weeks. They were familiar to any Omega: *Freak. Dead end.*

'You read it yourself,' Piper went on. 'You've seen how the people in the Ark argued about whether it's even worth fixing the twinning. They thought a race of people with mutations, people like us, might not be worth saving. Might be worse than the whole race dying out. That's why they stayed down there. They were hiding from us,' he said. 'And from the risk of becoming like us.'

CHAPTER 27

I returned to the pile of papers covered by Professor Heaton's distinctive scrawl.

'Not everyone in the Ark had given up on the surface survivors. Heaton kept writing about the untwinning, and arguing for it. He wasn't the only one.' I showed them the appeal written in Year 20, which made it clear that there was no prospect of the Ark residents continuing to breed and survive underground, and that at least some of them wanted to help the Topside survivors.

'This man,' Zoe said. 'Professor. He wrote –'

'That's not his name. Lots of the people in the Ark are Professors. It's some kind of title – like Councillor, I suppose. He's Professor Heaton.'

'And he wrote all this?' she gestured at the masses of paper bearing his crabbed handwriting.

'Yes.'

I guided them through my rough classification system. A big bundle of the papers in Joe's trunk had been Professor Heaton's. Another large collection was nothing but diagrams, blue lines intricately inked, to form shapes and designs that

I could not decipher. The largest grouping of papers, though, contained only numbers: column after column, zeroes in rows like blind eyes staring back at me. A few of the columns were labelled, but the words meant nothing to me: *Curie (Ci); Roentgen (R); Radiation Absorbed Dose (RAD)*. I remembered how The Confessor had spoken about the machines, using words that I'd never heard before. *Generators. Algorithms.* She had managed to become fluent in the language of the machines. To the rest of us, these words were just strings of letters.

'These don't tell us anything,' said Piper, throwing down another page of impenetrable numbers.

'They do,' I said. 'They confirm that the people in the Ark could do things that we can't. We know they were capable of preventing the twinning, even if they chose not to do it. If we could find the Ark, piece together more information, and get our best people working on this, we could do it. It could take years and years. Generations, maybe. But think of what Zach and the Council have been able to do, with the tanks.'

'You think that's something to aspire to?' The Ringmaster's words were like a whip, snapping at the air between us.

'You're deliberately misinterpreting me,' I said. 'You know what I meant. The tanks are hellish – but they show that we can do things with machines that we couldn't even imagine.'

'We don't need to imagine it,' Piper said. 'We have to live with it.'

'The machines have done terrible things,' I said, my voice rising. 'But we've lived in fear of them for so long, we haven't considered the possibility that they could also do amazing things.'

'You're sounding more and more like your brother,' The Ringmaster said.

'You know me better than that,' I said. 'The technology from the Ark can fix the twinning. If we find it, then we could change everything.'

'But can we? Find it, I mean,' Piper said. 'None of this counts for anything if we can't do that. If you're right, and the Council's found it, then your brother's probably been there. He could be there now, for all we know. Can't that help to lead you there?'

I exhaled heavily. 'Not so far. I've looked and looked, and there's nothing like a map, or even the names of any locations. And I've tried and tried to feel it.'

They were all watching me.

'You found your way to the island – even from hundreds of miles away,' The Ringmaster said.

'I know,' I snapped. 'But I'm not a machine. I'd been hearing about the island all my life, and dreaming about it for years. I'd never even imagined this Ark.'

There had been moments, during those long days and nights amongst the papers, that I'd thought I could start to feel something – some kind of pull towards the Ark. But to my erratic seer visions, the Ark was nothing more than a scent carried to me on the wind – enough to make me raise my head and sniff, but not enough to draw me in a specific direction.

'Being a seer doesn't work the way you want it to,' I said to The Ringmaster. 'It never has. Do you think, if I could control it, I'd be waking up screaming every day from the visions of the blast?'

I was grateful when Zoe changed the subject. 'Xander said he'd heard noises in the Ark. You haven't found anything to suggest that those people could have bred, and survived?'

I shook my head. 'Not for four hundred years, down there.' The last document that I'd found was dated Year

58. By then, things were already falling apart. In whole sections of the Ark the Electric had broken. They were living in darkness and damp. Almost all of them were old, and the madness had been spreading like the damp. 'They couldn't have clung on much longer. Xander said it used to feel quiet, and now that's changed. *People rattling the bones.* The original Ark dwellers didn't survive. If Xander says he can feel people again in the Ark, it's more proof that the Council's found it.'

'Then why haven't they acted on it?' Simon said. 'If the Council knows it's possible to end the twinning, and prob-ably know how, why aren't they doing it? They hate being bonded to us, even more than we do to them. They tried experiments and breeding programmes for decades – Sally and the other infiltrators confirmed that, when they were working inside the Council. And that was decades ago. Why try so hard to end it, for so long, and then not act on the solution, if they discovered it?'

'Because the Ark hasn't given them the perfect solution they were after,' I said, gesturing at the papers. 'Even assuming that they were able to replicate what the people in the Ark could do, that doesn't end the mutations – only the twinning. Everyone would have mutations, not just Omegas. They mightn't be as severe as the mutations we have now, but there'd be no flawless Alphas, either.'

'You really think they'd rather be bound to Omegas than see all their children with mutations?' Piper said. Next to him, Zoe's arms were folded across her chest.

'That's not the choice they have to make anymore,' I said. 'The tanks have changed everything. Now, they think they have a different choice. They can end the twinning, and everyone has to bear the burden of the mutations. Or keep the fatal bond, and tank the Omegas, so they have the best of both worlds. All the benefits of their strong, perfect Alpha bodies, risk-free, their Omega twins safely tanked.'

Piper exhaled heavily. 'They're not so different from the Ark people, are they,' he said. 'All those centuries ago, they had the chance to end the twinning, and they didn't take it either.'

Zoe's eyes were hard. 'I don't feel bad that they all died down there, in the rat-hole they'd created.'

'Not all of them.' I lifted one more document. It was one of the cross-hatched papers. The handwritten words were slotted in the gaps between printed rows of numbers, headed *Radiation readings: Surface Expedition 11.*

'This is the last thing I could find of Heaton's. It doesn't have his name, but it's his writing, I'm sure.'

I read it aloud.

July 19, Yr 52.
Attn: Interim Government.

Due to your continued failure to assist survivors Topside, despite repeated requests (both from me, and from others who have undertaken the increasingly rare surface expeditions), my role in the Ark is no longer reconcilable with either the oath I took as a doctor, or my personal conscience. In accepting a position in the Ark, I believed I was becoming part of a historic project necessary for the survival of our species. However, given the refusal of the government to assist those left Topside, let alone to implement the treatment that could stop the twinning, to remain in the Ark would be an act of selfishness. Now that surface expeditions have effectively been discontinued, there is no longer even any pretence that the Ark exists for the broader benefit of those

*I therefore resign my post with immediate
effect. By the time you find this, I will have left the Ark.
I do not expect to survive long, Topside. I entered the
Ark as a young man and now I am old, and in poor
health. But I hope nevertheless to be of some use to
those survivors I encounter in the time I have remaining.*

*I have no illusions that I will be
much missed in the Ark. In recent years I have been
increasingly ostracised, and have been characterised as
an 'agitator' or 'dissident', and even had my mental
health impugned, as a result of my objections to the
continued prioritisation of The Pandora Project, when
those resources could better be used to ease the
suffering of the Topside population, and to . . .*

Heaton's words disappeared in a blur of copper-green mould. The springs of the bed squeaked as I bent and placed the page carefully back on the pile.

'He was one person,' Zoe said. 'One old man, who finally left. How much could he really have helped them, on the surface?'

'Perhaps not much,' I said. 'But I'm glad he tried, at least. I wish I knew what had happened to him.'

There was no time to indulge in speculation. Piper was already on his knees and beginning to rifle through the papers laid out near him. 'This *Pandora Project* comes up again and again,' he said. 'Aren't there any more details about it?'

I shook my head. 'Only the mentions that I've already shown you. It comes up often enough to show that it was important to them. Even when things were falling apart, they were protecting it, keeping it going.'

'Then that's what we need to find,' Piper said.

*

For the rest of the day, and well into the night, the four of them worked their way through the papers that I'd sorted. I left them to it, and helped Elsa strip away a patch on the courtyard wall, where fire had charred the plaster. After the weeks of hunching over the documents, squatting on the floor of the dormitory, it felt good to throw myself into more physical work again. Although it left me with plaster dust in my hair, and hands greyed with dirt, it was a cleaner kind of work than grubbing through the papers of the long dead.

It was dark when I returned to the dormitory. Zoe and Simon had gone, and Piper was by the window, bundling together a small pile of papers to take with him. The Ringmaster was alone at the far end of the dormitory. He stood when I entered.

'I wanted to show you this, before I go,' he said.

He passed me a sheet that he had put aside. I scanned it briefly. It was one of the technical reports that I'd read already, and stacked alongside the others. Column after column of numbers, as meaningless to me as the diagrams.

'You missed something.' He pointed to the bottom half of the sheet, where the mildew was so thick that the paper wore a layer of fuzz. 'There's a handwritten bit. You can hardly make it out, but it's there.'

I bridled. 'Have you been waiting here, just to give me a hard time because I missed something? You've seen how many papers I've had to wade through.'

'I'm not trying to criticise you,' he said. 'I thought you'd want to see this.'

I took the sheet from him, and read the pale heading of the handwritten section: *Disciplinary Hearings (Yr. 52, Sept 10th).'*

'I did read this,' I said. 'There's a few pages like that – it's the list of their crimes and punishments. Like the record of hearings before a Councilman.'

Underneath the heading was a list of names, annotated.

Upcher, J.
Theft of supplies from mess hall. Convicted. Restricted rations, 6 months; relocated to Section D where extended electrical curfew is in effect.

Hawker, R.
Using electricity in curfew hours. Convicted. Restricted rations, 3 months.

Anderson, H.
Manslaughter. Acquitted. Convicted of lesser charge: Excessive use of force. Transferred to un-armed duties, 6 months.

I looked up at him. 'I told you – I read these already.'

He shook his head. 'Look more closely.' He pointed to the margin and turned the page so that it was horizontal. Then I saw it, scrawled sideways in the margin, the faded ink hard to differentiate from the mildew. It was barely visible, and I had to hold the paper close to the lamp to make it out.

Given that any unauthorised departures pose a clear security threat to the entire Ark, Anderson's actions were found to fall within his remit as security officer. However, he has been sanctioned for shooting to kill, without making any other attempt to subdue Heaton when he encountered H. attempting to enter the principal

*ventilation shaft. The disciplinary committee accepted that
Anderson had verbally warned H., but it was found
that . . .*

The rest was illegible.

'Heaton never got out of the Ark,' The Ringmaster said, taking back the page. 'We should've known they'd try to stop him. He knew the location; he knew how to get in and out. They must have been terrified that he'd unleash a torrent of survivors from Topside.'

'You sound like you agree with what they did. Killing him.'

'I never said that. But I can see what they were thinking.' He moved towards the door. 'Anyway, I thought you'd want to see it.'

'I wish you hadn't shown me,' I called after him.

He turned in the doorway. 'Even if he'd made it out of the Ark alive – what do you think would have happened to him, on the surface? You've seen the reports. It was a wasteland. The survivors were barely clinging on. Heaton wouldn't have survived up there. He was old, already. He'd have got sick, or starved. At least this way he probably had a quicker death. Their weapons would have been efficient.'

He discussed death so casually. It was simply part of his vocabulary, as everyday as patrols or weather.

'I know he probably wouldn't have survived up here,' I said. 'The thing is, he knew that too. And he went anyway.' I was thinking of what Piper had said to me before the battle, when we thought we could not win. *That's hope*, he'd said.

The Ringmaster shrugged. 'You said it yourself: you wanted to know what happened to him.'

He reached a hand for my face. For an instant it rested

against the side of my jaw. The last time he'd touched me, it had been to grab my wrist, when we'd argued in the tithe collector's rooms.

I jerked away, stepping backwards. He looked down at his hand as though it were a stranger's. The disgust on his face mirrored that on my own.

He stepped back into the dark of the courtyard and was gone. When I turned back to the dormitory, hand pressed to my face, Piper was still busy with the papers, and had noticed nothing.

That night, after Piper had gone, it wasn't The Ringmaster I thought of, but Heaton. It was true – I had said that I wanted to know. And it was also true that his death had probably been quicker and less painful than a slow death on the surface, poisoned with radiation, and starving. But as I lay in bed, I wished I could have left Heaton's story unfinished. I wanted to be able to imagine him climbing upwards, throwing open a hatch for the final time, seeing the light filtered through the sky's veil of ash, and stepping out into the world.

CHAPTER 28

Piper came back at dawn. I was already awake, and had been most of the night – a vision of the blast had ripped me from sleep not long after midnight, and I'd been lying there, trying to douse the flames that still smouldered in my mind. When I heard the footsteps in the courtyard I reached for the knife beneath my pillow.

'It's me,' he said, letting the door slam against the wall as he opened it. His eyes were swollen, the skin beneath them darkened.

'Did you sleep at all?' I said, as I sat up and swung my legs to the ground.

'I think I can find it,' he said. 'The Ark. Look here.'

He tried to pass me a sheet of paper, but I waved him away as I pulled on my jumper.

'At least let me get dressed,' I said. 'The Ark's been there for four hundred years. It's not going anywhere.'

It was so cold that I wrapped the blanket around my shoulders over my clothes, as I squatted to look at the papers he laid out on the floor.

'Here,' he said, sliding a page across to me. It wasn't

315

dated, but the neat printing marked it as being from the Ark's early years. It was one of the expedition logs, recording radiation levels on the surface.

'Look at the first column,' he said.

The heading read: *'Radiation readings (Bq) taken at mile intervals from the Ark (Entrance 1).'* Below it, the numbers unfurled: *'West 1; W. 2; W. 3;'* and so on down the page.

'But then the readings just stop,' Piper said 'W. sixty-one is the last one. But in this sheet –' he passed me a second sheet, similarly barred with columns of numbers '– another expedition goes east, and they get much further. Up to E. two-hundred-and-forty.'

'So? They had to turn back earlier when they headed west. Maybe they got as far as they planned; maybe they ran into some kind of trouble. Met some hostile survivors and had to leg it.'

He shook his head. 'They weren't in a hurry – they were taking measurements on the way back as well – look at the third column.' He looked up at me. 'They stopped because they hit the coast.'

'OK.' I paused and wiped the sleep from my eyes. 'But even if that's what happened, how much does that help us? It places the Ark about sixty miles inland. But which part of the coast? That's a strip more than six hundred miles long.'

'Look – here.' He rifled through the papers he'd arranged, and passed me a sheet. 'The bit at the bottom, about the water.'

It was one of the Ark's regular status reports, with updates on supplies, outbreaks of illness, and issues with the underground structure itself.

Yr 3, Aug 9th. INFRASTRUCTURE/RESOURCE
BRIEFING (MANAGEMENT COMMITTEE).

Potable water: tanked supplies should, at current rates, last
a further 26 months (shorter than anticipated, due to the
rupture of Tank 7 during the detonations) after which we
will be relying on the external water supply. The filtration
system for the external supply is functioning, but while the
removal of ash and residue has substantially reduced
radiation levels (to well below pre-filtration readings taken
by Surface Exp. 4), it remains significantly higher than . . .

I looked up at him. 'They had access to drinking water. So they're near some kind of stream or river?'

'There were more than a thousand people there. It'd have to have been a decent-sized water source.'

'OK – so we're talking about a river, passing sixty miles or so from the coast. It doesn't exactly pinpoint the location.'

'Here.' He was ready with another single sheet, its bottom half torn away.

I read the title:

Yr. 18, April 18th. SURFACE EXPEDITION 23:
OBSERVATIONS (TERRAIN RECONNAISSANCE W/
VIEW TO FUTURE RESETTLEMENT).

But Piper didn't wait for me to read it all – he reached over and tapped on a section near the page's truncated end. 'There – read that bit.'

. . . given that radiation levels have failed to subside at
expected rates, any surface resettlement in future
decades should ideally be located close enough to

*continue to use the Ark's facilities (espec. the water
filtration systems and*

*The Ark's location, while optimal for
minimising damage on impact, has limitations for surface
resettlement. The clay loam soil that made the area ideal
for stable excavation is poorly suited to farming. . .*

'Now turn it over,' Piper said.

Even my careful handling sent small flakes of paper and
dust drifting to the ground.

'There's nothing there,' I said. 'Just a stain.' The back
of the sheet had no writing – only a faded brown mark,
spreading from the bottom of the picture, as though tea
had long ago been spilled.

'That's what I thought at first,' he said. 'But then I
wondered why the back of the page hadn't been reused. All
the other papers have every spare space filled. Half a page
blank like that – they would have reused it.'

I bent to look more closely. There were overlapping
layers of discolouration, seeping from the left-hand side.

'It's a picture,' Piper said. He reached over my shoulder
and turned the page on its side. I could see it now – the
stains weren't stains after all, but mountains, reaching into
the bare sky. 'Not a picture like the ones in that pile,' he
said, gesturing to the technical diagrams that I'd massed on
one of the beds. 'It's not detailed, not there to show how
something works. It's more like the kind of pictures my
parents had hanging on the wall in their house.'

I wondered who had painted it. I tried to picture them
pausing, during one of the rare surface expeditions, wanting
to take back into the Ark an image of the world that had
been lost to them.

'Look,' he said. As he leaned forward from behind me to point at the picture, his arm rested on my shoulder. I could feel his warmth against my back. My whole body had shuddered from The Ringmaster's touch, but Piper's was as familiar as the weight of my rucksack on my shoulders, or the texture of my blanket against my neck.

'See that mountain,' he went on, 'with the peak that drops away on one side? That's Broken Mountain, viewed from the west. Next to it, the one with the plateau – that's got to be Mount Alsop.'

I turned so I could see his face. He was grinning. It had been a long time since I'd seen a smile like that.

'There's a plain, west of the Spine Mountains, about eighty miles north west of here. The Pelham River runs through it. It fits with the painting, and all the other stuff – the distance from the coast. Even the clay soil.'

I remembered all the maps, pinned to the walls in his tiny makeshift chamber on the island. Even before he joined the resistance, there were his years of travelling with Zoe. He knew the land in a way that I didn't. Not the vague groping knowledge of a seer, but the intimate knowledge of years of hard travel. He knew the best passes for crossing a patrolled mountain range; which coastal caves would flood at high tide; the quickest route through the swamps, avoiding all the roads.

'If I can get us to the right area,' he said, 'can you find it?'

'It'll be guarded,' I said.

'That's not what I asked,' he said. 'Can you find it?'

I closed my eyes. When I'd sought the island, it had been like a beacon, a light that I'd followed. The Ark felt different. It was a darkness, a blackness so complete that I couldn't even feel my way towards it. I tried, once again, to stop my mind's instinctive flinching from it, and instead to turn and face it. I tried to picture the plain, and the river, overlooked by the mountains. And I felt it, the slightest tug, gentle and unsettling as a tiny bug crawling in my hair. Something was waiting for me in that buried place, where we would go to ask the bones what they remembered.

I nodded.

He gave an answering nod. 'Then we leave today.'

*

I knocked at the door of Elsa's room and she came quickly, a shawl wrapped over her nightgown. When I told her we were leaving, she asked no questions, only pulled me to her, held me so close that I could smell the warmth of skin and sweat; the garlic tang of her hands. Neither of us said anything about meeting again. We had moved beyond the cheap consolation of words.

At the Tithe Collector's office the others were waiting.

'I've ordered three of our best horses to be made ready for you at the gates,' The Ringmaster said. 'I offered to send some soldiers with you, too, but Piper refused.'

'Piper's right,' I said quickly. 'We can travel more quickly, just the three of us, and without being seen.'

I was surprised that The Ringmaster hadn't insisted. I knew he didn't trust us, or this mission to the Ark.

He bent lower, speaking so that only I could hear. 'Do you think I need to waste troops on making sure you don't betray me?' He shook his head slowly. 'If you betray me, or risk us all by unleashing more machines, I have a whole town here, Cass. I have your Elsa, and Sally, and Xander.'

He made no explicit threats, but their names were enough.

He straightened. 'Be careful,' he said, louder. To the others, listening, it might have sounded like a benediction. I knew better.

Sally came in, unwrapping a scarf from her face.

'I've just spoken to the dawn patrol,' she said. 'It's the same as yesterday: smoke to the south, and more sightings of Council soldiers. They're keeping their distance from the town, but they're out there, more and more of them. You'll have to wait until the snow comes. You'll need the cover, to get clear of here.'

I looked out the window. The clouds overhead were murky and thick, but it hadn't snowed for two days. Footsteps on the road outside had churned the snow to grey slush.

Piper was staring out the window too. 'Lucia was good with weather,' he said. I glanced quickly at him, but he still had his face turned to the window. He rarely mentioned her, and now that he had, his voice was soft. 'She would've been able to tell us when the next snow was due.'

'Well she's not here.' Zoe's voice came down like an axe, cutting off Piper's words.

*

It was after sunset before the clouds made good their promise of snow. It fell thickly, fat dabs of whiteness in the dark. There was no time for long farewells. Sally embraced Piper and Zoe, and surprised me by squeezing my arm.

Xander wouldn't move from the window, where he was watching the snowflakes swarming in the gusty wind. He didn't turn as I approached. His chin rested on the window-sill, his breath blurring his reflection in the glass.

We'd thought about taking him – it was Xander, after

all, who'd first sensed the Ark. But with him and Sally in tow we couldn't evade the Council soldiers, or travel quickly, let alone penetrate the tightly guarded Ark.

'We have to go,' I said to him, 'and we can't take you with us.'

'Are you going to find *The Rosalind*?' he said. It was the clearest sentence he'd said in weeks. I couldn't bear to tell him about *The Rosalind*'s hacked-off figurehead, left in the snow on the eastern road, or about her crew setting sail again in the Council's tanks.

'We're looking for the Ark,' I said. 'The maze of bones.' If he understood what I said, he gave no sign of it.

'I'm sorry,' I said quietly. And I was. Not sorry for leaving him behind, because we had no choice. But sorry that I'd been avoiding him. Sorry that his mind was the clapper in the bell of my own madness, and that I had not been brave enough to share more time with him.

Now, watching the snow, he was calmer than I'd seen him in a long time. I touched his hand before I walked away.

'Forever fire,' he whispered, like a promise.

CHAPTER 29

When I hefted my rucksack onto my back it clanked, and jabbed me in the shoulder blades. Not knowing what to expect in the Ark, we'd packed a lantern and jars of oil, as well as food, water, and blankets. Sally, Simon and The Ringmaster watched us step into the snow.

At a crossroads near the gate, six of Simon's troops were waiting for us, including Crispin, holding the reins of our horses. Piper spoke quietly with him, out of hearing of the rest of the squadron, then nodded and returned to me and Zoe.

'We'll ride out with Crispin's patrol,' he said. 'It gives us the best chance to slip off unobserved, if the Council's soldiers are watching. Say nothing to the squadron of where we're headed, or why.'

Our horses were loaded with saddle bags, stuffed with oats. We mounted and filed out the eastern gate. Beyond the shelter of the walls, the snow battered our faces, and I wrapped my scarf up to my eyes. For ten minutes, we followed Crispin east along the main road, before turning south to trace a broad circle around the town's walls. Torches burned at intervals along the wall, each one illuminating a few yards of snow. In the watchtowers, lanterns glowed. The town's ring of light only made the darkness seem thicker where we rode.

At one point I could smell smoke, and Crispin pointed to the south.

'A few miles that way, there's a camp of Council soldiers,' he said. 'At least a hundred of them. We've had scouts watching them since last week.' In the dark, the sole sign of them was the trace of smoke in the snow-heavy air. 'The Ringmaster and Simon are planning a raid, soon,' said Crispin.

I nodded. A raid was the sensible thing to do, before more Council soldiers arrived and before New Hobart could be encircled. But the thought of another battle, however necessary, made vomit rise at the back of my throat. This was how violence worked, I was learning: it refused to be contained. It spread, a plague of blades.

The patrol rode in silence around the south of the city, the ghost of the burnt forest on our left. As we began to turn to the north, I heard music. It was snatched away by the wind in an instant, and when I raised myself in my stirrups and looked around, the others were riding on as though they'd heard nothing. Fragments of music kept coming, falling around me like the snow. I called ahead to Piper, but he said he heard nothing. I knew, then, that there was nothing to hear but the wind, and the hoof-falls of our horses on snow. The music was in my head.

Our route was about to cross the main road running from New Hobart to the west. Crispin, at the front of the patrol, raised his hand to halt us. There was something in the road ahead, beneath the lone oak. Crispin's troops fanned out, weapons at the ready. It was hard to make out the shape in the thick snowfall. It looked like a figure, but it was too high, and it wavered with the confused wind. For a surreal moment I thought the man was flying, as if we'd encountered a ghost, one of the unburied bodies from the battle, grown restless. Then another gust of wind swept aside the snow for a moment.

The man hung from the tree. There was an unmistakable wrongness to the angle of the neck. Three crows took flight from the branch above him as Crispin and two of his men rode towards the body.

'Stay back,' said Piper, throwing his arm out to stop me as I urged my horse forward. Piper had his knife out, and Zoe and the other soldiers were scanning the space around us.

'It's an Omega,' Crispin called back to Piper. 'He wasn't here when the last patrol came through, but there are no tracks – they must have strung him up around sunset, before the snow.'

The horses had picked up on our unease and were snorting, backing into each other.

'It's a message,' Piper said. 'They left him here for our patrols to find.'

'I need to see this,' I said.

'You want to see the inside of a Council cell again?' snapped Zoe. 'Because that's where you'll end up, if you don't listen. We're a mile from the walls. It could be an ambush, for all you know.'

I ignored her and kicked my horse forwards. Piper rode after me, shouting. But I wasn't listening to him. The music in my head – I knew what it was: the refuge song. The closer I got to the swinging man, the more the music was out of tune – the notes of the melody were wrong, as if played on slackened strings.

It was Leonard who had been hanged. His guitar had

been smashed and then the strap looped back over his head. The arm of the guitar made a crooked scarecrow out of him. When the wind spun him, I could see his hands tied behind his back. Some of the fingers stuck out at strange angles. I wasn't sure whether they'd been broken in the struggle, or in torture, or whether it was just his body's stiffening. I didn't want to know.

Piper and Zoe flanked me, looking up at Leonard as the wind turned his face away.

It wasn't even Leonard's broken body that I mourned – it was all those tunes still inside him. All those words still to be sung.

'We need to take him down,' I said.

'It's not safe,' said Piper. 'There are Council soldiers about. We need to leave the patrol and get out of here.'

I ignored him, dismounting and looping my reins around a low branch so I could set to work untying Leonard's hands. The twine was fastened tightly, the fibres rasping against one another as I tried to work the knots loose. The squeaking sound of it set my teeth on edge in a way that the touch of Leonard's cold flesh didn't.

'Can you take his body back to New Hobart, bury it properly?' I called up to Crispin, who was still surveying the road to the west.

He shook his head. 'They've enough bodies to deal with. This is a patrol, not a gravedigging service. I'll send a man to the town to report, and two to scout the area. The rest of us need to finish the patrol.'

'Fine,' I said. 'I'll bury him myself.'

'We don't have time for this,' hissed Zoe. I ignored her and kept on at the twine holding Leonard's hands behind his back.

When they were freed, Leonard's hands didn't fall to his

sides, but stayed bent behind his back, stiffened or frozen into place.

I couldn't reach the rope from which he hung. I jumped a few times, swiping at the rope with my dagger, but all I succeeded in doing was startling my horse, and setting Leonard's body spinning.

'It'd be quicker if you helped me,' I said to Piper, 'instead of just watching.'

'There's no time to dig a proper grave,' he said. 'We'll take him down, but then we have to move.'

'Fine,' I said, out of breath.

We did our best. From his saddle, Piper cut the rope while I held Leonard's body up, then together we lowered him to the ground, his weight unleashing fresh pains from my half-healed arm. Zoe held Piper's horse when he dismounted and lifted the guitar from Leonard's neck. The wood creaked, splinters snapping. I leaned over him and tried to loosen the noose that clutched at his neck. I slit the rope; the flesh beneath it was dark purple, and didn't spring back, instead preserving the rope's indentations.

Together we carried him to the ditch at the side of the road. When we lowered him to the ground, his body bent at the waist with a creaking sound. Every minute on that road was a risk, and there was no time to bury him properly, with our bare hands, and in the frozen earth. In the end I cut a small section from my blanket and laid it over his face, grateful that he had no eyes to close. We were about to re-mount when I ran back to the tree and retrieved the smashed guitar from where Piper had let it drop. I gathered the fragments and laid them next to Leonard in the ditch.

*

We headed north with Crispin and two of his soldiers, as they continued their circuit around the town, but once we were half a mile from the road Piper turned his horse west, and Zoe and I peeled off to follow him. The others didn't even slow their horses, though Crispin looked back and raised a hand. 'Go safely,' he said. Piper raised his hand too.

We rode far, and fast. In the snow and the darkness, it felt like we were travelling blind, and I thought of Leonard, and his perpetually dark world. Twice my horse almost lost its footing in the snow. Once I sensed people not far to the north of us, and we sheltered in a gully, glad of the snowfall that covered our tracks as the mounted men rode along the ridge above us.

We headed west until it was light enough to negotiate the rocky gullies that lay to the north. By noon, we were approaching the foothills of the Spine Mountains. The snow that we'd been thankful for earlier was now setting as a sheet of ice on the rocks. The horses, already tired, were shying and hesitant; several times we had to dismount and lead them.

As we rode, I kept thinking of what Piper had said: *Lucia was good with weather.* It was the first time he'd willingly raised the subject of the dead seer. Usually, he and Zoe edged around Lucia's name as though it were a thorn bush. When Piper had spoken of her, back in the tithe collector's office, Zoe had snapped at him. I remembered the loaded glances he and Zoe exchanged, whenever Lucia was mentioned. When Xander had asked after Lucia, Zoe had stiffened, while Piper's voice had been thick with grief. *She's gone*, he'd said.

It was like the Ark: it had been there the whole time, beneath the surface. And now I understood it, it changed everything. Now that I'd realised how Piper had felt about Lucia, so many things fell into place. How quickly he'd warmed to me on the island. His willingness to free me, against the will of the Assembly. It wasn't me who he'd warmed to: it was his memories of Lucia.

It explained, too, so much about Zoe. Her hostility to me, and her frustration with my visions. Even with Xander, she had been silent and brittle in the face of his brokenness.

All their lives it had been just the two of them: Zoe and Piper. I knew that bond, because I'd lived it myself, with Zach, before we were split. How much more intense the bond must have been for Zoe and Piper, who had chosen to stay together, even after he'd been branded and sent away. For Zoe, especially, who had made that choice, leaving her parents, and the ease of an Alpha life, to follow him. Choosing him, even though it meant a lifetime as a fugitive. And then he'd left her. He'd not only gone to the island, where she could never follow, but had also found a closer bond with somebody else. I understood how Zoe might still feel unmoored by this. I knew from experience that there were different kinds of intimacy, no less binding than the kind shared by lovers. I remembered Zoe's face when I'd come across her at the spring, listening to the bards' music with her eyes closed. It was the only time I'd caught her looking so unguarded. Her face had been turned upwards, showing her loneliness to the sky. Before she'd snapped at me and stormed away, she'd told me about how she and Piper used to sneak out together, as children, to hear a bard play.

When the dark came, we stopped in a copse through which a stream ran, frozen at the edges. We tethered the horses downstream and managed to get a fire started, though winter had stripped the trees and they gave little cover from the snow.

I waited until we'd eaten before I broached the subject. Zoe was sitting beside me, reaching her gloved hands so close to the fire that I could smell the singed wool. Piper sat with his back to us, looking out between the trees.

'I know what it's like to be close to your twin,' I said to Zoe. 'And I know you two are closest of all, sticking together the way you did.'

'What are you going on about?' She poked the fire with a long stick. Sparks darted upwards and were snuffed out by the darkness.

'I understand that it wasn't easy for you,' I went on. 'How the two of you must always have depended on each other.'

'Is there a point to this little monologue?' She still grasped the stick. The end had caught fire, and she held it upright, like a torch.

'I understand, now, about Lucia.'

She raised an eyebrow. Piper had turned so quickly that the knives on his belt clattered. I waited. The words I was about to speak were stones, and I tested their weight before I dropped them into the pool.

'You're jealous,' I said to Zoe. 'Because Piper loved her. You didn't want to share him then, and you don't want to share him now. Piper and I aren't even lovers, but having another seer around is too much for you, isn't it? That's why you always snap at me, always criticise me.'

'Cass,' said Piper, his voice measured as he stood and stepped towards us. 'You don't know what you're talking about.'

Zoe had dropped the flaming stick. It glowed, half an inch from my foot. Piper bent and tossed it back onto the fire.

I'd thought that Zoe might hit me, but she just shook her head slowly. 'You think you understand my life? You

330

think you understand me and Piper? Screaming about the blast in your sleep doesn't give you any special insights.' She leaned closer, speaking very slowly and clearly. 'You're pathetic. You think you're so wise, and so special, so much better than Xander and Lucia. I wish you'd hurry up and lose your mind entirely. You're harder to be around than Xander – at least he doesn't think he's special, and he shuts up sometimes.'

I had to raise my voice to compete with the wind. 'Did you hate Lucia as much as you hate me?' I asked. 'I bet you were glad when she died. Then you could have your precious Piper to yourself.'

Her hand moved toward her belt, and I wondered whether she would throw a knife, and whether Piper would defend me. If it came to blades and blows, who would he choose?

She turned her back on me and walked away. I watched her go until the night claimed her, and I could see nothing but the fire's light thrown against the tree trunks.

Piper took a few steps, too, as if to follow her.

'I'm sorry,' I called after him. 'Not sorry about what I said to her. She's had it coming for months. But I'm sorry for you.' I paused. 'I know how hard it is. I'm sorry that you lost Lucia.'

'You don't know what you're talking about,' he said.

'I lost Kip,' I said. 'If you'd told me about Lucia, I would have understood. You act like you want us to be close, but you didn't even tell me about her. You had to wait for me to work it out.'

Of all the responses I might have expected, his was the last. He looked at me, for a long moment, and then laughed. He arched his head back, his Adam's apple bobbing with each gasp of laughter.

I didn't know how to respond. Was he mocking Kip? Mocking the comparison I'd drawn, between my loss and his? His laughter echoed back at us from the tree trunks and the fire, until even the flames seemed to be laughing at me.

Finally he lowered his head again, and exhaled deeply.

'I shouldn't laugh,' he said, wiping his face with his hand. 'But there's not been much to laugh about for a while.'

'And this is funny to you, is it? Kip and Lucia are dead.'

'I know.' The creases around his eyes disappeared when he stopped smiling. 'And it's not funny. But it's not what you think.'

'Then tell me. Tell me what it is.'

'I can't speak for Zoe,' he said. 'You know what she's like.'

'Apparently not,' I said, my voice rising again. 'Apparently I'm so wrong about everything.'

'I know you meant no harm. But you'll need to make this right with her.'

He walked to the lookout spot, leaving me alone with the fire.

*

We'd rigged a canvas sheet against a tree trunk, to keep the snow off. I crawled into the space beneath, though I didn't sleep until Zoe came back, after midnight. She slipped, unspeaking, into the cramped space beside me. I felt her shivering as she fell asleep.

She dreamed of the sea. We'd slept apart for weeks, while I was in the holding house; now we had no choice but to sleep close, and I shared again her dreams of the sea, reliable as tides. Perhaps that was what made me realise my mistake. When Piper shook my shoulder to wake me for my lookout shift, I understood the truth about Lucia.

CHAPTER 30

Sitting at the lookout post, while Piper and Zoe slept, I traced each clue that I'd missed, or misinterpreted.

I thought of how Zoe knew how to deal with my visions, better than Piper. *She can't talk yet*, she'd said to him, when he tried to badger me about what I'd seen. *She'll stop carrying on in a minute.* I'd registered it only as dismissiveness. I hadn't recognised the confident familiarity of someone who'd seen this many times. Someone who'd passed many nights with a seer.

Her words to me: *You're not the first seer.*

Her reluctance to sail, and her clenched hands on the railing of the boat when we'd left the Sunken Shore.

I had taunted her: *I bet you were glad when Lucia died.* But it was the bones of her own lover that Zoe was searching for every night, when she slept.

I looked over my shoulder to where Piper and Zoe lay, sleeping. The canvas above them was sagging with the weight of snow. They slept back-to-back, just as they'd fought in the battle. In the cold, with the blanket pulled high around their necks, they looked like one creature with two heads.

I was always getting things wrong. I was more blind than Leonard. I'd been wrong about The Confessor, thinking that it was me she was hunting, instead of Kip. I'd been wrong about Zoe's dreams, and about Lucia. Getting the visions was one thing, but interpreting them was another. My visions had led me to the island, but our presence had led The Confessor there too. My visions had showed me the silo, and allowed us to destroy the database – but that had cost Kip his life. My visions had shown me so much, and I'd understood so little.

I didn't need to wake Zoe for her shift – she woke herself, as she usually did, and crawled from the shelter to stand behind where I sat at the lookout spot. It was still dark. Downstream, one of the horses gave a small whinny.

'Go to sleep,' she said. 'There's hours yet until dawn.'

'It was you, wasn't it,' I said. It wasn't a question. 'You loved Lucia.'

It was too dark to see her face clearly, but I could see the white clouds of her breath.

'We loved each other,' she said.

It was strange to hear her talk of love. Zoe of the rolled eyes and the shrugs. Of the poised knives.

'I'm sorry,' I said. 'I've been an idiot.'

'It's not the first time. I doubt it'll be the last.' There was no spite in her voice, just tiredness.

'I don't know why I didn't realise,' I said.

'I do,' she said. 'Because I'm a woman. Because I'm an Alpha, and she was an Omega. Because although you like to think you're so far above the assumptions and prejudices of the rest of the world, it turns out you're not so different from them after all.'

I had nothing to rebut her accusation. It settled on me like ash.

'Why didn't you tell me?' I asked eventually.

'It was mine.' She paused. A glimpse of her eyes, white in the dark, as she looked at me, and away again. 'I feel like there's so little that's left of her. I don't want to share it around.'

I thought of how I had been reluctant to speak about Kip. There'd been times that I'd felt as though his name were a relic – it was all that I had left of him, now, and it might be worn out if I used it too much.

'When you heard the bards' music, back at the spring that day, and told me about the bard you and Piper used to listen to when you were kids. I thought it was Piper you were thinking of.'

She snorted. 'I'd always remembered that bard. When I first met Lucia, that's who she reminded me of. They both had beautiful hands.' She gave a small laugh. 'And Lucia used to sing, too. She was always humming away to herself in the mornings, when she brushed her hair.'

She was quiet for a while.

'I wish you'd told me about her,' I said. 'I would have understood.'

'I don't need your understanding.'

'Maybe I could've used yours,' I said.

She shrugged. 'My relationship with Lucia didn't exist just to teach you a lesson about grief. She didn't die just so you and I could bond over our sob stories.'

She sat beside me on the log and leant her elbows on her knees. I could see her hands, the lighter skin of her fingertips, five pale points in the night as she reached to push her hair back from her face.

'I was used to not speaking about her, anyway. We had to be careful all the time. Working for the resistance, the last thing we needed was any more attention. An Alpha and

Omega relationship is a whipping offence, even without it being between two women. All that crap about Alphas having an obligation to breed.' She snorted. 'Like that would have made a difference with me. As if I'd otherwise have found some nice Alpha guy and started pumping out babies.' The chilled air seemed to absorb her laugh.

'It was hard for her, on the island. You know what people are like about seers at the best of times– always a bit suspicious, stand-offish. Then they found out about the two of us being together. After that, they just cut Lucia out.' Her hands tightened into fists. 'It didn't matter to them that I'd been working for them for years. That I'd done more for the resistance than most of them ever had. Or that Lucia was risking her life working for them too. They stopped speaking to her. They were happy enough to keep benefiting from her visions, and the work she did. But they wouldn't even talk to her. They forced her out of the house she'd lived in. They called her a traitor, an Alpha-lover.

'Piper did his best for her – found her somewhere to stay in the fort, and tried to tackle the worst of them about what they were doing. But he had the resistance to run. There was only so much he could do. That's when her mind started to go. I know it was the visions that did it, really, but she'd been able to manage them better, when she had friends – people to talk to. Once they left her on her own, she didn't have anything except the visions.'

I remembered my isolation in the Keeping Rooms, with the horizon shrunk to the grey walls of my cell, and nothing to distract me from the horror of my visions.

'And I wasn't there,' Zoe went on. 'She wanted to spend more time on the mainland – to move here full-time, even. But I told her it was too dangerous, until I could sort out a safe place for us, somewhere out east, away from the patrols. The more unstable she got, the harder it was to keep her hidden, and stay safe. She was getting really volatile. It wasn't just the screaming when the visions came. At other times, too, she couldn't control what she said. You've seen what Xander's like. We couldn't count on her to make sense, let alone stick to a cover story.'

Zoe paused, looked down at her hands. It was lighter, now, the wind nudging the clouds from the moon. She'd slipped one of her knives from her belt and was fiddling with it.

'I told her to get on that boat.' Silence. She rocked the tiny knife from side to side, slicing air. 'She hated going back to the island, by that stage. But I made her. I shouted at her, when she tried to refuse. Told her it was for her own safety.'

She gave a bleak laugh. 'Like Piper said the other day: she was good with weather. You know how you're good with places? Weather was one of her things. She could always sense a storm picking up. Even a change of wind coming. It was one of the reasons she was so useful to the resistance, over the years – letting them know when they could make a safe crossing.'

For once her hands were still, the knife resting inert on her palm, like an offering.

'She would have warned them about the storm. She always knew. But they didn't listen to her anymore. Because she'd started to behave oddly. And because they all despised her, because of us. Because of me. They called her a traitor. And they wanted to get back to their precious island.' She looked straight at me, defying me to deny it. 'I know she must have tried to warn them about the storm.'

The final word caught in her mouth. I waited, while she stared straight ahead and took several slow breaths.

'I saw how the madness crept up on her,' she said. 'And on Xander too. When you came along, I hoped at first that you might be different. Piper was so worked up about you. And you'd found your own way out to the island. I couldn't ignore that.

'Even after I met you, I hoped you might learn to control your visions, so you wouldn't fall into the same trap as her. As all the others. I tried to help you. But it's happening all over again. The visions, the screaming. The way your eyes shift around after you've seen the blast. Even when you talk to us, these days, sometimes it's like you're looking at something else going on, just behind us. Or through us.' She looked down. 'She used to do that too, towards the end.

'So that's why I'm done with seers,' said Zoe. 'When you wake up screaming, I already know what it means. And when you talk about the visions of the blast, especially, I've already heard it all. I know where it ends.'

I was used to her looking at me with disdain, or irritation. I was used to her snapping that my night screams would bring down a Council patrol on us, or complaining that she and Piper would be travelling at twice the speed without me slowing them down. The look she gave me now, though, was one I never thought I'd see: she pitied me. I pictured Xander's frantic hands, his restless eyes. I was remembering my own future.

She met my eyes. 'I can't pin everything on a seer again – not the future of the resistance, or even Piper's happiness. I can't watch it happening again.'

She turned away from me. I waited for a few minutes, but she said nothing more. I slipped back to the shelter, to Piper's warmth. For the few hours that I slept, I dreamed her dreams. Grey water, thrashing under a storm. The sea's black underbelly, keeping its secrets.

*

In the morning she was gone. I found Piper standing by the empty lookout post. I could see by the slump in his shoulders that he already knew.

The dawn was staining the eastern sky with light.

'She left us the lantern,' he said. 'All the jerky, too.'

'Can't you go after her?'

He shook his head. 'If she doesn't want to be found, I wouldn't have a chance.'

He looked at me. 'Did you talk to her, last night, about Lucia?'

I nodded. 'I thought it might be different, now that we'd spoken. That she might stop hating me.'

'It's not about you, Cass,' he said. 'It's never been about you.'

He went back to the shelter and squatted to unrig it, shaking off the snow before shoving the canvas into his rucksack.

'Did you know she was going to leave?' I asked.

'No,' he said. There was a long pause. 'But I'm not surprised.' He stood, shouldering his rucksack. 'I saw what losing Lucia did to her. Not just when Lucia drowned, but before then, when her mind started to go. Now Zoe's had to watch you and Xander struggle with your visions. I've seen what that cost her.'

That night, as we sat by the fire, I thought of how the sea refused to give up Lucia's bones. I thought of Leonard, in the shallow ditch. Kip's body on the silo floor. Had they taken him away, and buried him? Was the silo abandoned, and had it become his tomb, and The Confessor's too? I couldn't decide what was worse: the thought of strange soldiers shifting him, hauling his body away to bury somewhere. Or the thought of him being left there, where he lay.

That night, in my dreams, Kip was floating in a tank again. I woke to my own shouts, so loud that the horses panicked and yanked at their tethers. Piper wrapped his arm around me until the shaking stopped.

Later, when the sweat had cooled on my face, and the tremors had left my hands, I sat beside Piper and told him the truth about Kip's past. Some things are easier said in the dark. He listened in silence, without interrupting. Finally, he spoke.

'He did terrible things. But he suffered for them, didn't he? When they cut off his arm, put him in the tank for years? When he killed himself, to save you?'

I didn't know how to respond. How much forgiveness could be purchased with an arm, or a life? And who could decide the punishments, or make that kind of reckoning? Not me, I knew, with my own guilt and complicities to bear.

*

We rode for five more days. Only once did we see a sign of pursuit: a single rider who came upon us one night, not long after dusk had fallen. The terrain here was jagged with spars of rock and little shelter, and when we crossed the wide road running north, we'd decided to risk it for the short distance to the shelter of the forest visible a few miles away.

The soldier spotted us first – by the time I saw his red tunic, a few hundred yards ahead, he was already wheeling his horse around. Even from that distance, he would have seen Piper was missing an arm. For an Omega to ride a horse was already a whipping offence – if the rider made it to his garrison, they would send patrols to hunt us down.

Piper didn't consult me, he just leaned forward and pressed his horse to a gallop. I did the same, not sure if I was chasing the soldier or trying to stop Piper.

We were never going to catch up with the soldier – he had too great a start, and our horses were tired and hungry from long days of riding in snow and ice. But Piper wasn't aiming to catch him. We were thirty yards away when Piper threw the knife. At first I thought he'd missed – the rider didn't move, or cry out. But after a few yards, he began to slump forwards. When he was prone, face pressed to his horse's mane, I saw the glint of the blade in the back of his neck. Then, with a terrible slowness, he slid to one side. When he finally toppled from the saddle, one foot was stuck in his stirrup, so that when the horse panicked and sped away, the man was dragged along. The hoof-falls were joined by an extra beat, the soldier's skull bouncing on the iced road.

That surreal chase seemed to last forever: the horse frantic, bucking and shying, and us gaining on him only slowly. The soldier upside down, his head dragging, bouncing and for several seconds, even tangling between the horse's back legs. When we finally drew even, the horse was crazy-eyed, its dark coat striped with sweat. Piper grabbed the reins, and the horse recoiled as if trying to shake its head free of its own neck. Its hoofs clattered on the ice as it danced on the spot.

There had been a time when I would have screamed at Piper, and asked why the soldier and his twin had needed to die. Now I said nothing. If we were captured, the Ark and Elsewhere would slip further from the grasp of the resistance. Zach and The General would win, and the tanks would be fed.

Piper jumped down and freed the soldier's body from the stirrup. I dismounted and looped all three reins together, pinioning them with a heavy rock. We dragged the body from the road to the cover of the ditch; I knelt with Piper there, helping to scoop snow over the stiffening corpse. The blood was black where it pooled beneath the man's neck, and pink at the edges of the spreading stain.

I felt more than ever the truth of what Zach had said on the road outside New Hobart: I was poison. He was right. Even to glimpse me now, a hooded figure in the snow, meant death. My journeys in the last few months had left a map of bones laid across the land.

If I was a prophet, I foretold only death, and I fulfilled my own prophecies. Ever since the silo, I'd been struggling to recognise the Kip I knew in the person The Confessor had described. Now, for the first time, I wondered if he would recognise me.

Piper held out his hand, appraising the snow that still fell on it.

'It'll cover the tracks, at least. It should buy us some time – more time than if he'd raised the alarm tonight. They won't find the body before daylight, even if they realise he's missing by then. But we have to leave the road, now.'

We led the dead man's horse with us when we left. He was still skittish and nervy, jerking at his reins and Piper and I were both exhausted. By midnight we reached the forest, and there we tethered the horses and Piper took the first watch as I slept for a few hours. I woke to a vision of the blast, and couldn't reconcile the extremes – my body shaking with cold and my mind shimmering with flames.

Piper was watching me, but in the slightly distracted way that I'd grown used to in these last few days, since Zoe had left. He seemed a long way away - always scanning the distance beyond the horizon of my face.

He'd never accused me of driving Zoe away. He didn't need to. I saw myself through her eyes, now. I was both in my body and aware of it. Aware of how I shook when a vision came. How when I dreamed of the tanks, I woke with my mouth wide, greedy for air, as if I'd just surfaced from the tank's cloying liquid. I heard, as if for the first time, the noises I made when I had a vision of the blast. The strangled screams that never expected to be heard, because there was nobody left to hear, and no world left to hear in.

'Where do you think Zoe's gone?' I said to him.

'There's a place out east, where she used to think of building somewhere for her and Lucia. It's harsh country, right on the edge of the deadlands, but it's a long way away from all of this.' He didn't have to explain what he meant.

Once, I would have argued with him, said that I didn't think Zoe would give up on the resistance. But after the mistakes that I'd made, I had no right to claim that I knew her. Or to ask anything more of her than she had already given.

'Do you think she's coming back?' I asked him.

He didn't answer.

CHAPTER 31

I felt the river before I felt the Ark. We'd emerged from the forest onto the open grasslands, and I could sense the water's movement within the stillness of the plain. Piper pointed to the east, and the mountain range that squatted across the horizon. From the Ark painting, I could recognise the distinctive peak of Broken Mountain, and the plateau of Mount Alsop.

Within a few hours of riding, I began to feel the Ark itself. It was an aberration in the earth. Ahead of us, beneath the plain, I could sense the obstinate hardness that was neither soil nor stone. And within this buried carapace was air, where earth should be.

I could feel, too, the soldiers massed there. I heard Xander's voice: *noises in the maze of bones.* The whole Ark hummed. If I'd had any doubts that the Council had discovered the Ark, I had none now. It was a hive, ready to swarm.

A few miles from the river, we tethered the horses in a copse scattering most of the remaining oats amongst the sparse grass. I was reluctant to leave them like that: there was no water other than a few shallow puddles, half-frozen, and I didn't know how long we would be gone for. But it was too risky to set them free, where they could be noticed by the soldiers. 'And we might need them again,' said Piper. I noted the *might*; we were both thinking the same thing: *If we come back.*

We moved, hunching, through the long grass. Ahead, the plain rose to a broad hill, where trees fought the boulders and stones for a patch of earth. The river curved around the hill from the west. The winter hadn't caught this river – its dark water was too deep and too fast to freeze.

'Do we need to cross it?' Piper asked, eyeing the flow warily.

I shook my head, and pointed at the hill. 'The Ark's on this side, under there.' I could feel it more clearly than ever. There was metal beneath the hill – I tasted its iron tang. Doors and passageways, a tracery of metal and air under the earth.

I led Piper a little way up the base of the hill, amongst the trees, towards the point where I could feel one of the passages climb to meet the air. The trace of metal was strong here – I could sense the doors, iron slabs set into the slope.

Before we reached the doors we saw the first soldiers. A covered wagon, pulled by four horses, flanked by eight more riders. Piper and I dropped to a crouch in the snow. The grass was long enough to hide us, but each time one of the soldiers turned to scan the plain I found myself holding my breath. When they passed the curve in the road they were less than thirty yards from us. Close enough that I could see the red beard of the soldier driving the cart, and the rip in the tunic of the last rider, where his sword's hilt had worn away the fabric.

Then they had passed us. We watched them approach the scar in the hillside where the door must once have been.

But there was no door now: just a gouged space, forty yards across, in the earth. At some stage in the last four hundred years, the hill of scree and boulders had engulfed the doorway that I could sense, and claimed it as its own. By the looks of it, it hadn't been easy for the Council to excavate. To the side was a mound of earth and rocks, some of the boulders as large as a horse. Trees, too, had been uprooted and dragged there, roots groping at the air. The detritus of centuries. In front of the opening, a line of soldiers waited: at least ten of them, a tongue of red peeking from the hill's open mouth.

For an hour or more we watched the entrance. Soldiers came and went to the wagon, and in and out of the dark chasm, but the watching guards didn't move from their posts. They weren't alone, either. Piper pointed out to me the bowman waiting on the hill, twenty yards above the door. She was nearly concealed by the boulders amongst which she perched. If Piper hadn't told me what to look for, I might have mistaken the protruding tip of her bow for a sapling. But it moved slightly, when she turned to survey the hill below her. Anyone who stepped from the long grass of the plain would be dead before they got within fifty yards of the door.

Parting the grass with both hands, I scraped the snow clear, closed my eyes, and pressed my cheek against the iced ground, and tried to get a feel for the overall shape of the Ark that lay below. It took me a few moments to work out why it felt familiar. Then I recognised it: it was like the island, but inverted. Where the island had been a cone rising from the sea, this was an upside-down cone, tunnelling down to a central point. The outer corridors, at the surface level, traced a rough circle, several miles in diameter. Within this ring, narrower and deeper, a network of rooms and corridors burrowed. A nest of circular corridors, ever smaller and more deeply sunken. Even the outer ring of the Ark wasn't close to the surface. In front of us, beyond the buried doors, a passageway dropped steeply to join the outer corridor. And there was a symmetry to the Ark's layout, I realised, as my mind fumbled its way through the stone and steel. The passageway to the surface was repeated, at equal lengths around the Ark's circular rim.

'Remember what the papers said,' I whispered to Piper. 'The radiation measurements were taken from *Ark Entrance 1*. There are other entrances. I can feel three more, around the outer circle. One at each of the compass points, more or less.'

For the rest of the day we edged around the rock-strewn hill, crouching in the deep grass. Three times I sensed a passageway climbing to meet the air. But each time, when we crept close enough, we were greeted by the same sight: guards, swords, and bows. In front of the western door was a cluster of tents – enough to quarter at least a hundred soldiers.

The southern door, closest to the river, had been spared the hill's advances, and instead of a messy excavation, a steel structure was visible, at ground level, although rusted. It was circular, more a hatch than a door, and was the height of two men. It looked as though the Council had blasted it open, somehow: a hole was torn in the centre of the hatch, edged by sharpened spurs of metal, reaching inwards like monstrous teeth.

When we'd retreated out of sight of the door, Piper exhaled slowly, closing his eyes for a moment. 'We'll have to come back, with troops. Even with Zoe, we could never have taken one of those entrances. And even if we did, we'd only be trapped as soon as we entered.' He kicked at the snow. There was no time for this. No time to make the risky journey back to New Hobart, and to return again. No time for another battle, and more blood. How much luck, and how much time, did we have left? The Council's soldiers in the Ark were excavating more knowledge, more power, every day – and each day, the refuges swelled with more Omegas.

Piper sat on one of the boulders, and gave a desolate laugh. 'That poor bastard, Heaton, died trying to get out of this place, and here we are, struggling to get back in.'

At Heaton's name, my head jerked upwards.

'There's one more entrance.'

He sighed. 'Is there any point? They're not going to have left a door unguarded.'

'It's not like the others. It's not a door,' I said. 'It was what you said about Heaton that reminded me. Remember what The Ringmaster found in that report, about the guy who'd killed Heaton when he tried to get out?'

Piper nodded. I'd told him and Zoe about The Ringmaster's discovery, and the conclusion to Heaton's story.

'It said something about where it happened,' I went on. 'Something about him being killed while trying to get into a *ventilation shaft*. I didn't know what it meant – didn't really think about it. But it means he wasn't trying to get out of one of the main doors. It makes sense – they'd have been carefully guarded. He was trying to escape another way.'

'This *ventilation shaft* – so a kind of underground chimney?'

'I guess so. They must have needed to get fresh air down there, somehow.' A chimney was what it felt like, now that I trained my seeking onto it: a passage to the surface, both smaller and steeper than the main entrances.

'Is it big enough for a person to get through?' asked Piper. 'And is it safe?'

'Heaton thought so.'

'That didn't work out so well for him.'

'Not because he was wrong about the shaft, though,' I said. 'Only because they caught him doing it.'

'Then wouldn't they have done something to seal it up, if they caught him trying to get out that way?'

'If he'd succeeded, perhaps. But as it is, maybe not. He didn't manage, after all. From their perspective, their system worked: nobody escaped. And think about the name: *ventilation shaft*. It was part of how they got the air down there. Not an easy thing to seal up, especially with everything else they had on their plates.'

'And you don't think the Council found it, sealed it up?'

'Only if they know it's there,' I said.

It wasn't only the Council sealing it up that I worried about – it was the centuries, and the shifting of earth and roots that had buried three of the four main doors.

Those external doors were tightly guarded, but they stood miles apart. We positioned ourselves halfway between the eastern and northern doors, and waited for darkness before emerging from the deep grass of the plain. Before we crossed the rough road that snaked around the hill, Piper told me to jump from stone to stone, so that we left no footprints in the exposed snow where carts and soldiers would pass.

Across the road and up amongst the boulders of the hill itself, we were directly above the Ark, and in the middle of the Council's four watch posts. Now that the Ark lay beneath us, I could feel it more clearly. The size and the depth of it were astounding – all the more so because the hillside gave no sign of what lay below. My awareness of the empty spaces beneath me was so strong that I found myself step-ping tentatively on the snow, mistrusting the ground, even though I knew it was solid for hundreds of feet before the

Ark hollowed it out. And while parts of the Ark hummed with activity, there were whole sections in which I could sense nothing but gaps in the earth, air beneath the soil.

It wasn't easy, scrambling up the huge hill, negotiating the boulders and scrub by moonlight. Without my seer-sense guiding me, I doubt we'd ever have found the hatch. It looked like no more than a dip in the earth, just another hollow in the tussocked ground between the boulders and trees. But I could feel the opening, the absence of earth beneath it, like the covered pit trap on the path to Sally's house, though infinitely deeper. I knelt and looked more closely, parting the grass to expose a glimpse of rust, more orange than the dirt around it.

We scraped the snow to one side and pulled up the grass. Fibrous and sharp, it left slits on my fingers, and came out clotted with soil and moss at the base. When we'd cleared a round patch, it revealed the hatch. It was a circle barely two feet across, set deep in a metal rim. The lid wasn't solid, but a steel grid, still partly obscured by soil. Around its edge, four steel poles emerged from the earth, each of them ending in a jagged gnarl of rust just above the ground.

'It must have had some kind of structure over it, once. A cover, or something,' Piper said.

Whatever it was, it was gone now, whether in the blast itself, or in the centuries that followed.

I bent to the hatch. It looked tiny to me – barely the width of my shoulders. It must have looked even smaller to Piper, his back twice as broad as mine.

'Hell on earth, Cass. How big do you think this Heaton guy was?'

'There are other tunnels near here, too.' I could sense them – air tunnels running from the surface to the Ark's core, as if the hill beneath us had been pierced with a skewer, like a cake being tested for readiness.

'Bigger than this one?'

I shook my head. 'A fraction of the size.' From what I could feel they would be barely a few inches across. 'And think what it said on that bit of paper: *principal ventilation shaft*. This is the biggest one.'

Piper was probing the edge of the hatch with his dagger, dislodging a trail of dirt and moss. When he'd traced the entire circle, I reached for the hatch, hooked my fingers through the gaps in the grid, and pulled. It didn't move, though it gave a reluctant creak.

Piper worked his way around the edge again. Curls of rust settled in the snow, staining it a lurid orange. He muttered about blunting his dagger, but persevered, both of us gritting our teeth against the screech of steel on rust.

He nodded to me, shaking his blade clean, I tried again. Nothing. But when he reached down and pulled with me, his hand between the two of mine, the hatch gave a final rasp and came away.

We dragged the hatch to the side and let it drop onto the snow, but the tunnel mouth was still concealed from us by what looked at first like a layer of dirt. Piper reached down and prodded it with the tip of his dagger. The blade sank into the dirt, more than an inch deep. When he swept the knife sideways it left a trail behind it, revealing a fine mesh beneath the dust. It was a filter, sieving the air and catching the particles big enough to slip through the steel lattice above. When I ran my blade around the edge, the thin wire mesh barely resisted, and I was able to pick it up, a disc of dust and netting, the dust shearing away as I lifted the mesh. It didn't fall far, though – after we'd removed that first filter, we had to slice away at least four more layers, each a few inches deeper than the last, the final one set several feet below the surface. Piper had to hold on to my belt as I lay on the ground to cut away the last layer, my whole torso hanging down the tunnel.

He hauled me back up, and I tossed the final filter down beside the hatch. The filters crafted more finely than anything I'd seen, were so weightless that they didn't even dent the snow. Each strand of metal mesh was spiderweb thin. A membrane between the Ark and the world.

The dust and dirt that we'd dislodged were layers of sediment probably undisturbed for centuries. If we'd sifted through each filter, we might have traced the years through their remnants. On top, the snow of this winter, and the familiar dust of every day: dirt, and grass seeds. Beneath it, the dust of the bleak years, when the recovery was tenuous, tentative. Perhaps the first fragments of plants, as they began to regenerate. Under that, the dogged ash of the Long Winter, thick enough to darken the skies for years. And, last of all, the ash of the blast itself. Fragments of buildings and bones.

We peered down the tunnel, a steel tube, not vertical but steeply angled. It was night where we stood, but the darkness seemed merciful compared to the total blackness of that hole below.

'I'm glad that we're following Heaton, at least,' I said. 'It's like he's showing us the way.'

'He was trying to get out,' said Piper. 'We're doing the exact opposite of what he wanted to do.'

I ignored his words, instead sized up the breadth of his shoulders.

'It's too small for you,' I said.

'You're not going down there by yourself.'

He took off his rucksack and set it on the ground, and

knelt at the edge of the tunnel. And although I didn't say it to him, I was relieved that I wasn't going to be offering myself to the darkness alone.

The tube was too narrow even for me to wear my rucksack. We stuffed our pockets with matches and jerky, and filled the oil lamp. I looped the strap of the water flask over my shoulder, and we hid the bags in the shelter of a nearby rock.

Piper lit the lamp. 'I'll go first,' he said.

'That won't work. I need to feel the way.'

I took the lamp, though it wasn't my eyes that would guide me but my faltering mind, edging forwards, sensing the spaces, the gaps, the obstacles.

'Are you ready?' I said.

He smiled. 'Of course I'm ready,' he said. 'I'm following a seer, who's following a dead stranger's failed escape attempt from hundreds of years ago, into an underground ruin full of Council soldiers. What could possibly go wrong?'

CHAPTER 32

I'd been in cramped spaces before. The tunnels through which Kip and I had escaped from Wyndham had been dark and low-ceilinged. And the chute that had expelled us from the tank room had been airless and dark – but we'd had no time to prepare, to dwell in our fear. Nothing had compared to this: the slow descent into a chute so narrow that I had to keep my arms stretched out in front of me, because there was no room for them at my sides. When I tried to look back to see Piper, my face was pressed against the metal. All I could make out was the shape of my own body, and the tunnel's metal walls reflecting back the lamplight. Ahead of me, beyond the lamp's small sphere of light, there was a wall of absolute darkness, receding inch by inch as we crawled our way further down.

Turning around would be impossible. I tried not to think about how we would manage if the way ahead were blocked. With the chute descending so steeply, it was hard to see how we could ever reverse our way up it. I could hear Piper behind me; his breaths, and the scrape that the knives on his belt made on the chute's roof. It quickly grew warmer, as we descended – the Ark was its own climate, unrelated to the chilled night we'd left behind on the surface. My sweat mixed with the dust of the tunnel to make a sticky paste. With my slippery hands, I couldn't get a purchase on the smooth walls, so I was sliding as much as crawling. I began to sense the river above us. We couldn't hear it, but I could feel its ceaseless flow, adding to the sense of weight crushing me.

The tunnel was growing even narrower. I was sure I could feel it constricting my chest. I tried to calm myself, but my body refused to be placated. Each breath shorter than the last, until my breathing was a fever dance.

The tunnel distorted Piper's voice into unfamiliar shapes. 'Cass, I need you to stay calm,' he said. His voice was steady, although his chest must have been even more tightly squashed than mine.

My words were short, each one the length of a racing breath. 'I. Can't.' I said. 'Can't. Breathe.'

'I've followed you in here. You're the only one who knows the way. I need you to do this.'

If he'd tried to order me, I might have sunk further into panic. But he said he needed my help, and I knew it was true. We would both die, if I didn't pull myself together. Zoe and Zach too. It would all be over, and nobody would ever find our bodies. We would be beneath the earth, but forever unburied.

I thought again of Kip, and his unclaimed body.

I shook the idea from my mind, and began moving again. There could be no darkness in the tunnel ahead of me that would be harder than the memory of him. I shuffled onwards, bracing my hands against the tunnel's rounded sides.

Twice the chute bent at a sharp angle, so that we had to

wiggle painfully around a tight corner, the first time leaving us crawling horizontally for a respite, before another bend returned us to near vertical. Three times the tunnel branched, and I tried to fathom the way. I clenched my eyes and let my mind grope ahead, waiting until I could feel the route opening before us. It was like tossing a stone down a well and waiting for the sound. Piper asked no questions, and didn't complain while I hesitated. He just waited until I was sure enough to move on. Ahead of me, beyond the lamp's feeble glow, it was so dark that in the end I kept my eyes closed, to allow me to concentrate without scanning the tunnel walls for hints that weren't there. The one reassurance that I had was that I could sense nobody anywhere near us. I could still feel the thrum of people to our east, in the deeper sections of the Ark, but the spaces below us, although bleak and black, were at least empty of breath and voices. I knew better than to trust these senses entirely – places had always been easier for me to feel than people, and both required intense concentration. My mind's giddy slippage between past, present and future had always added another dimension of risk. But here, in the tightly enclosed spaces of the Ark, the presence of people seemed to echo, while other sections of the warren were heavy with undisturbed air.

It was impossible to guess how far we'd descended – surely, I thought, it must be hundreds of feet? It was so warm down here, and damp, that the snowy grass above us felt like it belonged to a different time, and a different world.

I'd felt the way before us widening, but the end of the tunnel caught me by surprise. When I reached forward there was no further chute for me to grab, and I slithered out and fell a few feet onto a floor. I wasn't hurt, though I gasped, and called out to warn Piper. The dust on the floor was more than an inch deep, and I'd landed hands and face first. I stuck my tongue out, grimacing, and tried to spit out the claggy mixture of dust and saliva. One of the glass panels in the lantern had smashed when I fell, but the lantern itself still burned. I looked down for the broken pieces, but they had been lost in the dust. When I turned, Piper's arm emerged from the chute. He swung himself neatly down to land on his feet, dust rising and settling.

I didn't realise how afraid Piper must have been until I saw the relief on his face, lit from below by my swinging lamp. He was jubilant, his teeth catching the light as he beamed.

'Don't move,' I said.

He looked down and saw what I meant. The tube had spat us out into a round chamber, perhaps fifteen yards wide. At its centre was a circular hole, several times wider than the chute from which we'd emerged. If Piper had taken one step backwards, he'd have fallen over the edge.

'You can't sense any soldiers near here?' he said.

I shook my head. 'Nobody,' I said. 'They're deeper. We're not in the main bit of the Ark yet – these chambers aren't built for people. It's just the air passage.'

We kept our voices down, nonetheless. Piper took the lamp and lowered it. The hole in the floor wasn't empty. From a central axis, flat blades radiated, like the spokes of a wheel. Each blade was six feet long, and more than a foot wide. They were like the sails of a windmill, but rendered in unforgiving metal, and laid on their side.

Piper nudged the nearest one with his boot and the whole structure creaked into motion, executing a slow half turn.

'I bet it used to spin by itself, when the Electric was still working,' I said.

'Heaton was going to climb up through that, while it was spinning?'

'He was a smart man. He must have known how to stop it, at least for long enough to get through.'

Piper prodded one of the blades with his boot.

'It must be another part of the air filter system,' I said. 'To get fresh air down here, and to keep the blast ash out. There's a reason they didn't get mutations down here, or twins. Look at all of this stuff.' I gestured at the walls, which crawled with wires and thick tubes. At foot-long intervals along the walls were circular holes as big as a hand. Some had tubes feeding out of them, others were open, like screaming mouths. There were labels affixed to the wall beneath each one, engraved on metal plates, but when I wiped the dust from them they were still unintelligible: *VAC. EXTRACT 471. RECIRC. 2 (INTAKE). EXHAUST VALVE.*

I had expected to find machines inside the Ark. I hadn't realised that the Ark itself was a kind of machine: its very structure was a contraption, rigged to allow life to exist so far underground. There was so much between the Ark and the world above. For those who'd built this place, it wasn't enough to bury themselves several hundred yards under the ground. They'd mistrusted even the air, and put it through an obstacle course before it could reach them. Survivors on the surface had contended with the blighted world, without the shelter of hatches, filters, or sealed tunnels, while the Ark dwellers had sheltered below them, hidden.

Piper was squatting at the edge of the hole, peering down through the gaps between the blades.

'It's not a long drop,' he said.

The floor of the room beneath us was visible, probably only five or six feet below the blades. Between each pair of blades there was a gap just about wide enough to climb through.

'I'll go first,' I said, turning my back to the hole so I could lower myself. 'Then you can pass down the lantern.' I was on all fours, about to drop my legs over the edge, when Piper hissed.

'Stop. Look at the dust.'

I looked down, but could see nothing remarkable about the fine grey silt that coated the concrete. My hands were buried in it knuckle-deep.

'Not there – on the blades.'

I knelt, turning to look at the blades behind me.

'There isn't any on the blades,' I said.

'Exactly.'

He reached down to me, jerked me upright.

'This wheel thing – it still turns – and regularly enough to keep the dust off.'

It seemed impossible that anything could still work down here. But he was right – the blades were dustless. And now I looked more closely, I saw how the dust in the rest of the small room was thinner by the edge of the hole, and banked deeper at the edges of the room, as if blown away from that central point.

'It's been four hundred years,' I said. 'More, probably. You read what it said in all those papers: things stopped working.'

'Not completely,' he said. And I remembered the occasional faltering of the electric light in my cell in the Keeping Rooms. Had it been like that, in the Ark – just a gradual stuttering in and out of darkness? 'And we don't understand how their machines worked,' he went on. 'Just wait, for a while at least. If it starts up while you're climbing through, it'll cut you clean in half.'

We moved away from the blades and sat in the dust by the wall. It was an odd kind of vigil, watching this machine to see if it might spring back to life. We hardly spoke. It was stuffy, and sound moved strangely in the small room, muffled by the dust.

'It won't change anything, even if we see it move,' I said. 'We still have to get through it.'

'Let's just see what we're dealing with,' he said.

We'd been waiting for the wheel to turn, but the light came first. Without noise or warning, the room was lit, as though the darkness were a curtain that had been snatched away. I cowered, my back to the wall. Piper leapt to his feet, his drawn blade sweeping from side to side as he scanned the room. It was painfully bright, after the subdued glow of the lamp. The lights were different from the one in my Keeping Room cell, which had hung on a wire. These were set into the ceiling itself, in lines of solid glowing white. There were glowing panels in the walls, too, so we cast no shadows. We had left our shadows on the surface, along with the fresh air and the sky.

Seconds after the lights came on, the noise began: a grinding sound like broken glass underfoot. The blades began to turn. Slowly, at first, but within seconds the wheel whirred faster than I could ever have imagined. It became impossible to distinguish the individual blades, and the chamber beyond disappeared entirely from view, the blades converging into a single spinning mass. My hair was blown back from my face, and I raised my arm to shield my eyes as the fan whipped the dust into a frenzy.

Piper shielded his face too, his gaze shifting from the lights to the spinning blades and back again. I remembered that he'd never seen the Electric before. I'd lived beneath its artificial light for four years in the Keeping Rooms, and seen the intricate machinery of the tank rooms and The Confessor's database. But all of this would be new to him. The white sheen of the lights. The sounds: not just the noisy buzz of the fan, but the low hum of the lights themselves, a burr as insistent as dragonfly wings. After a few moments he'd slipped his knife back into his belt, but his knees stayed bent, ready to move quickly, and he kept his arm raised, fist braced, as though the Electric could be parried with punches.

'Amazing,' he said to me over the fan's whirr. 'After all these centuries.'

I stared up again at the lights. Piper was right – there was awe amidst my horror. I dared to lean forward, closer to the fan, my face pummelled by the air that the blades threw upwards. The illusion of wind, down here where no wind could ever reach.

I couldn't stop myself from picturing what would have happened had I been lowering myself through at the instant the blades started up. It would at least have been quick, I thought. A slicing so swift that there would be no time for pain. And Zach, somewhere, would have died just as quickly. Perhaps in a Council meeting, or inspecting the tanks in one of his new buildings at the refuge. He would suddenly have dropped to the floor, a puppet with the strings cut.

The brightness and the sound lasted for several minutes, although time was uncertain in that bunkered world. Then the lights blinked twice and failed completely, and the lamp became our only bulwark against the darkness. For a few moments more the blades continued to spin, but without the manic propulsion that we'd just witnessed. Instead, there were several revolutions, each one slower than the last, before the wheel settled into stillness.

'We still have to get through it,' I said.

'I know.' Piper held the lamp out over the blades, their sharpened edges glinting.

I wished he hadn't realised the wheel still turned. We were going to have to submit to the blades' mercy anyway. It had been easier before Piper had stripped away the illusion of safety.

He swung the lamp around the chamber. 'There's nothing here that we could use to jam it,' he said. He was right – no furniture, no panels that looked as though they could be prised loose and jammed between the blades and the hole's edge.

'We can't just lower ourselves through,' he said. 'We have to jump. The faster we get through it, the smaller the risk.'

Together we ventured again to the hole's rim. At the edge, where the spaces between the blades were widest, each gap was still barely two feet wide. Narrow enough that we'd have to jump with absolute precision to avoid hitting the blades. A painful knock at best. Sliced flesh at worst. And that was if the blades stayed motionless. If the Electric came back while we were passing through, there was no best or worst scenario – only one outcome.

We waited a while longer, to see whether there was any pattern to the outbursts of the Electric. It must have been about an hour that we sat there, and in that time the lights came on three more times, heralding the fan's spinning too. But there was no pattern that we could detect. The first two times were close together – only minutes separated them. The third came after a long period of darkness, and lasted only a few seconds, barely long enough for the wheel to achieve full speed.

The Electric was a ghost, trapped in the wires of the Ark. Its erratic presence added a new dimension of terror to the place, and making me wince at each new flaring of light and sound.

A few seconds after the last flicker of lights had left us, the blades were slowing.

'Now,' I said. I stepped to the edge of the hole again. Everything seemed hazy, my eyes still readjusting to the lamp-lit half dark.

'I'll go first,' he said. 'If something goes wrong, on my way through, you go back up.'

Back up to what? If he died, Zoe would be dead too. She would never come back, would never be found. The thought of making that cramped ascent, with Piper's body below me and Zoe's somewhere above, was worse than the thought of the fan itself.

'We'll do it at the same time,' I said.

He looked at me, then nodded. We stood on opposite sides of the hole.

'It's only a short drop,' he said. But we both knew it wasn't the drop that was making the sweat prickle my forehead. It was what we had to pass through, before we landed.

'You can't feel anything?' he asked. 'Any sense of when it might start up again?'

I shook my head. 'I didn't even realise it still went around at all.'

'Fine,' he said. 'We'll jump on three. Do you want to count?'

'Do you have a lucky number?' I said.

He gave a quiet laugh. 'Let's not rely on my luck.'

So I counted to three. I cringed away from the final syllable, but *three* came anyway, and we jumped.

I didn't get it quite right – my left knee clipped a blade's edge as I dropped through, propelling the next blade into my right shoulder. Piper, the lamp still in his hand, was a blur of light dropping opposite me. And there we both were, on the floor below. Piper exhaled, and I heard myself laughing, even as I was inspecting my shoulder for blood. Our smiles were quashed by the sound of the fan starting up again.

The wheel began spinning close above our heads. Directly under it, where we crouched, the force of the movement was overwhelming, gusting air pushing us to the ground.

'If we'd waited a few more seconds,' Piper shouted over the noise. 'If my lucky number had been ten, we'd be landing in pieces.'

'Maybe you're not so unlucky after all,' I yelled back, crawling to the wall, where the wind's buffeting was less forceful.

We scanned the room. Like the one above, the walls were packed with wires, tubes, and buttons – more than the previous room, in fact. The labels on the engraved plates were once again a frustrating mixture of the familiar and the incomprehensible: *VENT DUCT LEVEL 4*; *RE-ROUTE VIA DECONTAMINATION SLUICE*. On three of the four walls there were large metal hatches, each one sealed with a black material, cracked and perished.

'Which one of these is the right way?' asked Piper. He pulled at some of the black edging. It crumbled in his hand. I could see him sizing up the hatches. 'Hell on earth,' he shouted in my ear, 'I thought we'd finished with tunnels.'

'We have,' I said. 'Look.'

The lights failed at that instant, throwing us back into lamplit gloom.

'OK,' I said, into the merciful quiet. 'Listen, then.' I stepped back the way I'd come a moment before, and stamped gently. The dust on the ground subdued the sound slightly, but the clang was still audible. Something shifted beneath my foot: a loose panel in the steel floor.

Piper brought the lamp across, and we knelt together.

As we swept the dust aside from the concealed hatch, writing appeared, engraved in the metal of the panel itself.

EMERGENCY MAINTENANCE ACCESS ONLY.
DE-ACTIVATE INTAKE VALVES WHILE HATCH OPEN.
FOLLOW DECONTAMINATION PROCEDURES
WHEN LEAVING CONTROL ROOM.

'Does this count as an emergency?' Piper asked with a sideways smile.

The floor panel was rimmed in the same black material as the wall hatches, perished and crumbly to touch. When Piper pulled at the handle, the whole hatch came smoothly away. The tunnel below was wider than any of the other chutes we'd seen so far. Mounted on one side was a steel ladder.

Thirty or forty yards down the ladder, my feet struck another hatch. I paused for a while, to be sure that I could still feel no movement in the corridor below us. There was nothing but dust, and the residual hum of the Electric. Nonetheless, I moved as quietly as I could, placing the lantern carefully on the floor while I reached down to shift the hatch and push it to the side.

I lowered myself through the opening, dropping the final few feet to the ground. Piper followed. We were in the Ark.

CHAPTER 33

Here, at last, we'd been returned to an environment that was on a human scale. Not that it was hospitable: hard grey floors and low ceilings, and a long corridor receding into darkness in both directions. Every few yards a grille was set into the ceiling, and above them I could feel the network of ventilation tunnels that we had just left. Where we walked, in the main corridor, the lamp illuminated only a few square yards at a time. There, a steel door, open. Here, a corner, all the straight lines softened by dust. There, when Piper swung the light around, another door, opening onto another corridor, another shade of darkness.

Months before, when Zoe, Kip, and I had passed through the taboo city on the mountain pass, my mind had been jostled by the clamour of the dead. There was none of that here. I wondered if it was because the people of that city had died suddenly, when the blast came – ripped from their lives without warning. In the Ark, there was a different heaviness in the air, choking with silence. A slower dying. Years, then decades, of darkness and creeping and steel doors above them. An unease heavier than the hundreds of feet of stone and earth and river above us.

'Grim, isn't it,' said Piper, as he turned the lamp from side to side.

There was no point answering. Every inch of the place declared its bleakness.

'I thought it would be different,' he said. 'More comfortable, I suppose. I thought they were the lucky ones – but I can't imagine being stuck down here for long.'

I remembered too well, from my time in the Keeping Rooms, what conditions like this could do to a person. In those years in the cell, my nerves had been rubbed raw on all the hard surfaces, the locked doors, until each of my senses grated and jangled, and the low ceiling became a mockery of the unseen sky above.

I led us westward, in the circuitous manner that the Ark's geography permitted. Even here, out of the cramped ventilation tunnels, the dust was thick enough to mute the sound of our footsteps. Nobody had passed this way for a long time. I didn't doubt that the Council would have explored the whole Ark, but I could sense that nobody moved or breathed within this layer of the structure. I didn't even need to look into each room to be sure – their emptiness was as tangible to me as the dust. It was like picking up a water flask, and testing its weight – I had no need to unscrew the lid to know that it was empty.

Doorways on both sides stood ajar. For now, though, we kept to the main corridor. At regular intervals it passed through thick steel doors. They looked imposing, with elaborate locks, steel tumblers and bars, but each of them was open. I examined one of the locks. There was no keyhole, only a metal cube near the tumblers, studded with buttons, each with a number engraved on it, 0 to 9. These cubes had been unscrewed from the door and hung now from their own exposed wires.

Each time the sporadic bursts of the Electric unleashed the light, sound came with them. Above the insect buzz of the lights themselves came a whirring noise and occasional clanks from above, where air vents traced the corridors. When the lights went out, we were dropped into silence.

'No wonder so many of them went mad,' Piper said. 'It gives me the creeps just being in here.'

In some sections, water had penetrated the walls. The river above us had been kept at bay, but it had never stopped its stubborn groping downwards. Mould spread from the ceiling, a mass of black fur, like the pelt of some huge animal stretched across the right-hand wall of the corridor. We peered into a room in which a foetid puddle covered the entire floor, fed by a slow drip of water from the ceiling. The drips fell at the pace of footsteps, and as we walked away I had to steel myself not to check over my shoulder that we weren't being followed.

*

We stepped into a large room where the darkness seemed to push back against the edges of the lamp's glow. There was a long table, neatly laid: knives and forks set out, along with plates, each one offering up their meal of dust. I ran my hand down the back of one of the chairs. It wasn't wood, nor leather, nor any other material that I recognised. In the four centuries here, in this underground world, it hadn't mouldered or splintered. It was hard, but not cool under my touch in the way that metal would be.

Except for the grime, it was an everyday scene – the sort of thing that I would have expected to encounter in a kitchen or an inn. Piper put the lamp on the table and picked up one of the forks, lichened with rust. It clattered when he let it drop back down on the tabletop. I leaned over to set it back into its place, parallel with the knife, then realised how ridiculous it was, re-laying this table for ghosts.

The next door, like all the others, was open, the tumblers of the lock exposed. I brushed my hand across the front of the door and felt the engraving beneath my palm. When Piper raised the lamp, we could read it clearly, despite the dust still nested in the grooves of the engraved letters: *SECTION F.*

'This is where they put the crazy ones, right?' Piper said.

As I stepped through the doorway, something crumbled beneath my foot, with no more resistance than a dry biscuit. At my gasp he swung the lantern around.

My boot had crushed the thigh-bone of a skeleton. The bones lay around my feet, just inside the door.

Against the far wall, more skeletons lay. The lights came on in the corridor behind us, but the chamber we'd entered remained dark, and I recalled what it had said in the papers: *Electricity (excluding ventilation) has been disconnected, to prioritise the needs of the rest of the population.*

I looked back at the bones by the door. How long had those locked in Section F waited by the locked door, in the darkness? Had they clawed at the door, screamed and begged for release? The metal of the door bore no marks, told no stories.

Before we'd descended into the Ark, it was the soldiers and the unknown machines that I'd feared. I hadn't realised how much horror could lie in something much simpler: a steel door, and a cluster of bones.

*

We came across other bones soon. In a small room, a skeleton was curled on its side on a bunk bed, dust covering it like snow. Further down the corridor, a scattering of bones lay on the floor. They looked as though they had been kicked aside. A few yards from the rest of the skeletons, a lone skull rested upside down, a bowl of teeth.

'Did the Council soldiers do this?' I said.

Piper knelt, examined the bones.

'It's recent, whoever it was – look at the colour, where the bones've been broken.'

I bent to see. Where the bones had snapped, the lantern revealed bright white, a cross section of clean bone contrasting with the browned surface.

He moved off down the corridor, taking the light with him.

The door marked *SECTION G* had jammed half-closed. We had to sidle in, the jutting tumblers of the lock catching at my shirt.

There were no beds here. Instead, a row of benches was topped with tubes and handles, and basins set into the steel surface. I peered into one; it had a drainage hole at the bottom, with a dead spider next to it.

Along the back of the room, shelves were crammed with huge jars, the glass clouded by centuries. Where a jar had crumbled or broken, a ring of sharpened dust remained.

I drew near to the shelves. Once there might have been liquid inside the jars, preserving their contents like brine in my mother's pickle jars. Or like the Council's tanks. There was no liquid left now – just a dirty line of residue below each lid. At the bottom of every jar was a nest of tiny bones.

If I hadn't already seen the baby skeletons in the grotto beneath the Council fort at Wyndham, I might have allowed myself to hope that these were the skeletons of some kind of small animals. But denial was a luxury I couldn't permit myself, and when I forced myself to look closely, it was clear that the small skulls were human, each one tiny enough to sit in my palm.

'Look,' Piper said. He placed the lantern on the shelf, picked up one of the skulls and held it out to me.

I took it. It weighed almost nothing, eggshell-light, and had turned a yellow brown. When I turned it over in my hand, I saw what Piper had noticed: the three eye sockets. I balanced it gently back amongst the other bones, its three eyes looking out.

'These were some of the *involuntary subjects*, then, from Topside,' Piper said.

In the next room the shelves were larger, and the jars they held were the size of small barrels. At the bottom of each jar were two skeletons, two skulls. These must have been amongst the earliest of the twins. I bent to stare through the clouded glass into the closest jar. The two skulls had rolled together. One of the tiny jawbones had fallen open, as if mid-cry. The rest of the bones were all dislodged, piled loosely like kindling set for a fire.

Most of the labels were perished to nothing, or blackened with fungus. On some, though, we could still make out words:

Pair 4 (Secondary twin: Hyperdontia)
7 (Secondary twin: Polycephalic)

One of the skulls had row after row of teeth, overlapping. In another jar, the larger of the two skulls sported four eye sockets, and two noses.

I tried to picture these people, the Ark dwellers, labelling the jars. Attaching convoluted names to Omegas, as if these labels would make our bodies less unruly. Seeking out all the ways in which we diverged from them. Cutting open the children; assembling and reassembling them; counting their bones.

The back wall of the next room was constructed entirely of drawers, floor to ceiling. I pulled one open. It was deeper than I could have imagined; it slid out more than a yard, and would have slid further if I hadn't been stopped by the rattle of loose bones. Staring up at me was a skull, still rocking slightly.

Each of the drawers we opened was the same. I was beginning to feel that the whole Ark was constructed not of steel and concrete but of bones.

Piper saw me blanching, and pushed shut the drawer that I was holding.

'These bones don't tell us anything,' he said. 'Why are there no papers? No records?'

'The Council's cleared it out.'

There was nothing here to show us how the Ark dwellers had managed to undo the fatal bond. If that information still existed, it had been taken or destroyed by Zach and The General.

Piper kicked the drawer nearest to him. Something inside it dislodged and clanged against the steel.

'There are still more levels to search,' I said, trying to keep the hopelessness from my voice. 'And they haven't finished with the Ark yet. There's a reason the soldiers are still here.'

We trawled those dusty rooms for hours. Walls with a tracery of rust and damp. A baby's skull the exact weight of a nightmare. A bench with bones laid out like a shop display.

*

Now, in the corridors below us, the soldiers were moving. I could feel them, just as I could feel the river moving above us. It was an awareness that was neither hearing nor sight, but was no less vivid. Once or twice, noises did penetrate from below. The clank of metal on metal; a distant shout. I was afraid to lead us down there, but hours of searching the two upper levels had revealed nothing but mildew and bones. The Council, or somebody before them, had taken everything that could be of any use. And the soldiers themselves had long ago abandoned these higher levels – the dust confirmed that.

I dragged a chair to beneath one of the ventilation grilles in the ceiling, and Piper stepped up onto it and used his knife to unscrew the metal grate. The rust had done its work, so it took him a while, but when the grille was laid on the floor we hauled ourselves through the gap and back into the network of tunnels.

There were grates every few yards, so as we crawled along the tunnels that traced the corridors, we could peer down periodically and catch glimpses of the empty rooms and corridors that we passed. I guided us to where the tunnel sloped down, following a flight of stairs to the next level, and then I extinguished the lantern, so that our own light wouldn't betray us. From then on, we could see only when the Electric flashed on, the grilles casting stripes of light in the tunnel, and allowing us to look down to the concrete floors below.

The lights were off when we heard the soldiers coming. Two of them, from the sound of the footsteps, accompanied by the noisy rattling of a handcart. They rounded the corner, the lantern mounted on the cart swinging from side to side and throwing seasick shadows on the corridor walls.

I froze, and tried not to panic at how the steel tube amplified even the sound of my breath.

There was a jolt as the cart scraped against the wall, and one of the men swore.

'Go steady. That's not hay you're pushing.'

They were almost below us now. I could see the sweat on the balding head of the older soldier, as he paused to steady the cart.

The second man grunted. 'Hot as hell down here. Can't blame me for being in a hurry to get outside.'

I squinted, trying to make out what was inside the cart itself, but all I could see was a bundle of wires, and the glint of metal.

'You tip the cart and break this stuff and neither of us is going anywhere,' the bald man said. 'You saw what happened to Cliff.'

The younger man said nothing, but slowed his pace. 'Won't be sorry to see the back of this place,' he said.

'You're not staying on with the technicians?'

The younger man shook his head. 'I'll be working on the installation at the new bunker, once this is all sorted.'

They had moved out of sight, but not out of earshot. I didn't dare to follow them – the sound of our crawling, only a yard above their heads, was too great a risk.

The older man spoke. 'You won't have too long to wait. Two weeks, if all goes smoothly, they were saying in the mess tent yesterday. But three's more like it, I reckon.'

'Three at least,' his companion said. I had to strain to catch his words as the men drew further away. 'Unless they start having us pull night shifts. Going to be a bitch of a job, clearing those last few rooms. The corridors down there are only just wide enough for the mobile generators. Some of it's going to have to be taken apart on site.'

For a while longer we could hear the rattle of the cart, and then nothing. After that we moved even more slowly, and flinched at each accidental thud of our knees and elbows on the echoing metal tunnel. A lone soldier passed below us, and then another pair with a cart, but they moved too fast for us to see any detail through the grates. Sometimes fragments of conversation reached us, from soldiers we couldn't even see, the sound garbled by the pipes. *Back to the comms room . . . Without the batteries ... If it's fish again tonight I swear . . . Check under the converter rig . . .*

After an hour or more I noted that they had all begun to head in the same direction: outward, towards the stairs that led to the western door.

We forced ourselves to wait another hour. Counting the seconds helped to keep my mind off the heat and the hunger, and the pain of my knees and elbows from dragging myself through the tunnels.

When an hour had passed without soldiers, and I could sense no movement in the area around us, I relit the lamp. There was no quiet way to leave the tunnels. I managed to blunt my knife scraping at the rusted bolts, and in the end I had to shuffle forwards so that Piper could dislodge the final screw with several blows from his elbow, sending the panel crashing down to the concrete floor six feet below. Here, where the soldiers had been working and walking, there wasn't even a layer of dust to muffle the clang.

Piper dropped quickly after the grate, and I followed, half convinced that I was lowering myself into an ambush. But there was only Piper, knife in hand, slightly hunched in the low-roofed corridor.

'Help me put the panel back,' I whispered.

'If they didn't come at that noise, there's no point whispering,' he replied, but he did as I said, taking the other side of the grille and helping me to rest it back into position.

A soldier would have needed to look closely to see that it was no longer fixed in place.

Night must have come to the surface, where the soldiers guarded the entrances on the hill above us. My hunger reminded me, too, how long we'd spent in the Ark, and Piper and I ate some of the jerky, which my pockets had not protected from the dust. As we chewed, we walked in silence along the narrow corridors inspecting the many rooms leading off it. Some were empty; others contained furniture, but all the shelves had been stripped, and the drawers sat open and bare.

The small room at the end of the corridor was different. Instead of furniture, the walls were covered with machines, metal boxes built into the walls. Dust had settled on the buttons and dials, but it was nowhere near as thick as in the upper levels. Some of the machine casings were opened, and partly dismantled. From one panel, a tangle of wires spilled, reminding me of the man I'd seen during the battle of New Hobart, his guts unspooling from his sliced stomach.

The lights came on. I moved to one of the walls, and tried to read what I could of the labels, but the words meant nothing to me: *Satellite 4. Triangulate. Radio Rec 2.*

Next to me, Piper ran his hand along the smooth front of a piece of black glass, his finger leaving a line in the dust.

The voice that filled the room was at once too loud, and too distant. Piper spun, pushing me between him and the door as he pulled out his knife. But the noise didn't come from the door, or from any single place. It seemed to echo throughout the room, from all sides at once.

My hand, too, was on my knife. But there was no soldier to aim at, or to cower from. I couldn't match the evidence of my ears to what I could see: the empty room. And what I could feel: the absence of any living person, other than the two of us, frozen by the doorway.

The voice stopped and started, like Xander when he hurled himself again and again at the locked door of language. In between the fragments of words, there were bursts of noise. A crackling like a fire catching on in dry hay.

> . . . *is a recorded transmiss. . . from the Confederacy of the Scattered Islands . . . in the detonations, and suffered direct strikes on ... survivors, but the southern and western regions remain uninhabitable . . . despite massive loss of life . . . agriculture re-established, and progress in . . . the plague of twins successfully treated, except in outlying islands . . . mutations widespread but varying in severity . . . latitude, and . . .. please respond. . . . se respond . . .*
> . . . *is a recorded transmiss . . . from the Confederacy of the Scattered Islands . . . in the detonations . . .*

Six times we listened to it. The same words, and the same blasts of raw noise. Then the lights went out again, and the darkness extinguished the sound.

I had thought the Electric was like a ghost, trapped in the wires of the Ark. But this was the real ghost: a voice from Elsewhere, captured here in this airless room. Somehow, through the miles and the years and the machines, this message had come through.

My heart battered at my ribs like a fist. Piper and I didn't speak. What was there to say? I felt as though language itself had taken on a new gravity, as if I had understood, for the first time, the power of words. That string of broken words, spat out by the machine, came from Elsewhere. Each word was a new blast, reshaping our world.

For the next hour, each time the Electric returned, we

explored the machines in that room. But all we succeeded in doing was starting and stopping the voice, by pressing the panel that Piper had touched. The rest of the machines yielded nothing to our frantic fingers. Many were half-disassembled; all were coated in dust. And there was nothing else to find: no papers, no maps. Nothing more tangible than the voice.

Even as we searched, I knew that it was futile. If these machines were still working, and if they were capable of receiving any further messages from Elsewhere, there would be soldiers here night and day. The Council had searched this room more thoroughly than we ever could. The only thing that the machines could do now was to regurgitate that single message. We had found all that there was to find, and it was enough. It proved that Elsewhere had survived, and that they had ended the twinning. And it proved that the Council knew it too.

CHAPTER 34

It was hard to keep track of time down there, where sunlight was a memory, and even the air was heavy with dust. But we knew that the soldiers must return, and that when they did we'd have to retreat back to the ventilation tunnels, or to the upper levels. I knew also that the Ark had not revealed all its secrets to us. Elsewhere had survived, but we still had to find it. Undoing the twinning was possible, but we still needed to know how. So we left the room of the sporadic voice, and I led Piper down the eastern corridor, and down the stairs.

At the base of the staircase, the door had been blasted open - only a margin of steel remained, hanging from the twisted hinges. A sign on the wall read: *SECTION A – RESTRICTED ACCESS (level 6a)*. Beyond the doorway, the lights in the corridors no longer flared on and off, but were constant and unflickering. It felt strange that the deepest levels of the Ark were the brightest. But the papers had shown that the Pandora Project had been kept going, even when the Ark residents were rationing the lights, and locking some people away in the dark. Here, in the belly of the

Ark, the Electric was still working properly. There had been hints, in Joe's papers, that the Ark had some fuels that wouldn't fail: *the nuclear power cells will outlast us all*. But it was one thing to have read it on a mouldering page, in words whose meanings had been buried along with the Ark, and another to see it here: the light that had endured all this time. It seemed a kind of magic, some witchery of machines.

Piper had passed through the doorway. I paused for a moment behind him. The horrors of the Ark had been vivid enough by lamplight, and in the inconsistent electric lights that had flared on from time to time. Whatever was in Section A we would have to face without the mercy of darkness. I took two slow breaths before I followed Piper through the door.

For an instant I thought I'd been hit on the head. The blast was so vivid, the explosion of light so forceful, that I screamed, stumbling forwards and reeling into Piper, my hands clutched to my face. Piper's lips were moving, but the snarl of flames in my head swallowed all other noise. He propped me upright but I shrugged him off, blundering past him to crouch against the wall, my head squeezed between my forearms.

When the vision had receded I was able to stand once again, but white spots still blurred my sight, and the smell of scorching was thick in my nostrils.

'Keep going,' I said to Piper, waving him forward, and shaking my head to try to clear it. I kept one hand on the wall to steady myself as we walked further down the corridor. There was a noise here that had been absent from the rest of the Ark. I closed my eyes to listen to it: the hiss of water. I'd felt the river above us ever since we'd entered the Ark, but now I could hear it too. As well as the ventilation tunnels, huge water pipes traced the ceiling, and they rumbled with the river's black current.

Room after room was empty. Not empty in the same way as the upper levels that we'd wandered, where the stark grey walls appeared always to have been bare. The rooms in Section A had been hollowed, stripped of their contents. The walls themselves were half removed, whole panels missing, the wiring and tubes exposed. Elsewhere the wires had been cut, close to the walls. Copper tendrils sprouted from the frayed stumps.

The blast recurred in my head, aftershocks stuttering like the lights in the Ark's upper levels. I clenched my teeth together and tried to concentrate on the wreckage of these rooms. There were so many of them: huge chambers, and small rooms that branched off them. All had been stripped.

There was no trail of smashed equipment like the one Kip and I had left behind in the silo when we'd tried to break the machines. There were no machines here, broken or otherwise, except a few trailing wires. Where things had been removed from the walls, they'd been carefully excised: neat saw-marks on the concrete showed where whole structures had been excavated. All that remained were labels on doors or walls, for things that were no longer there:

COOLANT PUMP (3)
CONDENSATE OUTLET
VALVE PRESSURE (AUX)

'The Council haven't destroyed anything,' I said. 'They're just moving it to somewhere else.' I thought of *the new bunker* that the soldier had mentioned a few hours earlier.

They hadn't quite finished stripping Section A yet. Further into the warren of rooms, we found some that had not been cleared, or not entirely. Wall panels were still intact, each one crowded with dials and buttons. Several had constellations of lights, too, flashing green or orange. In some of the rooms, the dismantling was halfway completed, panels removed and their workings exposed. A parchment lay on the floor, a detailed drawing mirroring the panel nearby, with each wire and socket numbered. Beside it sat a handcart, half-loaded with the disassembled machines, each item tagged with a numbered label. When I examined the diagram on the floor, I could make nothing of it: only numbers, and the odd unfamiliar word: *Launch coordinates. Manual override.* The complexity of the machines was overwhelming – it was clear that shifting the equipment had been the work of years. It was like dismantling and relocating an entire beach, with each grain of sand meticulously labelled.

The next room, though it was only small, hummed with noise. The open door wore an engraved placard:

H_2S *PROJECT*
CLASSIFIED
ACCESS RESTRICTED – CERTIFIED H_2S
TECHNICIANS ONLY

I looked up at Piper, but his face was as blank as mine. 'You didn't find anything about this in Joe's papers?' he said.

I shook my head and stepped inside.

I had expected some new horror, but what greeted us in the half-dark room was familiar. I knew by the smell, even before I saw the shape of the tanks, lit only by the flashing lights above them. The air of the room was thick with the too-sweet stench of the tank liquid, overlaid with a sour taint of dust and decades.

There were ten tanks, in two neat rows. The glass was smeared with grime. From the metal ring that encased the base of each tank, a rash of orange rust crept up the glass.

In most of the tanks, a figure floated. I'd thought that Sally was old, but these figures had passed beyond old age and back into a kind of fleshy babyhood. They curled in the water, their bloated skin puffy. Their flesh was loose on them, and it was pale and wet as the skin under a freshly-peeled scab. Their noses and ears seemed too large, as if these had kept growing while the rest of their bodies wasted.

They were all men. If they'd once had hair, it had gone now, the skin bare even where their eyebrows and eyelashes should have been. Their fingernails were so long that they dragged on the base of the tanks, tangled like the dangling roots of the swamp trees near New Hobart. The nails on their toes had browned and curled tightly. One of the men had his eyes slightly open, but they revealed only whiteness. It was impossible to tell whether his eyes were rolled back, or whether all the years of immersion had bleached his irises.

When we'd sailed to the island, Kip and I had seen jellyfish floating in the dark water. The men in the tanks reminded me of those: the formlessness, and the puffy, sodden texture of their flesh.

Piper moved closer to the tanks. His mouth was twisted, his nostrils narrowed – his whole face distorted with disgust.

'Are they alive?' he asked.

I looked more closely. In the front row of tanks, nearest to the door, there were still tubes in the men's noses and wrists. The flesh had grown around the tubes so that it was hard to tell where the skin ended and the tubes began. I pressed my face to the glass, and stared at one of the men's wrists, where a fleshy tuber protruded, swallowing the first few inches of the tube. The machines above the tanks still thrummed, and the man vibrated, nearly imperceptibly, with the machine's pulse.

In the back row of the tanks, however, the machines had been dismantled, and the tubes stripped away. Two of them still held men, but they floated utterly motionless, the surface of the liquid undisturbed by the electric hum.

I pointed to them. 'These ones are dead,' I said. 'The liquid's kept them from rotting, but the Council must've taken the machines apart, to see how they worked.'

The last three tanks in the back row were empty, their lids open. The liquid had been drained – only a few inches remained, a sticky puddle at the floor of each tank. Over the lip of one of the tanks, two tubes hung limply.

'And these ones?' Piper gestured his head at the front row, below the intact machines.

'Not dead,' I said. 'But not alive, either. There's nothing there – just their bodies.'

'Are they really from the Before?'

I didn't need to tell him. The scene in front of us was its own answer. The ancient tanks; the flesh that had grown over the tubes; the skin bleached of colour, steeped in centuries of silence.

'Who did this to them?' Piper said. 'I thought this started with Zach. Why would somebody tank these people in the Before? They didn't even have twins – not proper ones like we do.'

I shook my head. 'I think they did it to themselves.'

I should have known that the idea for the tanks would have its origin here. The Council, or perhaps Zach himself, had found this and replicated it. In Zach's hands, these ten tanks had spawned thousands of others. The ten glass tanks in this room had begun something that would be the end of all Omegas. Where Piper and I saw a ghoulish and futile exercise, Zach and The General had seen an opportunity.

I walked to the side wall. A plaque was mounted there. Rust from the wall had corroded it, but when I raised the lamp, I could see that somebody in recent years had scraped clean the words engraved in the centre, so that they were legible.

HERE THE SURVIVING MEMBERS OF THE ARK'S INTERIM GOVERNMENT ARE PRESERVED, IN THE HOPE THAT IF HUMANITY HAS SURVIVED ELSEWHERE, WE MAY BE FOUND, AND AWAKENED, TO SHARE THE KNOWLEDGE OF OUR TIME, AND TO PASS IT ON TO NEWER GENERATIONS.

'*The knowledge of our time?*' I said. And I found myself laughing – a hacking laughter that my body threw up as a final defence against what I was seeing. 'Waiting, all this time, for *humanity* to find them. When they knew, all along, about the survivors above them.'

I moved to join Piper, back by the tanks.

'They must've realised, in the end,' I went on, 'that nobody was coming to find them. They'd heard the message from Elsewhere, but nothing else. All those years. Decades.' I wrinkled my nose as I stared at the bodies. Despite the bloatedness, the men had no deformations. No extra limbs, or missing eyes. Each of the floating men a piece of pickled perfection. They were saving themselves – but not for us. I stood next to Piper, his single arm touching the glass beside my own raised hands. To these men, Piper and I would have been no more than abominations.

He was staring at the nearest man's wrist, where tube had become flesh, or flesh had become tube.

'If they're alive,' Piper said, 'should we try to wake them? Talk to them? Hell on earth, if these are really people from the Ark, from the Before, then think what they could tell us. More about Elsewhere, for one thing.'

'The Council's already tried that,' I said, gesturing at the three empty tanks. 'But I could've saved them the effort: these men can't tell us anything.' Stepping closer to the glass, I watched the white eyes of the floating man. I pressed my hands against the tank, but I could feel nothing but the glass against my palms. When I'd seen the unconscious Omegas in the tanks beneath Wyndham, I'd felt a spark of presence within each of them. That was what had made their suspended state so appalling: knowing that trapped within each stranded body was a mind. But the man who drifted in front of me now was simply a sack of flesh, with no consciousness to animate it.

'They're not dead,' I said, 'but there's nothing left of them.'

These were not people, any more than driftwood was a tree.

We left them there, in the tanks they'd built for themselves. The smell clung to us long after we'd gone.

We moved through more half-emptied rooms and echoing corridors. We were at the southern end of Section A when the blast came again. Just ahead of me, Piper had entered a large room. When I followed him, the memory of flames radiated from the doorway, in a blast so total that my eyes rolled back in my head. I reeled backwards, and I must have cried out, because I felt Piper grab me round the waist as I fell, and then everything went. It didn't go black – it just went. The world was ripped away by flame, and I was unconscious before Piper had lowered me to the ground.

*

When I woke, I was lying on the concrete floor. I put my hand to my face and felt the furring of dust, where it had stuck to my sweaty skin.

Another flash of light erupted behind my eyes.

'I can't handle this now,' I said, shaking my head as if that would make it stop.

'Calm down,' he said. 'Listen to me.'

'Don't tell me how to handle it,' I barked at him. 'It's the end of the world, and it's happening in my head. Again and again. You have no idea what it's like.' The only person who did know was Xander. And Lucia, before the water took her. These were the only ones who would understand me now: the dead and the mad.

'What if it's not what you think it is?' Piper said quietly.

I stared at him. 'You're not the one who has to live with it every day. You think you can do a better job of dealing with it or understanding it?'

'I didn't say that,' he said. 'I'm just asking you to think about it.' He bent close to me. 'Why do you see the past in that one vision, and not in any of the others?'

It was hard to concentrate on his question, with the flames still burning in the edges of my mind, and the earth and the river above bearing down on me.

'I do have other visions of the past, sometimes.' I sat up. 'Impressions of it, anyway.' I couldn't always disentangle my visions from my dreams or my memories, and time was capricious in all of them. In the taboo town, on the mountaintop, I'd felt the lives and deaths of four hundred years ago hanging over the town like a fog. And when Piper had told me about the massacre on the island, a week or more after it had happened, I'd seen it unfolding. At other times, I saw distant events at the same time as they happened. I'd learnt too well that if I witnessed a death then my visions would probably force me to witness the twin's death at the same moment.

'I know it's not straightforward,' Piper said. 'But almost all of your visions – the real ones – they're of the future, not the past. Why would the blast be different?'

I shook my head. 'The blast isn't just the past, though. It doesn't fit into time like other things do.' Piper had ridden through the ash drifts of the deadlands beside me. He of all people should know that the blast had never ended. In our crooked bodies and our blighted world, we lived it every day.

'Listen to me,' he said. 'You've always assumed that your blast visions are flashbacks. But what if you stop trying to justify why they're different from your other visions, and consider that they might be just the same?' His eyes didn't leave mine. 'Why else would the visions of the blast be happening more and more often? Not just for you, but for Xander too. Even for Lucia, before she died.' He paused. I could hear the river above us, and the hum of the Electric. My own pulse pounding in my head, urgent as running footsteps. 'Something's coming, Cass. What if it's not the past you're seeing, when you see the blast? What if it's the future?'

'No,' I said. My voice sounded strange to me: high and quavering.

'That's the Pandora Project, that they were working on here in Section A – it's not about finding Elsewhere, or splitting the twins. It's the blast. The machines to do it again.'

'No.' It was a shout, a plea. I wanted to hush him – I felt as if his words themselves might unleash the flames. If he'd seen what I'd seen – if he'd witnessed the world burn, again and again – he couldn't have knelt there and offered the suggestion as if it were a thing that could be contained.

There was something else stirring in me, alongside my raw terror. It was recognition. The *yes* of my whole body, seeing the blasts at last for what they were: visions, not memories.

It was going to happen again.

CHAPTER 35

We sat together on the floor amidst the gritty dust, the dander of the concrete that had been sawn away. There was a buzzing in my ears. I couldn't tell if it was the ringing that my blast visions sometimes left me with, or just the hum of the Electric.

I stared at the concrete wall. I was grateful to focus on one simple thing, amongst a world in which everything was its own opposite. Zach was my twin, and also my enemy. I had loved Kip but he was also a stranger. The blast was the past, but also the future. Xander was mad, but his words would come true: forever fire.

'I've feared it,' Piper said, 'ever since I saw how the blast was coming to you more and more. But I still don't understand it. They can't use the blast machines against us. The casualties would be just as high on their own side. It's the one blessing of the twinning: it makes mass killing pointless. There's nowhere here that wouldn't be a disaster – for them as much as us. If they could deal with us that way, they would've done it a long time ago. That's why they'v bothered with the weapons that they had in the Be

393

'They're bothering now,' I said.

'But why? Why go to all this effort to create another blast, when they can never use it against us?'

I looked up at him, and the awful weight of words settled on me. I didn't want to tell him what I knew. He had enough burdens. But I couldn't carry this alone.

'They're not going to use the blast on us. They're going to use it on Elsewhere.'

I gestured at the room, and the others that led off it, most of them meticulously emptied. 'They know that Elsewhere is out there – maybe they've even found out where it is. And they know that Elsewhere can undo the twinning, and that we've been seeking it too. If they think Elsewhere could become a threat to their rule, they won't hesitate to use the blast.'

I remembered again The General, the lizard stillness of her eyes when she'd smiled. And Zach, the anger that coursed through him like the river through the pipes above us.

'I was wrong again,' I said. The steel and concrete walls threw my words back at me as echoes. 'I've had visions of the blast my whole life, and I've been wrong that whole time. Everything I see gets twisted.' I rubbed my hands to my eyes as though I could polish my visions into focus, somehow scour them clear.

'You found Joe's papers,' Piper said. 'You found the way into the Ark. We couldn't have done any of this without you.'

'I thought we were going to find the answer down here,' I said flatly.

'We did,' Piper said. 'It just wasn't the answer that we wanted.'

*

There was one more level of the Ark still underneath us, unexplored, but I was beginning feel the first stirrings of movement in the outer corridors, where they led to the surface doors. A shifting in the air, disturbing the dust. Then noises, reaching us through the pipes. We left the brightly lit lower levels and sprinted up the stairs to where we'd left the ventilation grille unscrewed. The first soldiers passed below us just as we'd hoisted ourselves back into the pipe and were replacing the hatch. But they were too noisy and busy, pushing their empty handcarts, to note the muted scrape of metal, or the hushed breath coming from somewhere above them. When they'd passed, we moved again, dragging our exhausted bodies towards the upper layers of the Ark. Five more groups of soldiers passed below us. Their discussions were at once familiar and unfamiliar: the everyday chatter of bored soldiers mixed with the strange language of the Ark.

Not likely, unless the betavoltaic batteries go too. . . Two more trolleys coming from the western door, to meet the next wagon. . . Been there since the blast – what's the rush?... Under the coolant pipes. Couldn't shift the casing without a drill.

One word, though, made me jerk my head so sharply that it hit the roof of the pipe. *Reformer.* I heard, too, Piper's intake of breath behind me. Motionless, I listened. There were no soldiers within sight, but the voices and footsteps came from somewhere nearby.

Said he wants to inspect it himself, so get it cleared. You know what he's like.

The voices were gone.

Somewhere in the Ark my brother waited. The last time I'd seen him had been on the road outside New Hobart, the knees of my trousers still wet from where I'd knelt to shroud the bodies of the drowned children. I remembered the sight of Louisa's small teeth, rounded like gravestones.

For a long time, as Piper and I crawled our way back to the upper levels, I thought about what we'd heard the soldier say: *You know what he's like.* Did it apply to me, anymore? Could I claim to know Zach now, after all that he'd done? And did he know me?

More than a decade ago, he'd relied on his knowledge of me to have me exposed and branded. When he declared himself the Omega, he'd known that I would step forward. He'd known me well enough to be sure that I wouldn't let him be branded and sent away. He had made our closeness into a weapon, and turned it on me. And I had allowed him to do it, when I'd chosen to protect him, whatever it had cost me. Now, the man waiting somewhere in the Ark wasn't even Zach anymore – he was The Reformer. Was I a different person too?

When Piper and I reached the abandoned upper levels we lowered ourselves from the pipe into the dusty rooms near Section F. Amongst the jars of bones, we sat and ate more of the jerky, and drank most of the water. I'd thought that rest would be impossible, after all that we had seen and learned since entering the Ark, but it had been at least two nights since we'd last slept. We found a small room, free of bones, and slept.

Instead of the blast, I dreamed of Kip. His body was blurred by the glass and by the liquid in which it floated. But the hazy silhouette was enough – I would know his body anywhere.

I woke and I knew, with a certainty that nested in my flesh like frostbite, that these visions of Kip in the tank were not from the past, any more than the blast visions were. On the road outside New Hobart, Zach had told me that he had something of mine. When he'd tossed the figureheads onto the ground in front of me, I'd thought he'd been talking about the ships, and their crews. But I understood now what he'd meant.

'He's here,' I said. 'In the Ark.'

'We know that already,' Piper said, his voice still groggy with sleep. 'You heard what the soldiers said.'

'Not Zach,' I said. 'Kip.'

Piper pushed himself up, leaning on his elbow. Dust from the ground had caught in his hair, and in the stubble on his chin. When he spoke his voice was patient.

'You're tired. What we've learned is a lot to take in. For anyone, and especially for you.'

I threw off his pity like an unwelcome embrace.

'I'm not mad. I've been seeing it, ever since he died. I thought it was just memories from when I found him under Wyndham. But you were right – that's not how it works.' I thought of how vivid it was, when I saw Kip in the tank, and of how the sight ambushed me even when I slept. 'It's a vision, not a memory. If even the blast is the future, then this is too. They have Kip. And he's in a tank again, or will be.'

It wasn't hope that had driven me to my feet. I knew Kip had died. I had seen the damage to him – nobody could survive that fall. I'd heard the sound of his landing, so wet that it had swallowed its own echo. And I'd seen The Confessor's body, too, the breath wrung from it like water from a rag.

So it was anger that ran through me now, not hope. I had seen what his years in the tank had done to him. The thought of him being returned to the tanks now was a horror so heavy that it choked words in my throat.

When I'd freed him from the tank beneath Wyndham and we were scrambling away, on the cliff above the river, he'd told me that he would jump to his death rather than be caught and taken back to the tanks. Months later, in the silo, that was what he'd done. I was the seer, but Kip had made his own prophecy, and kept it.

Now Zach had taken even that from him.

*

We had to wait a few more hours for the night's exodus of soldiers through the western door to the camp outside. When it came, it felt like the Ark exhaling slowly. I was impatient, but now that I knew what waited for me on the lowest level, my terror had taken on new shapes. I kept thinking of Xander's words to me, when I'd mentioned Kip: *It's not finished.*

When all seemed quiet in the corridors below us, we crawled along the tunnels, clambering down from level to level. This time, when we passed above the emptied rooms of Section A, I knew what to expect, and I clamped my teeth together and vowed not to cry out when the blast visions came. We had come too far now to be caught by a careless cry, to be flushed out like rats by some soldier on a night patrol. When the blast tore through my mind, I braced my body against the walls of the pipe and thought of Kip. When the flames released me, my tongue was bleeding from where I'd bitten it, but I had not made a sound.

The pipe traced the final staircase to the Ark's lowest level, below the rooms we'd explored the night before. The door at the base of the stairs was closed, and the lock looked intact, but in the ventilation pipe we passed unimpeded over the doorway. Beyond it, the Electric still hummed noisily, but the only light visible was an ambient green glow, leaking through the grate ahead. I pressed my face to it and looked down.

A single huge room occupied nearly the entire level, pillars supporting the high ceiling. Like the rooms above, it had been stripped back to its concrete bones: the walls were chipped and scarred, wires protruding from the wall and floor. But where the rooms above had been left bare, this vast chamber had been filled again, with row after row of tanks. Those that I could see, in the rows closest to us, were empty. The glow that suffused the room came from above the tanks, where panels blinked with tiny green lights.

The tanks in the central rows were big enough for one person, while the tanks lined up at each side were massive – the size of the tanks we'd found in New Hobart. As I'd seen there, and in the tank room beneath Wyndham, raised gangways ran beside each row, to allow access to the tanks from above. Suspended over the tanks was a network of pipes and wires; amidst them, running along the centre of the ceiling, loomed a huge pipe, several yards wide. It rumbled with the sound of the impatient river.

On my elbows, I dragged myself forward to the next grate, which was directly above one of the gangways. I had to kindle the lantern again to give me enough light to undo the screws. My knife was already blunted, and my hands were shaky with exhaustion and anger, but there was less rust on these bolts, and within minutes the grate was free. I lifted it carefully into the pipe, slid it out of the way, and dropped to the gangway just a few feet below.

I'd tried to land gently, but at the sound of my feet hitting the metal, footsteps echoed near the middle of the room. In the dim light, and through the ranks of glass, I couldn't see him, but I knew that he had seen me.

CHAPTER 36

Zach was twenty yards away, and sidling to the far door when I finally spotted him. He stopped the instant that Piper landed beside me. Before Piper's boots had sounded on the gangway, his arm was already drawn back, knife poised to throw. He held the blade so delicately, between thumb and one finger, but I'd seen him kill enough times to know that there'd be nothing delicate about the impact if he launched the knife at Zach's throat.

'Kill me, and you kill her too,' Zach said, his voice a breathless yell.

'If you raise the alarm, I'm dead anyway,' said Piper. 'Tortured too, and Cass'll be tanked. She and I both know what choice we'd make, if it comes to that.' I know that Piper was remembering the same thing that I was: the moment outside New Hobart, when the battle had turned against us, and his knife had been pointed at me. We'd never discussed it. We'd never needed to.

'Don't think about running,' Piper went on. 'Even if you dodge my knife, she won't.'

'Hell on earth, put out the lantern, at least,' Zach shouted at me. 'There's hydrogen sulphide in some of these pipes – you'll blow your hand off.'

I didn't understand all of Zach's words, but the panic in his eyes, as they darted from the lantern to the pipes above us, was real enough. I lifted the lantern's shutter and blew out the flame, returning us to the dim green glow of the machines' lights.

'You can point your knife at me all you like,' Zach called up to Piper. 'But you'll never get out of the Ark.'

'I know what you're doing,' I said. 'I know about the blast machine, and Elsewhere.'

'You don't know anything,' he said.

'You said to me, years ago, in the Keeping Rooms, that you wanted to do something with your life. You said you wanted to change the world. You could have done that, with what you found here. Not the blast machine. The other things: you could have ended the twinning. You know it's possible. Elsewhere did it.'

'And make us all into freaks, like the two of you? That's what it does, you know, ending the twinning. It doesn't free us of Omegas after all. It makes us all into Omegas.'

'You'd rather that people are stuck with the fatal bond, instead?' said Piper.

Zach waved his arm dismissively. 'We found a way round that,' he said. 'I found a way to be free of you after all, with the tanks. We don't need Elsewhere. For four hundred years, we've managed to preserve humanity. Proper humanity. It survived the blast itself, and the Long Winter, and four hundred years of deadlands and droughts and everything else we've had to contend with. And after all that, Elsewhere would end it, if you drag them into this. Just when we've found a way to be free of Omegas, Elsewhere could make us all into freaks.'

I shook my head. 'And you honestly think there's more humanity in what you're suggesting? Making another blast, and destroying Elsewhere, rather than ending the twinning and accepting that there'll be mutations?'

'If you really think that being an Omega is nothing to be ashamed of,' Zach hissed, 'then why did you hide it? Why did you lie for so long, right through our childhoods, and work so hard at pretending to be one of us?'

'Because I wanted to stay with my family,' I said. I didn't take my eyes from his. 'I wanted to stay with you.'

'No,' he said. 'You wanted to pass yourself off as an Alpha. To take what was mine.'

With Zach, that was where it always ended up. We'd been talking about the blast, about the future of whole lands, the fate of everyone, both here and in Elsewhere. But if I followed his arguments deep enough, we always ended up at the same place: him as a frightened, resentful child, afraid that he would never get to claim his birthright. That people would think he was the freak, and not me.

It seemed such a little thing for the fate of our world to rest on. But I could feel it in him, the source of everything. If you stripped away the tanks and the Council and Ark and the blast machine, there he'd be: my brother, a small boy, angry and afraid.

Piper interrupted my thoughts. 'Are you stupid enough to think that the blast can be contained?' he said to Zach. 'That if you unleash it on Elsewhere, it won't hurt us here as well?'

Zach shook his head impatiently. 'They're a long way away.'

'You haven't found them yet,' I said. It was a prayer as much as a statement.

'We will,' he said. 'And we'll find them before the resistance

does. We know they're out there. We know what they can
do, and what they've done.'

'Then let them do it,' I said. 'What does it matter, what
they do across the oceans?'

Zach's nostrils were pinched as he inhaled. 'They're seeking
us. Even if you and the resistance never manage to find them,
they're still seeking us. They sent a message. We found it
here. Just a single message, a few words, that reached here
hundreds of years ago. It came through too late for the Ark
builders – it was right at the end, when things were falling
apart for them down here. They couldn't even reply, let alone
seek out Elsewhere. But they kept the message. We know
Elsewhere's out there. And we know they've still got machines.
They were able to send that message, all those years ago.
And they'd already ended the twinning, even then.'

'You can't do this,' I said.

He laughed at me. 'Can't? We already have. We've nearly
finished moving the blast machine. Everything else that I've
found, over the years, I've had to piece together, bit by bit.
Nothing was ever complete; nothing ever worked, and we
were always short of fuel. But everything we've found here
has been protected so carefully, documented so thoroughly.
You've seen what we've managed to do with the tanks. We'll
do it with the blast machine too. Maybe not perfectly – it's
harder without The Confessor.' A pause. He swallowed.
The mention of The Confessor seemed to trouble him
more than Piper's knife, still cocked towards him. 'She had
a talent for the machines,' he went on eventually. 'It was
incredible to watch – she understood them like nobody else.
Taught me more than you can imagine. But even without
her, you can't stop us. She oversaw most of the work, before
she died, and my best people are finishing it. We've already
got most of what we need out of this place.

'You might have found your way here. I wondered if you would – we knew those papers were at large, and you're like a tick I can't shake off. But you're no more than that. You can't stop us.' He turned to Piper. 'You could kill me now, and her with me, and it still wouldn't stop the blast, or the tanks. You think The General's going to stop any of this, if I'm gone? She's the one who ordered us to set up more tanks here. Room for five thousand Omegas on this level alone.' He gave a smile. 'It's the perfect place for them, now the blast machine's been moved from here. And it's not like they're going to need a view.'

I felt suddenly very weary, and tired of listening to him. 'Take me to Kip,' I said.

I saw how the tendons in his neck tensed. 'I don't know what you're talking about,' he said.

I climbed down the ladder from the gangway. Now that I was amongst the tanks, the curved glass and the dim light distorted the space in the room, as if the air itself was bulbous and thickened.

I walked past Zach without a word, leaving Piper to guard him. I headed to where Zach had been coming from, when we'd first entered the room. I knew what he had been doing, here alone at night, while the soldiers retreated to their camps and watch posts. And I knew already what I would find.

Near the centre of the room, amongst the rows of empty tanks, stood two that were filled. I pressed my face against the glass of the tank closest to me.

It was like the first time I saw him.

Except it wasn't. Years before, when they'd cut off Kip's arm to make him pass for an Omega, they'd stitched him up so carefully that even I had never seen the scar. There had been no such delicacy this time. His whole torso had been bound with scars, like a stuffed joint of meat held tightly by twine. A wide scar curved from his back around to his stomach; another one ran straight down the middle of his chest. Along the side of his head, roughly healed stitches pulled at the skin, so tightly that his left ear was stretched out of shape. I didn't realise that I'd reached out to press it flat until my fingers hit the glass.

The scars weren't the only difference. This time, his eyes were closed, and they stayed that way. As I leant towards him, the glass unyielding against my cheek, I knew that Kip was gone. Nothing of him remained but the wreckage of his body. It was a ship, dredged up from the ocean floor, but all the crew were lost.

In the next tank was The Confessor. She had none of Kip's scars – her naked body was unmarked, except for where the tubes entered her wrists. I had feared her for years, but she was not frightening now. She was suspended with her knees curved up towards her chin, and she looked smaller than I'd have believed possible. I looked at her fingers, curled into fists, and I knew they would not open again.

'I had to keep her.' Zach had followed me, Piper and his knife staying close behind him. 'There's too much valuable stuff in there,' Zach said, gesturing at The Confessor's tank. 'The database relied on her mind, as much as on the machines. And she was the one who deciphered the blast machine, worked out how to get it out of here. She was my trump card. Without her, The General's just taking over.' His voice had crept higher and higher. 'Taking everything that I've been working for.'

I saw how Zach had moved between me and The Confessor's tank. His hand was pressed against the glass, as though to shield her.

'Look how we both ended up,' I said to him.

'What are you talking about?' He didn't even look up at me, his eyes still fixed on The Confessor.

'You couldn't wait to push me out of your life,' I said. 'And then look who you found yourself close to.'

'You're not like her.'

I nodded. 'But she was a seer, all the same. And she was probably the only person whose childhood comes close to my own.'

Once, I might have said that person was Zach. I knew better now. He'd been there, with me, but our experience had been utterly different. We'd both been afraid, but they were different fears. I had feared being exposed and separated from him. He'd feared that I would never be sent away, that he would be stuck with me forever.

'It's not only you,' I said. 'I did it too, ended up with someone just like you. The Confessor told me about Kip's past, just before he died. He was just like you.' I ignored the expression of disgust on Zach's face as he glanced at Kip's wasted, floating body. 'I realise it now,' I went on. 'Before he was tanked, he hated her, just like you hated me. He struggled to expose her, and to have her sent away. And then he came after her, later, to have her locked up.

'So we did the same thing, you see.' I shrugged. 'Neither of us knew we were doing it, but in the end we both found ourselves closest to somebody just like each other.'

It was all a circle, as round as the tanks themselves. Zach and me, parted and brought back together. Kip, taken from the tank and returned to it. The blast that had been and would be again.

'You want to end the tanks,' he said. 'But they're the only thing keeping him and The Confessor alive.'

'They're not alive,' I said. Kip's body mightn't have been

bloated and faded like those of the tanked Ark dwellers in Section A, but it was just as empty of presence. 'You might have managed to drag him and The Confessor halfway back from death, but that's it. You knew they couldn't be saved. You knew you were never going to be able to use her again. You kept them like this because you didn't have the courage to let her go.'

'Don't say that,' said Zach, his voice shrill now, his hand pressing harder against the glass of The Confessor's tank, where she floated, oblivious. 'It could change,' he said. 'You could help me,' he said. 'If you worked with me, helped the doctors, we could find new ways to heal them. You can't just give up on them.'

I'd seen what being tanked had done to Kip, his mind hollowed of its memories. What could Zach possibly imagine would be salvaged from him and The Confessor after the fall, and this second tanking? Would he keep them preserved for decades, until they became like the tanked men I'd seen upstairs?

'You're counting on me clinging to some kind of hope?' I said.

He was watching me minutely. Zach, who had done everything he could to teach me that hope was for other people, in other times.

I turned back to the glass of Kip's tank. 'It's not about hope, or giving up on him,' I said to Zach, so quietly that my words were barely more than a shape my lips made against the glass. 'It's about choice, and what he would want. He wouldn't want this. Not ever.' I thought again of those grotesque figures, floating above us in Section A. 'Not even The Confessor would have chosen this.'

I walked to the steel ladder, climbing to the gangway that ran at the level of the tank's lids.

'Are you sure you want to do this?' Piper said.

I kept climbing, until I stood above Kip.

I swung the lid aside and shared the tank's sickly breath. When I'd first found Kip, beneath Wyndham, I'd been unable to lift him out. But that was after I'd spent four years in the Keeping Rooms. I was stronger now, and he was lighter than he had been even then. I wrapped both arms around his torso, feeling the raised ridges of his scars, and pulled.

As the liquid released him and he took on his own weight, I had to haul hard, but nothing could have made me let go. When I'd dragged him over the glass rim, I laid him on his back on the gangway. His face was slicked with the viscous liquid. Twice his arm moved, a random jerking, as if his hand were a fish thrown on a ship's deck, thrashing. The liquid dripped from him through the metal grille of the gangway to land on the floor below. Fast, at first, in trickles and splashes, and then slowly, hitting the concrete floor one drip at a time. I tugged the tube from his wrist, and watched the hole fill with sluggish blood. From his mouth I pulled another tube, a second tongue.

Zach rushed at the ladder, but Piper tackled him, grappling him to the ground. If Zach said anything, I didn't listen. I turned back to Kip, and bent low over his face.

He gave two exhalations, each one a tiny benediction of warm air on my cheek. The third breath wasn't a breath at all – just an opening of his mouth. His eyes stayed closed, and I was glad.

I turned my face to the side, cheek pressed against his chest. I didn't pretend, even to myself, that I was comforting him. I knew there was nothing left inside him. If there was any comfort in that last embrace, it was all for me.

I held his spent body and looked at his closed eyes and his slim fingers. I slipped my palm under the back of his neck and let my hand take on the familiar weight of his head. He took no more breaths. For the first time since the silo, I cried.

*

I stood and looked back down at The Confessor, in her tank. She had sunk to the bottom, her neck arched backwards. Her eyes were open but her face was expressionless. In death, she was no more inscrutable than she had been in life. Zach sat leaning against her tank, head thrown back, not hiding his tears.

'You'll never get out of here,' he said. Piper let him stand, but kept his knife pointed at Zach's back. 'All the entrances are guarded,' Zach went on. 'You'll be caught. He'll end up back in the tank. And we'll drag them back to life again.'

'It's not life,' I said. I stepped carefully over Kip's body on the gangway, and back to where I'd left the lantern. The matches were in my pocket. I fumbled at the first attempt, the match scraping limply and then snapping. The second time, the flame flared and caught.

'What the hell are you doing?' said Zach, as I lit the lantern's wick. 'I've told you already. It's not safe.'

This time I laughed out loud. 'Safe' had become nothing more than a syllable. What could it mean, here in the Ark, in this maze of bones in which Kip lay dead and the empty tanks waited?

'What are you doing?' Zach said again as I lifted the bright lantern. The river's churning in the pipes seemed to grow louder in my head. Piper stood behind Zach, keeping his knife trained on him.

I weighed the lantern carefully in my hand while I looked down at Zach.

'When we were split,' I said, 'I took the branding and

the exile for you. You knew I'd do it, to protect you. And I've been protecting you, one way or another, ever since then. That ends now.' I raised the lantern high. 'There'll be no more tanks here. And you're not getting the last pieces of the blast machine, either.'

I stared right into Zach's eyes. 'You think you know me?' I said. 'You don't know me at all.'

I glanced to Piper. We knew each other well enough, I prayed, for him to see what was coming.

'Run,' I said.

I threw the lantern. Not at Zach, or even at the tanks. But at the ceiling, where the smaller pipes clung to the bottom of the huge central water pipe.

The air above us shattered into sound and light. The blast knocked me onto my back, hand raised to shield my face. Piper had dived to the side when he saw the lantern's trajectory. Zach was slower to react and was propelled backwards by the explosion, crashing into one of the tanks.

After the wave of heat there was a shriek of scraping glass, and the two empty tanks closest to the blast collapsed into themselves. A third tank stayed upright, but the glass had become opaque, a lacework of fissures. I looked up at the central pipe. Where the blast had hit and the smaller pipes had ruptured, a dark hairline crack was visible. Water dripped through it. The drops were speeding up, keeping time with my pulse.

Zach scrabbled back to his feet. The broken glass had left a small cut on his temple, and his face was white with dust. 'That's it?' I could hardly hear him, my ears still echoing from the explosion. 'You've managed to break three tanks. That's your grand gesture?'

When the pipe burst open, the water drowned his laughter. The river had come to claim us.

CHAPTER 37

Zach was knocked backwards and swept towards the door. He grabbed at the door handle and staggered to his feet, gasping. It took him only seconds to jab at the metal panel, and then a green light flashed and the tumblers slid back. As soon as he began to push the door open, the force of the water tore it from his grasp and slammed it against the wall of the corridor. He looked back at me one more time, but the water was already approaching his waist. A whole section of the overhead pipe tore loose, smashing two more tanks as it fell. The green lights on all the panels began to flash, a synchronised blinking that set the whole room shimmering, green stars on black water. Then the lights turned red, and disappeared, so that the only light came from beyond the door through which Zach had run.

There was nothing else to do. Our footsteps on the metal gangway were almost drowned out by the torrent of water. By the time we reached the missing grille, the water was already grasping at our feet. Somewhere behind us, I knew that the dark water would be scooping up Kip's body. I didn't look back. I hauled myself into the tunnel, and heard the banging as Piper followed me.

Our whole time in the Ark, I'd been able to feel the river above us. Now, as we crawled, heaving ourselves up the incline of the tunnel to the next level, I could feel the river below us, too, filling every space it could find.

We reached the next level just before the water, but I knew that our cramped progress through the tunnels would be too slow to save us. When we got to the grate that we'd dislodged the day before, I dropped back down to the corridor. Here, the lights were still on, but soon water was clutching at my ankles. The cold of the river was sharp, even through my boots. Then the ceiling lights spat blue sparks, and went out. In the dark, Piper was only a sound of splashing beside me. By the time we got to the next flight of stairs, the water was at my hips.

It didn't matter how fast we ran. Somewhere in the Ark, Zach was running too, and if he didn't make it, nor would I. But he knew these corridors, and could head straight for the main doors. If any guards remained at the exits, after the river's bursting, Zach wouldn't need to fear them.

We ran. The lights on the upper levels weren't lit, and the blackness was thickened by the sound of rising water. It caught up with us in the top level - when the river reached the main corridor, sparks sprayed from the ceiling, with a sizzling sound like hot steel plunged into water. In the instant of light, I saw a skull bob past my feet. A boat of bone. Then the darkness returned. I tried to concentrate on finding the main ventilation tunnel, but the messy and insistent currents of the water changed the way the corridors tugged at my mind. We ran through Section F, its silent rooms now noisy with water. At one point I led us the wrong way, and we had to backtrack twenty yards, against the current. We were almost swimming now, the water at our chests, the cold so extreme that my lungs clenched, refusing air. The sounds of Piper behind me grew fainter; with only one arm to pull himself through the water, he was dropping behind.

If the water's current had not been heading in the right direction down that final corridor, we would never have reached the open ventilation hatch leading to the main shaft. My feet could no longer touch the ground, and I was propelled by the water rather than my own flailing movements. But when I gripped the sides of the open hatch and tried to pull myself up, the current was no longer an ally. It refused to let me go, dragging me so mercilessly that when I finally managed to pull myself through the hatch, my legs scraped against it and left filings of flesh on the steel edge.

Here, in the narrower space, I had the ladder to hang on to, though my frozen hands kept slipping from the rungs. Piper grabbed from below, clutching my foot for a moment before he, too, found the rungs.

When we pulled ourselves into the control room, with the wheel of blades above us, the water followed. Each time a spark from above illuminated the room, I could see how the water had crept further up the walls. One of the sealed hatches on the side of the room gave way, the dislodged door crashing into my hip as the water burst through.

The gap between the blades and the water had shrunk to only a few feet, the water at our waists. The dwindling space amplified the sounds, and our breathing was loud, each breath the quick rasp of a handsaw through wood.

There was no time to worry about the Electric or the sharpened fan – the death offered by the water was certain, unlike the blades. Piper knelt so that I could clamber on to his knee, just as I'd once seen him kneel to help Zoe. He steadied me while I groped up through the darkness to find the blades with my hands. The lights stayed off, and the blades stayed still. Even the sparks had finished flaring now – perhaps the river had done what four hundred years had not, and drowned the Electric for good.

Piper had nobody to lift him. The first two times he jumped, I heard the splash that followed as he fell back down. Kneeling at the edge of the hole that I could not see, I tried to gauge how fast the water was rising, and how much air was left. How many breaths remained to us, and whether I would wait for him if he fell another time.

It was a calculation I never had to complete. The third time he jumped, his hand thudded on the rim of the concrete floor. I grasped his forearm with both of my hands, throwing myself flat against the ground to counteract his greater weight. Our skin was slippery and numb with the water. As he heaved himself upwards, his whole arm shook. His hand was a vice, squeezing my wrist so tightly that my skin was crushed between our bones. My newly-healed right wrist remembered its pain; when I gasped, the sound was lost in the hiss of water beneath us.

He made it through the gap. We didn't speak – there was no time, and not enough air in the small space, with the river whispering at us from below. In minutes, it would pass the fan and join us in this final chamber. I clambered into the tunnel. No time for hesitation, now, and no choices to make. Only water below us, and air above. I braced my wet boots against the outsides of the tunnel and reached my arms in front of me. The steepest sections, though far from vertical, still took all my strength. Each jerky movement gained only a few inches, and often my hands or feet slipped on the rounded piping. My body's giddy shaking

produced no warmth, and I was utterly depleted as I nego-
tiated the turns in the tunnel, forcing my body around the
tight corners. The only comfort was the sound of Piper
behind me. Then another sound began to follow me up the
tunnel: the creeping of water. It was quiet at first – just a
dampening of the echoes as our knees and elbows bumped
against the steel. But within minutes every movement of
Piper's legs was a splash. Before, I had been relieved that
the tunnel wasn't vertical. Now I realised what it meant.
Even I, higher than Piper, would never be able to stay afloat,
or to keep up with the water and let it carry me upwards
– the angled pipe would trap me.

For a second, I wished we'd stayed down there, in the
base of the Ark with the tanks, and taken the quick death
that the flood had promised us. I could have gone to Kip's
body, and been with him at the end. Worse to die slowly
here, and to have to listen to Piper drowning below me.
To hear his death, and Zoe's death nestled within it. I would
die in this tunnel, cramped so tightly that I couldn't so
much as wrap my arms around myself in the final moments.
No consolation but the grip of the steel.

It seemed strange, after all my dreams of fire, that it
should end like this: death by water.

My pulse became a cry that only I could hear: *Zach. Kip.
Zach. Kip.*

Two flecks of white appeared before my eyes. Was I dying
now? Was my body so numb with cold that the water had
overtaken me before I could even realise? Or had Zach,
somewhere else in the Ark, succumbed to the water?

But the lights stayed steady. They were not spots on my
vision, not the last flarings of consciousness. They were
stars.

CHAPTER 38

In those last few hundred yards, with the night sky in my sight, we climbed higher than the river's level, and the water stopped pursuing us up the tunnel. There were no more splashes from behind me as Piper crawled – just the dulled thuds of metal set in concrete.

The moonlight outside couldn't penetrate the tunnel properly, but the darkness around me changed. I could see the seams of the metal, where the sections of pipe had been joined. Above us, at the rim of the opening, I saw the silhouette of the long grass swiping at the air, blown by a wind that I'd never expected to feel again.

After all that had happened in the Ark, it was strange to find the surface world unchanged. Snow lay on the boulders, and the wind scudded clouds in front of the stars. Unconcerned by floods, Arks, or blasts, the moon continued its progress across the sky. But as I slumped on my hands and knees in the snow, I could still hear the rumble of the river beneath us as it forced its new course through the Ark.

We were soaked, and the cold night air felt like an attack.

When I looked down at my hands, they were blurred with tremors. Piper had dropped to his knees on the grass. I stared beyond him at the earth's dark mouth, and thought of everything that had been drowned when I unleashed the river. The ghost voice of Elsewhere. The remnants of the blast machine that Zach had not yet salvaged. The thousands of tanks, awash now with all the Ark's old bones. And Kip, free of the tank and of his broken body.

The next hours passed in a haze of cold. As we retrieved our rucksacks, there was shouting to the east, where the nearest door to the Ark lay. Lamps were moving in the distance. We ran, skidding amongst the boulders in their shrouds of snow. When we were off the hill and back in the long grass of the plain, we kept running. Even when there were no sounds of pursuit, we kept moving. To stop and sleep in the snow, in our soaking clothes, would be to die. The cuffs of my soaked trousers hardened with ice, clipping at my ankles with each step. The sun rose and revealed my blue-white skin. By the time we reached the copse and found the horses, new snow was falling. I knew I should be glad that it would cover our trail, but pursuit seemed a less immediate concern than the cold. I rode slumped forwards, pressed to the warmth of my horse's neck. Piper rode beside me, leading the horse of the soldier we'd killed on the road on the way to the Ark. It seemed a long time ago – so much had changed during those few days and nights underground.

I looked back to the south. I could see the hill that squatted over the Ark, and the wreckage of the camp where the Ark's western door had spat out the river. The tents had been swept away. White canvas snagged on trees downstream.

When I slowed, and half-slipped from the horse, Piper shouted at me to keep moving. He rode close and shook my shoulder. I tried to brush him away, but my hands were so cold that I could no longer move my fingers. My body had become nothing more than an encumbrance, a block of chilled flesh that my horse hauled.

Some time shortly after dawn, when we were beyond the plains and back in wooded country, Piper led me to a shallow cave, and tethered the horses when my fingers refused to grasp the reins. Inside the stone shelter, we stripped off our ice-stiffened clothes and huddled in our underwear under the dry blanket. His skin next to mine was no comfort – we were as cold as each other. There was a rawness to the cold, as though not just our clothes but our skin had been stripped away. I put my frozen fingers, one at a time, in my mouth, to coax them back to life. When the warmth returned, it brought pain with it, the blood forcing its way back into flesh. Could Zach feel it too? I wondered. How close to death would I have to be, before Zach's body would begin to tremor in unison with mine? I closed my eyes against the world and slipped into sleep.

I dreamed of the coast. I'd shared Zoe's dreams of the indifferent waves many times, when she was with us. But this was different. Instead of a featureless expanse of ocean, I saw a white cliff, standing bulwark between the land and sea. I saw a sail that scooped up the wind. Sea spray on wood.

I'd never seen those white cliffs before. But their strangeness was nothing compared to what the ship carried.

I woke, shouting of Elsewhere.

Piper turned from the cave entrance, where he'd been hunched over a small fire.

'You were with me at New Hobart,' he said, when I'd thrown on my clothes and told him what I'd seen. 'Zach showed us the figureheads. There was no mistaking them

– I know every ship in my fleet. They had Hobb and the crews – The General mentioned Hobb by name. *The Rosalind* and *The Evelyn* are taken, Cass.'

I couldn't argue with him. I couldn't even give him details about the ship that I had seen. A white sail, against a white cliff, and the sulky-mouthed curve of the horizon. But I knew we had to go there. And when I described the white cliff to him, he nodded.

'Sounds like Cape Bleak, sure enough. But there are no ships left to come in. We need to go back to New Hobart, and tell Simon and The Ringmaster what we found in the Ark. Now we know the Council's plans for the blast, we need to consolidate the resistance if we're going to fight back. And what about the others in New Hobart? What about The Ringmaster's threat?'

I'd been thinking of it too – Elsa, Sally and Xander at The Ringmaster's mercy. 'We did what The Ringmaster would've wanted, in the end,' I said. 'If his network of spies brings him any news of us, it'll be that we destroyed the Ark, and whatever machines remained there. Even he could ask no more of us than that. He won't betray us while he thinks we can help him work against the machines.'

I squeezed my fingernails into my palms. Since I'd found out that Zach was rebuilding the blast machine, time had felt finite – it was running out, like the air above us when we were in the flooding Ark. I might have slowed Zach's plans, by drowning the last pieces of the blast machine and destroying the huge chamber of tanks, but it was still not enough. Elsewhere existed, and if Zach and The General found it before us, it would burn.

'A ship's coming,' I went on. 'I don't know what ship it is, or how it will come. But I know it's got something to do with Elsewhere. I felt it.' There were no words to explain what I had sensed, when the ship had sailed into my vision. The knowledge, as immovable as the cave wall behind me, that the ship carried with it a trace of Elsewhere. Something beneath those full sails that was so entirely alien that it both fascinated and repulsed me.

'It's coming, and soon,' I said. 'And we have to find it before the Council does, or any chance we have will be lost. There isn't time to go back to New Hobart.' I stood up. 'And I'm not asking for your permission. I'm going, with or without you.'

He was staring at his scarred knuckles. How many times had he unleashed his blades from those fingers, I wondered? How many lives had that hand taken? Would he stop me, if I tried to walk away?

His face was grave. 'If we're going to stop the Council, the resistance is going to need you more than ever. You nearly got us both killed in the Ark. You can't just go off now, taking more risks.'

'You say the resistance needs me,' I said. 'That's why you spared me, on the island. But if the resistance needs me, it's because my visions are valuable. So listen to me.'

When he spoke, his voice had dropped low. 'The resistance has needed me, too.' A pause. 'Needed me to do things. To make decisions. To be certain, even when I haven't had much certainty left.'

He looked up at me, the flames lighting the underside of his face, leaving his eyes in darkness. Outside, the snow had stopped, and the night was hushed.

I remembered what he'd said to Leonard, months ago: *There are different kinds of courage*. I'd seen Piper fight, and I'd seen him stand before the assembled troops and rally them to battle. But it would take a different kind of courage, now, for him to choose to follow me.

'If I set off now,' I said, 'I might be able to cross the western ridge while the snow holds off.'

'I'm coming with you,' he said.

'I'm glad,' I said. And it wasn't until I spoke the words that I knew they were true.

*

In the long days of riding westward, my mind kept returning to those final moments in the ventilation pipe. How I had reached for Kip's and Zach's names, instinctive as breath.

I thought often of Zoe, too, though Piper never spoke of her. All that we knew of her was that she lived. And although I found myself missing the click of her knife on her nails, I thought she was better off, wherever she was, not knowing the news that Piper and I had dredged up from the Ark. Zoe had enough burdens already.

At night, I dreamed of the blast, and of the cliff that waited for the ship. There were no more visions of Kip in the tanks, and that was a mercy. But the blast dreams took on a new potency, now that I knew their true significance.

'I used to think my visions were letting me down,' I said to Piper one night, after the blast had left my sleep in ashes. 'Because they were unclear, or inconsistent. That they were failing me somehow. Now I know it was me failing them. I only saw what I wanted to see.'

'Maybe you saw what you needed to see.'

I kept staring at the night sky.

'Maybe you had enough to deal with,' he went on. 'If you'd known all along about the blast, it would have been too much. Perhaps you would've gone mad. Or given up.'

Sometimes I thought my madness was an Ark, buried deep within me. I could feel it, even if he couldn't. Soon enough it would be found.

*

Our escape from the Ark, drenched and nearly frozen, had left me with a fever. For three days I'd been sweat-soaked and shivery, my neck swollen and my throat inflamed. Piper wouldn't admit it, but he was unwell too – his skin was clammy, and he'd picked up a wheezing cough. When we crossed the high pass over the mountains, the snow drifts were so deep in places that we had to dismount and lead the horses. By the time we were on the far side of the pass, my teeth were chattering loudly and Piper could no longer conceal his own body's shaking.

We both knew we could not continue like this much longer. When we came across the small settlement clustered by the stream, it was after midnight, and there were no lamps visible in the windows. We decided to tether the horses in the woods upstream, and risk sneaking into the barn at the settlement's edge. We climbed up to the loft, and lay in the mounded hay. I ignored the itching and spiking of the hay, and burrowed deep for warmth. Beside me, Piper was trying to silence his cough. I was both cold and hot at once, my swollen neck pulsing with pain. We didn't sleep so much as pass out.

Our sickness had made us careless – we didn't take lookout shifts, and woke at dawn to the sound of the barn door slamming open below us.

I heard the chink of metal as Piper slipped a knife from his belt. But nobody came up the ladder, and the sounds from below were the unhurried noises of daily work. A barrow was wheeled inside, and then came thuds of wood on wood. I was lying facedown, and I moved slowly to scrape aside the hay, uncovering cracks in the rough floor to peer through. Below, the barn door stood open, admitting the first hints of dawn, and a woman with a single eye was loading a barrow with logs of wood from a pile in the corner.

That's when I heard the whistling. The chilled air blurred the notes at the edges, but I knew the tune immediately: Leonard's song. She was whistling the chorus, pausing between lines as she bent to grab another armful of wood, and huffing in the cold so that half the notes were more breath than tune. But it was clear enough, and in my mind I matched the words to the notes as they reached me on the lazy wind:

> *Oh, you'll never be tired, you'll never be cold*
> *And you'll never ever ever grow old,*
> *And the only price you'll have to pay*
> *Is to give your life away.*

Like me, Piper was smiling. I closed my eyes and found his hand. Here, at least a hundred miles north-west of where we'd last seen Leonard alive, the song had found its way. It wasn't much – just a scattering of notes, hanging for a moment in the air. The song had seemed such a slight thing to carry the message of the tanks – but it was spreading.

We slipped from the hayloft as soon as the woman had gone, and ran from the settlement in the hesitant dawn light. I was thinking of Leonard – the chill of his dead flesh, and the broken guitar around his neck. I'd seen enough of death, these last few months, to know its absoluteness. I'd seen the dead bodies on the island, and at the battle of New Hobart. I'd seen Kip on the silo floor, each angle of his body wrong, and seen him again, his double death, preserved in the tank. There was nothing romantic in death, and nothing that would bring those dead back: not tanks, not tears, and not songs. But having heard Leonard's music in the barn, I was assured that at least some part of him had slipped that noose.

*

It took two more weeks to reach Cape Bleak. The snow had melted, and our fevers receded. The spare horse meant we could rotate mounts, and we made good progress, even though we had to travel at night once we'd reached Alpha country. For more than a week we passed through hills richly populated with villages and towns. We moved through the darkness, unseen, and I didn't feel afraid, even when Piper told me that we were passing within miles of the biggest Council squadron in the west. I'd seen the Ark, and knew its secrets. I passed through the blast each time I slept. Little else could scare me now. And the half-heard song from the hayloft sustained me, and helped to heal my sick body, more than any of the sinewy hares that Piper caught.

Eventually the land grew scrappy again, gnarled by the coastal winds, and there were no more Alphas to avoid. Then we came within sight of the sea. Inhospitable cliffs cut away into the ocean. I knew them at once for the cliffs I had dreamed of. White as sliced flesh, before the blood springs to the wound.

There I dreamed of the sea. When I woke, I knew that the waves that had broken on the edges of my sleep were not my own dreams. I sat up quickly, almost expecting to find Zoe there, sleeping beside me as if she'd never gone. But there was only Piper's back as he sat looking out from the cave's entrance, watching the sun set over the water.

'That headland, there.' He jerked his head to the north,

to a finger of land that pointed accusingly at the ocean. 'That's Cape Bleak. It doesn't look like it, but on the northern face there's a path down to a small cove. When courier ships from the island were due to come this way, our scouts on the mainland would light a signal fire on the point, to let them know it was safe to send in the landing craft.'

It was full dark by the time we reached the tip of the headland. The wood that we'd scavenged was damp, and Piper had to tip the last of the lamp oil on the mound to coax it into flames.

We waited all night, but there was no answering gleam of flame from the sea – only an occasional flash of white where the waves broke below the cliffs. The cries of gulls scraped at the night.

At dawn, the fire had subsided into ashes.

Piper exhaled as he rubbed his face with his hand.

'So we try again tomorrow night,' he said. But I noted the slump of his shoulders, the set of his mouth.

We should have learned it after the island, and after the tanks of dead children in New Hobart. After Zach had thrown the ships' figureheads at our feet. And after the Ark, which held nothing for us but another blast. Nothing was more dangerous than hope.

*

We sat for a long time. We should have been sleeping, but neither of us wanted to go back to the cave, and to be cramped in there with nothing to speak of but the ship that might never come. So we waited on the cliff, watching the light from behind us spread over the sea.

In my vision, the ship had cut cleanly through the water.

The ship that we saw, rounding the point, moved sluggishly. It lurched when the wind picked up, wallowing to the left. The mast was crooked, and the sail puckered where it had been stitched. The figurehead wasn't the only thing missing; all along the prow the wood was gouged. Sections had been patched with tar and boards, but the wounds still showed.

People were busy on the deck, and another was clambering in the rigging. But one figure was motionless at the bow, hands on the rail.

A whistle came to us. The wind on the headland was gusty, and it stretched the notes and then snatched them away. But I'd heard enough to know. Piper stood, and we both ran to the cliffside path, while the chorus of Leonard's song was carried past us on the wind.

CHAPTER 39

By the time we'd scrambled down to the rocky cove, a dinghy had been lowered and was halfway to shore. Piper waded thigh-deep into the water to meet it. I watched while he embraced Zoe, his arm so tight around her waist that for a moment he lifted her, and the other sailors had to move quickly to steady the small boat. Then he lowered her into the water beside him. She smiled as she walked towards the beach, where I waited. I wished I could have stopped time there: Zoe smiling, Piper grinning behind her in the water. I didn't want to speak – our news was too grim to give to her, on this bright morning, when she'd just found us.

'I thought you'd gone east,' I said. 'Got away from all of this.' From me, I meant.

She shook her head. 'I was going to.' She was unabashed. 'For the first day I did head eastward.' She paused, squinting into the glare of the sun on the water. 'But then I kept thinking about Xander.'

Piper was listening too, but Zoe wasn't looking at either of us. She was staring beyond *The Rosalind* at the low waves.

'I kept thinking of how he was always telling us *The Rosalind* was coming in, and how we'd dismissed him.' She spoke very quietly. 'I thought I should try, at least. That one of us should believe in him.'

I watched her staring at the waves, and I knew that it wasn't only Xander who she had been keeping faith with, but Lucia, whom nobody had listened to, at the end.

The crew had jumped from the dinghy, and three of them began to haul it on to the beach. The fourth sailor limped as he waded to Piper. They shook hands, the man grasping Piper's hand with both of his.

'This is Thomas,' Piper said, turning to me. 'Captain of *The Rosalind*.'

'We didn't see the signal fire until just before dawn,' he said. 'I wasn't sure if we'd get here in time to catch you.'

'We thought you'd been taken,' I said.

'We nearly were,' Thomas said. 'We hit a bad summer storm in the western straits, barely a month after we'd left the island. We got off fairly lightly, but *The Evelyn* was driven aground on a reef. The damage was bad, and half of their water tanks were wrecked too, so Hobb had to turn back.' He looked grim. 'Zoe told us about what's happened: the island. The figureheads. What The General said, about Hobb and the crew being captured. They must have got back just after the Council seized the island. Probably sailed right into the Council's fleet.'

'And your figurehead?' said Piper, turning to look at the ship's patched prow. 'I saw it myself. How the hell did they get hold of that?'

'When we eventually came back, we didn't make it back to the island - a Council ship gave chase just outside the reef. Got close enough to do some damage to our mast, but we managed to lose them in the western reef and get clear. We

432

knew then that the island must have fallen. We limped back to the mainland, and came here first, like we'd agreed. But there was no signal, no sign of anyone from the resistance. After that we tried all the usual places, but there were no signal fires, and more and more Council ships about. In Chantler Bay there were three of them at anchor – we only got past there unseen because it was dark. The winter storms were well and truly starting by then, and we got desperate – even dropped anchor by Atkin Point and sent four scouts inland to the safehouse, but it was burnt out. Had to keep moving – they're patrolling the coast more tightly than ever. We'd been spotted again, and had one of their brigs on our tail, when the big storm blew in from the north, a month back. Seas as high as I've seen. We shook off the Council ship, but lost two men. Ran aground on some rocks, just off Chantler Bay, started taking on water. That's when we lost the figurehead, and half the prow with it. The brig that was chasing us must have come across it. Who knows if they really thought we'd gone down, or if they just wanted you to think we had?

'When the storm was over, we couldn't even find some-where safe to beach and fix the hull. I had to keep the crew on the pumps night and day.'

'I came here first,' Zoe said, taking over the story. 'Right after I'd left you. Waited a few nights. Tried Chantler Bay, but drew a blank. But a fisherwoman in a tavern there said she'd seen a ship, listing badly, and heading south. She said it wasn't one of the Council's, but too big to be a local fishing boat. I went down to Siddle Point, lit the signal fire on the old lookout post, three nights running. A patrol came through, too, on the second day, passed not a hundred yards from where I was hiding. I was about to give up. I could hardly believe it, on the third night, when I saw the lantern flashing back at me.

'When I was aboard, we sailed back here.' I thought of
Zoe's nightly dreams, and knew what it must have cost her,
to take to the sea again. 'The patrol ships hardly ever come
this far north,' she went on, 'so we were able to beach *The
Rosalind* in Coldharbour Bay. It took almost a week just to
fix the hull.' She looked at me and Piper. 'If you'd come a
few days later, you'd have missed us. I was going to head
back to New Hobart, to Simon, and leave the crew here to
guard Paloma.'

'Is that another ship?' I said.

Zoe shook her head.

*

They rowed us out to *The Rosalind*. Two sailors threw down
the rope ladder. When they saw Piper, they jumped to
attention, saluting him. Thomas led us towards the prow.
The sailors stood in silence as they watched us pass. Their
clothes were bleached by sun and salt, and they looked as
battered as *The Rosalind* itself. Many were thin, and some
had the blue-red blotching of scurvy on their arms and
hands.

A group of sailors was seated by the prow, where the
stump of the broken figurehead jutted at the sky. Only one
of them stood as we approached.

She left the group, limping slightly as she walked towards
us. At first I thought one foot was bare, though it made no
sense, on the frosty deck. But as she drew closer I could
see that the bare leg was false. Not a wooden stump, such
as I'd seen often enough. Instead, it was made from a
smooth, harder material with a flesh-like texture, carefully
crafted to look like a foot, although it didn't bend at the
ankle when she walked.

It wasn't the uncanny replica foot that made me stare at her. Nor was it the fact that the other sailors all wore the blue of the island's guards, and she did not. There was something else different that I could feel: a thinness about her, an insubstantiality that I couldn't grasp. As though she would cast no shadow.

She was solid enough – when I shook her hand, her grip was strong.

'I'm Paloma,' she said, turning from me to shake Piper's hand. But I still couldn't stop staring. Piper seemed oblivious – why didn't he flinch from her as I did?

'She doesn't have a twin,' I said. I heard the fear in my own voice. I hadn't meant it to be so obvious. But it was as if I could see a wound on her that the others couldn't see. She was incomplete. Half a person.

'None of us do, in the Scattered Islands,' the woman said. 'I gather that you call it Elsewhere.'

*

Thomas and Paloma told us their story first. *The Rosalind* hadn't found Elsewhere, despite a tortuous journey through the northern ice-straits, further than any other resistance ship had ever travelled. Instead, Paloma's ship had found them.

'There used to be machines for sending and receiving messages,' she said, 'even after the detonations. But no messages ever came, and we never knew whether anyone was out there to hear ours. Then the communication machines stopped working altogether. So the Confederacy's been sending out ships, almost every year, for as long as anyone can remember.'

The cadence of her voice was unlike any I'd heard before.

I shouldn't have been surprised. Even within the mainland, there were variations in accents. When I'd met people from the east, close to the deadlands, their voices usually marked them as decisively as their ragged clothes or starved faces. A drawling tone, some words musically elongated. Up north, people shortened their vowels. My own father had spoken in the slightly clipped accent of the northern regions, where he'd been raised. Paloma's accent was far stronger than any I'd encountered. It made familiar words strange, stretching them in unexpected directions.

'When we found *The Rosalind*, my crew sailed back to Broken Harbour to report the news,' she said. 'But two of us came aboard your ship, to be the first emissaries. Then Caleb died in the storm.' She looked down. 'So it's just me now.'

Silence fell. Where could we begin? What questions came first, when encountering a new world? It had felt so audacious even to dream of Elsewhere that I'd never allowed myself to give the dreams detail, or to imagine what people from Elsewhere might be like. This twinless woman, pale and alone, was more like us than I'd imagined, but more alien than I could grasp.

Thomas was showing Piper a map, he and Paloma bending over it to gesture towards Elsewhere's location, somewhere beyond the map's edge. Zoe stood nearby, watching.

I couldn't face being there when Piper told Zoe and Paloma about the Ark, and what we'd discovered there. It was cowardly of me, perhaps. Paloma's twinless state was like a high-pitched sound that only I could hear, and when I was standing close to her, my teeth clenched tight and my breath evaded me. I left them talking, and walked back to the stern, to share my unease with the restless sea.

*

After a while, I heard Zoe's footsteps on the deck.

'Piper told us about what you found in the Ark,' she said. 'About the blast.'

I nodded, still staring at the water.

'I'm glad,' she said, stepping to the railing beside me. I raised my eyebrows. 'Not about the blast, obviously,' she went on. 'But I'm glad I know now. It makes me understand Lucia more, I think.' She paused. 'Why the visions of the blast damaged her the way they did. On some level, she must have known that it was coming.'

I nodded, thinking of Xander, too, and his scattered mind. He, Lucia, and I had all borne witness to what was coming.

'Piper told me about Kip, too,' said Zoe. 'That you found him.'

'It wasn't Kip that I found,' I said. 'It was just his body.'

She offered me no words of comfort, and I was grateful. She had dispensed enough death herself to know that it wasn't something that could be softened. Instead, she stood with me and watched the sea.

'Even though he looked so different,' I went on, 'it was the first time, since The Confessor told me about his past, that I could remember him properly.'

'It wasn't Kip she was telling you about,' she said impatiently. 'Any more than it was him who you found in the Ark. Why don't you get it? Whoever he was when they put him into that tank, he wasn't the same person when they took him out. Nobody could be.'

She turned to face me. 'The Confessor didn't know him,' she said. 'That was her big mistake. She let you and Kip find her in the silo that night, because she thought her twinship with him meant you'd be helpless. She thought she was drawing you into a trap. The Kip that she grew up with wouldn't have done what he did. He wouldn't have jumped to save you.'

A gull swooped low over the water.

'If you assume that Kip's past defines him,' she said, 'you'll be making the same mistake The Confessor made. And you'll be letting her take him from you twice.'

Further out, beyond the breaking waves, the sea reflected the clouds. A doubled sky.

'I know what you're doing, when you focus on Kip's past,' she said. 'Because I did it too. I focused on the bad stuff, so I wouldn't have to mourn Lucia.'

She closed her eyes for a few moments. When she opened them, she spoke quietly. 'Instead of dreaming about the sea every night, I wish I could dream about her. Not her death, or her madness, but who she actually was. About the way her nose wrinkled when she smiled. How she could fall asleep anywhere, anytime. How, when she'd been sweating, the back of her neck smelled like pine shavings.' She gave half a smile. 'The madness took her away from me, and then the sea did it again. But I betrayed her, too, when I only remembered the bad parts. I should have remembered her properly, even though it's harder.'

*

The sun was high before Piper came to join us at the railing. He stood on the other side of me, his feet planted wide on the shifting deck.

'Did Paloma tell you?' Zoe asked him.

He nodded, and turned to me. 'She confirmed what we heard in the Ark: they found a way to end the twinning. Just like the people in the Ark did, except that in the Scattered Islands they actually went through with it. It's not simple, and it's not a magic cure. It's the same as it said in Joe's papers: no fatal bond, but everyone has mutations.

Maybe always will have. And they can't undo existing twins – only the next generation. But we already knew that.'

'And you've told her about the Council,' I said, 'and the blast?'

He nodded. 'I don't know if she's taken it in properly yet. But she said she's staying. She said she wants to help.'

My life was a map of other people's sacrifices. Bodies marked it like wayposts. Now all of Elsewhere was in jeopardy.

'There's something else,' Piper said. 'Thomas told me something, about Leonard's song. You know Thomas said he sent some of his sailors inland, to the safehouse? They heard the song in a settlement along the way. And that's how they first heard about the battle of New Hobart – there was a verse about how the Council was defeated there.'

'That wasn't in the song,' I said. 'Leonard wrote it a month before we freed New Hobart.'

Piper smiled. 'It's changing, like Leonard said it would. Growing. More and more people hearing it, and adding to it.'

'Not Leonard, though,' I said picturing Leonard's body hanging from the tree.

Piper saw my lips tighten. 'It's not hopeless, Cass. We have the alliance with The Ringmaster, and his army. We freed New Hobart. The news of the refuges and the tanking is spreading fast. We've found out the truth about the Council's plans for the blast. You destroyed the Ark, with all those tanks, and whatever pieces of the blast machine they hadn't already taken. And we've found Elsewhere.'

What he said was true. But like everything, these days, it was doubled. New Hobart was safe from the Council for now – but I wasn't sure how long we could trust The Ringmaster. He would approve of us destroying the Ark, but his reaction to Paloma, and the news of Elsewhere's cure for twinning, was less certain.

We had found Elsewhere, but the Council and their blast machine were searching too. Either the people of Elsewhere would be our saviours, or we would be their doom.

I stared down at my hands, holding the wooden rail at the stern of *The Rosalind*. Since that day in the silo, I sometimes looked at my own body with incredulity. Zach was my twin, but it had felt as though it was Kip's death that I could not possibly survive. But here I was. The same hands. The same heart, still churning blood. Since Kip had taken that leap, I'd punished my traitorous body every day, for continuing. I'd embraced the cold, and the hunger, and the exhaustion, as if they were my due - until those moments in the flooded Ark, when I'd caught myself fighting for my life. And there'd been no noble desire to save the resistance in my mind, during those breathless moments in the tunnels. Only my own desire for life. Hope was not a decision I made. It was a stubborn reflex. The body squirming towards the air. The taking of the next breath, and the one after that.

Months ago, when we'd looked down towards the distant sea from McCarthy's Pass, Piper had told me that there wasn't only ugliness left in the world. Believing that had very often felt like more of a stretch than believing in Elsewhere. But in the flooded Ark, I'd fought for life. And I was glad of it – glad to feel the ship's wood beneath my hands, as I stood and watched the horizon with Zoe and Piper at my side.

Paloma would be waiting for us at the prow, and there would be information to share, plans to be made. The conflict had spread, somehow, to encompass the world. For all my visions, I could not see my way through it. But for these few moments I stopped trying. I allowed my body to be enough. I remembered what I had said to myself, as a child, when I was trying to resign myself to my newly branded face: *This is my life now*. Here, on *The Rosalind*, I let the words unfold in my mind once more: *This is my life now*. The emphasis had shifted.

I spoke out loud to Zoe and Piper the words I'd not yet admitted to myself. 'Before, when I refused to kill myself, it was because I was protecting Zach. Now, it's not Zach I want to save.' I looked up at them. 'It's myself. I want more days. I want to see more things like this.' I gestured at the sea below us, the gulls hoisting themselves on the wind coming off the cliffs. 'I want to listen to bards again. I want to get old, as old as Sally, and have a head full of memories instead of visions.'

It felt wrong to be smiling. That small declaration, *more days*, felt more audacious than ever in the face of the Ark's secret.

All my memories were entangled with death. But I claimed them, nonetheless, gathering them up as I'd gathered the fragments of Leonard's guitar. There, facing the sea, I closed my eyes and let myself remember.

ACKNOWLEDGEMENTS

My exemplary agent, Juliet Mushens, has been the best possible partner for this series, with invaluable support from Sarah Manning, and from Sasha Raskin in the US.

For their clear and insightful reading and advice, I warmly thank my editors, Natasha Bardon at HarperVoyager (UK) and Adam Wilson at Gallery Books (USA). I would also like to thank my excellent copy-editors, Joy Chamberlain and Erica Ferguson.

Clara Haig-White and Andrew North have been patient and thoughtful advisors throughout the writing process. Sarah Heaton helped me to arrive at the title.

I am enormously grateful for the work of Florence Laty, Aysel Durmaz, and Julie Bonaparte, who helped to care for my son while I wrote this book.